P9-DCC-873

By Lisa Black

TRAIL OF BLOOD
EVIDENCE OF MURDER
TAKEOVER

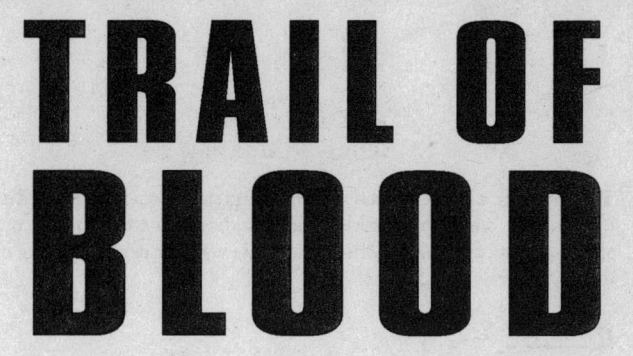

TRAIL OF BLOOD

LISA BLACK

HARPER

An Imprint of HarperCollinsPublishers

This book is a work of fiction. The characters, incidents, and dia-
logue are drawn from the author's imagination and are not to be con-
strued as real. Any resemblance to actual events or persons, living or
dead, is entirely coincidental.

HARPER

An *Imprint* of HarperCollins*Publishers*
10 East 53rd Street
New York, New York 10022-5299

Copyright © 2010 by Lisa Black
Excerpt from *Defensive Wounds* copyright © 2011 by Lisa Black
Map by Nick Springer, Springer Cartographics, LLC.
ISBN 978-0-06-198936-0

First Harper mass market printing: August 2011
First William Morrow hardcover printing: September 2010

Printed in the United States of America

Visit Harper paperbacks on the World Wide Web at
www.harpercollins.com

10 9 8 7 6 5 4 3 2 1

for my dad
who would have loved all this

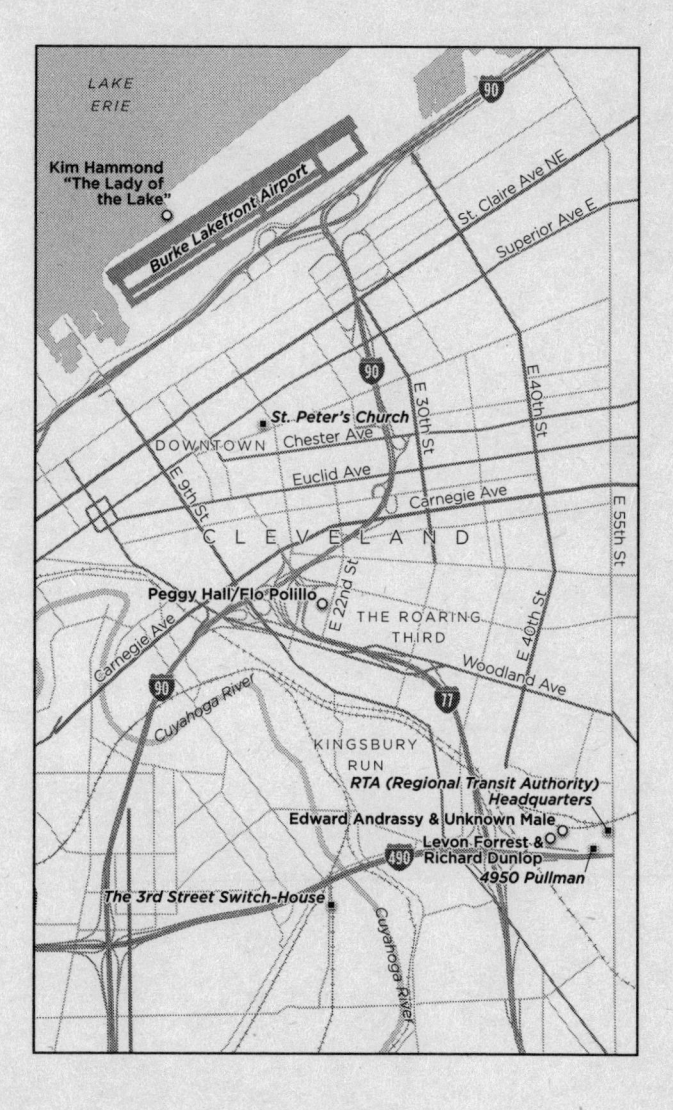

TRAIL OF
BLOOD

CHAPTER 1

THURSDAY, SEPTEMBER 2

Fall had come early this year, and Theresa could see why people considered it the season of death. With the sun behind clouds the trees appeared as a palette of dull browns. Weeds had overtaken the train tracks below, though she knew a rapid transit car would rattle by at any moment. The only spots of color belonged to graffiti on the pylons supporting the bridge. It was Labor Day weekend according to the calendar, but it might as well have been the middle of winter on this edge of the city.

"Why am I here?" she asked the cop. He stood next to her, further crumbling the edge of the asphalt street with one toe.

"Metaphorically speaking?" The brown autumn tableau did not seem to bother him and he drew in the crisp air with relish; but then he was young, and in uniform, and would not get a chance to deal with homicides very often. "That I couldn't say. But probably because I called the sergeant and the sergeant called Homicide and Homicide called Dispatch and Dispatch called the Medical Examiner's Office. 'Sounds weird,' the sergeant told me. 'I'll call Forensics.' And here you are."

"What's weird about it?"

He waved at the valley and its train tracks. "Know what that is?"

She declined to answer, tired of playing Q & A with a boy half her age, and gave him a mild glare instead.

"Kingsbury Run," he said.

She knew the term, of course. Everyone in Cleveland did. "So?"

"Come with me." He turned away from the valley he'd just pointed out without waiting to see if she would follow or offering to carry her crime scene kit. And she was an old woman now. Forty, as of next Friday.

She left her car parked along Pullman. Traffic did not present a hazard—no one ventured up this deserted road on the edge of the downtown area except for employees at the electrical station on the corner. A white car labeled SECURITY sat at the entrance; its lone occupant watched her progress with great suspicion, as if he could see no reason why terrorists would not arrive in a Medical Examiner's Office station wagon or appear as a mild-mannered forensic scientist.

The two-story structure had been constructed with stone instead of brick and had probably been an attractive building a century ago, before the property hedged on one side by train tracks became trapped by the tail end of I-490 on the other. Square, about a hundred feet by a hundred feet. The lawn around it had long since descended into weeds and garbage. The building had no glass in its window spaces, no door at its threshold. Obviously empty, obviously a victim of fire at some point. Obviously dead.

Her phone trilled with a text message from Chris. She did not send a reply.

The cop strolled up to another young officer guarding the entrance—that was when you knew you had aged, when they all started looking not old enough to drive—and exchanged some sort of wisecrack. The one guarding the door, however, did not find the fall air or the weird homicide as invigorating as his compatriot. He broke off a yawn to shout something to the interior of the building, and the detective appeared just as she reached the front stoop.

"I might have known this would be your doing," she said to him.

"What, like it's my fault?" Frank Patrick had been a Homicide detective for ten of his years and her first cousin for all of them. Pinpricks of sweat appeared around his mustache and a swipe of dust marred his dark slacks. "Watch your step."

She moved into the dank interior. Chunks of plaster and concrete lay on top of ancient pop cans and other garbage, and gaping holes appeared in the ceiling, but the floor felt plenty solid enough to support her one hundred and thirty pounds. A film of white dust still hung in the air. Some of the walls had been removed from the area to her left and gray light from the far windows provided a hazy illumination. On her right a dim maze of rooms still existed. It smelled of urine, decomposed fast food, and old smoke, which explained the blackened surfaces on the south wall of the building.

"Arson," Frank said without being asked. "That keeps happening to the collection of old warehouses that cluster this dying city. I quote a particularly depressing columnist. It's either kids with nothing better to do or some homeless guy trying to get cozy."

"You got me out here for an arson?" Theresa had been trained in many avenues of forensic investigation. Arson was not one of them.

"You got something better to do?"

"Just my job." This overstated the case a bit. Leo and Don were at the lab, surely keeping things under control.

"Your job includes getting away from the microscopes now and then," he reminded her. "Forget the arson, that happened weeks ago. The fire guys came with their shiny trucks and took out what little structural integrity this building had left."

She glanced up at the ceiling. "It's not going to cave in on us right this minute, is it?"

"No guarantees. Think anyone would miss us?"

Good question. Her fiancé had been dead for over a year and her ex-husband was probably out with the latest in a line of pole dancers. But her mother certainly would, and her daughter would notice when the tuition check didn't clear. Chris—who knew? She stumbled over a collection of crushed Coke cans and decided to concentrate on her cousin's gray blazer as it advanced into the gloom.

He went on. "This prompted the city council to once again address the issue of empty buildings and their absentee landlords and file a claim to seize the property for destruction. Councilman Greer, as you know, has made it clear that cleaning up the city of Cleveland is his personal mission in life and only he can save us from ourselves. No protests ensued to save this little blight on the landscape, so they hired Mr. Lansky's construction company"—he gestured toward a man up ahead, who was standing off to the side with a paunch and an unlit cigar—"to demolish the place lest it just up and collapse one day on a homeless squatter or some innocent but high-spirited youth."

Another glance at the ceiling. It did not appear to have moved. "Or us."

"So far, so good. The construction guys, or rather

the deconstruction guys, started from the top down and tossed the walls through those holes in the ceiling. Upstairs is just empty space. But when they started taking out the sections on the ground floor, well"—he stopped at the edge of an incomplete wall, his tall frame outlined by light from the other side of it—"they found this."

She reached the area, blinking in the brilliance provided by portable halogen lights. Bordered by two walls and a collection of two-by-four studs stood a table. It had been roughly but sturdily constructed of unfinished wood and bolted to the floor.

On that table stretched the body of a man. And that man had been dead for a very long time. His flesh had sunk to only a papery, peeling cover over the bones and left no odor in the air. The body's arms and legs lay straight, the back flat against the surface of the table. It would have seemed a fairly peaceful repose, were it not for the white vertebrae protruding from the collar of the shirt without a skull to cap them off.

Theresa approached the table, thrown into erratic shadow by the lights crouching along the floor. She only assumed the body to be male—the shapeless pants and leather belt did not suggest femininity, and neither did the dark, long-sleeved shirt. She touched a fold at the elbow and the material became dust under her finger. "It's desiccated, like a mummy."

She picked up one of the halogen lights, careful to use the handle and not the hot casing. Its electrical cord snaked off through the structure to where a generator hummed in the distance.

The head had been removed from its rightful place, but not from the area. It rested between the flopped-open feet in their brown leather shoes. The hollow eye sockets stared up at her. It had retained some flesh and even some hair, yes, but not enough to resemble a face, not something human, just a badly done Halloween decoration.

"See what I mean?" The young cop had followed them. "Weird."

The damp of the surrounding gloom finally reached her bones, and she shuddered. Now she knew what he had meant about Kingsbury Run and its very special history.

"What do you think?" Frank asked her.

"I think I'm going to need coffee," she told him.

CHAPTER 2

THURSDAY, SEPTEMBER 2

Theresa's hands probed gently but insistently as she checked the clothing both for identifying objects and for a clue to the body's condition. Would the papery flesh hold it together in transport? She couldn't wait for the anthropologist, two and a half hours away at his university—plus, with the current budget crisis the county wouldn't want to pay his consultant's fee to assist with the body's recovery, only to examine its skeleton. She puffed in exasperation as one sleeve disintegrated in her fingers.

"How's it going?" Frank asked.

"It's got to be cotton, or wool. Some natural fiber. Synthetics would hold together better. If he'd have been in the ground wearing this there'd be nothing left at all." The man had carried something in his shirt pocket as well; she worked at it with her fingers but it had been melded into place as the body had decomposed and saturated the clothing and its contents. It felt like a small notebook, malleable, so she did not force it. It could remain in place until they got the whole setup in the lab and could examine it with proper lighting.

"He? You sure it's a man?"

"The anthropologist will have to say for sure, but he's got that bump at the back of the skull that men have."

Frank probed the sandy hair on the back of his head as an apparent fact-checking exercise but said only: "How long has he been here?"

"A long time. That's all I'm prepared to say for now." Even when disturbed the body did not smell bad, only a bit musty. The many foul odors from the decomposition process had long ago dissipated along with the flesh. Theresa pulled gently on the leather belt, hoping for a wallet in the back pocket. It held together only slightly better than the pants, though the steel buckle merely needed a little polishing. A triangular object, previously hidden underneath the body, came along with the belt.

"Is that a gun?" Frank asked.

She slid the dusty object from its case, tilted it under the bright light. "Smith and Wesson thirty-eight."

"Let me see."

"Do not break it open and/or unload it," she ordered him before she handed it over. No matter how versed a cop became in forensic principles, they never quite lost that "making the gun safe" habit.

"I know, I know." He, too, held the weapon under one of the portable lights for a better look.

Theresa took a moment to retrieve an important piece of her crime scene kit—the emergency hair clip. The red curls kept tickling her cheeks as she looked down at the corpse. The movement kept her warm as the sun rose enough to burn off the fog. Mourning doves sighed and cars buzzed along 490 in the distance. "Where's your partner today?"

"Sanchez is at city hall, running down the building history."

Never too busy to tease her cousin, she said, "You've been partners for six months. You can't call her Angela?"

"We're cops. We don't do that first-name stuff."

"Yeah, sure. How about Angie?"

"How about you get this wrapped up so I can get back to murders that happened this week and not this decade?"

"Maybe it's not a homicide."

"Besides," he went on, "she hates *Angie*. Not a homicide? He's carrying a gun, and do you think his head wound up between his legs by accident?"

"I'm saying that this table, even though it's made out of wood, reminds me of our autopsy tables. It has a lip installed around the edge, as if to keep the blood in or to keep the patient from sliding off. There's a hole at the bottom that might have had a drain attached to it, with a hole in the floor underneath it that's been filled in with some sort of rubber. Was there a funeral home at this address? A medical school?"

"And they just happened to leave a body behind when they cleared out?"

"Stranger things have happened. It could even be some sort of shrine."

"Removing someone's head and placing it between his feet is not normally considered a sign of respect."

"Again, stranger things, and if that's the case then this is just abuse of a corpse, not murder. That's why we need a list of tenants. Also, I haven't found any signs of violence. No gunshots or blunt force trauma to the skull, no visible breaks or nicks in what I can see of the ribs. His bones seem intact."

"Aside from the head having been removed."

"Yeah, aside from that."

Theresa checked the right back pocket of the trousers, reaching in with a cautious and gloved hand. Technically she should have patted them or removed the pants first. Reaching into unknown pockets could result in disastrous encounters with dirty needles or other unpleasant items. But the extremely delicate condition of the clothing made her put aside her own rules. The man had six cents on him, a nickel and a penny. Again, she picked up the halogen lamp for a closer look. "I don't even know about this decade."

Frank had been inspecting the one remaining wall. "What do you mean?"

"I don't know if you're going to want to hear this. *I* don't even want to hear this."

"What?"

"It may sound simplistic, but pocket change is generally a reliable indicator of the time a body went missing. You would think we would carry around coins from any year in the past twenty or so, but as a practical matter—"

He came closer, peered over her shoulder at the items in her palm. "Spit it out, Tess. What year are they?"

"The penny," she told him, "is from 1931. The nickel says 1935."

He picked up the copper coin with Lincoln's head on one side and sheaves of wheat on the reverse, gently, as if it might disintegrate as easily as the man's shirt. Theresa flipped over the nickel, viewing the standard American Indian and buffalo reliefs.

"You mean this body's been here for seventy-five years?" Frank demanded.

Several things occurred to Theresa.

First, that—assuming the man had been murdered—at least they did not have a deranged, decapitating killer running around the city. The killer would almost certainly be as deceased as his victim by now, or at least too frail to be hefting bodies onto dissecting tables.

Second, that given the time lapse, this case would be very difficult, if not impossible, to solve.

Third, that the year 1935 put this man's death in the midst of the infamous Torso Murder spree, in which at least a dozen people were killed, usually dismembered and scattered about the Cleveland area like the seeds for a grisly harvest. The killer had never been caught and all but three of the victims remained unidentified.

Most had been found in or near the desolate valley outside, called Kingsbury Run. Oh, and the press would fall on the story like cats on an open can of tuna.

"Crap," she said.

"Yeah," her cousin said, seconding that.

Six cents. Had the killer robbed the victim and not bothered with the coins? Or had six cents been a reasonable amount of pocket change at that time? She found herself glancing at the skull, as if it could tell her. How had he come to be walled up? Hadn't anyone missed him? "Who owned this patch of floor, that they could brick it in without anyone else noticing? Was this one big room, or apartments, or what?"

"I'm a little fuzzy on that myself," Frank told her. "Yo! Mr. Lansky!"

The man approached, holding his unlit cigar in front of him like a talisman, stopping at the two-by-fours that marked the edge of the small room. When asked, he explained what he had found when they first began clearing the building, three weeks before. His gaze settled on the bones laid out on the table and stayed there throughout the conversation.

"The south side of the ground floor had serious fire

damage, really blackened. The upper floors weren't bad. The hallway passed through the center of the building, so that the offices had exterior windows."

"How many separate units were on this floor?" Theresa asked.

"Four or five. I didn't really pay attention. From the variety of materials I'd guess it's been divided and subdivided plenty of times over the years. I don't have any idea what it looked like originally."

"Did they have plumbing? Drains?"

"Sure. They all had lavatories, sinks, and toilets, I think at least four on each floor. We've ripped them all out."

"Which suite did this little room open to?"

He stopped looking at the corpse just long enough to blink at her, check out her legs in their khaki trousers, and blink again.

She rephrased. "Where was the door?"

"What door?" he finally asked.

"The door into this room." She spoke with more patience than she felt.

He put the unlit cigar to his lips and, she swore, puffed on it. "That's what I'm trying to tell you. There wasn't any door. Anywhere. If there had been, we'd have emptied the room before we used the sledgehammers. It's so damn dark in here that my guys took out most of the opposite wall before they saw—that."

Theresa waved the halogen light at what remained of the other walls. They appeared unbroken, though hardly finished—merely rough wooden strips with plaster oozing through their cracks from the other side.

Frank's phone rang, and he walked away to answer the call.

"The door had been bricked up?" she asked Lansky.

"No brick. Plaster and furring strips."

"So the door had been plastered over?" she persisted.

"Or there never was a door, and whoever did—this"—he nodded at the body with revulsion—"added a whole wall to block it up."

"Or it was in the sections that you already took out."

"Nah," he argued. "Guys would have noticed. No door, no molding. They said straight plaster and furring, nothing odd the whole length. There are some dry-walled areas in the southwest corner, but they were at least thirty feet away. I'm telling you, a building this old, the walls have probably been moved and rebuilt a dozen times."

"But no one ever found this."

He visibly shivered. "Or they did and didn't want to tell anybody. Is there anything else you need from me? I'm going to send my guys to another job, unless there's a chance we're going to be able to do anything here today. . . ."

"No chance," she assured him.

"Mr. Greer isn't going to like that." This seemed to bother him even more than the corpse.

The hole at the bottom of the table still intrigued her. "Was there a bathroom or kitchen adjacent to this room?"

"Half bath. No tubs or kitchens in the building. I think it was all office space, maybe used as a warehouse later on. We took out plumbing here." He tapped his foot on the floor where he stood, to the south of the mystery room, near the row of studs.

Perhaps that had been part of the original space—otherwise where did the water come from that then drained out? "Where did all this plumbing dump to?"

He had grown sufficiently accustomed to the corpse to look away from it for up to ten seconds, and did so now to give her an incredulous look. "Sewer."

"I mean, where did the pipes go?"

"Cellar."

"This building has a basement?"

"I wouldn't call it that. Just an access area for pipes and wires."

"I want to see that."

"No," he told her in a solemn tone. "I don't think you do."

She pointed out the hole in the table and the apparently corresponding hole in the floor. "I think he had a drain system here that he dismantled when he bricked— closed—this space up. He filled in the hole in the floor with some sort of putty so that it wouldn't be noticed from the basement. I need to see where a pipe would have gone."

He sighed. "Don't say I didn't warn you."

Frank returned to fall in line with her as she followed the construction manager. "Warn you about what?"

"I hope you didn't wear a good suit today." Theresa pulled a diminutive but powerful flashlight from her pocket as they descended from the gloom of the empty building to the outright dark of the basement. *Cellar,* she thought, correcting herself.

"I've learned never to wear a good suit. Hey, how is Rachael getting along at OSU?"

"Still bouncing off the walls with excitement. She talks almost too fast to understand when she calls, but apparently her classes are going well. Of course she's too busy studying to call very often."

He put his hand on the back of her neck as they reached the bottom of the stairs, pulling her hair slightly, letting her know that he knew she was a little bit miserable and would not admit it. It had been three weeks and two days, not long enough for Theresa to adjust to the emptiness of her nest.

Mr. Lansky had not exaggerated. Theresa didn't

need to duck her five-foot-seven-inch frame to avoid coating her hair with cobwebs but felt like she did. Columns of stone, here and there, supported the structure above. Noises from the city outside faded to a vague hum. The floor consisted of hard dirt and still appeared much cleaner than the surfaces upstairs. Flashlights lost strength by the time the beams found the outer walls, leaving the edges of their new world hovering in gloom. It smelled of coolness and silence.

The construction manager aimed his flashlight upward and silently illuminated the copper piping, green with age, traveling along the underside of the ground-level floor. Next to them ran a much wider, darker tube.

She tapped it with one latex-gloved finger and moved to avoid the shower of dust that action produced. "Is that the drainpipe?"

"Yep. Cast iron."

Frank said, "Iron? Odd that they hadn't replaced that by now."

"If it ain't broke," Mr. Lansky intoned, "don't fix it."

They continued their cautious shuffle across the open space with only three flashlights for illumination. Theresa wished she could have brought one of the halogens, trailing its electrical cord behind her like a line of bread crumbs.

The construction manager stopped at the approximate center of the building's foundation and all three of them looked up. Theresa located the hole, neatly drilled through the floor and then filled in. Perhaps twelve inches of space separated it from the drainpipe. "Could there have been a smaller pipe through that hole that emptied into the drainpipe?"

"Sure," the man said at once. "There's a clean-out right here; he could have hooked up to that. Of course then it's not available to you as a clean-out if you need one, though it's probably got one or two more along the length—yeah, there's another one. This is a quality pipe. They built things to last in those days, gotta hand them that."

"Can you tell if there had been a pipe attached to it?"

"No, lady, I can't." Then he added more patiently, "That little bit of space, they wouldn't have had to install brackets or anything even. Just a pipe that hasn't been there for a long, long time. If it ever was. You don't need me, you need a psychic. One of them ghost hunters."

He found this amusing and began to laugh, only to cut the chuckle off into a strangled sound when a footstep creaked overhead.

"Our patrol officer," Theresa assured him, but no color returned to the man's face and he hunched into himself.

Frank had lost interest in the piping and now directed his light into the dimness around them. "Dirt floor," he said to Theresa.

"I know. Visions of John Wayne Gacy. But the ground is so steady—I don't see any depressions." If bodies had been buried in the basement—always a popular location for one's victims—they would see irregularities in the surface where the bodies decomposed and created a hollow deep in the ground. The dirt on top would settle inward, making a dip. They could probe, piercing the ground with a metal rod to see if they hit a soft area, but she was not certain that would even work for ancient graves. Ground-penetrating radar would be better, if they could talk one of the universities or maybe an engineering firm into doing it for them. The county would never pay for the equipment.

Besides, they had no reason to believe other victims existed, even if the man upstairs turned out to be a victim of homicide. He had been not buried but walled up in a hidden shrine, as if the killer felt guilt.

She didn't believe that, though. The type of people who decapitated other people didn't usually stop at one. He could have brought in more dirt to fill in the depressions and then smoothed the floor of the cellar flat again.

Their patrol officer paced, finding another loose floorboard to give off a deep *creeeeeak*. The construction manager decided it was time to leave and headed for the stairway.

"You see anything of note?" Frank asked her.

"A lot of dust."

"Me neither."

She followed him up the steps. "We need to hang on to this building for another day or two, you know. There're no signs of other victims, but I'd hate to think of bodies lying down here and then we pile the building on top of them and bury them deeper."

"Depends on what they're going to do with this property. They'll probably dig it out for a new building, put in a better foundation and more subground levels."

"In which case I'd still rather find them before a backhoe does."

"Don't talk about *them*. There is no them. There's just this one guy."

"Right. There is no them," she repeated like a mantra as they emerged onto the ground floor.

Unless they had, at long last, uncovered the lair of the Torso killer. Then there could be half of Depression-era Cleveland buried under the rock-hard dirt beneath them. The thought made her ill, and yet a little frisson of excitement ruffled the tiny hairs on the back of her neck.

It would be horrible.

It would also be the case of a lifetime.

Grandpa would be so proud.

She asked Mr. Lansky: "Was the stairway to the second floor here? It couldn't have been convenient for all the second-floor tenants to have to go past one of the offices to get there."

"Naw, there was an outside stairway to the second floor. We took that down last week."

The construction manager didn't pause as he spoke, just continued through the cleared area and kept on going until he had left the structure entirely. Their patrol officer, by contrast, stood entirely too close to the body for her comfort. "You didn't touch anything, did you?"

"No," he said insistently with a convincing shudder.

"What are you going to do with this body, Tess?" Frank asked, most likely impatient for his midmorning cigarette break.

"I don't know. If I scoop him into a bag, the anthropologist is going to have to sort out every tiny bone all over again. I'm thinking of taking the entire tabletop. We can saw through the two-by-four legs and carry it like a tray." It wouldn't be the biggest thing she'd ever hauled back to the lab. That honor went to a three-bedroom recreational vehicle with four flat tires. "I wish I could Saran Wrap him to it first."

"Why can't you?"

"I hate plastic wrap. Too much static electricity. It would take half of our trace evidence away with it. I suppose I could cover him with brown paper, though. . . ." She pondered various ideas while prodding gently at the left back pocket, which contained a firm, rectangular object. The trousers held together better than the shirt had but still ripped at the slightest stress. "I need an archaeologist. Someone trained in handling ancient things."

"Seventy-five years isn't exactly ancient." Frank crouched, examining the rubble of plaster and wood covering the floor. He began to pick up pieces, give them a glance, and toss them outside the area of the room, searching for anything that had been inside the room before the walls tumbled down.

"The pocket change could be misleading us. He might have been a coin collector and kept them aside to take home. He could have died in 1940, or 1950, or 1960, for all we know." Concentrating mightily, she managed to slip the object out of the pocket with minimal tearing. A wallet? No.

He scattered more plaster stones. "And this still could be some kind of natural death. Like the guy who leaves Mom's corpse in her bedroom for twenty years, that sort of thing."

"Then again"—she stared at the object in her hand as her heart began to beat a few pulses faster—"maybe not."

Frank looked up. "What is it?"

She tilted it toward him, the hard leather case with its gold-colored shield nestled inside. "He was a cop."

THURSDAY, SEPTEMBER 2

The Torso Murders of Kingsbury Run began in 1935, unless one counted the pieces of a woman washed up by Lake Erie the year before, in which case they would have begun in 1934. The murders stopped in 1938, or perhaps 1950, if one could accept a twelve-year gap in the killer's activities or supposed that he became more circumspect in hiding his victims—while aware that circumspection had never been part of his style. When victims weren't cut into pieces and dropped into either the lake or the river, they were wrapped in paper and left like parcels for unsuspecting passersby to find. Some particularly unlucky male victims were divested of not only their heads but their genitalia. Sometimes the heads remained missing, sometimes only the heads were found, and sometimes the heads were placed near the body, in one case buried close by with the hair quite noticeably visible above the earth. He killed both men and women; only three of the victims were ever identified, and one of those tentatively.

His reign produced either twelve or fourteen victims, depending on which individuals were included or excluded. Unless one considered the rash of skeletons and other bodies found around New Castle, Pennsylvania, and one found in Youngstown, in which case the list of murders added up to twenty-six occurring between 1923 and 1950.

He was never caught.

The Torso murderer, also known as the Mad Butcher or the Mad Butcher of Kingsbury Run if you really wanted to get dramatic, was Cleveland's very own serial killer, more prolific, equally as bent, but slightly tidier than Jack the Ripper.

Standing over the body, Theresa asked herself if she could really solve this, finish the case that her cop grandfather had told her about, repeated over and over at her request like a macabre bedtime story. He would have been thrilled at this development. He would have—

She stopped herself. Time to get real. If the case couldn't be solved in its own time, what could she hope to do so many years later? All the city would get out of this latest chapter would be more frustration. Not to mention the maelstrom of media attention any whiff of it would inevitably produce. And this dead cop would give off more than a whiff . . . more like a sirocco.

Theresa swept her thumb over the gold badge. "It looks just like yours."

"It would," Frank told her. "The design hasn't changed since 1906. Unfortunately detective shields don't have numbers, so we can't run him down that way."

"You'd have lists of which cop had what number, three-quarters of a century back?"

"A police department is a bureaucracy. It keeps lists of everything, including the serial numbers of department-issued weapons." He plucked the gun from the table and pulled out his phone, squinting at both of them—the little numbers on the phone and the little numbers on the gun. He had not yet given in to reading glasses. Neither had Theresa.

Her phone rang. Chris again. She snapped it shut without answering.

"Is that Leo?" Frank asked, referring to her problematic boss. He watched her with the phone to his ear, obviously on hold.

"No." She brushed the last specks off the badge, avoiding her cousin's eye. He had many of the characteristics of an older brother—the annoying ones. If he sniffed an uncomfortable subject, he'd run that rabbit to ground every time.

He merely raised an eyebrow, phone still clamped to his ear. "Who, then?"

"Chris."

"Cavanaugh?"

"Yep."

"You're not taking his calls? Why?"

"Because I have more important things to do right now."

"What'd that showy ass do, stand you up for a date?" Frank had never been a fan of the high-profile hostage negotiator.

"That wouldn't be possible, since we're not even really dating."

"I should think not—what? Yes, I'm here." He relayed the gun information to the person on the phone, and Theresa turned back to the body.

Besides, if she and Chris were really dating, he would call her more than once a month before texting for a lunch date as if she'd drop everything for the opportunity to see him. And he wouldn't have taken the city manager's daughter to the Cleveland Playhouse benefit last week.

Of course it was okay that he did, because they

weren't really dating. Besides, the benefit was more of a political event.

She set the badge next to the left foot. The shoe on that foot had what appeared to be masking tape wrapped around the toe.

The body snatchers, the Medical Examiner's Office transport ambulance, were on their way with a Sawzall. She would cover the body with paper but still refused the plastic wrap idea.

Frank snapped his phone shut. "James Miller."

"What?"

"CPD assigned a Smith and Wesson with that serial number to a James Miller."

"How did you find that out so fast?"

"We got a great guy running our history museum and he's got all the rolls from back then. Miller joined the force in 1929, was promoted to detective in 1932, was dismissed in 1936 for dereliction of duty."

"Don't you have to turn in your gun and badge when you get fired?"

"Usually. The historian has got to check some other records but says it isn't clear why he was fired—the way the notes he could locate are worded, they could mean that Miller *became* derelict and was therefore fired. In other words, went AWOL."

Theresa looked down, automatically directing her gaze to the head of the body when of course the head no longer sat at its usual spot at the top of the spinal cord. "Wouldn't a cop suddenly going missing cause a stir?"

"Of course it would. I'm sure they investigated, but it will take a while to track down those reports. That's *if* this is even him, and not someone who stole James Miller's badge and gun either to pawn it or use it. Those were desperate times. The Torso killer wasn't the only one operating in Cleveland."

"What do you mean? We had another serial killer?"

"I meant the other kind of serial killers—mobsters. Cleveland was a wide-open town then. They'd cracked down in New York and Chicago, but here they stayed under the radar and had most of the cops on the force on their payrolls. That Untouchable guy had to come here and clean it up."

"Eliot Ness. I know, but I thought hit men dumped their bodies, not constructed little shrines to them."

"It's not a shrine. I've gone through every pebble on the floor and they left nothing in this room but the body. And they would have wanted to make absolutely sure this body did not turn up—even then, they didn't kill cops if they could help it. This table could have been here for another reason, gambling, making bathtub gin. Miller finds them, or wants a bigger cut or something, so they slit his throat, wall the place up, and conceal two crimes at once."

"I don't know," she said skeptically. "Why make such a statement with the beheading if you didn't want to display it as an object lesson for everyone else?"

"We don't know that they didn't. There could have been a gap of time between the murder and closing the room."

She didn't want to picture a line of delinquent clients traipsing past to gape at the body of James Miller. Spreading the brown paper shroud over the bones, she tucked it in at the edges. Officer Miller would be subjected to only empathetic gazes from now on.

Theresa picked up one of the halogen lights, aimed it at the remaining wall. The light danced off the ancient wood and the plaster welling up through its cracks. The construction appeared steady and strong; the job had not been done in haste. It might be the original structure, but then they had no way to tell what the two and a half missing walls had been like before their destruction. If the walling up of James Miller had been flimsily done it wouldn't have kept him secret all these years.

The wood had aged over the years with a speckled pattern of discoloration. She took a small bottle of Hemastix test strips out of her crime scene kit and dampened the ends with distilled water. Then she got Frank to hold the light for her while she pressed a wet yellow tip to a large stain, dark against the dark wood. The feltlike yellow material instantly turned a deep blue. "There's blood on the walls."

"Wow, what a shock. Wouldn't cutting someone's head off produce a lot of blood?"

"That depends on how it's done. If it takes a number of cuts to the carotids, then there would be blood spraying everywhere for a few seconds. Even if there's only one quick stroke severing the neck, the heart could keep pumping out the rest of the blood since cardiac tissue can function more or less independently of the brain—assuming the victim is still alive, of course. But this"—she stood back, taking in all the darkened spots as a pattern and not merely a characteristic of the wood—"isn't one or two arterial spurts. The drops are more discrete, separated."

"Castoff?" Frank suggested.

"Upon castoff upon castoff, upon castoff."

"As if someone got really medieval on his ass?"

Theresa couldn't help but picture the Mad Butcher, dancing around the room covered in his victim's blood, each thrust of the knife scattering red liquid across the wood and plaster. A fall breeze drifted through the windows behind her, carrying with it a hint of winter, and brushed the back of her neck.

She tested a few more stains. They all reacted positively. "Yes, it's only four feet from the table, but it seems like an awful lot of drops for a relatively small amount of damage to the body. There's no evidence of multiple stab wounds and/or bludgeoning, and no fractures."

"If it's mob work, it could have been something more subtle, some technique that hurts a lot but doesn't kill quickly. Maybe they had questions for Officer Miller he didn't want to answer. Or asked for something he didn't want to give back. Though I can't see why they'd leave him armed, in that case."

Theresa dug a sliver of wood from one stain with a disposable scalpel, dropping it into a small manila envelope. She marked the location on her crime scene sketch before moving on to another stain. "Or this guy isn't the only person who was killed in this room."

"You really do think this is the Torso killer's workshop?"

"I think I need to sit down." A joke, with no place to sit—but it really was too much: the bizarre circumstances, the time warp, the victim being a cop, the possible connection to a historic serial killer. "Who's going to tell Mr. Lansky that we need to hang on to this building for a while?"

"I vote for you."

"I vote for Leo." Her boss had a deft hand for dealing with anyone he thought potentially useful to him—i.e., anyone outside the Medical Examiner's Office—and would have the clout to hold up even a city councilman's pet project. Whether he would have the fortitude, of course . . . Leo's grasp of local politics exceeded even his considerable grasp of forensics.

"Good luck with that," her cousin told her.

The plastic scalpel, meant to slice soft flesh and perhaps fabric, snapped in two and left the blade stuck in the hard wood. She couldn't waste supplies and continued to work with it, careful not to let her fingers slide down to the cutting edge. "There isn't any huge hurry, is there? Jacobs isn't planning to build a mall here or anything?"

"Not that I know of."

"Then we need to keep this. Besides, if we really can link it to the Torso killer, it will probably beat out the Rock and Roll Hall of Fame to become the city's number one tourist attraction."

"You sound almost hopeful."

She started on a third stain, snapped the scalpel further. "I can't decide what to hope for. I'd love to *know*, like everyone else in Cleveland. But I don't want to jump to conclusions. And how do we go about investigating a seventy-four-year-old crime? We may not be able to get DNA out of such old bones, or this ancient wood. What if all this blood doesn't belong to him? What if he slaughtered half a dozen victims in this little den—how do we find reference samples after so many years?"

"Cheer up, cuz. You and I have worked cold cases before."

She sealed another manila envelope with red tape. A metallic rattle from the building's entrance told her the body snatcher team now approached with a gurney and, she hoped, a big-ass electric saw. "This case isn't just cold. It's frozen-solid cold. It's liquid-nitrogen cold."

"That's why I need you."

Monday, September 23
1935

The lines scared him.

Snaking up the street and around the corner, a single-file assortment of men in worn clothing and beat-up shoes ended at the door to the soup kitchen. Each of them would get what they could, eat the soup and maybe shove the roll into their pocket for later or to take home to their families. It would almost certainly be their only meal today.

Some days James looked away. Other days he forced himself to stare at them, to see each man as an individual and not a piece of society's offal. To remind himself how lucky he was to still have a job and the semblance of a normal life. They came with a price, yes, but the alternative remained more costly.

The driver's door opened and his partner, Walter McKenna, dropped into the driver's seat. Worn-out seat springs protested at his weight. "He didn't see nothing."

They'd spent the morning working their way down

Prospect, inquiring with the merchants who were either friendly to cops or known for associating with those who weren't, trying to scare up information about the burglary of a Euclid jewelry store the previous week. So far they had been "treated" by various shop owners to three cups of coffee each as well as a piece of apple pie, two cigarettes, and a cigar (for Walter) but had not learned anything about the burglary.

"Let's go to lunch." Walter started the car, and after the engine thought about it for a moment or two, it coughed to life. "You worry too much. Stop looking at them."

"I know."

"That's not going to be you."

"I know," he repeated, though he didn't.

They drove one block over and parked at the curb outside the Arcade—one of the advantages of having a car that said POLICE on the side was the ability to park wherever you wanted, Eliot Ness and his traffic safety program notwithstanding—and went inside. Walter liked what he called "decent" food. No five-bit diner for him, so they often stopped at this collection of offices, eateries, and shops arranged in rings around five stories of open air, topped by a glass ceiling. Throngs of office workers, young clerks with out-of-style ties, and secretaries in modest skirts, swirled around them.

They sat in the diner window to watch the people going by, recognizing a good number of them. James pointed out a wiry guy skulking along with another man. "What about Henry?"

"Only hits groceries. He'd never try a jewelry store, he doesn't have the contacts to unload the goods."

"Maybe he's trying to come up in the world."

"Ain't we all."

The waitress came by. James ordered the cheapest

thing on the menu—a ten-cent ham sandwich—instead of the tuna fish he would have preferred, because he knew he wouldn't have to pay for it. An inefficient sop to his conscience—or his ego.

"How's Helen?" Walter asked.

Not a non sequitur. Helen definitely planned to move up in the world. "She wants a refrigerator."

"Can't blame her," Walter said. "They're great. No more dealing with the iceman, having that damn drip pan overflow and flood the kitchen. I couldn't stand our iceman. Always showing off his muscles to my wife. You lift blocks of ice for a living, idiot, and she's supposed to be impressed with you? I mean, you and Helen got electricity, right?"

"I have electricity. I don't have the five hundred bucks a refrigerator would cost. I could buy a new car for that."

"You don't need a car. You do need to eat."

"We eat fine." He shouldn't have said anything, knowing his partner would take his wife's side. Walter's spouse got whatever she wanted, because Walter's police salary came with a healthy supplement from appreciative citizens—people who appreciated not being arrested for gambling, speeding, bootlegging, or beating up a business rival. Walter's wife had a refrigerator. And a new dress every month. And their kids went to the parish school.

Helen, on the other hand, altered her dresses once in a while for a fresh look, made leftovers last for days, and saved her mascara for social occasions.

The other cop persisted. "Stuff lasts longer, because the temperature don't go up and down as the ice melts."

"Uh-huh."

"I trust you, Jimmy. You know that, right?"

Again, the path his partner's mind took did not present a mystery. James would have had plenty of money if he were a "normal" cop. Refusing to take it only gave the other "normal" cops a reason to think he might not be a stand-up kind of guy. Cops who weren't stand-up guys made other cops nervous. "I know. I'm just careful, Walter. Maybe you should be, too."

"What does that mean?"

"Nothing from me, you know that. But once Ness takes over—"

Walter dropped his sandwich back onto his plate with disgust. "I don't care about what that pretty-boy newshound did to Capone! Anybody could have gotten Capone, the guy did everything but piss in full view of the entire city! The ones operating here are a lot smarter."

James waited until Walter went to work on another mouthful and kept his voice low. "Smarts may not have anything to do with it. You know Burton is going to win the mayoral race and his entire platform seems to be police corruption. Even without Ness, people are going to go down and I don't want to be one of them."

Walter licked his fingers and winked at the waitress. "I don't get you, Jimmy. Without even blinking you'll go up against a drunk with a gun who's beating his wife, but let some politician shake his fist and you quiver."

James had no trade to fall back on, no extended family to help him along, and the army didn't have the budget to take guys back. He pictured himself waiting in a line of hungry men. "I can't lose my job."

Walter's soft face softened even more, and he shook his head. He understood, really. Walter wasn't a bad guy. Not cruel, loved his wife despite his big talk about women, a good father. He would be right behind James against any criminal element . . . if only James felt comfortable enough to turn his back.

Now his partner leaned forward as if he might pat James's hand. "It's an election year, Jimmy. Guys say stuff like that every election year. Once the votes are counted it will be a different story. He can't throw out the whole entire force, so he'll concentrate on the big shots, fire a few captains to make it look good, and things will go on as before. Guys like you and me will always be here."

He wiped his mouth with a napkin and got up; no need to wait for a check that wouldn't come. James examined his pockets—sixty-five cents. He left five of them on the table as a tip for the waitress, or a hedge against completely giving in, the best he could do in the fight for his soul.

Then he followed his partner's broad back out to the car, thinking: *There is no you and me. There is no me and anybody. There's just me.*

Walter used one of the blue call boxes, placed on every other street corner, to check in. As rookie detectives, they didn't warrant one of the new radio cars. They could have gone back to the station but Walter preferred to stay out and about rather than hang around the smoky, cramped building. So did James.

Fall had come but no scent of dead leaves made it past the gasoline fumes and market stands. A horn blared. James watched a particularly pretty girl step off the curb and cross the street, her skirt brushing the backs of her calves. Funny how hemlines went back down after the flapper dresses of the last decade. He would have preferred they kept going up. Had the crash sobered the country? Did Americans believe that because of their loose ways in the twenties they had somehow brought the Depression on themselves?

One year ago, a woman—or rather, *parts* of a woman—had washed up on the beach over in Euclid, a different precinct. Now and then Walter would wonder aloud what kind of pervert she must have been keeping company with to wind up like that, and the victim had never been identified, nor the case solved. If the city's police force didn't need Eliot Ness, why couldn't it solve such a brutal crime? No, the modern age had arrived, and James wanted to ride its crest instead of dragging his feet trying to hold it back.

Then Walter threw himself into the car with more than his customary enthusiasm. "You are not gonna believe this."

CHAPTER 5

FRIDAY, SEPTEMBER 3
PRESENT DAY

The bizarre circumstances of James Miller's death did not automatically confer top billing at the Medical Examiner's Office. He had not been the only citizen found dead during the previous twenty-four hours, so Theresa spent the morning with clothing examinations on two unrelated suicides and then returned to the lab to set up the spectrometer to run the gunshot residue analyses. The lab felt comfortable, for a change, now that the summer heat had faded. Once the snows came the building would always be either too hot or too cold, depending on how the furnace felt like working that day, but for these few weeks they could achieve a happy medium.

The notebook in Miller's pocket had not been cooperative, its pages fused together with decomposition fluid. She had placed it in the fume hood with a little humidity; if that could unstick the pages, then the alternate light source might be able to see the writing underneath the staining.

Theresa swallowed the dregs from her coffee cup, booted up her computer, swiveled to the other counter, and mounted the crumbling shirt fibers on a glass slide. It took her approximately two seconds to decide the shirt fibers were cotton.

Theresa swiveled back to her microscope to make some notes on the cotton fibers.

"That from your long-lost Torso victim?" The DNA analyst, Don Delgado, hitched one long leg over the corner of her workbench. Dark eyes in an olive-skinned face watched her rotate the lens to a higher magnification.

"I see the word's out."

"Faster than a defense attorney's motion to suppress," he said in agreement. "You think it's the guy Ness couldn't catch?"

"I think you're too young to even know who Eliot Ness was."

He unhitched his leg, his foot slapping the floor with a sharp crack. "Come off it, Theresa. You're only a few years older than me."

"Eleven," she muttered, her head still bent to the microscope.

"You counted?"

"Wait until you hit forty. Numbers take on a new importance."

"Really."

"For instance, last week my butt fell. Overnight. I went to bed and everything's fine, I wake up and my buttocks are resting on the tops of my thighs."

"Want me to take a look?" he asked.

"If exercise and dieting won't budge them, there's nothing you can do."

"Can I try anyway?"

She glared.

"That hostage negotiator guy still calling you?"

She glared again. The city manager's daughter had just turned twenty-five. She went on. "*Anyway,* Frank and his partner learned, from the city building department, that the building on Pullman went up in 1933. A railroad guy named Arthur Corliss owned the place and rented out the offices, eight separate units, four on each floor. Then Frank and Angela went to the Western Reserve Historical Society to look through phone books. *Dusty* phone books, he whined at me. The city directories listed the tenants at that address."

"I didn't know they even had phone books in 1935."

Theresa made a note of the fibers' original colors—blue and brown—as well as the dried decomposition fluid coating them. "They came up with a list of unit numbers, but there's no way to know how the suites were numbered. The owner had unit one, but we don't know if that was on the upper floor or the lower floor or *where* on the lower floor. There was also a tutor named Metetsky, a few architects, a medium. Like a talking-to-the-dead medium. Oh, and a nutritionist named Louis Odessa."

"They had *nutritionists* in 1935?"

Theresa examined a slide of the dead man's sock fibers. Wool. "Americans' obsession with health started in the twenties. Until then no one had heard of a balanced diet or the idea of *losing* weight instead of gaining it, or that kitchens were supposed to be sanitary. Plus, it was the roaring twenties. Times were good and new ideas were welcomed with open arms as Americans discovered a desire to be sophisticated and cosmopolitan. Until the 1929 crash, of course. Then people went back to eating what they could find."

"Did you major in history or something?" Don demanded.

"As far as my mother is concerned, the TV set has two channels, the Food Network and the Discovery Channel."

"So you can't figure out whose apartment he was in. What did the anthropologist say?"

The doctor had driven up from Kent State University after his morning classes to consult with Theresa. "He says the guy was decapitated, neatly, without nicking a bone. Not an easy thing to do, especially if the victim's still alive while you do it."

"Is that the COD?"

She hoped not. The idea of James Miller being conscious while a man cut his head off gave her an uncomfortable twinge in her heart. Being able to do her job meant *not* picturing the victim's last moments. "There could be another cause of death, sure, like poison or suffocation, something that wouldn't leave a mark on bones or clothing. Maybe toxicology can help. They should at least be able to find any heavy metal poisons in the hair, or perhaps the dried-up little prune thing that the stomach has shriveled to."

"Yuck. You know Leo's already been on the phone with Court TV."

Now she looked up from the ocular lenses. "Oh, no."

"Oh, yes. And *Unsolved Mysteries*. Just giving them the heads-up. So now I'm giving you the heads-up that where you want to keep your head is down. Leo's going to want results on this one, like, yesterday, so he can go on camera with all this new information."

"Better him than me."

"Don't worry about that. Leo's smart enough to know that the camera will love your pretty face a lot better than his. He'll make sure you're locked in the cellar if any Hollywood princes call."

"Me and the rats."

"I'll rescue you," he promised.

Theresa said good night to a smoking deskman on the loading dock and walked through the cool night air to her car. She had grabbed the last space in the farthest corner of the lot, blocked from the streetlights by the building next door, tucked up against the small copse of trees between the M.E.'s and University Hospital's medical school.

She had always loved September, the month of her birth, the end of humid summer days, the start of a new school year, which a bookworm like her did not consider torture. Now she took a deep breath to clear the dust of 1935 from her sinuses. A different age. What would have been the effect of Cleveland's first serial killer on its citizenry and its police force? Surely neither group could fully comprehend what they'd come up against.

The populace simply felt beleaguered, under attack by a faceless monster who lurked in the shadows, a specter they could have written off as an urban myth useful for scaring their children into good behavior, were the tale printed in a storybook instead of the newspaper.

Theresa pulled a heavy sweater more tightly around her body. The police, she knew, had approached the crime as they would any other, searching for men who frequented the areas where the bodies turned up, men with criminal records and a documented propensity for violence, men who were "perverted"—a word defined much more broadly then than in the current day. The second victim, and one of the very few identified, Edward Andrassy, had possibly been bisexual, since rumors of homosexuality dogged him. Yet he had also been considered a ladies' man. This started police on a running hunt for perverts and others who lived outside society's norm. Much had changed in three-quarters of a century. If the events of the 1930s occurred today, with the experience of too many serial killers to comfortably count, police would hunt for a man with a minor criminal record or none at all, a man with a steady job, unsuspecting neighbors, and an ordinary appearance who remained quite firmly below the radar.

Different, but not easier. It had taken twenty years to catch the Green River Killer.

Theresa had parked under what turned out to be the only nonfunctioning light in the lot. A few more leaves scuttled by as she reached into her pocket for her keys. A door slammed behind her, most likely the deskman returning to work after his cigarette.

Of course police today might not meet with any more success than in the past. "That description fit so many people." She found herself talking aloud, a common exercise for those too often alone. "Though forensic science—"

A scraping sound behind her, too big to be caused by a leaf, stopped her midsentence.

"Hello, ma'am—"

She whirled, hand still in her pocket. The man had at least six inches and seventy pounds on her. He stepped closer, his face thrown into shadow by the light behind him. He wore dark pants and a dark jacket, and carried something in his hand.

Her hand came out of her pocket, clutching a small canister of pepper spray. "Stop right there! Don't come any closer!"

He stopped and put his hands in the air, dropping whatever it was he held. It fell to the asphalt with a harmless splat. A notebook. "Whoa, hold it. Don't spray, please. Look, Ms. MacLean—"

"How do you know my name?" She glanced across the lot behind him, hoping the deskman would reappear on the dock, and did not lower the spray.

"That's my job." He turned slightly, so that the vague light showed her a shock of stylishly tousled brown hair and an angular nose, but his eyes were lost in the shadows of his face. "I'm a stringer—a researcher for the *Plain Dealer*. My name is Brandon Jablonski. We heard about you finding another Torso killer victim over on Pullman and want to do an in-depth piece on it, the Torso Murders, the history, the effect on Cleveland. Can I ask you a few questions?" He lowered his hands, scooped up his notebook, and got out a pen in one smooth movement.

But he did not move closer, so she did not depress the tiny plunger. "Where did you hear that?"

He gave her a grin, with straight teeth and a chiseled jaw, looking less and less like some psychotic stalker every minute. "I have my sources. What can you tell me about the victim?"

"Nothing," she said, "yet. What makes you think he's a victim of the Torso killer?"

The hands holding his pad and pencil flopped to his sides. "Come on—decapitated on some kind of autopsy table?"

She wondered again where he got this information. The construction workers? Mr. Lansky? The patrol officers?

He went on: "The Torso killer terrorized Cleveland for four years, more really. He was America's version of Jack the Ripper, unparalleled in savagery and never caught. He cut off heads, limbs, genitals. But he wasn't some kind of monster."

"Could have fooled me."

"I mean, he was a monster, but he wasn't insane. The entire city was keeping an eye out for this guy in a day when no one had televisions or iPods or the Internet—in other words, people actually paid attention to what occurred outside their own doors. People knew their neighbors. People, well, people read the friggin' paper. And he still moved around as if invisible."

"I know," she said. "But I can't—"

"He took his victims, he did whatever he felt like to them, and then he dumped them in public areas. And he *still* wasn't caught. He was so unique, as serial killers go. I've read book after book on criminal profiling and still can't get a picture of this guy, who he was, what motivated him. Ms. MacLean—" He took a step toward her.

Her arm with the canister had begun to slump, but now it snapped to attention. "Stay right there."

"I only want to ask a few—"

"I can't answer them. All inquiries must be directed to Medical Examiner Elliott Stone. I'm sure you know the number. Call in the morning and make an appointment."

Another step. "But—"

"No buts. I'm getting into my car now. Do *not* come any closer."

"We need to work together on this, Ms. MacLean. I know you must be as obsessed with it as I am—"

She slammed the driver's door shut and cranked the engine until it gave a whining sound. Brandon Jablonski made no attempt to stop her.

She pulled out, careful not to hit him and careful not to get close enough for him to strike one of the windows. In the rearview mirror she saw the man watching her, rooted to his original spot, a contradictory morass of dark colors and perky smile. Whatever else, he had a healthy respect for pepper spray. It made her wonder if he'd been on the receiving end of it before.

She also wondered if he would skip the helpful "Hello, ma'am" warning next time.

It didn't matter. She could not discuss James Miller's death or its possible connection to the Torso Murders. She might say too much, turn the cop's killing into a media event and reveal too much about herself in the process.

Because she was *exactly* as obsessed with the case as he was.

CHAPTER 6

MONDAY, SEPTEMBER 6
PRESENT DAY

Theresa yawned her way into the laboratory Monday morning, catching the eye of her boss.

"Hot date?" Leo wanted to know, watching her pour a cup of what smelled like burned caffeine. "Did you finally do the dirty with that hostage negotiator?"

"Fell asleep rereading Badal's *In the Wake of the Butcher*."

"That's a sad commentary on your social life. You need to get married again, or at least get a dog."

"I have a dog, and I was never lonelier than when I was married."

"How about some Visine, then?"

She didn't tell him that red eyes were a small price to pay for having her mind occupied instead of lying in bed listening to every sound, automatically assuming it to be Rachael and then having to remind herself it wasn't, that Rachael was away at college, growing up and growing away. "How about the day off, then? It *is* a holiday."

"You had the weekend off. One more day and we'll be buried."

"*You* had the weekend off," she said, correcting him. "I had a bar brawl in the Flats that produced three dead bodies and a lot of blood spatter. I haven't even examined James Miller's clothing yet."

"Better get to it. I got a phone call about you last night. At home, no less," Leo said.

Her stomach did that little dipping maneuver, exactly as it did when she'd been called to the principal's office or her doctor said he needed to discuss some test results. "Why?"

"You have to release that building today. The one on Pullman. Finish up whatever you've got to do and get out of there."

"What? Why?"

"Why? Because the cops can't spare two patrol officers twenty-four/seven to keep an eye on it. Because it's practically rubble now, so what is it going to tell you about a seventy-five-year-old crime? Because Councilman Greer talked the city council into condemning the place and they in turn made a sweetheart deal with Ricardo Griffin and company to build a recycling plant there, and there's a completion clause in the contract."

"But it could be another Torso killing—Cleveland's claim to fame, true-crime-wise! I thought you wanted to make some Hollywood magic with it."

"Turns out Hollywood likes stories that have endings and the local paparazzi are already tired of staring at an empty building."

"Not all of them," Theresa muttered, recalling Friday night's visitor.

"Besides, after their cameras go on to the next warehouse fire or school shooting, I'm still going to be dealing with Greer, and the police chief, and their overtime budget."

"But what's the freakin' hurry? That building has been there for, what, seventy-eight years?"

"Exactly—it's unsafe, about to fall in on itself. If murder groupies turn the place into a shrine, one of them is eventually going to get hurt. Or killed. Besides, shrines don't make money. Getting a huge federal grant to increase 'green' processes, *that* makes money."

"Huh. Well, what else could they do with a location like that, between a freeway and the railroad tracks?"

Leo sipped his coffee, apparently the only nutrient he needed or wanted. "What I'm saying is, get done with what you need to do and release the location, just like you would do for any other crime scene."

She counter-offered. "Can you get your buddy at the college of engineering to GPR the cellar?"

"Ground-penetrating radar? You think he buried bodies down there?"

"I think if he did, we should find them before the backhoes do."

He considered this. "Okay. I'll give him a call. But if he can't work us in by tomorrow at the latest, we forget it."

She nodded, yawned again, refilled her cup, and walked down the three flights of steps to the amphitheater.

Theresa examined most clothing and evidence in the old teaching amphitheater, since it minimized contamination to the lab and also had more room. The lab and its wide windows had better lighting, but the amphitheater worked well when one wanted no lighting at all. The small windows had been boarded over years ago to make slide shows more visible, and if she needed pitch dark all she had to do was hit the wall switch.

Never mind that most people would not want to find themselves standing in complete dark while inside a morgue. Theresa had worked there long enough to know that the dead will not bother you.

The living were, of course, another story entirely.

The back of the victim's shirt, having been soaked in the decomposition fluid that seeped out as the body mummified, held together much better than the front of it. It had hardened into a sort of shield, which Theresa now slid underneath an infrared light.

She had observed the clothing first under ultraviolet light to see if any foreign fibers glowed or any defects—holes—showed up. Then she changed to infrared, which washed out blood and decomposition fluid and illuminated only the material underneath. Nothing of any interest. She switched to the trousers, and what she saw surprised her.

She went next door to the photography department and fetched Zoe, explaining, "I need to do pictures as I go. This material is so fragile I'm afraid I'll make a hole by touching it."

The photographer sighed deeply. Then she made several trips between the two rooms, setting up two lights, a tripod for the camera, the red filter, and the remote shutter release, and sighed again. Infrared photography had to be done in the dark with an open shutter, so the subject—the pants—had to be completely still. Easy enough, but so did the camera. On top of that the camera had to be focused before the red filter blocked the view and then the filter added to the lens without disturbing the adjustment. "What is it that you're trying to get?"

"Fouling," Theresa told her. "There's a little hole just under his waistband, which I thought had just been the belt loop tearing away from the pants, but I saw what might be an oval of fouling around it. The killer might have shot him at close range with the barrel angled upward so the bullet traveled up the internal organs; that would explain why the anthropologist didn't find any marks on the bones. When we're done I'll do a Griess test, which will probably dissolve what's left of these pants." She had hoped, against all probability, that James Miller had had a peaceful death. No such luck.

"Gunpowder will show up after a hundred years?"

"It's only been seventy-four, but I don't really know. I've never tested clothing more than a few days postmortem, that I can think of. I'll have to hope that nitrites don't decompose."

"People do," Zoe warned her.

"Thanks for the news flash."

"I mean, I was just thinking . . . is that hostage negotiator still calling you?"

"I believe his interest has decomposed." He would never be able to take anything as seriously as she took everything, and his hot and cold behavior must have been his way of telling her so. The irony of a man who made his living getting people to express their feelings not being able to express his own did not appeal to her. Theresa did not care for irony, which was too often cruel.

Zoe tested the shutter-release cable. "Are you sure? He's been asking you out for, what, a year?"

Theresa didn't glare at the photographer as she had at Don. Women were *supposed* to talk about these things, at least according to TV commercials, and she'd grown tired of talking to herself about it. "Chris Cavanaugh never wanted to date me. He wanted to sleep with me. God knows why."

"Yeah, that's such a mystery. Can you get the lights?"

Theresa flicked the switch, plunging the room into darkness. The dark brown trousers sat illuminated under a ghostly circle of red light. The body fluid stains receded into the cloth and the sooty area around the tiny hole got darker.

"That could be fouling," Zoe said.

Theresa hesitated to call it. "It could be, but I've never worked on something so old before. Why would he be shot? None of the Torso victims were shot."

"Why is there a problem if you make it with the hostage negotiator?"

"But then the way he left the body—that wasn't the Torso killer's MO either."

The photographer persisted. "You aren't married. Neither is he."

"Because then I'd be one more notch on Cavanaugh's bedpost or gun belt or whatever analogy would be appropriate to him, me and the city manager's daughter and whomever else he winks at. And then he'd move on to the next negotiation. It's what he does."

Zoe depressed the plunger on the remote cable. "So the surest way to get rid of him would be to hop in the sack? And the best way to keep him coming around is to stay out of it?"

And there Theresa stood, caught in the net of her own logic.

"Um—yeah."

Zoe advanced the film, depressed the plunger again. "That *is* a pickle."

The door to the hallway cracked open, which let in the whining sound of a bone saw from down the hallway. Christine Johnson's exquisite face poked in.

"Hey," the pathologist told Theresa, "did you know your guy was shot?"

CHAPTER 7

MONDAY, SEPTEMBER 6
PRESENT DAY

"Unfortunately," Theresa told her cousin, "that counts against it being one of the Torso Murders."

He stopped at a red light on Lakeshore, giving her a good view of the stadium. She still missed the old one, that oversize and clunky edifice that had housed both football and baseball fans for sixty-four years. The modern structure had crystal video screens and more bathrooms but held no memories for her.

"That's unfortunate?" Frank asked.

"If James Miller has nothing to do with the Torso killings, then his murder exists only in the little vacuum we found him in. All attendant information has almost certainly been lost over the years."

"We may never find answers, then," Frank said.

"We will," Theresa said insistently. "I will. But if he was a Torso victim it would have given us a place to start—we'd have had information from the other murders to consider. And it certainly would have made things interesting. Think how pleased Grandpa would be that we got to work on the case."

The light changed. Frank said, "Arthur Corliss sold his building in 1959, died ten years later. We don't know what happened to the wife, but they had one child, Edward Corliss, born 1950."

"And that's who we're going to see?"

"Yep."

"Where's your partner?"

"Sanchez is taking the construction crew through their statements again, trying to figure out which unit our murder room belonged to. She might get somewhere if those guys can keep their eyes off her chest, but that will be difficult. The lavatories were the only concession to modernity; each unit added closets and storage space piecemeal over the years until the interior walls were jumbled. The fire took some walls down and the crew did the rest, but they weren't paying much attention to what partitions were where, not with Councilman Greer breathing down their necks. He's in some kind of hurry for this project to go through. He says it's because the grant will expire, but he's probably got a kickback check waiting on a completion date."

"They knocked down half the walls to that little room without noticing the table?"

"They saw it, but between the dim light and the plaster dust covering their goggles they couldn't see what was *on* it until they were close enough to touch."

"The building is still secured, right?" Theresa asked.

"For the moment," Frank said. "The chief's already gotten a call from Greer. The councilman really has a hard-on for the demolition and is already laying down threats of unfavorable voting come budget time. Happily for us, the chief hates the good councilman's guts. Something about a round of buyouts in the late nineties."

"Do you have a photograph of him? Miller?" she asked.

"I think we're past the point of a visual ID, cuz."

"Very funny. I'd just like to see what he looked like. Was he married? Any children?"

"Wife named Helen, don't know about kids. I can't tell if anyone investigated her. He wasn't considered a homicide, just a deserter."

"Which he wasn't."

"How do you know that?"

"I just do."

Frank chuckled and hit the gas, and the car shot from the I-90 on-ramp to a precarious position between a tractor-trailer and a school bus in less time than even Ford advertisements predicted.

Theresa stifled a gasp, then averted her eyes from the HOW'S MY DRIVING? sign nearly touching their front bumper by glancing into the backseat. "Why did you bring the stalker along?"

"I'm not a stalker," Brandon Jablonski said mildly. "What was that you said about your grandfather?"

"Relax, I'm kidding." At least she thought she was. He didn't look at all sinister in the cold light of day; in fact he seemed to be all lean determination and stubbled good looks, notebook at the ready. "It's just that I've never seen my cousin bring a reporter to an interview before."

Frank made a face he didn't bother to hide from the rearview mirror. "The chief—the police chief, not the homicide chief—considered this a good PR opportunity. After the media ran the story of James Miller and his Torso killer–like death, we've been deluged with calls, so he figures we should use it to make us look good."

"Bringing a reporter along on an investigation."

"The chief also figured that since it's the coldest case Cleveland PD's ever worked, the killer has to be as dead as his victim, so publicity won't cause a problem at a trial."

"I don't know. Some people can be pretty hardy."

Every time Theresa glanced at the rearview mirror she met Brandon Jablonski's warm brown eyes, as if they shared some secret joke—probably how he thought of scaring the crap out of her in the parking lot last night. Now he said, "What would you do if you find the guy and he's ninety-six years old?"

"Arrest him," Frank said.

"Really," the man said thoughtfully.

"Yep."

Theresa stole another look at Brandon Jablonski. "PR," she said. "Sometimes I swear your chief and Leo must be twins. They never miss a trick."

"They could be, since that's why you're here as well as Mr. Jablonski."

"What?"

They continued through Lakewood, crossed the Rocky River, and took a right. "The chief likes the cousins angle."

Jablonski added, "The combination of police work and forensic science, represented by two members of the same family, tackling Cleveland's toughest case. You can't make up stuff better than that."

Frank made that face again. "He thinks it's cute."

"Well, we *are* sort of cute," she admitted.

"Especially you." Jablonski grinned. "What was that you said about your grandfather?"

Theresa hesitated. Speaking of her family out of pride was one thing, speaking of it for possible publication quite another. But she had opened the door, so she said, "Our grandfather and great-grandfather were cops."

"Really," Jablonski said. "Did they teach you about the Torso Murders?"

"Not really. They occurred before Grandpa Joe's

time, and our great-grandfather was a juvenile probation officer, more of a social worker. He met Eliot Ness,
though."

"Yeah?" The researcher leaned forward, resting his
elbows on the back of the front seat like a restless teenager. "The great man himself?"

"Yeah, when Ness founded the Cleveland Boys'
Town. Great-grandpa didn't care for him, though. Too
dapper."

Jablonski frowned. "Dapper?"

"Something of a ladies' man."

"Oh." She could feel his breath on her neck. "Am I
dapper?"

"I wouldn't have any idea. And shouldn't you be
wearing a seat belt?"

He sat back, lips curved. "Still, that's intriguing. Can
the current generation solve the crime that stumped their
forefathers?"

Frank went on as if neither she nor Jablonski had spoken. "Also, you see bodies cut open every day. We need
to figure out who installed a dismemberment chamber in
that building, and you'll probably know what to look for
more than I will. Like that drain hole."

Jablonski promptly returned his face to the back of
the front seat. "You think that was how he got rid of the
blood? They always theorized that the Torso killer had
to have medical or surgical—or even pathology—training, since he decapitated his victims so neatly."

Theresa didn't ask how he knew the details of the
table in the building, only said, "Yeah, but I don't buy
that. One summer—I call it the Summer of the Stab-
bings—"

Her cousin gave a small groan. "Not this story again."

"One each, in June, July, and August, I had a guy
come in dead of a single stab wound. Big guys, healthy

guys. All three hit in the upper left shoulder, because when a killer is right-handed and faces their victim for their Norman Bates moment, they stab the left shoulder. The knife went down behind the rib cage and nicked the heart. All three died before help could arrive, even though at least one had another person present who promptly called 911. All three had been stabbed by their girlfriends or ex-girlfriends."

Frank tried to cut in. "Now—"

She didn't let him. "Now, these girls weren't med students, and they certainly weren't doctors."

"Still," Jablonski said, his attention pinging back and forth between them, "it can't be easy to cut someone's head off. So how do you learn to do it without nicking a bone if you're not a doctor or a surgeon, or a butcher?"

"Same way you learn anything else. Practice. And," she added, "he practiced a *lot*."

"We're here," Frank said.

Edward Corliss lived in the smallest house on a very expensive street, with nothing on the other side of the structure but Lake Erie. The home had stained glass in the front door, marble steps, and a modest but expensive dark sedan in the drive, but Theresa considered its prettiest asset to be the sweeping maple tree in the center of the yard, its leaves ablaze in red, yellow, and orange. The private cocoon of fall foliage nearly hid the neighboring drives, but she could just glimpse a man in a white lab coat stepping into a Mercedes.

She stepped out of the car and sucked in the smell of autumn.

Frank walked beside her and Jablonski took up the rear, following too closely for comfort. She sidled over a bit, uncomfortable with a man both flirtatious and too young for her. She had not encountered one before this.

Most men flirting with her these days were in the midst of retirement planning.

Their peal went unanswered. Frank, never one for patience, suggested they look around back.

"It might take him a while to get to the door," Theresa pointed out. "How old is he?"

Already walking away, Frank said, "Sixty-one. And he sounded hearty enough on the phone."

Theresa followed her cousin and Jablonski followed her. "Tell me about your grandfather. He was a cop?"

"Forty years," she replied. Ivy covered the wall on her left and shrubs lined up to her right. She brushed her hand along their piney branches as they filed to the back. There, the blue expanse of water with the sun reflecting from each wave both greeted and blinded them.

A single dock jutted from the shore, with a small sailboat tied up at its end. Frank had been right; a man made his surefooted way along the bow as he wrapped the sail—though Theresa doubted this could be Edward Corliss. Perhaps he had a son.

When Frank reached the dock and kept going, Theresa followed eagerly. Like any Clevelander, she never needed an excuse to go near the water and breathe in that familiar scent of gasoline and dead fish that meant family vacations on Catawba Island and that feeling of peace a body of water always conferred.

The man on the boat heard them and turned. Wearing a plain burgundy sweatshirt and jeans, he had blue eyes and silvered hair and appeared delighted to see them. "Hello! You must be the detectives."

He leapt to the dock, causing only a minor tremor in the wood, and Frank completed the introductions. Edward Corliss shook hands with each of them, pressing Theresa's gently in his firm fingers. He had an easy smile and the trimness of one who had long ago embraced whole wheat tortillas.

"I'm sorry if you waited at the front—I didn't expect you to get here so quickly."

"Are you getting it ready for winter?" Frank asked, nodding at the sailboat.

"No! It's too early yet. I don't put Jenny away until the lake threatens to freeze. Let's go inside and see if I can help you, shall we?"

He took up the rear, guiding them off the dock like a good captain, and they followed him inside. Theresa ran her fingers through her hair to repair whatever damage the lake's gusty winds had done to it.

Corliss ushered them into an oversize front room done up in russet and gold tones, the colors splashing against the white walls. Windows made up most of the north wall, from which every whitecap on the lake could be seen in frothing clarity. Scarlet carpeting, jacquard sofas, a vast fireplace.

And trains. Lots of trains.

They collected on every surface, end tables, the high mantel, and circled the room on three high shelves. A mahogany table that could have seated twelve had been given over to a mountaintop village with miniature houses and farms and more train tracks than any real mountaintop village would have. Two engines with several cars wound through it, occasionally passing but not colliding with each other. She swore she could smell the evergreens.

"Wow," Theresa said.

"Yes," Corliss said. "I went a little overboard in here. One of the hazards of bachelorhood, not having a wife to stop me. But you're here about my father's building, right? Would you like to sit down?"

Theresa would rather have studied the snow-covered

village and its trains but followed her cousin to the crisp settee. Jablonski perched on the edge of a wing chair, pulling a tiny camcorder from one of his two camera bags. He clicked it on and aimed it at Theresa.

"Your father constructed the building at 4950 Pullman?" Frank began.

"Yes. I mean, he contracted for it to be built."

"Did he have any other buildings in Cleveland?"

"No, no. My father was a railroad man; he only dabbled in landlordship that one time, and only as an investment. My father—his name was Arthur—"

"We know."

Corliss spoke of the large train systems with the same enthusiasm he showed for his miniature ones. "He started working in the rail yards as a boy, moving through every job they had, from loading to shoveling coal to coupler, eventually to detective—like you—with a small railroad company in Pennsylvania. By the time the line's owner began to fall into ill health, my father had enough saved to buy the line. You see, around the turn of the century there were hundreds of small, limited-span lines. In the 1910s and '20s, bigger companies began to buy up the mom-and-pop lines and turned into conglomerates like the Pennsylvania Railroad and the B&O."

Theresa fingered a pair of binoculars on the end table, wondering how close they would bring the whitecaps and seagulls. But she didn't pick them up. They looked too heavy and too expensive.

"Oh," Frank said. Jablonski finally switched the camcorder's gaze from Theresa to Corliss.

"My point is, Pennsylvania bought my father's company and made him one of their vice presidents, as well as a very wealthy man. Rich enough that he could have retired right then, but he loved the trains too much, and besides, the Depression had arrived. He needed a safe investment for his money and figured real estate would be as safe as any."

Frank made a note. Jablonski, the camera perched on one knee, plucked a gold figurine of a steam engine off the coffee table in front of him. Corliss looked askance, and the researcher put it back with the gentlest *clink*.

Frank went on. "He kept an office there for himself?"

"I believe so, yes. He'd take me around there during my younger days, before he sold the place. He also had a desk at the rail yard station—big brick place right on the river, they tore it down in the sixties—and he'd spend a lot of time there, too. He used the office on Pullman more for managing his personal affairs, the building, other investments, and as a place to store his growing collection." The man waved his hand to take in the room. One of the moving trains gave a toot and released a puff of smoke into the air. The not-terrifically-pleasant smell of burned oil reached Theresa's nose. "He passed a lot of these pieces down to me. Could I serve you some coffee, or tea? Ms. MacLean? You look a bit chilly."

"No, thank you. I'm fine."

He seemed to glow a bit at her smile, though it could have simply been from talking about trains. Or his father.

Frank got him back on topic. "Do you remember the building's tenants? From the 1930s?"

"Oh, my, let's see. I remember the architects most, I guess. They rented a unit nearly the entire time my dad owned it. They were always very late or very early with the rent, depending on how their contracts came along. He also had an artist, just after the Second World War— until the guy ran out of canvases one day and painted all over the walls; then my dad kicked him out. Didn't care for the man's taste, he said, nor his judgment." Corliss chuckled over that until Theresa laughed with him.

Frank asked, "How were the units numbered? One through four were the ground floor?"

Jablonski pulled a camera from the second bag. An older digital model, it had double the bulk of the camcorder.

"Yes, and five through eight the second story. He had a medium for a couple of years—a woman who said she could communicate with the dead. My father loved stuff like that. And, as he always said, *she* paid the rent on time. Unlike the doctor."

"Doctor?"

"In the office next to his. Every month my father would have to threaten him with eviction to get the rent, but he'd cough it up at the last minute and buy himself another thirty days."

"What kind of medicine did this man practice?" Frank asked ever so casually. Theresa wished she could hide so much with her voice.

The model train let out another toot. Jablonski took a few quick snaps, all of Theresa. When she frowned at him, he aimed the lens at Corliss.

"Some sort of dietary therapist."

"A nutritionist?"

"I suppose. A bit of a quack, according to my father— there were plenty of them around in those days. You have to remember that antibiotics hadn't been discovered yet and people would try anything. But my dad must have liked the man, or he wouldn't have put up with the rent always being late. He could be very softhearted."

"Must have been a lot of people late with the rent then," Jablonski put in. "Unemployment in Cleveland reached twenty-three percent during the Depression, and most households had a single wage earner. That's why there were so many homeless and transients for the Torso killer to choose from."

"Torso killer?" Edward Corliss blinked at the younger man.

"Would you have any records from your father's ownership of the building?" Frank asked before Jablonski could expound upon the infamous murderer and all his crimes.

Now the silver-haired man blinked at him.

"Any receipts from his tenants? Leases? Tax returns?"

"Oh, I see what you mean. No, no, I'm sure I don't. He sold that building in—um . . ."

"Nineteen fifty-nine."

"Yes. I cleaned this house from end to end after he died, when I moved back from England. My father was not a pack rat, all the trains notwithstanding. I don't recall finding anything related to the building. He had tax returns, but supposedly you only have to keep those for seven years, so I destroyed them."

"What about photographs?" Theresa suggested. "Did your father have any pictures of his building, especially from the 1930s?"

He considered this, hand to chin. "I don't believe so. People didn't take photos of every single thing the way they do now. But we could look." He stood up with the energy of a man half his age and held out his hand to her.

After being helped to her feet in such a courtly manner, she followed him from the room, past the mountaintop village.

"This must have taken years to build," she told her host.

"Oh, this is merely an introduction to my world," Edward Corliss told her. "Let me show you my real pride and joy."

MONDAY, SEPTEMBER 6
PRESENT DAY

They passed through a white-on-white hallway and into a completely changed environment from the front room. No carpets interrupted the light hardwood floor and no draperies blocked the high windows. No furniture save for a waist-high platform in the center of the room, which had to measure ten feet by fifteen.

Corliss stood at one end and turned a crank to roll up the clear plastic sheet that floated on the top, supported by metal rods placed in strategic locations.

No quaint village here. Highways, skyscrapers, and houses upon houses, through which the trains flowed, met, separated, and looped around again on the shores of a blue— "It's Cleveland," Theresa exclaimed. "You've modeled Cleveland."

"From Rocky River to Shaker Heights." Corliss bent over one corner of the platform, opened an electrical box, and flipped several switches. Tiny bulbs lit up in the windows of the office buildings, the airport, gas stations. Trains chugged to life.

"You even have the rapid transit cars." Theresa watched one of the electric commuter vehicles, on which she'd spent so many hours over the years, glide along beside a locomotive. Both at 1:64 scale, of course.

Even Jablonski seemed impressed. He took some stills, then switched back to the camcorder, its lens sweeping the model city from end to end.

Frank said nothing but circled the tableau as if he expected to witness the model citizenry engaging in various crimes. He needn't have worried. The replicated city had every accoutrement down to park benches but not one citizen. Theresa did not find that surprising—they'd have had to be the size of ants and number in the hundreds to populate this metropolis.

"Here's the Medical Examiner's Office." Theresa could have spent an hour noting every detail to the display. "How long did this take you to build?"

"About a year, I suppose. But I'm never really done. I'm always tinkering with it—I spent three days on the swing bridge this past week after its motor decided to quit. Then I decided to make it winter—at least in part of the city. Here, let me show you."

He picked up a pint-sized plastic container and popped off the lid. Before she could react, he scooped up her hand and immersed her fingers into the white goo. "Brush it on the trees like this, lightly, so it sort of frosts them but not completely."

It had been a long time since a man held her hand. The white stuff felt like cottage cheese but drier, the tiny plastic limbs rough but flexible. Under her fingers, Christmas came to Cleveland.

"Do you ever crash them?" Jablonski asked, tapping one engine as it went by.

"Of course not!" its creator snapped. "And don't touch that!"

"Sorry."

"I could stand here all day." Frank's voice sounded patently unconvincing, but perhaps only to someone who'd known him since her birth. "But we really do need to learn more about your father's building."

"It's here." Theresa pointed out the stone structure's miniature copy. It looked better in the model than in real life—tidy and still alive.

Frank raised an eyebrow to let her know she was being less than helpful. "Can we check for the photographs, please?"

"Certainly. You have to excuse me, I don't get many opportunities to show it off. My neighbor is a fan, but other than him . . ." Edward Corliss handed Theresa a rag for her fingers, switched off his tiny city with obvious regret, carefully replaced the plastic dust cover, and took them to a much smaller room off the back of the house. Bookshelves covered nearly every inch of wall space except for framed prints and drawings of trains, and it smelled of dust and pipe tobacco.

"They're not in an album, I'm afraid, only loose in a box," Corliss warned them as he dug through one of the lower cabinets. "Father didn't always have my sense of order. Or Mother's."

"Where is your mother?" Frank asked.

"She passed away, oh, must be more than forty years now. Before father did. Let's see what we have here." He sat at a wooden desk that would have required six bodybuilders to lift and flipped the top of a box that had once held Audubon Society note cards. The other three people in the room watched over his shoulder, Theresa leaning close enough to pick up the scent of Old Spice. She loathed Old Spice because her first boyfriend had worn it. She decided not to hold that against Edward Corliss.

After donning a pair of reading glasses, he turned the photos over, one by one, gently but methodically. "This is my baptism, you don't need to see that . . . those were our neighbors, they've since moved . . . my flat in England, I still regret selling that, the prices have shot up in the past few years . . . my graduation . . . ah, here's one. It's the outside of the building, though."

Theresa peered at the black-and-white image, still sharp after so many years. "Which one is your father?"

He tapped a lean finger on the man in the center, who was wearing creased trousers and a white shirt with a tie. He bore some resemblance to his son, mainly in the deep-set eyes, but seemed taller. He carried his suit coat tossed over one shoulder, and a rounded hat had been pushed back from his forehead. He posed in front of the same entrance Theresa had passed through yesterday morning; his clothing and the shadow behind him told her the picture had been taken in summertime, when the sun hung to the north.

"Who are the other people?" Frank asked.

On Arthur's right stood a gaunt man in similar clothing and a young woman in a long black skirt and a coat festooned with chiffon scarves. She had wavy dark hair and smiled. The man didn't. On the other side of the owner, two young men seemed to be jostling with each other and their images had blurred. Behind them and off to the side sat a man with less-neat clothing and a ruined expression.

Corliss said, "I'm only guessing, you understand, but I'm sure my father told me at some point that these two young men are the architects I spoke of. And—again, I'm not sure—this man could be that doctor."

"The nutritionist?" Theresa asked.

"The dietician, yes."

"Who's the woman? Is that your mother?"

"No." Edward Corliss brought the photo closer to his face and then backed it away again, as if that might help jog his memory. "I have no idea. She could be the medium. Father always described her as an outlandish dresser."

"What about this man, in the background?"

Corliss shrugged. "Again, no idea. He could be anyone, someone working for the other tenants, a passerby. He could have been a bum, I mean, a hobo. My father used to try to help them during the Depression, give them a meal, let them sleep there a night or two if he had any vacant units. I said he had a soft heart, and during those years there were plenty of men who needed one."

"When was this photo taken?" she asked.

Corliss turned it over, showed them the *May 5, 1936,* printed in block letters. "The man could have been a messenger for the railroads or one of the other businesses, I suppose, or he could have spent the night on the front stoop and hadn't left before they snapped the picture. As I said, a common occurrence then as now, the poor souls sleeping on the sidewalk. Sometimes I think not much has changed."

Jablonski spoke, startling Theresa. He had moved to just behind her left shoulder. "Who took the picture?"

All four people peered at the snap with new interest.

"Your mother?" Theresa suggested.

"No, they didn't meet until after the war. I really don't know. A friend, I suppose, or another tenant."

Frank asked, "Did he ever mention someone disappearing from his building? A tenant? A client? Even a hobo?"

Corliss considered the question, shook his head. "I'm sure I would remember something like that."

"Did he ever mention a James Miller?"

"Not that I recall."

"So you have no idea who this dead man we found could be?"

"I've been thinking of nothing else since you called this morning. No. I have no idea." His eyelids fluttered suddenly. "Surely you don't think my father had something to do with that."

"We don't have any theories at present. Do you mind if we borrow this picture?"

Corliss pulled it away, toward his own chest. "My father wouldn't kill anyone. No one."

"I understand," Theresa said.

"Unless they deserved it," he added, and turned over the picture. The sentiment did not seem too odd; Theresa had heard it before. Corliss continued to sort through the photos but the only other find, from an investigator's point of view, came near the bottom of the box.

"This is my father's office at the Pullman building," Corliss told them.

Corliss Sr.'s office bore a great resemblance to Corliss Jr.'s study, aside from the color of the walls—white in the photo, pale caramel in the room in which they currently stood. Plenty of bookshelves supporting model trains instead of books, and framed pictures of same. Arthur Corliss stood by himself, facing the camera with crossed arms and a self-satisfied expression. A notation at the bottom read: *November 1935*.

"This is the same desk," Theresa said.

Edward patted the worn surface as if pleased she had noticed. "Solid cherry. An unusual design for the time, the flat top. Office desks were always rolltops, with all those little cubbies for storing things, but as office work increased in the new century, efficiency experts decided that a plain top minimized clutter and backlog. The pigeonholes made it too easy for workers to stash their work and forget it."

"Interesting," Theresa said.

Frank didn't find the historical trivia quite as fascinating. "There's a door."

"Door?" Corliss asked.

"Door?" Jablonski asked.

Theresa noted the opening, framed by wooden molding, in the wall behind the desk. "Is that the bathroom? Did you ever visit your father's office, Mr. Corliss? Do you remember its arrangement?"

He frowned in concentration, peering at the photograph. "Vaguely. I would have been only seven or eight, you understand."

"Did it have a small lavatory?"

"It had a sink. I remember how old the fixtures seemed. And a bit rusty."

"Anything else? A closet? A storage space?"

"I don't think so, but I really can't be sure. I had just turned nine when he sold the place." He handed the photo to Frank and went through the rest of the box but did not find any more of the building at 4950 Pullman.

With the interview winding down, Jablonski the stringer came to life. "Did you work for your father's railroad, Mr. Corliss?"

"A bit, in my younger days. I ran the dispatch office for a few years, but then decided to break away to the more sophisticated climes in Europe and England. Silly, as it turned out, but not entirely unproductive: I read mechanics and chemistry at Oxford and then settled down to a respectable job as a civil engineer."

"Buildings?"

"No, roads. Traffic patterns were our main concern." He stood up, visibly stretching his legs, and plucked a four-inch-long locomotive carved from ivory from a shelf. He pressed it into Theresa's hands, guiding her fingers over the glossy surface. His eyes, she noticed, were blue with blue-gray flecks, like bubbles in champagne. "I bought that from a pipe maker in Bath . . . remarkably smooth, don't you think? Anyway, then my father died and I returned to manage his estate. I also took over his position in the preservation society."

Jablonski pounced on this. "The what?"

Frank's pager buzzed, that angry-bee sound.

Corliss answered without looking away from Theresa. She had not been a tactile person for many years but somehow didn't mind the warmth of his hands wrapping hers around the ivory train. "The American Railroad History Preservation Society. I'm the vice president. We're hosting a cocktail party–slash–fund-raiser at the art museum next month. You should come."

Was this older man hitting on her?

Of course as her officially ancient birthday loomed, sixty-one no longer seemed too far out of line, especially a well-spoken and interesting sixty-one, so perhaps she should consider—

Then she thought of her fiancé, dead for fifteen months now, and it all seemed absurd. Her, her job, a seventy-four-year-old corpse.

"All of you," Corliss added.

"It's beautiful," she said of the train, and placed it back on the shelf. "Thank you for showing us around."

"Any time. I'm only too happy to share my collection. See this gear? It's from an original Union Pacific steam locomotive."

"We have to go," Frank said.

"Mr. Corliss, did your father ever mention the Torso Murders?" Jablonski asked.

"The what? Oh, those, the bodies in the river. I'm not *that* old, young man. Those things happened long before I was born."

"*Now,*" Frank added.

Both host and reporter seemed disappointed as the party moved back to the front door, their voices echoing slightly against the foyer's high ceiling. Corliss said, "Do come back if I can help in any other way. Take my card, Detective—there's my phone number. It's been a pleasure to meet you."

"Thanks," Frank said.

Jablonski asked if he could come back with follow-up questions, perhaps in the next day or two, and Corliss agreed.

"Thank you," Theresa told him. He responded by touching her elbow as she made her way over the threshold, a courteous gesture, gentlemanly, except for the way his thumb caressed her forearm as he did it.

As she slid into the passenger seat, she noticed Corliss still watching from the open door. "That was interesting."

Frank mumbled under his breath.

"Did you get a call?"

"I'm going to drop you off at your car, Mr. Jablonski," he said by way of response, and nosed the car out onto the boulevard.

"Your boss said I could stay with you two all afternoon, following the investigation. . . ."

"Only the cold case. Not a current one."

The grim way he said it convinced Theresa that the rest of her day had just been claimed as well.

Jablonski sprang forward like a pointer catching a whiff of quail. "You mean there's been a homicide?"

"No comment."

"Oh, come *on*!" he protested. Theresa could hear real frustration bubbling up from his carefully maintained persona.

"No."

The reporter threw himself back in the seat. "We'll see about that."

MONDAY, SEPTEMBER 6
PRESENT DAY

The Cleveland Air Show began as national air races, an idea brought to the United States from Europe by Joseph Pulitzer, the man for whom those prizes are named. The purpose in 1920, as now, was to encourage interest in aviation. The show rotated through several cities until Cleveland hosted the largest and most (indeed *only*, to that point) financially successful show in 1929. Fully three times larger and longer than today's shows, the 1929 show established Cleveland's ownership of the event.

Particularly in these early days, the work could be dangerous. Occasionally a pilot would be lost. But in 1949 a racer banked his Mustang too sharply at one turn and crashed into a house in Berea, killing a young mother and her baby son. The air show shut down for the next fifteen years.

Today, the usual commercial and air taxi services at Burke Lakefront Airport are suspended every Labor Day weekend as citizens pack the bleachers to watch pilots, wing walkers, and parachutists defy the law of gravity. Nearly all of them would remain unaware of this year's tragedy, but then, this death had nothing to do with airplanes.

When Clevelanders say "lakefront airport," they mean it. Walk north one hundred and some feet from the runway and your shoes will get wet. The edge is built up with piled rock to keep the grassy buffer from washing away, though the Port Authority officers patrolling this Labor Day were not concerned about natural predators. Only human ones. Cleveland did not have a large number of possible terrorist targets (much to the relief of its citizenry), but the air show, with its large military presence, had to qualify.

And so the Port Authority officer had been policing the perimeter on foot when he discovered the girl's body. Or rather, part of it. He stared at it for a long time, that completely obvious yet somehow indecipherable object. Then the officer took out his radio, called his supervisor, and said a silent prayer of thanks that the piled stones sloped downward to the water and therefore the body or part of a body lay just below the line of sight from the bleachers. There were a hundred thousand spectators on the south side of the tarmac. At least half of them carried binoculars.

Theresa had attended the show in exactly two of her (almost) forty years. She wondered if this visit counted as number three, though they didn't enter the show, only skirted around it down a small access road between the runways and the water.

A marked patrol vehicle led the way, without activating his lights or sirens—the air show organizers wanted only scripted drama for the customers. Theresa did not feel discretion to be the better part of valor while on such an active tarmac and tried to look in all directions at once as she drove. Did someone tell the pilots that they were coming? Around her were biplanes, fighter jets, and one massive thing that had to be some kind of military transport. What if one landed on her?

The patrol car ahead pulled off the road and parked on the patchy lawn next to the seawall.

Noise assaulted her ears as she stepped from the car. A deafening, thorough noise that invaded the head and then bounced around inside, crowding out the smell of gasoline and dead fish and the excited hum of the spectators. Theresa forgot all about the dead body she had come to see, forgot about getting her camera or crime scene kit, nearly forgot her own name, just stared at the sharp-edged jet suspended in space between her and the bleachers. The people in those seats appeared as oscillating pixels of color through the light-bending waves of heat put out by its engines.

Frank appeared at her elbow. "Come on."

"What *is* that thing?"

"Harrier. It hovers. Come on."

He helped by carrying the toolbox with the large plastic markers numbered one through thirty. She would use them to photograph small pieces of evidence within the scene. She also took her camera case, her sketching kit, and a plastic crate stuffed with paper bags, evidence stickers, and measuring tape. That covered the necessary equipment for most of her duties, though if there had been a shooting she would have had to get the laser trajectory kit and maybe the metal detector to find spent casings. If there had been a sexual assault, she'd have needed the battery-operated alternate light source, so that the semen would glow in the ultraviolet light. If the body had been buried, she'd have had to get the shovels and the sieves to sift the dirt. This was why Frank had driven Theresa back to her office, to pick up the battered county station wagon with all her equipment. At least they had gotten rid of the persistent Mr. Jablonski.

Another officer, in a uniform Theresa did not recognize, waited at the water with Frank's partner, Angela Sanchez. They watched her approach with ominous solemnity. Frank had told her only that a body had been found near the air show. Driving separately, she could not get any further details and now guessed she would not care for any details once learned.

The edge of the land crumbled into a protective wall of large stones before dipping into Lake Erie. She could not hear the water lapping on the rocks but caught its fishy smell. The officer, she noted from his uniform, was from the Port Authority.

Spread out over the rocks lay a woman's body, back to the rocks, chest to the sun, the right hand trailing lazily into the water as if she had been trying to get one last tan this summer. But only part of her. The torso ended at the waist, and at the neck.

No lower body, no head.

No sun would tan this now-bloodless corpse.

Theresa said, "Wow."

"Yeah," Angela said. "Not something you see every day."

"Something I could have happily never seen." Theresa shivered, only, she told herself, because the brisk lake breeze carried a hint of winter.

"Any chance that's a very early and very effectively rendered Halloween decoration?"

Theresa shook her head. "Definitely a real human being. Or at least she used to be."

The woman had been skinny, with the perky breasts of youth. No jewelry or nail polish, no injuries other than the obvious, except for a scratch on her left middle finger. The nails, bitten down until the ends of the fingers bulged past them with that puffy, rounded shape, would tell them nothing about defensive actions. There would be no skin cells from the killer left under that worn-down keratin.

Theresa moved closer, tested the piled rocks before depositing her weight, and steeled herself before examining the torn neck and bisected waist. She might have seen blood and guts every day on the autopsy table, but encountering it in a new way could still come as a shock. The white vertebra surrounded by dark red muscle was gross to look at and didn't tell her much. Nevertheless she would safeguard that area in particular since a pathologist could garner a great amount of information from it—what weapon had been used, how it had been used, whether any trace evidence had been left in the mess.

Frank stepped gingerly onto the rocks behind her. "Please tell me it's a boating accident. She got drunk, fell overboard, and got run over. The boat's owner didn't report it because he's married and didn't want his wife to find out he was pleasure-boating in more ways than one."

He didn't have to shout anymore; the Harrier had finally landed and its engines eased down into quiet. Now Theresa could hear the crowd, the sound of distant milling and conversation. "I'll let the pathologist make that determination—but I doubt it. It depends on the size of the propeller, of course, but I have a feeling there would be more cuts, and of varying depth."

Frank sighed. "This day is just getting better and better. So it's deliberate—probably still a boyfriend."

"Probably." To do such damage to a body required a great deal of energy and the rage to fuel it. Unless the killer turned out to be the rare complete psychotic, he most likely felt quite personal about the victim. A criminal mob might use beheading to strike fear in their enemies, but throwing the body away where it might never be recovered would defeat the purpose. Dismemberment might make a body easier to conceal, but the lake could handle any size corpse. A killer might dismember the body to hamper identification, but leaving the hands with potentially recoverable fingerprints would defeat *that* purpose. This killer had no purpose in mind other than hatred. While she lived, the victim most likely received a healthy amount of attention from the opposite sex. Perhaps it had turned into an unhealthy amount.

"A personal connection would be a really good thing in this case. If we can identify her, the killer will pop up somewhere in her circle." Angela's optimism sounded forced.

Theresa said, "It would be helpful, because chances of finding trace evidence are slim to none. Smart money's on none. There's nothing quite like soaking in a large body of water to wash any incriminating hairs and fibers away."

"How long do you think she's been in there?"

"Not long. She's only just beginning to bloat. I'm surprised she surfaced at all." Usually bodies didn't float until they had decomposed enough for the tissues to fill with gas. This one should still have been on the bottom, and each wave bubbling up through the piled stones threatened to carry the body away again. Theresa poised herself to grab the left wrist should it become necessary.

"There was a lot of activity inside the breakwall this morning," the Port Authority officer informed them. "Anyone who has a boat is out on it, watching the air show. The water got churned up."

The low concrete breakwall, designed to keep the treacherously shallow Lake Erie from eroding the shoreline, lay slightly more than a quarter mile offshore.

"That must stretch at least two miles in either direction," Theresa pointed out. "How likely is it that she got in here from the open water?"

The officer squinted at the sun reflecting off the waves, pondered the breakwall, and took a deep breath. Theresa expected him to lick one finger and hold it up, but instead he said, "I'd guess she was inside the breakwall to begin with, since you say she hasn't been in there long. But there's really no way to be sure. That's the thing about water. It does what it wants."

Another noise ramped up, higher in pitch than the Harrier but equally loud. "Is that the Blue Angels?" Theresa asked, trying not to sound like a teenage girl and having a hard time of it. The Navy jets had been the stars of the air show for as long as she could remember.

"Thunderbirds," Frank said, correcting her. "We get the Thunderbirds now. They're Air Force."

Six jets passed overhead, flying, of course, in perfect formation. The sound of them seemed to come up from the ground and invade her body like an electric shock, reverberating in her heart. That sound, not quite like any other in her experience, had always been her favorite part of their act. Once again she neglected the victim to gaze, unabashedly, at the sky. "Wow."

"Yeah, wow," Frank said. "Can we get back to the dead person, please?"

"Mm-hmm, okay—hey."

"What?"

Out on the tarmac, the air made hazy by the dust and heat the planes kicked up, something appeared to be moving toward them. Not a plane. A person.

She squinted. Two people, strolling across the runways with complete disregard for the dozen planes possibly taking off or landing at any moment. "Should they be doing that?"

The Port Authority guy looked, swore, but stayed by their side as he radioed the situation to his colleagues. "What kind of nuts are these?"

"Probably drunk bigwigs," Angela Sanchez guessed. "They came from the VIP tent."

"Why didn't you say something?"

"I thought it was part of the show."

The Port Authority guy scowled, moved out in front of them, and put his hand on the butt of his gun.

Neither of the two people appeared to be Brandon Jablonski, so Theresa left him to it and returned her attention to the body. Four inches below the dead woman's right elbow, on the outside of the forearm, something triangular and very thin had left a light singe mark in the skin and pale hair. Not torture—right on the surface, as if she had brushed up against something small and hot, rather than its being pressed into her flesh.

A voice made her look up. The two walking people had crossed the road nearest them and wound past their vehicles. A car with flashing lights—Theresa assumed it to be the Port Authority reinforcements—came tearing up the entry road from the far west edge of the airport but would not reach them before the people did. Not that this gave her any cause for concern, since the two people approaching them did not appear threatening: a young woman in a body-hugging miniskirt, making impressive time in strappy platform sandals, and a man wearing a well-cut suit and tie. He did not seem as enthusiastic about their little jaunt as his girlfriend and scowled at her back.

"Stop right there," the Port Authority cop said. Frank said nothing, only watched with a tight face. They were on the port department's turf, Theresa realized. You don't poach another man's authority, no matter how tempted.

"OMG," the woman said, pronouncing each initial. Her face seemed familiar, as if Theresa might have seen it on the society pages or a billboard. "What's going on? Did you find a bomb? Or is it a dead body?"

"You just walked across an active airfield, ma'am," the cop said. "Don't you think that's a little dangerous?"

"There weren't any planes coming or going. The Thunderbirds are going to be up for the next fifteen minutes."

As if to emphasize her point, the team of jets zoomed overhead again, and again Theresa could not resist watching them until they became minimized by distance.

Unfortunately they proved equally irresistible to the Port Authority officer, and the woman advanced another five feet before he noticed and said, "This is an active crime scene, ma'am. You'll have to leave."

"It's okay," she assured him with the confidence of the clueless and waved a hand at her companion. "This is Councilman Greer."

The man in question said, "Tasha—"

"I don't care who he is." The Port Authority officer had run low on patience, or perhaps he also didn't care for the councilman's voting record. "You're leaving the area. Now. This car pulling up will give you a ride back to the bleachers so you don't have to walk across the tarmac—"

Tasha had pointed the toes of her impressively long legs, and the extra few inches were all she needed to see down the slope. "Oh my—look, Benjy, it really *is* a body! Look at that! It's all torn up!"

The Port Authority officer waved to his colleague, who was now crossing the grass, and repeated his order that they leave the area immediately.

"Oh, for heaven's sake, she's just looking," the coun-

cilman snapped. He was a handsome man of indeterminate age, indeterminate race, and, if today's exhibition
gave any indication, indeterminate sense.

Tasha had grasped his arm, but not for support or
comfort. She nearly jumped up and down in excitement.
"This is so *cool*! It's so gross!"

At this Theresa stood up and planted her feet directly
in front of the body. "This isn't TV, ma'am. This was
a *person*, not an object for you to gawk at just to put a
thrill into your perfect little life."

Tasha had apparently made a lifetime habit of simply ignoring anything unpleasant and only twisted her
body to see around Theresa. The councilman flushed.
"There's no need to get insulting. You do this for a living—how ghoulish does that make *you*?"

The second Port Authority officer reached them, as-
sessed the situation with one glance, and took Tasha by
the forearm. "This way, ma'am." She could have moved
or been gently pulled off her feet, so she walked, her face
still turned toward the water, while dipping and turning
to get one more glimpse of the mutilated corpse.

When the first officer tried the same technique on
Councilman Greer, however, the man snapped his arm
away. "Get your hands off me. I have an honorary
badge, you know."

"That's the only reason I'm not putting you in cuffs, *sir*."

"Fine, I—" The man turned. Moving away from the
officer brought him one step closer to the shore, and
suddenly the councilman, too, caught sight of the dead
body. The blood left his face and it turned a ghastly sort
of orange.

"Better catch him," Frank said. "I think the good
councilman's going to faint."

Greer didn't, though, merely turned away and took
a few unsteady steps. The Thunderbirds did a vertical

climb over the lake, their engines whining, their sharp outlines silhouetted against the cobalt-blue sky. The cops present watched, of course, as anyone would, but Theresa stopped to swat a late-season mosquito and therefore witnessed the councilman drop to one knee and lose his lunch onto the grass.

Theresa wrinkled her nose, grateful that the planes drowned out the sound of retching. Talk about gross.

The man glanced up, wiping his mouth, noting that the three officers were turned away from him. Then his eye fell on Theresa.

She couldn't resist. She smiled.

He gave her one malevolent glare before bounding up to be escorted away by the officer with his girlfriend, as if the officers would not be able to conclude how a cup or two of vomit had suddenly appeared on the turf.

Men and their egos.

Theresa went back to the body, lifting the left hand and turning it over. Still no signs of defensive wounds. She had a tattoo of a bleeding rose on the inside of her pale wrist.

Frank leaned over her shoulder. "Finding anything? Other than that she liked roses?"

"No bruises or sticky residue around the wrists—no indication that she was bound."

"So she must have been unconscious when he took her head off, or already dead. Right?"

"That would be my guess. We should at least be able to get some tox results, see if she'd been drugged."

Angela crouched near the woman's shoulder. With the Thunderbirds in the distance a quiet fell over the shoreline, broken only by the lapping waves and the occasional gust of wind. "Kind of weird, isn't it?"

"Finding a chunk of a dismembered body on the banks of the air show?" Theresa asked. "Yeah, I guess."

"No, I meant two beheaded corpses in the same week. What are the odds?"

"We only *found* them in the same week. The murders themselves took place seventy-five years apart. Hardly a pattern."

"I didn't think you believed in coincidence."

"I have to. I've seen them. Once I had two women come in within a half hour of each other with the same relatively unusual method of suicide, gassed by a propane tank and a plastic bag."

"That is kind of odd."

"No, I found their home addresses odd. They lived around the corner from each other. At first I thought it must be some kind of suicide pact."

"What changed your mind?"

"Their suicide notes. They both left one—unusual in itself, only about a quarter do—but one was a shopping list of instructions and the other a booklet of poetry, a perfect illustration of right-brain and left-brain orientations. Same action, very different methods and motivations."

"And you think our two headless corpses are the same thing?"

"Unless we have a ninety-year-old serial killer running around, yes. Miller probably died at the hands of a mobster or Cleveland's Mad Butcher. This girl either had the bad luck to cross the path of a modern-day serial, or she had a fight with her boyfriend."

"Remind me not to date." Angela shrugged. "Oh, wait, after the last guy I'll never need reminding again."

"Now there's a story I need to hear," Theresa said as she checked between the fingers for trace evidence, finding none.

"No, you really don't."

Most men were murdered by enemies or business

rivals. Most women were murdered by someone who had promised to love them. And now Rachael would be meeting boys, young men, who didn't have to stand in Theresa's foyer and introduce themselves when they picked her up. Only a roommate Rachael had described as silly and neurotic to witness in whose company Rachael left the dorm, the campus. . . .

The county's ambulance crew arrived. Two men, one white, one black, both gently unhurried and neither appearing strong enough to lift the sometimes quite hefty victims who needed a ride to the autopsy room. They stopped at the edge of the seawall and simply absorbed the scene for a moment or two, as every other person present had. The two Port Authority cops conferred in the background, apparently having a good gripe session about the gall of Councilman Greer.

"You're killing me, missy," one of the body snatchers said to Theresa.

"Come on, Duane. I don't get to pick 'em."

"Twice in one week," the other, Tom, intoned. "You must not be living right."

"I don't see how I could live any *more* right. I sleep alone, exercise, go to church, and eat tofu, for cryin' out loud. This isn't my fault. At least she's not heavy."

"You sleep alone?" Tom said. "I know guys who would pay for that information."

Duane merely handed her the edge of a white sheet to spread over the rocks so they could flip the torso onto its chest. Moving a dead body could often produce noxious odors as fluids in the body shifted and released, but Theresa smelled only the brisk, fishy water. The skin appeared clean except for some dirt adhering from the rocks.

"Well, she wasn't shot, stabbed, or bludgeoned," Theresa concluded. "At least not in this part of her body." She held up a corner of the sheet and they used it as a hammock, lifting the torso and moving it to an open body bag spread out on the grass. They avoided the remains of the councilman's last meal.

Theresa pulled off her latex gloves. "I doubt there's going to be much I can tell you, but we'll see what Toxicology says about her fluids and what the pathologist says about the injuries. I'm sure you've already contacted Missing Pers—"

"Wait." The first Port Authority officer had returned and interrupted her. "There's more."

"More?"

He jerked his thumb over his shoulder, indicating the coastline that spread into the east. "Another piece."

"The other half of her body?"

"Not exactly . . . just a *piece*."

The boom of the Thunderbirds, roaring back into the grandstand area, covered Theresa's response.

The group moved half a mile along the seawall to view what else the Port Authority staff had found. Theresa once again crouched on wet rocks with water flooding up beneath her shoes, and saw what the cop had meant. One piece. The head.

Theresa had no doubt it belonged to the same victim. Female, underweight, short blond hair. Eyes glazed over as if she no longer cared to see the world around her.

Theresa examined the ruined flesh at the neck, looked around for trace evidence, and steeled herself to pick it up and place it on a clean sheet for the body removal crew. *Think of it as a basketball,* she told herself. *A ten- or eleven-pound basketball, with eyes. And a mouth, which might have spoken to her killer, asked him to spare her life. A brain that had held feelings and hopes and dreams. A-okay, now. One. Two. Three.*

Theresa lifted and deposited and managed to do it with her eyes open. Well, half open.

Two beheaded victims in the same week.

The lake could have been the one area of Cleveland that hadn't changed since their dead detective's day. If James Miller could have been transported forward seventy-four years to this spot, he wouldn't know any time had passed. The water remained the same, knowing, silent, treacherous. The first victim of the Torso killer had washed up in pieces from this same body of water, though not connected to the murderous series for well over a year. The Lady of the Lake, they had called her. She had never been identified. Theresa decided this girl would not suffer the same fate. She would have a name to put on her headstone.

She felt Frank's hand on her shoulder, warm and squeezing gently. "By the way," he said, "happy birthday."

"Not yet," she reminded him. "I have four days left."

MONDAY, SEPTEMBER 23
1935

Everyone called it Jackass Hill, the origins of which had been lost in time. A steep slope of Kingsbury Run between the dead ends of East Forty-ninth and Fiftieth, it made for excellent sled riding in the winter but seemed dull and forlorn during fall, that period of time when death stalked the flora. Sparse weeds and other haphazard growth covered the ground from the ridge to the valley and poked up between the train tracks. Weeds and cops. Half the detectives in the city had beaten James and Walter there, as well as a good portion of the uniformed division; no matter, since the case would be assigned to more experienced detectives, not them. They had shown up for the same reason everyone else had—curiosity.

Though once James saw what the knot of officers had gathered around, he reminded himself what had killed the cat.

A dead white male lay on his side in the twigs and

brush. One leg stretched out at an angle and the forearms flopped in a relaxed position in front of the chest. The man would have appeared to be asleep were it not for the fact that the body was nude (except for a pair of socks) and headless. James could only assume it was male, since those distinguishing parts had been removed along with the head.

He stopped, looked down, concentrated on his shoes for a moment. The leather had begun to part from the sole on his left one.

Walter reached his side, got his look at it, stared like a moth at the sun. James waited for the cursing, but all his partner could muster was: "Wow." After a moment, he added, "Did you see stuff like this in the war?"

James had seen every type of injury a soldier could suffer, delivered by everything from a bayonet to heavy artillery, every way men could use machines to kill other men, but that had been different, impersonal, cold. "Not like this," James said. "Nothing like this."

"It doesn't stop there," a nearby cop told them. Jazzed by the drama, he promptly became their tour guide and led them to a second body that had been treated just as the first. No head. The missing genitalia from both men had been left together in a sad little heap.

James noticed two uniformed guys using trowels to turn over the earth where a dark material mixed in with the weeds. "What are they doing?"

"Digging up the head. The—whatever he is buried both heads but left their hair sticking up through the dirt." The cop shrugged, one sharp spasm of movement. "Buries them and then leaves it so they're found. Why do that?"

James nodded at the small pile of severed parts. "Why do *that*?"

Walter took out a cigarette, lit it, and puffed deeply

without once looking away from the decomposing tissue. "I've seen a lot of weird things on this job, Jimmy. Bad things. Sick things."

James nodded again. "But nothing like this."

"*Shit* no."

It should smell like a slaughterhouse, James thought, *but it doesn't.* A whiff of death, yes, but not the metallic, turned-meat odor of carnage. He looked again, this time pushing the horror to a far corner of his mind. "They're awfully clean, the bodies. I don't even see any blood soaked into the ground. One guy strafed with a German machine gun would leave a puddle three feet in diameter."

"Coroner says they were moved," the uniformed cop told him.

"Haven't been dead that long, either," James said. "It hasn't rained in the past few days, so that wouldn't have washed all the blood away."

His reasoning failed to impress the uniform. "You're about the tenth cop to point that out. They were dumped here, like the coroner said. We've searched all the open areas out about two square miles, and there's no pools of blood anywhere."

James moved back to the first body, taking in the lack of scratches and the relatively clean socks. "These are two good-size guys, and they weren't dragged. This guy carried them down here?"

"He must be a moose," Walter said, trailing behind him. "Or he had a partner. Maybe partner*s*."

"There's nothing here—no houses, stores. He must have a car, got them as far as the top of the hill. Why not toss them out and go?"

"Because he wanted to do the little burying-the-heads thing. And leaving the . . . in a pile," Walter answered.

"Because he *wanted* to," James mused, staring hard

at the body now. "So much so it made the risk worthwhile."

The uniformed guy shook his head hard enough to loosen a few Brylcreemed locks. "Pervert. Killing guys like—*that*. Got to be some kind of queenie."

"Or he didn't come down the hill," James added.

Walter had gotten over the first shock of seeing the bodies and now took refuge in sarcasm. "What, he flew?"

"No, he definitely didn't fly. I'm just saying maybe he didn't come from the road."

"From where, then?"

James did a quick 360 scan. "A train?"

Walter turned to the myriad of rails crossing the valley floor, beginning two hundred feet behind them, glinting in the slanted afternoon rays. "He hopped off a train with a dead body tucked under each arm? Jimmy boy, you've got to stop going to bank nights at the Allen. Those movies are giving you a wild imagination."

"He didn't need to bring both at once. And it would explain where all our blood is."

"It rode away in a boxcar? A bull would have found it by now. They inspect those cars every day."

"Unless it was on its way out, turned up in some other town where the railroad police are puzzling over it right now."

"I think it would be easier to come down Jackass Hill with one of these guys hefted over your shoulder than jump off a moving train with one. You'd break both legs. Unless he really is some kind of giant."

"No. Nah, you're probably right. Or he—"

"McKenna! Miller! Get over here!"

Their captain, short but hefty, his hair a crawling fringe around a widening bald spot, and a uniformed guy had been inventorying a pile of clothing left by the bodies. *Very neat,* James thought, *he stacks the clothes in one spot, the cutoff body parts in another,* and reached out to accept the brown paper sack the captain held toward him. "That's a coat. We think it belongs to the second guy, from the size of him. Find out where it came from and who it belonged to and don't let me see you again until you do."

"Sure thing." The captain didn't seem to trust James any more than the rest of the cops and didn't speak to him often. Encouraged, James held the paper bag out for Walter to see as if it were a new nickel.

His partner screwed up his face. "You carry it. I'm not touching anything this murdering pervert had his mitts on."

James did not relish the idea himself but put the distaste out of his mind. How to proceed? Most of his detective work so far had been questioning witnesses and informants until one coughed up a name. But once he had tracked down a hammer used in a burglary by finding the store that sold it and visiting every one of the customers they sold that brand to until one of those customers bolted at the sight of him. He and Walter would have to do similar work now.

Once in the car, he shuffled the garment around within its bag until he found a label. "B. R. Baker Company. I guess we'll have to find a store that carries these."

"They'll be closed now. We'll have to start again in the morning."

"We could find the owners at home, get them to open up."

"Then they'll have to call in the department managers, and they'll have to call up the sales managers and then the floor men—it will take two hours tonight to do what we could do in ten minutes tomorrow when everybody's there. Applesauce. It's been a long enough day as it is."

James gave up. The most bizarre homicides this city had ever seen, and his partner wanted to go to sleep.

But he hung on to the bag, didn't leave it at the station. The captain had given it to him and with him it would stay. He hadn't even wanted to leave the station itself, a situation as unusual as the two bodies on the hill in its way. For one evening he didn't feel like an outsider with his own coworkers. For one short period the other cops forgot all about who was on the level and who was bent and who was out-and-out crooked, united by a common horror.

He walked home from the precinct house at Wilson and East Fifty-fifth, dead leaves scuffling under his feet, fresh air in his lungs, carrying the paper bag.

CHAPTER 11

TUESDAY, SEPTEMBER 7
PRESENT DAY

Theresa picked up the miniature notebook, which James Miller had left folded open to the most recent page; many of the preceding pages were covered in writing, stuck to each other in some spots, and the sheets after that point were blank. The first section of the notebook had wound up in the center; thus protected, the writing remained relatively clear.

James had begun his notes on April 20, 1936, with the case of a purse snatched from a lady's arm outside the Playhouse Square movie theater. His handwriting could get murky, but it seemed James had noted the woman's description of the perpetrator (twenty-five to thirty, torn brown jacket) and the movie she had intended to see (*A Quiet Fourth* with Betty Grable). He had interviewed a few witnesses, expressing his opinion of their veracity with a system of exclamation points and question marks. Theresa could picture him, in a brown suit coat with a hat pulled low on his brow, the marquee lightbulb glinting off his eyes as he stared down a squirrely customer.

Leo's voice at her elbow made her jump. "So is it him?"

"Who?"

"The Mad Butcher of Kingsbury Run."

"Leo, aren't we going to look a bit foolish if we suggest to the population of Cleveland that we have a nonagenarian serial killer in our midst?"

"They'd love it. If we can link this guy to the Torso killer the national outlets will pick it up. Then these local TV wimps will have to run the story, councilman or no councilman. What's that? Is that from the girl?"

"No, our 1935 victim." She began to separate the pages, gently, using a plastic set of tweezers. "The girl didn't have anything on her but a tiny blob of brown paint in her hair. It's got a fiber in it, though, probably carpeting, red polyester in a trilobal shape. Oh, and also two little flecks of white stuff."

"*Stuff* is not a forensic conclusion."

"I'll run it through the FTIR. Otherwise the lake scrubbed her poor little body 'til it gleamed. There was no one in Latent Prints on the holiday, but I suspect they'll turn up her ID today—she looks unnaturally skinny to me, with that junkie pallor." The tips of the notebook pages crumbled as she pulled on them to open the book flat.

"You going to put that under the ALS? I'll go with you."

She protested. "You really don't have to do that. . . ."

"Don't be silly. I'm always ready to help one of my staff with a thorny problem. Besides, *U.S. News and World Report* will be calling this afternoon and I'd like to have something to tell them."

"But I thought we never released information on an open ca—"

"I'd like," he repeated, holding the door open for her, "to have something to tell them."

She kept her sigh to herself and carried the notebook in its tray down the two flights of steps. The ultraviolet light apparatus stayed in the amphitheater, since she normally used it for clothing examinations.

They were in luck. The decomp fluid hadn't caused the ink to run, and the ultraviolet light moved past the decades-old blood and decomposition fluid as if they weren't there, then sank into the writing as if filling up its indentations with blackness.

"It seems to be a list." She stared at the page, sorting out the words in her head.

"One would assume he took notes on his investigation, just like any detective," Leo mused, breathing into the cubic foot of air surrounding their work. He had lunched on something with curry in it. "I wonder if he was working on the Torso Murders. Hey—maybe he *is* the Torso killer. Wouldn't that be great?"

"No," Theresa snapped. "That wouldn't be great at all."

"Well, interesting, anyway. Famous serial killer turns out to be cop. It's usually the number three theory anyway, after 'doctor' and 'spoiled son of a wealthy family.' The same ideas they had about Jack the Ripper."

Theresa wrote her translations onto her worksheet, squinting in the near dark. "Any theories about why the Torso guy took their heads off?"

"He thought they were vampires and wanted to make sure they stayed dead?"

"I've been reviewing the literature. Decapitation as a method of murder is very rare, so rare I can't find anything written on the subject. Bodies are often dismembered to make them easier to dispose of, but the Torso killer must have had other reasons. Sometimes he divided his victims into pieces but then left them where they were sure to be found, so it wasn't done to hide the body. Sometimes he scattered them about town."

"Proving that no man is an island, that sort of thing?" Leo guessed.

"Then some he hung on to for a while. And yet he had such an eclectic mix of victims—all genders and ages, like the Zodiac killer or the Night Stalker. So maybe it's not a sexual thing."

"Are you kidding? He emasculated a couple of them. Besides, is serial murder ever *not* a sexual thing?"

"Good point," Theresa said. "Then with a number of his victims, he removed only the head. Why the head?"

"They do it in the Middle East."

"But that's more of a political statement. I suppose it's always been popular for political murders, from the samurai to Vlad the Impaler to the French Revolution. But for your average psychopath, not so much."

"Maybe both our killers wanted to be different."

"But why decapitation?"

"I don't *know,* okay? Can you figure out what that says?"

James Miller had written:

> *pills*
> *dog hair*
> *newspaper*
> *food in stomach*
> *RR tar?*
> *bull?*

"How are you making that out?" Leo demanded.

"If I can read my own handwriting, I can read anyone's."

"His lists are just like yours. A bunch of words that don't mean anything."

"My lists mean something to me." She turned a page, moving backward into the notebook. "These must have meant something to him."

> Kingsbury—June 5, 1936
> decapitated WM, about 20s
> slim, many tattoos
> naked
> no blood!
> right in front of RR police—why?
> clothes piled—J.D.

"So he was definitely still alive in 1936," she said. "And he *was* investigating the Torso Murders."

"And solved them. He caught up with the guy."

Theresa stared at her boss, his face a ghostly echo in the weak UV light.

"What?" Leo said. "That didn't occur to you?"

"Yes, but—" The idea had been there since they had found the body, of course, but putting it into words forced her to picture it: A dedicated cop tracked down the monster the entire city had been looking for. He solved the crime of the century but never had a chance to tell anyone. His only legacy came to be that of a deserter, a bum who walked off the job.

In a split second James Miller went from being an intellectual exercise to a tragedy.

"What?" Leo said again. "What are you looking all sniffly about?"

They were jumping to conclusions, of course, not just jumping but leaping with reckless abandon, both feet off the ground. Yet she had never been more certain of anything in her life.

A beam of light split the room, cleaving her and Leo to opposite sides. Christine appeared in a white coat, backlit like an angel. "Here you are again. What is it about you forensic types and the dark?"

Theresa cleared her throat. "We're used to it. Years of working for the county have taught us to burrow."

"Well, dig yourself out and come see this."

Theresa sidled over to where she knew the light switch would be and flicked the lights. Leo blinked.

"You're not going to tell *U.S. News* about this, are you?" she said to him.

He shook his head, chin in hand. "No. No, I think we're going to keep this to ourselves for a while, until we can flesh out every detail possible."

"Good."

"Then it's straight to TruTV."

Theresa followed Christine to the autopsy suite, where her eyes reacted badly to the brilliant light and therefore she viewed the girl's corpse from under lowered lids until her pupils adjusted. The torso had been opened and the organs removed through the Y incision. The head lay on the steel table, nearly touching the shoulder. The killer had left the top of the neck nearly level with the shoulders, with the raw circle in the center making a crater in the body rather than anything resembling a neck. The head had a short stem at its base.

"What?" Theresa asked.

"The head has been removed from the shoulders," Christine stated.

Leo let out a puff of impatient air.

Theresa said, "I had noticed that. You might say it jumped right out at me. Looks like he did a rather tidy job of it, all things considered."

"Actually, it's fairly messy. He stopped and started again, downright hacked in places."

"So not as neat as the Torso killer."

"You mean the Torso killer who would be about

ninety or a hundred years old now? Okaaay. Well, from the condition of the wounds I think it's safe to say it's not the same guy. My *point* is, when I tried to piece the two together"—she slid the head toward its rightful place, stopping with no more than a quarter inch to go.

"You do that?" It had never occurred to Theresa to reassemble a body like a macabre jigsaw puzzle.

Apparently it had never occurred to Christine not to. "Of course. Now, see how it looks?"

"Gross?"

"Missing. If we took a needle and thread and did a Dr. Frankenstein, this girl would look like an NFL quarterback. No neck. She's lost about two inches of neck, including two vertebrae."

Theresa and Leo exchanged a look. "He wanted to hide something," Leo said.

"A tattoo?"

"He left the roses."

"She might have had something more distinctive on her neck. Her name, or his."

"A bite mark," he suggested. Christine and the diener waited, the doctor patiently, the diener a little less so, their heads swinging back and forth with each new theory.

"We can't know about sexual activity," Theresa said. "Not without the rest of her. What about tool marks from a particular weapon, a unique knife?"

"Nothing unique about the knife," Christine told them. "A single edge, serrated, could be part of any kitchen set. Also, she still had a good amount of blood in her heart."

Theresa considered this. "So her heart had stopped beating before the decapitation, otherwise it would have pumped itself dry with the carotids opened like that?"

"Even with no head?" Leo asked.

"The heart is fairly autonomous," Christine replied. "It would keep going at least long enough to empty most of the five or six quarts. A girl this skinny, perhaps only four."

Theresa said, "So she was already dead when he cut her head off. Given the choice, I'm sure she preferred it that way."

"Maybe she had a heart attack when she saw that knife coming at her," Leo said. "I know I would."

Christine nixed that theory. "No, her coronary arteries weren't bad, considering the tar in her lungs and the old needle tracks in her arms. She could have been poisoned, somehow OD'd . . . though I didn't see any obvious foaming in the lungs. . . . I don't know. We'll have to wait for the tox results, and for me to get a closer look at the organs. We might find a tumor or aneurysm in the brain, too, but I wanted to show you the missing section before I started on the head."

Theresa's phone rang and she unclipped it from her belt.

"Our lady of the lake is Kim Hammond," her cousin reported. "Arrested three times for drug possession, once for solicitation, over the past six years."

"Interesting. I'm standing next to her now." She summarized Christine's findings. Frank listened, then said he and Sanchez were going to try to track down Kim's mother.

"See if she's got a soldering iron," Theresa said before hanging up, her gaze on the small burn on the dead girl's arm. "If the killer knew this girl at all, he had to know we would ID her instantly through her prints."

"Therefore he didn't remove any part to hide her identity," Leo said, continuing her reasoning.

"Therefore he removed it to hide his own."

"Or he didn't know her at all," Christine put in. "And

he didn't guess she'd have prints on file. He removed parts because he wanted to, because it made sense to him. Though usually they take something more—melodramatic. A breast, or the heart."

Theresa sighed. They could stand there and throw out theories all day, for all the good it would do them. "True. Okay, let me know if there's anything else you find, or that I can find out for you."

"How about who killed her?"

"Give me time."

"Oh, and before I forget," Christine said, "happy birthday."

So much for time.

CHAPTER 12

MONDAY, SEPTEMBER 23
1935

Helen had already eaten. James didn't care, didn't feel hungry anyway. He washed the table free of every speck of toast and jam and then spread out the coat, faceup. It smelled a bit musty but not offensive, with an almost chemical scent. The second victim, the one who most likely owned the coat, had had leathery-looking, almost tanned skin. No one at the scene knew what could have caused that. James had never seen anything quite like it, not even during the Battle of Belleau Wood. Twenty-six days with no place to put the dead had given him a close look at the stages of decomposition. It had also given him a reason to become a cop, figuring that if he could withstand that experience without losing his mind, he could withstand anything.

Except the lines.

"What's that?"

Helen leaned against the doorjamb, soft brown hair back in a braid, flannel nightgown reaching her ankles.

He didn't dare tell her the origin of the coat. Helen didn't like to hear about his job at all; his exploits as a Marine on a heroic field of battle made good dinnertime conversation for their few friends, but not breaking up a brawl or wrestling with a teenage house thief. Especially if the story involved blood, immoral behavior, or dirt.

Besides, he wouldn't know where to begin describing what he'd seen on that hill. "I worked on a burglary case this evening."

"Wash that table good when you're done. And there's coffee in the pot, if you want to warm it up."

"Thanks. Is Johnny sleeping?"

"Like the baby he is," she joked. Helen was a decade his junior, and it had taken seven years of marriage to conceive John; no matter what else occurred she and James remained united in their adoration of the tow-headed infant—even if Helen had expected more amenities in a marriage to a man with a steady job. She winced as someone thumped a chair on the floor in the apartment upstairs. "Even through the Taylors' nightly argument."

"Good." He bent over the coat once more. Walking home from the station he had formed more theories about how the bodies came to rest where they did. Perhaps the killer had thrown them from the trains and then jumped himself, or perhaps he had dragged them down the hill fully dressed, removed the clothing at the scene, and took most of it away with him. That way the skin would not have been scratched or poked.

Helen said, "Have you heard of Fiestaware?"

"Hmm? No."

She pulled out a chair, sat down, then must have caught the faint funk of the dead man's coat and pushed herself backward a foot. "It's a new line of dishes. They're heavy pottery and they come in all these bright colors."

"Honey? Do you have a magnifying glass?"

She left the room, returning with the round glass and a magazine, already opened to a dog-eared page. "See? This is Fiestaware. It should be available around Christmas."

He glanced at the ad featuring a tomato-red plate, glossy, concentric circles the only design element. Tacky, he thought, but knew better than to say so. "Looks kind of—garish."

"Bright," Helen corrected him. "It would give the kitchen some color."

He glanced around. "You wanted everything white. You said it was sanitary."

The magnifying glass confirmed his observations. No slivers of weeds or broken leaves. This coat had not been dragged down the hill or thrown from a train. The guys at the scene were right. This monster had carried both men, both nearly as tall and a little heavier than James, a considerable distance.

"It is sanitary. But it will also make the dishes stand out."

"What's wrong with china?" He should just shut up, he knew, but failing to keep up-to-date with Helen's budget could have consequences, and besides, he needed to get this conversation over with so he could concentrate.

"China's old-fashioned. You can't have a spaghetti party on china."

"Now we're having people over for spaghetti?"

Back in her chair, she flipped another page in her magazine but declined to show it to him. He knew it would feature a photo of a group of well-dressed, laughing people eating the Italian import, another new craze that didn't appeal to him.

He turned the left front pocket out, slowly pushing the fabric out from the inside, with the glass held above it. Lint, a dried and crumbled sprig of clover, and some brown shards. He moved the glass up and down to bring them into clearer focus, decided they were most likely tobacco. He had rolled enough cigarettes to know. "Do we have an envelope?"

"Yes. Why?"

"I need to put this in something. To keep it."

She looked up from the magazine. "Pocket lint? You've been reading Sherlock Holmes stories again, haven't you?"

"Helen!"

"I have two envelopes left and I need one to pay the electric bill."

He couldn't argue with that. "All right. How about a piece of paper?"

"I keep some scraps in the knife drawer."

When James had folded the motley collection into the center of a department store advertisement, he turned his attention to the right pocket. A hole had worn through the thin cotton, and nothing save some fuzz remained. Items in the pocket would have fallen into the lining. He flipped the coat open.

Helen sighed audibly. "It would be nice to have a spaghetti party," she said now. "It would be even nicer to have some friends to invite to it."

"Sure." He patted the lining with his fingers, detecting a coin, a sticklike object, and two small, hard nubs. Now, how to get them out?

"We could invite Walter and his wife."

His fingers barely fit through the hole. He couldn't rip the lining out; that might get him in trouble with the very captain who had entrusted him with the item. Besides, the Bertillon guys would examine the coat for pieces of evidence; he and Walter were merely supposed to trace it. But he didn't want to wait. "Where's your sewing scissors?"

She crossed her legs. "Who else besides the McKennas?"

Quicker to get the scissors himself. He sliced through a mere four sets of stitches at the bottom of the liner, figuring he could explain it to the Bertillon unit when he turned it over to them. James also figured he'd better address Helen's latest gambit before she invited half the neighborhood. "I'm not sure we can afford new dishes. I'm not sure we can afford spaghetti."

"I don't see why not."

"Can you hold this up? By the shoulders, like this. I need to work out whatever's in the lining." He hoped any future newspaper accounts would not mention this coat. If Helen ever found out what she'd put her hands on, they'd have another murder to investigate—his own.

She took her time about it but helped him suspend the coat over the kitchen table. He shook the lining and worked one side of the coat's layers toward the tiny opening he'd created. Along with the lint and grains of dirt, a penny and two pills fell out. "I know it's hard for you to stretch this household as far as you do, honey. But the whole country's in a depression."

"We don't have to be. You choose to."

He started on the other side of the coat instead of responding. His fingers worked out the stick, and that's all it was, a thin twig from some kind of plant. Why would a guy have something like that in his pocket? But he had clover in the other one, so why not?

"All I'm saying is, next time a butcher wants to give you a roast or a grocer offers you a sack of apples, take it. Just take it. If they want to give you gifts, who are you to turn them down?"

He snorted, unable to ignore the terminology. "Gifts? Is that what Walter's wife calls them?"

Helen dropped the coat onto the table and resumed her seat.

The 1932 penny had a spot of tar on its reverse. The

pills were different, both round and white, but one had an *A* stamped into it and a slightly larger diameter. "What are these?"

"How should I know?" Helen leaned forward to glance at them. "Aspirin? Ask a pharmacist."

His breath whistled through his teeth in frustration. "They'll be closed this time of night."

"Yes, they will. At least take it from the guys running numbers, or the—what d'ya call them, the bad men—pimps. At least take *their* 'gift.' It will just go back into their business if you don't."

"Well, that's a handy bit of reasoning."

"You'd let your son starve for your pride?"

They'd had this conversation so many times now that he wouldn't have believed it could still wound him. "Of course not. But Johnny's not starving, and it's not just my pride."

"Then what is it? Don't tell me you're afraid of losing your job, James, because they can't fire the whole force. You're more likely to lose it because your superiors don't trust you because you're not like them."

Helen was not stupid.

Maybe I am, James thought, unable to find the words to describe what he meant. "It's not pride—it's not *only* pride. It's because if I'm like everyone else, if being a cop doesn't stand for something but makes me just one more hustler in with all the other hustlers, then . . . what's the point?"

"Point? Your life has to have a *point*?"

It sounded ridiculous the way she said it, and yet . . . "Yes. Doesn't everyone's?"

She stared at him so long that he expected a burst of either tears or laughter. But in the end she merely stood up and walked out, taking her magazine with her, their inability to communicate intact.

Helen had buried both her parents, left her family farm, and withstood the birth of Johnny with barely a whimper. She could handle adversity when she knew no alternative existed. But what James saw as integrity looked to her like a willful, purposeless deprivation. A seething anger had replaced any former admiration for him, but he didn't know what to do about it. They had no one in the city to talk to except each other, and lately they couldn't even do that.

James warmed up the coffee and, not for the first time, wished he could afford a shot of bourbon in it. But if it meant depriving his wife of her Fiesta whatsits, then he could not indulge himself. He thought perhaps he *should* give in. What difference would one more corrupt cop make, in a city crawling with them?

His gaze fell on the two pills, a more concrete topic than his marriage, and one with concrete answers. When did the drugstore open?

Theresa finished transcribing the notebook found in James Miller's pocket, except for several pages too badly stuck together by decomposition fluid. He had definitely investigated some of the Torso killings. He had even sketched one of the crime scenes at Kingsbury Run, the area that used to be known as Jackass Hill, with two sad stick figures without heads to represent the victims. One had been labeled "A" for Edward Andrassy, she guessed, one of the few identified victims. The other had a question mark.

In the margin, he'd noted, *Don't tell Helen.*

His wife? What couldn't he tell her? And why?

Not that there wasn't a mountain of daily details Theresa had kept from her daughter, ex-husband, and mother over the years. Tiny facts that could not be gossiped about at the workplace or beauty salon because you never knew who talked to whom, and knowledge or lack of it could convict or exonerate a suspect. Or items that were simply too gruesome or disturbing to unleash upon those who weren't trained to live among them. It could be a lonely line of work, always filtering one's speech, always compartmentalizing one's life for the protection of others.

The infrared spectrometer gave a beep; it had finished searching its database for a spectrum like that from the two white flecks found on Kim Hammond. The specks had appeared to be nearly circular under the stereomicroscope, bright white and soft, like plastic. The Fourier Transform Infrared Spectrometer interpreted a transmission of light through the specks and produced a spectrum showing the functional groups present in its molecules. Polyethylene. Great. One of the most common polymers around.

The lines wavered before her eyes and she yawned. Sleeping hadn't been so easy in the past few years, especially since the incident at the Federal Reserve. Sometimes she could still feel the barrel of a gun grinding into her flesh—another thing she and James Miller had in common. But she had lived through her experience. James had not been as lucky.

Her desk phone rang, and she bruised one shin getting around the FTIR in time to answer it.

"Is this Theresa MacLean?" a woman demanded, her aged voice quavering a bit.

"Yes."

"Are you investigating the Torso Murders?"

How did this get past the switchboard? All calls had been routed to the police department, where they had more operators and were used to dealing with the cranks and the nuts and the people who simply wanted to chat about Cleveland's colorful past. "I need to refer you to—"

"I saw your name in the paper. I want to talk to you

about who killed that man you found in the building on Pullman."

"You need to speak to the police."

"I've already spoken to the police. I've spoken to the police for the past eighty years and they've never done me a bit of good. I want to speak to you."

Eighty years? "I appreciate that, but I doubt I can help you—"

"Never doubt, young lady. The world is just waiting for a sign of doubt to pin your feet to the floor and keep you in your place. I signed up to be an army nurse and spent the Second World War in the Pacific. Then I built an orphanage, walked along the Great Wall, knocked over a bank, and had three children. Never doubt."

"Okay," Theresa said. "And you know something about who killed James Miller?"

"I should."

"Why?"

"Because he almost killed me, too."

She called Frank, who assured her that since the murder had occurred seventy-four years previously she should feel free to investigate to her heart's content and not worry about stepping on CPD toes, especially since his toes were currently following the trail of the murder that had occurred that week. "You want to go visit some old lady, go right ahead."

"Her name is Irene Schaffer Martin—but she was Irene Schaffer then, a young girl. If she can actually recall the players in that building—"

"—and she's not completely senile," Frank added, "then sure, it could be helpful."

"I would think you'd be more interested in the murder of a fellow police officer."

"Notes made at the time suggest that my fellow police officer was up to his neck with a local boss named Harwood, and I'm not seeing anything to refute that."

"Did this Harwood make a habit of beheading his victims like the Torso killer?" she shot back.

"Speaking of that," he answered without answering, "the homicide unit received twenty-five phone calls just this morning from people whose great-grandpa or distant uncle or ex-neighbor told them who the Torso killer was. We even had one who said *he* was the Torso killer despite the fact that he wasn't born until the late fifties. Recall also that the entire police force worked on this case for over a decade and got nowhere. The freakin' untouchable Eliot *Ness* got nowhere. My own captain says he can't decide if he's assigning it to me as a reward or a punishment. Meanwhile I got a twenty-two-year-old with her head cut off, so excuse me if I find that a little more pressing, especially since nothing gets the media's attention like the brutal murder of the young and nubile. So go ahead and talk to this lady, and if she's got anything real or even plausible to say, I'll come out and take a statement. Deal?"

"All right." Perhaps that would be best, anyway. The woman had been firm about not wanting the police, and given Frank's mood, Theresa didn't want him either.

"Did you hear about—"

"Speaking of James Miller," she said at the same time, "did you get the ballistics back?"

"They've got to work the rust out before they can do a test-fire. Say, you might want to check out that nursing home while you're there. Now that you've passed over the hill."

"You're farther down the other side than I am. And it's a retirement community." She placed the receiver in its cradle and enjoyed approximately ten seconds undisturbed by any male animal before Leo stood in front of her desk with a mass spec report and a cell phone, as if ready to dial up *U.S. News & World Report* at any moment. "What's up?"

"Um . . . nothing."

Better to beg forgiveness than ask permission, and better to check out Irene Schaffer before unleashing the hounds of gonzo journalism on her. Or Leo.

Theresa went looking for Christine Johnson. She found the doctor in the autopsy room reserved for decomposed bodies—an odor-soaked room that could make grown men ill—snipping the fingers off James Miller's desiccated body. Theresa averted her eyes. "I *hate* it when you do that."

"Cleveland PD wants 'em." The doctor brought the handles of the pruning shears together, the *snap* sound identical to the sound of a small branch breaking. "They think if they work with the skin enough they can tease out a positive ID with prints. Apparently all cops were fingerprinted, even back then. Good luck to them, I say—these suckers are dry."

Of course merely finding James Miller's gun and badge on the corpse would not be sufficient identification. But the man being made to suffer this final indignity overwhelmed her. She tried to focus on an empty latex glove box on the counter. No one ever stocked the decomp room. "I wanted to know if you'd reached any conclusions about Kim Hammond and her missing section of neck."

"Nope." *Snap.*

"No?"

"I can't really be sure what killed her, much less what happened to her neck."

"Having her head cut off didn't do it?"

"She had too much blood left in her heart to have died of exsanguination. But so far tox is negative, no drugs, certainly no OD. She had edema in the lungs, no edema in the heart, and petechiae in the eyes." *Snap.* "That might mean asphyxiation, but pulmonary edema can result from a dozen different things, probably three dozen."

Theresa turned to ask, "Could she have been—augh. How many times are you going to have to do that?"

"Ten. I should think that would be obvious. Ten fingers, five on each hand. Humans are remarkably consistent that way."

"Could Kim have been smothered?"

"Doubt it. There were no impressions of her teeth against the inside of her mouth."

"Strangled?"

"Possibly."

Theresa watched her drop a severed, shriveled digit into a small jar of 70 percent alcohol and tried not to picture James Miller's hands as he took his careful notes. "You think someone could have cut out part of her neck to disguise the fact that she'd been strangled and not decapitated?"

"Or he saw a TV show where the cops got a fingerprint or the precise and unique size of the killer's hand from a bruise on the victim's skin or some such nonsense. Or he doesn't care what we think the cause of death is but does care what we think of his handiwork, and"— *snap*—"he did such a hack job taking the head off that he kept trying to neaten up the edges, which would be no easy task once the head had been disarticulated. Then he wound up shaving a lot more off than intended."

Theresa helped her zip up James Miller's body bag. "It just seems weird."

"Really? You mean the part where he killed her or the part where he cut her body into pieces and threw them in the lake?"

"I mean assuming Kim is a strangulation that looks like a decapitation. James Miller is a gunshot that looked like a decapitation."

Christine screwed lids onto the jars, tightening each one. "Oh, sure. The two have a lot in common, except that one occurred seventy-five years before the other. That kind of sets them apart."

"Seventy-four. I don't think they were committed by the same person. I just think it's weird."

"Maybe your respective killers don't care about official cause of death. They just like removing people's heads."

Theresa nodded.

"Or the pathologists who worked here in the 1930s got so distracted by the headlessness of the bodies that they missed other CODs. They wouldn't have had any women in the autopsy room then, you know," Christine added, as if this would explain any errors. "All men. Too many egos getting in the way of accuracy."

"I doubt it—chauvinistic or not, scores of people observed every last bit of flesh and evidence in the Torso killings. I wonder sometimes if they were more thorough than we are today—they didn't have technology to fall back on, no DNA or infrared spectroscopy or databases. Every piece of trace evidence had to be run down by old-fashioned legwork. And I don't think *headlessness* is a word."

"If it's not," Christine said as she stacked the jars into a small box, "it should be."

"What are you going to put on the death certificate?"

"I don't know yet. Why do you think I'm down here dodging the phones? Members of the media are calling me every five minutes wanting to know if she was dismembered alive. What is *wrong* with people?"

"I don't know, but if I did it would certainly explain the appeal of certain Hollywood offerings."

"I keep telling them that I'm waiting for the medical records and that will buy me some time. At least I can fill in one box with absolute certainty."

"What's that?"

"It's definitely a homicide."

Theresa left the fusty decomposed autopsy room and climbed the two flights of steps to the third floor to knock for admittance to the toxicology department. Unfortunately the team of pleasant, younger women who largely staffed the place had gone to lunch, and that left Oliver.

Theresa tiptoed into his lair, a corner bordered by a window, a workbench, a barrier of tall gas tanks, and the mass spectrometer. Oliver sat with his body mass spilling over the edges of the task chair, reading a gas chromatograph spectrum as if it were a racing form. And ignored her.

She watched the mass spec twirl its samples for a while and then said, "Kim Hammond."

Oliver turned a page. "The inside of that girl's body must have borne some resemblance to a nuclear plant after meltdown."

"Actually it wasn't bad. But that's youth."

Oliver grunted.

"I take it you found drugs in her hair?"

The dead cells of the hair shaft had long been used to detect drugs and poisons and their metabolites. Since hair generally grew at the rate of half an inch per month, it could provide a timeline for that activity as well.

"It would be simpler to tell you what I *didn't* find. To put it in layman's terms, cocaine, heroin, Xanax, THC—that's marijuana—"

"Thanks." She gritted her teeth. Putting up with Oliver's rampant self-esteem was the price one paid for prompt and thorough information. "I know."

"—oxycodone, and some little gobbledygook I think might be airplane glue. Plus amounts of caffeine and nicotine that should have been fatal in a little thing like her. This girl was an omnivore."

"What's in the last half inch or so?" The hair that grew during the past month would tell them of her most recent activity.

"Nothing. Sad, I suppose. She got off the stuff and died anyway." He did not sound sad. He sounded as if he were observing an unusual but not particularly interesting peak on a mass spec graph, which, to him, was all Kim Hammond represented.

"Poisons?"

"If you mean toxic compounds, no, not that they would have had time to grow into her hair anyway. But of course I checked the blood, urine, and gastric as well, since that's what I live to do here, one might call it my raison d'être, to put disgusting things into little tubes so it can tell us disgusting secrets."

"No obvious poisons."

"I refuse to repeat myself."

"Not even alcohol."

"I'm not sure I would call alcohol a poison, but that's for the do-gooders to debate. No alcohol."

"She was clean."

"And still dead," Oliver pointed out. "Rather turns the whole concept of karma on its ear, don't you think?"

CHAPTER 14

Returning to the lab, Theresa walked right into an ambush. Leo waited at the laboratory door for her, his body between her and the coffee machine. Never a good sign.

"We have a visitor."

In a rare absence, the Medical Examiner was away presenting a seminar in Columbus, so city councilman Greer had been shown into the conference room, where the battered 1950s décor had done nothing to improve his mood.

He invaded her personal space immediately, towering over her in a suit too heavy for the weather. She hadn't noticed the watery eyes or the weak chin upon their first acquaintance, but then they'd been separated by some distance and a dead body. "Are you the one holding up my building?"

"Um." She puzzled over this choice of words for a moment, then said, "No. I—we're—investigating a homicide that occurred there."

"Yeah, seventy-four years ago, and you've already removed the body and all your clues or whatever. Yet you need to turn my building into your own little stage. This isn't about you, Ms. MacLean, get that?"

"Of course it isn't—I don't know what would make you think—"

He held up that morning's edition of the *Plain Dealer*. "This, maybe?"

Metro Section, first page: *New Torso Victim Discovered in Downtown Building*. A subheading went on: *Third generation of Cleveland law tackle the case dads couldn't solve.*

He slapped the paper down onto the conference table. "Next you'll be declaring the place a historic landmark, I suppose, just to draw out your fifteen minutes of fame."

"Absolutely not." She glanced at Leo, who stood away from them, off in neutral territory between the file boxes of old records and a broken X-ray machine. In true Leo fashion, he would wait to see who won before choosing his side.

"You have no idea what you're interfering with, Ms. MacLean." He managed to make her name sound like an obscenity, standing close enough for her to feel the heat from his chest and smell the garlic from his lunch.

"I know a man was murdered—"

"The economy of this city is being murdered every day! Every minute we delay a recovery project, more Clevelanders have to declare bankruptcy and face foreclosure. I want that building released immediately."

"You were right in the first place, Councilman. This has nothing to do with me personally. We investigate every homicide thoroughly and we will do so in this case. After we examine the cellar with ground-penetrating radar, we will promptly release the building."

"I'll bill the county for lost ti—what?"

"I have someone lined up to do it this afternoon. If no new information turns up, then we are done with the building." She hated to do it, but she would have to let the site of James Miller's murder go. "Provided my supervisor concurs."

Her supervisor nodded feverishly.

The councilman backed off a few inches, allowing her a half-fresh breath of air. "That's what we're waiting on? For some egghead to look for buried bodies?"

She would not have expected the councilman to be aware of the uses of ground-penetrating radar. "Yes. The time elapsed since the murder occurred doesn't mean we investigate with any less diligence—"

"It's that bastard from the Twenty-second Ward, isn't it? He put you up to this."

"Councilman," she said with a sigh, preparing to tell him that she wouldn't know the Twenty-second Ward if her car broke down in the middle of it, but he stepped up to her again until his blue pinstriped shirt blotted the rest of the room from her vision.

"Don't bother, I don't care who it is. But understand this: This is a very important project. *Very* important. So if I get one more problem from this office, if you affect this project in any way again, you'll never get another job in this county. Got it?"

Too surprised to be afraid or even angry, she said, "Yes. And I'm sure Officer Miller sends his posthumous apologies for getting himself murdered in a building you want to sell."

His eyebrows knitted themselves together as he tried to work out those words into a statement relevant to him, apparently failed, and turned to go. Leo hurried after him, echoing cries of "So glad we could be of assistance, Councilman," down the hall.

Theresa waited for her heartbeat to return to normal. "I hope you don't mind me speaking for you, James," she muttered. "But I thought it appropriate."

Somewhere in the next world, she felt sure, James Miller chuckled.

In the empty room, she sat down at the conference table to read the article. Brandon Jablonski had not written it, though his name appeared as a contributor. But the wording and the enthusiasm for the Torso Murders sounded like him.

It began with a brief recap of the Torso killings and their impact on a depressed Cleveland. By the sixth murder, twenty-five detectives were working the case full-time, the most assigned in Cleveland history. They investigated every missing or suspicious person report; traced every piece of clothing found with the bodies; ran down even trivial, backstabbing complaints citizens made against their husbands, coworkers, or neighbors. The city counted on the great Eliot Ness to solve the case, but he never personally took the reins of the effort, instead working on a widespread police corruption case that resulted in thirteen convictions, two hundred suspensions, and a host of reassignments and resignations. A different kind of authority figure began to spearhead the mass of information being accumulated about the killer—the slight, scholarly county coroner Dr. Samuel Gerber. The case had fascinated him.

As always, Theresa had to smile at the mention of his name. Her first supervisor in the trace evidence section, Mary Cowan, had worked with Dr. Gerber during the infamous Sam Sheppard trial.

Neither famous man nor the battalion of law enforcement officers working for them could find the Torso killer, but that is not a reflection of their abilities or determination. The Torso killer defied efforts at capture because he did not behave like a serial killer on TV. He did not adhere to a rigid process for

selecting each victim or disposing of each corpse.
He did nothing to make his behavior predictable so
that some well-dressed team of agents could swoop
in before the last commercial break. No one could
have caught him unless by the sheerest luck.

The Depression had hit this industrial city
hard and nearly one-quarter of the population de-
pended on some form of government aid to sur-
vive. It fell to juvenile probation officer Gabriel
Beck to help the smallest victims of this crisis, kids
we would call "at risk" today.

His son, Joseph Beck, became a police officer
as well, patrolling the streets of Cleveland as it
moved into postwar prosperity and saw the birth
of rock and roll.

His grandchildren diversified the family effort.
One a cop and one a forensic scientist, the bet-
ter to surround and choke off today's criminals.
Citizens hope these two have inherited more than
just their crystal-blue eyes from their ancestors,
because they're going to need it to solve their latest
case: a newly discovered victim of the same Torso
killer that prowled Cleveland all those years ago.

History has come full circle.

Jablonski had included two photos, a famous grainy
black-and-white photo of a decapitated body from the
original case, and a snap of her and Frank on the dock
behind Edward Corliss's house. They were both identified by name in the caption. A profile, she decided, was
not her best angle—

Her phone rang.

"Did you see the paper?" her cousin demanded as
soon as she flipped it open.

WEDNESDAY, SEPTEMBER 8
PRESENT DAY

Theresa began to wind the extension cord, looping it around one elbow. "Thanks for coming out at such short notice."

"No problem." The balding geology professor patted the square, squat machine—Cleveland State had the only ground-penetrating radar within the city limits, so far as Theresa knew. "You know I'm always happy to get out of the office. I'm only sorry we couldn't find a body for you."

Theresa sneezed the dust out of her nose. They had crossed the hard dirt floor of the cellar at 4950 Pullman enough times to assure Theresa that no victims of the Torso murderer, or anyone else, had been interred there. Just as well. She had frustrated Councilman Greer for as long as she dared. Now his demolition could proceed.

"You find out who killed that girl? The one in the lake?" The professor stood backward on the steps, yanked until the machine was perched on the edge of the riser, risking back injury. Theresa lifted at the same time, the metal bars cool against her palms.

"Not yet."

"I hope you do soon. It's all my giggling mass of America's future leaders can talk about when they should be reviewing for the quiz."

Theresa lifted in unison, passing another step.

"I try to tell them it will be the boyfriend. It always is."

"They disagree, I'm sure."

"To a man—woman, I mean. 'Oh no,' they'll say, 'he loves me.' Sweet things. Makes me glad I have sons."

Theresa didn't distress him with tales of men killed by their girlfriends, only helped him heft the machine's bulk out to his car, thanked him again, and said good-bye. It had been daylight when she and the professor had arrived, but now the haze of dusk had settled over the city. Time to go. Yet she drifted away from her car, over to the brush-covered slope.

The Kingsbury Run valley—named for the first white settler in this western reserve, who purchased land that would later become the city of Cleveland—traveled in a meandering slash across northeast Ohio. It began two miles away at the West Third Street train switch-house on the Cuyahoga River, on the southern edge of downtown Cleveland. Theresa now stood at, roughly, the opposite end of it. The run officially continued for another four miles into the eastern suburbs, but past Fifty-fifth the tracks diverged and the valley grew less defined.

Cleveland was safer than a lot of large cities, but no one hung around East Fifty-fifth and Kingsbury Run after dark. Not unless they were very tough, which she wasn't, and not if they valued their personal safety, which she did.

Still.

She swung her head to the right and left. Tall dried

weeds persisted between the rails. A Red Line car of the rapid transit system took off from the East Fifty-fifth station and moved slowly west toward Tower City, its windows sparsely populated with commuters who hadn't gotten the day off or kids and young adults going downtown to enjoy the long weekend to its last drop. As the clatter of the train car died away, it left only the hum of vehicles on 490 behind her and the breeze whispering through the undergrowth.

The Torso killer had also been known as the Mad Butcher of Kingsbury Run, though only three of his twelve or so known victims were found there. But those three were arguably the most dramatic; one, under the huge East Fifty-fifth bridge to her right, and two on this same bank, about—she looked to her left—forty feet from where she stood.

Men used to sleep on this hillside while "riding the rails" during the Depression. A current of warm air kissed her cheek; maybe the impromptu camping wasn't as bad as it sounded. Until the Torso killer came by, looking for his next victim. Some aspects of serial killing had not changed much. The destitute and disassociated—like Kim Hammond—were still vulnerable to an offer of money, drugs, food, or friendship.

A distant twig snapped, too large a sound for a raccoon or an overgrown rat. Was someone actually sleeping outside here, one of the current era's homeless? She moved to the edge of the slope, tried to see around the lush Ohio growth. Ghosts of the Torso killer's victims didn't scare her, but modern-day, very real predators were another story.

One step down the hill, then two. The car sat not twenty feet behind her—she could make it there if someone gave chase. The lights of the Fifty-fifth rapid transit station glowed off to her right, but still a thousand feet away and over numerous sets of train tracks. Another step.

She set her feet carefully—not to be silent, she told herself, but because the uneven ground presented too many weeds and small bushes and discarded trash to move quickly. Before she knew it she had reached the bottom, where a path ran next to the tracks. Now she could see around the trees spotting the slope. In the west, the sun had fallen completely behind the city in the distance, abandoning her. A train approaching from the east rumbled and projected a glow forward along the tracks. It lightened the valley from dark back to dusk.

A form, large enough to be a man, moved on the hillside approximately sixty feet away to her left, to the west, toward downtown. She could scarcely see him, dark against darker, and wondered if her eyes were imagining things. But the movement seemed familiar, sensible. The up and down, pushing with one foot—yes, someone digging a hole.

Hardly a thrilling thing to witness. *Time to go, Theresa, instead of standing around an inner-city rail yard after dark*.

Yet she kept watching, growing more positive of her assessment with each second. Worse, she now noticed other shadings in the night around this activity. Another form, near the digger, this one also large enough to be a man, but stretched along the ground and unmoving. Maybe a friend waiting to take his turn with the shovel, but even a barely discernible shadow couldn't stay *that* still.

And with that, Theresa knew exactly what she was looking at.

She did not move. She unclipped her cell phone from her belt and spoke Frank's name into it, not wanting to take the time to dial his number. The digging man wouldn't hear her, not with the distance between them and the intense rumbling that grew to a crescendo as the train from the east arrived. Its track sat closer to her than she had expected, not dangerous but able to jar her bones with its earsplitting whistle and shake the ground beneath her. She pressed the phone to her ear.

"Hello?" Frank said. "Who the hell is this?"

She screamed his name, hoping he would hear her over the train. "Hang on, I'm next to a railroad."

"Then call me back," he screamed in return. "We're doing the notification."

"The building at 4950 Pullman," she shouted. "The hillside west of it. Send a car."

An army could have come up behind her under the cover of all that noise. Or a gang. She did a frantic 360 but saw nothing but weeds and heard nothing but Frank saying, "What? Tess, you're not making any sense."

"I think I see someone burying a body."

Frank expressed more disbelief at the fact that she would be walking around in the dark at that location than at the idea that she was currently witnessing a killer. "Are you nuts? Get back in your car."

"I'm not going to walk in front of a train."

"It's not the trains I'm worried about, idiot!"

The figure on the hill kept working, at a point halfway up Jackass Hill, about thirty feet from her path next to the tracks. Another train approached from the west on the outermost track, or second-outermost track, moving toward her. This new noise would cover her phone conversation—hell, it would cover a small explosion. But to be sure, she cupped her hand over her mouth and the receiver.

"Send someone."

"I will. But get out of there!"

"Just a welfare check. You don't have to tell them I actually see a dead body."

"Don't worry, I wasn't going to. Hang on."

He put her on hold as she moved closer to the man and the train moved closer to her. She hadn't intended either to occur, but her feet wandered forward of their own accord and the train did not pause. It had a light at its peak, bright and piercing.

BBBLLLAAATTT!!!

The figure on the hill—sharper now, with the edge of the approaching light behind it—stopped moving.

It straightened up.

It turned.

Theresa, trapped in the train's floodlight as if she were on a stage, stopped as well.

It—he or she—looked at her. She could feel that gaze even though she could discern no other details, not if it was a male or female, height, weight, or clothing, only the outline of a shape and how that shape went from still to deathly still as its invisible face lighted on her.

For a moment, neither of them moved.

The train from the east kept coming. Its driver gave her a second, irritated blast to tell her to get away from the tracks.

She left the path next to the track and charged the hill, forcing extra energy into her legs, pulling her feet from the brambles before they could trip her, nearly blind from the train light and wondering what the hell she would do if she caught up with this person. She had no flashlight, no weapon, and no illusions about her skills at hand-to-hand combat.

Not to worry. By squinting hard she could sort of see the hillside and the man, running away from her, shovel in hand.

She landed at the gravesite, her right foot sliding into the unfinished hole. The lights from the passing train, its driver still expressing his annoyance at her at an earsplitting decibel level, erased some of the shadows from the hillside and let her see the unmoving form.

A man's body lay on its side. It had no clothes. It also had no head.

The digging man couldn't have gotten far. She could probably still have heard him moving through the bushes that lined the top of the ridge, if not for the cacophony of that damn train in the valley.

Don't chase the man. You're not going to chase the man, who has at least one thing he could use as a weapon. You have none.

She ran after the man.

And promptly tripped over the second body.

CHAPTER 16

WEDNESDAY, SEPTEMBER 8
PRESENT DAY

Frank Patrick walked up the flight of steps behind his
partner. It gave him an opportunity to watch her hips in
action, and they were the only pleasant thing on the horizon of his next hour or two. Mrs. Lily Hammond lived
on the third floor of Riverview Apartments, across the
Cuyahoga River from the trendy downtown condos but
light-years down the socioeconomic scale. From each
door they passed emanated cries of babies or dogs or
both, and from the smell of the place the babies didn't
get changed, nor the dogs walked, often enough. Frank's
eyes darted to every shadow; he had investigated enough
homicides on this crowded piece of real estate to keep
his hand close to his gun. They'd made three trips here
already, and he hoped that this time Mrs. Hammond
would be at home and receiving visitors because he'd
really have liked to get this part of the job over with
already.

He would bet dinner at Lola's that Kim Hammond

had been killed by a violent lover. She would not have been the only Cleveland girl in recent memory to meet such a fate. No, Frank figured James Miller's death to be the more puzzling, not to mention unsettling. What was the point of being a cop if you still weren't safe from something like that? And why did it have to be the Torso killer, getting Theresa all riled up and talking about their grandfather? What sort of bad-humored jokester god had Frank offended lately?

The door quivered a bit when Sanchez knocked on it, loose in its moorings, and a woman inside called out. When Frank said they had come about her daughter, they heard shuffling sounds and the darkness behind the peephole became temporarily darker. Then a clink of security chain and the door opened. Between her daughter and her neighbors, Mrs. Hammond had no doubt grown used to the occasional visit from the CPD.

Kim's petite stature had not been purely the result of drug use; Lily Hammond would not have reached Frank's chin and a strong lake breeze would have threatened her stability. But her eyes and voice were calm and sober. "What has she done now, and don't expect me to know anything about it. I work two jobs; I'm hardly ever home."

Frank shut the door behind him as best he could. The knob no longer worked at all, only the chain at the top. From grooves worn in the carpeting he guessed the tenant secured herself by sliding a short bureau in front of it. "We're very sorry, Mrs. Hammond."

She had covered the room's only window with a thin blanket to block the view of other tenants in the courtyard, or perhaps to block her view of them, and the room was dim. She crossed her arms over a worn but clean orange sweatshirt, which featured a jack-o'-lantern and two black cats. "That's a switch. Usually you jump right to possible contempt-of-court charges if I don't tell you—" Then the significance of their wording sunk in and she paled. "Is she dead?"

A skilled interrogator might have asked, *What makes you think she's dead?* and received all sorts of tidbits of information in response. Frank could not be that cruel. "Yes."

The woman sank to a stained plaid sofa. Frank and Angela Sanchez sat as well, using two worn wooden chairs from the breakfast nook. Frank avoided upholstered furniture in other people's homes—cloth hid dirt and fleas a bit too easily.

Mrs. Hammond made all the right queries—when, where, how, and who? Frank couldn't answer any of them, especially the last. Sanchez made the woman a cup of tea and then they settled into the same series of questions they'd asked a thousand other grieving mothers.

Kim, her only child, would have turned twenty-three in a few weeks. She had been keeping away from the drugs since her last stint in jail. She did not have a boyfriend, violent or non-, so far as Lily Hammond knew, but then Kim did not bring her friends home. She would disappear for days on end and return to say she had been sleeping on so-and-so's couch, so her absence did not immediately alarm her mother. Kim did not have a job, though she had recently applied at several department stores downtown. She wanted to work in retail to get an employee discount. "A five-fingered discount, more likely," her mother admitted. "I loved my daughter, but I know how she thought. She figured that she had it tough so the world owed her a break. I could never convince her that she didn't have it all that tough, that it could be worse. It could be a lot worse."

Frank didn't ask what could be worse than poverty. The way Mrs. Hammond stared off into the middle distance made him think she could give him a laundry list. A television blared to life in the next apartment; in fact, televisions maintained a steady murmur throughout the building. Tenants left them on to make their unit seem occupied to would-be thieves.

"Kim wasn't always that way," the woman went on, her voice catching as grief began to blossom. "She held it together in high school, waitressed at Denny's, and even worked for a summer at city hall. But then she started up with the wrong kind of boys, and that led to the drugs."

Frank tried to look sympathetic, though he heard the "good kid, just fell in with the wrong crowd" story from virtually every parent he had ever interviewed. It never occurred to them that their kid *was* the wrong crowd. "So Kim stayed here more or less consistently from her release in June until yesterday morning."

"Yes."

"How did she spend her time?" Frank asked.

"She'd watch TV, maybe talk to the neighbors." A smile curved her lips for the first time since they'd arrived. "Once in a while she'd get ambitious and walk up the street to the market and then cook dinner. She liked to cook, when the mood hit her."

"The West Side Market?"

"Yeah."

"Did she have a car?"

"*I* don't even have a car."

"What did she watch on TV?" Sanchez asked.

Frank sighed. If his partner had a fault, it was this weird curiosity with the trivia of victim's lives, what kind of music they liked or which pet they doted on. To him, all the prior questions simply served to warm up the mother for the only relevant one: Did Kim have any enemies? Most whodunits solved themselves with that one inquiry.

"Lots of shows. Kim controlled the remote when she was home—those reality shows, usually the ones with cameras following spoiled Hollywood people around. I couldn't stand them. They always wind up with people screaming at each other about some stupid detail. I'd love to have their problems."

"Where is Kim's father?" Frank asked.

Mrs. Hammond frowned. "He's not in the picture."

"All right. But where is he?"

"Kim had just started junior high when he dumped us. By the time family court tracked him down for child support, he was dead. Killed in a traffic accident in Chicago."

"I'm sorry to hear that. Mrs. Hammond, could we see Kim's room?"

The woman snorted. "I'm sitting on it. This place has one bedroom and it's mine. When Kim stayed here, she slept on the couch."

The cops looked around. "Where did she keep her belongings?" Sanchez asked.

"She hangs some clothes in the closet there. Otherwise it's all stuffed under this couch—it's a futon, really. Take a look if you want." She traded seats with Frank, warming her hands on the mug of tea.

Frank knelt, gingerly, on the least-stained section of carpet and reached under the metal frame. The sum total of the twenty-two-year-old's worldly possessions filled two cardboard boxes. He slid one over to Sanchez and donned latex gloves to go through the other. This way he would not leave fingerprints on any item they decided to analyze, and he disliked touching other people's stuff with bare hands. Especially dusty stuff crammed beneath ratty furniture in a run-down apartment.

Kim had owned a few necklaces of plastic beads, hoop earrings, a cigar box, a letter from her parole officer and her high school report cards (which weren't entirely bad, he noticed), various makeup items that leaked trails of glittery powder throughout the collection, and a pile of socks, bras, and panties. He couldn't tell if they were clean or dirty, doubly grateful for the latex gloves.

The cigar box revealed a grimy array of two pencils, a medal—an eagle against a cross—on a faded ribbon, a black-and-white shot of a round-faced baby framed in silver, and a small spiral notebook with a worn cardboard cover. Frank flipped through a few pages. The random jottings in close script did not suggest anything to him.

"That was her father's stuff," Mrs. Hammond told him. "I don't know why she kept it."

Sanchez held up the picture of a young man from the other box. "Who is this?"

Kim's mother squinted. "I think he went to her high school. They didn't keep in touch so far as I know."

The detective then held up a birthday card. "This says *Love Always, Bubba*. Who's Bubba?"

"Me." Tears began to leak from the woman's eyes. "She would get her B's and M's mixed up when she first started to talk. Instead of Mama, I was Bubba."

Frank replaced his box under the futon and moved on before Mrs. Hammond's composure could dissolve completely. "You said she had been friendly with your neighbors? Which ones?"

She thought, then gestured to the north wall. "She would say hi to the Taylor girl, in the next apartment, but not talk much. Kim would chat with old Mrs. Evanston on the second floor, but everyone does; she haunts the lobby and blocks the elevator until she can bend your ear for five or ten minutes. Then that son of a bitch at the end of the hall always flirted with her."

"A man?"

"A man old enough to be her grandfather, practically,

a smooth-talking, drug-dealing bastard. Kim usually knew how to blow off scum, but him—she seemed to find him funny. Like his age made him harmless. I kept trying to tell her otherwise, but of course I'm old-fashioned and paranoid."

"What's his name?"

"Leroy Turner."

"Does he live alone?"

"Not so you can tell. Always a parade of people coming and going from that place."

"We'll talk to him. Did you notice any difference in her this past week? Changes in eating or sleeping habits? Did she keep different hours, make a new friend, seem depressed?"

"No," the woman said with a tone of surprise. "Not depressed at all. Tuesday morning—the last time I saw her—she had that sneaky little attitude going again that used to mean she'd gotten up to something, but sober . . . maybe a bit restless. I think she couldn't make up her mind to get a legitimate job or . . . find an alternative. She hated being broke."

"Anything else?"

The dead girl's mother thought, frowned, and bit the tip of one thumb. "I don't know if it means anything, but I remember being pleased about it on—Friday night, I think it was. I got bad food at lunchtime and I spent the evening throwing up every twenty minutes. So I didn't pay a lot of attention, but I remember she finally laid off the reality shows."

"Oh, yeah?"

"Got real interested in watching the news. Flicked through every channel, all evening long. She muttered some stuff to herself, but like I said, I was so sick I didn't listen to anything except my stomach. But later on that night—"

"Yes?"

"She went down to the pop machine in the lobby and bought me a can of ginger ale. For my stomach. That was new, for her to do something like that."

At the door nearest the stairwell, Leroy Turner opened up before Frank could finish knocking and invited them in with great courtesy. This told Frank three things: one, that Turner had been informed of their presence from the moment they set foot on the property, through that uncanny network of interested tenants that made it seem as though the building itself lived and breathed and thought; two, that during their interviews of Mrs. Hammond and her neighbors, Turner had had ample time to hide or give to others any evidence of his dealings; and three, that Turner wanted them to know all these things to illustrate why he should not, and would not, be the slightest bit afraid of them.

Short, a bit stocky, with graying hair, he wore a brown T-shirt with long sleeves and a logo of some obscure indie band on the front. The shabby but relatively uncluttered surroundings could have belonged to any law-abiding pensioner. He leaned back in his chair and made an expansive gesture at the empty chairs on the other side of the cracked Formica-covered table.

Sanchez sat on one of the upholstered cushions, but Frank remained standing. Open windows and a helping of Febreze almost hid the lingering smell of pot, but the faint reek of sauerkraut concerned him more. How did people eat that stuff?

"Now," Leroy Turner began, "how can I help you officers?"

"Did you know Kim Hammond?" Frank asked.

The man blinked, and for a split second his expressive face went still. *Is he relieved,* Frank wondered, *that we're here about Kim instead of the drugs, or dismayed because we're here about Kim and not the drugs?*

"Yes," Turner answered. "Nice girl. Lives up the hall."

"Lived," Sanchez corrected.

Now he did not try to hide the surprise. "What happened to her?"

"When did you see her last?" Frank asked. With this witness, cruelty didn't apply.

"What happened to her?"

"Answer our questions first."

"Why?"

"So we don't have to get a warrant to toss your place. Did you consider Kim your friend?"

If Frank hadn't been lied to by every person he had ever encountered in the drug trade, he would have eliminated Turner as a suspect in Kim's death purely by the fleeting glimpse of true sadness in his face. "Yes. I did. I assume from the past tense that I shouldn't anymore. What happened to her?"

"Did you sell her drugs?"

"In the past. Not since this last time she got locked up. Did she OD?"

"Was she using again?"

The aging man shook his head. "Not that I know of. But people backslide. How she die?" he asked, of Sanchez this time, perhaps thinking the woman would be more forthcoming, but, of course, he didn't know Sanchez. She said nothing.

Frank said that she had been murdered and that they were still working on exactly how.

Turner spoke without hesitation—again, not afraid of them. Kim had stopped by his apartment on both Thursday and Friday evenings. She had been sober and upbeat, chatting animatedly, "finally acting the way a young girl oughta, showing me a little optimism for a change." He did not see her after that and did not really have an alibi for Friday night or Saturday. He had been home alone for most of the weekend but had also spent part of Saturday down at the West Side Market. With friends.

Frank asked his standard enemies question.

"Kim never hung here long enough to grow enemies. She been inside for a while, she flits in and out of her mama's. Nobody in this building took much notice of her."

"Except you."

"She and me got along." Again, that glimpse of true regret on his face. Frank had no doubt the man could kill, but in such a melodramatic way? It didn't fit with Turner's ability to stay under the radar—if he wanted her dead as a lesson to other acquaintances, he would have left her body in the alley behind the building. If he only wanted to get rid of the body he could have dropped it in the river behind the building without the effort of cutting it up first. "She could talk to me about stuff she couldn't say to her mama."

"Like drugs?"

The man nodded. "Yeah. And being inside."

"What did she talk about on Thursday and Friday?"

He appeared uncertain for the first time. "Thursday, nothin', just the same old bull. Friday, she kept asking what I would do if I had a bunch of money."

"Money?"

"Yeah. Like if I won the lottery or something."

"Where was she going to get this money?"

"She didn't say *she* was going to get it. She asked me what I would do if I got it. Just talking. She'd go off into these fantasies now and then, get all excited about one of them Hollywood skanks and their cars and their clothes and how she'd have stuff just like that someday. Kid talk."

"So what did you tell her?"

Turner settled back again, the chair creaking under his shifting weight. "I said I'd put it in a bank in the Caymans and retire to Cancún. You ever been to Cancún?" he asked Sanchez, his eyes roaming her figure.

"What did Kim plan to do with her theoretical windfall?" Frank's partner asked.

"Get Hollywood skank clothes and cars, mostly." He rubbed long fingers over his shiny face. "And a house for her mama. Some place better to live than here."

Just then Frank's phone rang.

CHAPTER 17

WEDNESDAY, SEPTEMBER 8
PRESENT DAY

"What were you thinking?" Frank asked for the third time.

"I was thinking I'd like to get a look at the guy who was burying two dead bodies."

"You didn't know that when you started out to take a stroll among the train tracks and the winos and maybe a few gang wars!"

"Are you looking at this? Besides, I called you, didn't I?"

"So I'd know where to pick up your body! Thanks a lot." Frank rubbed the bridge of his nose, not because it hurt but because he and Theresa both had picked it up from a TV detective when they were kids as a way of expressing exasperation. Somehow exasperation came up a lot when they were together. "Look, just promise me that you'll never wander through a train yard after dark again. First, that you'll never tell a reporter our family history again, and second, that you won't wander through train yards."

It seemed unlikely that she would make a habit of either, so she figured it to be a safe bet. "Okay. But are you *looking* at this?"

"Yeah," he said. "I see it."

The first corpse lay on its left side, calves separated, arms loosely bent as if he were sleeping. That victim wore no clothes except for a pair of socks. The second victim, about twenty feet away and a little farther up the hill, lay on his back in a patch of dead goldenrod, with no clothes at all. The heads and male organs had been removed from both victims, the latter parts found together in a pile next to the second body. The killer had been working on the heads when Theresa interrupted him.

"I don't get it," Angela Sanchez said, staring down, not at the severed cranium of a youngish man with brown hair, but at the foot-in-diameter hole dug into the ground next to it. "He wasn't going to bury the bodies?"

Theresa shook her head. "No. Just the heads. With enough of the hair sticking out of the dirt so that we'd be sure to find them."

"*Why?*"

"Because that's what the original Torso killer did," Theresa said.

"Victims one and two," Frank intoned, "were found here, in exactly these positions."

"Victim one, anyway." Theresa pointed at the corpse lying on its side. "A photograph still exists of that one. We can't really be sure how he posed the other one. The records don't specify."

"And the pile of clothing?" Angela asked. "Is that like the original murders?"

"That, too." Theresa had made another trip, a more cautious one this time, up the valley to retrieve her camera. She snapped another photo of the material stacked between a worn brick and a crushed McDonald's cup with at least a month of grime on it. "It should be a coat, a shirt, pants, I think, maybe a hat. When Don gets here with the crime scene equipment I can examine it further."

"That's only enough clothes for one guy, though."

"I know, but that's what the first Torso killer did. This guy might deviate, though. He's already got a few details wrong."

Angela waited until a rapid transit train passed by, though the electric cars made much less noise than the diesel locomotives. "Such as?"

"In the Torso killings, they were both white, and victim two was older than victim one—this one on his side—and had been killed at least a week before victim one. He also had something poured on him, possibly calcium hypochlorite, that made his skin leathery. Now these two guys—victim two appears older than one, yes, but he's also black; his skin has not been treated; and he certainly hasn't been dead for a week. I'd be surprised if it were more than a few hours. He either hasn't studied his history or he's not as patient as his predecessor. He doesn't want to wait a week. He certainly didn't want to wait a year."

"I'm sure I'll regret asking this," Angela said, "but what do you mean by a year?"

"I'm sure I'll regret answering it. Monday's victim? The woman cut into pieces and thrown in Lake Erie?"

"Copying another one of the Torso killer's?"

"His first, so far as anyone knows. They called her the Lady of the Lake. Some of her—not the head—washed up on Euclid Beach, but because a year went by before the two men on the hillside were found, no one connected her murder to the series until much later. That's why they went back and called her victim zero."

Frank said, "So—assuming that woman *wasn't* killed by a boyfriend or a freak boating accident—our new guy decided to collapse the timeline. A year became two days."

Theresa tried to talk herself out of the theory. "But the first Lady of the Lake had been dead for months when she surfaced, and her skin had been turned to leather as well. That's not consistent with Kim."

Angela looked around, frowning in the bright halogens. "Zero, one, and two. How many were there, again?"

"Twelve," Frank said, "officially."

"Probably twice that in reality," Theresa added.

Frank asked, "Tess, can you identify him?"

"I can't even swear it *was* a him. I assume so, from the size of it—him—whatever I saw. One person, in dark clothes. I didn't see hair, whether he wore a coat or a hoodie or a mask or just had dark hair."

"Weight?"

"Big, I guess. You know I'm lousy at that."

"Well, *think*."

They stood side by side, backs to the tracks, facing the corpses, waiting for more reinforcements to arrive so that the scene could be documented and collected with all possible accuracy. She knew Frank had to draw every detail he could before the incident faded from her mind, *if* it faded. She just wished he would be a little more gentle about it. Her system had had a shock, even if she did not want to admit it.

"Think," he said again. "Bigger than me?"

"I think so, yes." Theresa frowned; it felt like a guess and guessing was the one thing she was not supposed to do. *Verifiable facts only, ma'am.*

"Loose clothing?"

"I think so."

"Glasses?"

"Didn't see a reflection."

"A glint from anything? Jewelry? A watch? A logo on his shirt?"

"No. Nothing."

Frank sighed his exasperation, then pointed out, "He took the shovel."

"Worried that it could be traced to him. Where did he go? I thought this road ended."

"No. It's more or less a dirt road for railroad use only, but it follows the tracks for two miles and over two bridges, then turns into Canal. From there he could get onto Carnegie and disappear."

"Great. We get to check for tire tracks up two miles of dirt road."

"That's what road guys are for. Tess"—Frank's voice grew harsh—"did he *see* you?"

Once again she was standing next to the tracks as a train bore down on her, its spotlight illuminating most of the valley but especially her, glinting off her white skin and the highlights in her hair. The explosion of the train's horn pounded her heart until it ached. The shadow turned. The shadow looked.

Now she shivered from more than the drop in temperature that came with the night. "Yes. He saw me."

CHAPTER 18

WEDNESDAY, SEPTEMBER 8
PRESENT DAY

The former army nurse lived in a tall building in West-lake. The sign read "Gracious Community Living" but, as Irene Schaffer Martin told Theresa immediately after introducing herself, "This is one of those places that old folks go to die."

Theresa had made her way through the lobby, which was elegantly decorated with washable plastic and vinyl furniture designed—well designed—to look old and rich, and now glanced around at the room Irene shared with a bedridden roommate who snored. The bed and the nightstand matched the rest of the facility, but Irene must have brought the other furnishings with her, including an elaborately carved bookcase crammed with knickknacks, reading material, and photos. The room and the building had a particular odor, not of anything unpleasant but of air that had recycled through mechanical systems one too many times without drawing in any new stuff from outside. "It doesn't look too bad."

"It's not," the old lady said. "You got to go some-where. Not cheap, though."

"How did you pay for it? The profit from knocking over the bank?"

Irene née Schaffer laughed, not a cackle but a full-throated belly laugh that shook her still-fleshy shoulders. She had a decent head of hair dyed a chestnut brown, worn straight to below her chin and then flipped out like a fifties teen. "Sort of. So you work with stiffs?" She sat in a wheelchair but twitched one leg, stretching out the ankle.

"Yes."

"I saw plenty of those in the war." The loose skin on her neck followed where the chin led as she shook her head.

"World War Two?"

"Yes. I almost went back for Korea, but I'd had my first one then, my daughter, and I couldn't take her along, now, could I?"

So many questions occurred to Theresa that she didn't know where to begin, but she figured it couldn't hurt to ease into the topic of the dead man. "When did you join the service?"

"When they bombed our damn harbor, that's when. Everybody did. Would you like some tea, dear?"

Theresa glanced at the window, where a few drops of rain had decided to fall; they'd caught her shoulders in the twenty steps from her car to the building's door. On top of that, her heartbeat had not yet returned to normal after stumbling over two dead bodies. "I'd love some."

The woman filled a Pyrex measuring cup with water and popped it into an undersize microwave. While it hummed, she got out two cups and saucers with a gold-edged floral pattern and went on answering the question as if she hadn't paused. "Though I can't say my decision was based on patriotism alone. I was twenty-one, all my friends were married or engaged—did your mother ever tell you that boys may fool around with the bad girls, but they don't marry them?"

"Yes."

"She was right. Though I wasn't bad, not really—hell, I qualified for sainthood compared to kids nowadays."

The microwave went *bing*, and she wheeled over to retrieve the cup of water. Then she made two cups of tea from the same bag and pushed one over to Theresa, who preferred cream and sugar in hers and also preferred to drink it from a cup she had washed herself. She concentrated on the delicate design of the flowers instead.

"But I could be wild. My father ran out on us, my mother and me and my little brother. So many men did during the Depression. The humiliation was too great, not having a job, not being able to provide for their families. No one had heard of welfare then, and charity was only for the very poor or the infirm."

Theresa sipped and nodded.

"My mother worked at the feed store, stocking shelves, lifting things that were too heavy for her to lift. We moved in with her sister and lived in their attic, which kept a roof—a leaking roof—over our heads. She charged us, my aunt did, fifty cents a week, which as a kid I thought was a pretty rotten thing to do to your own sister, but my aunt had three of her own kids to feed and she could have rented out the space for three times as much."

Theresa said, "Ms. Martin—"

"Stick with Schaffer. It's a good name. And I'm getting to it—I'm not senile, you know, I'm only trying to explain that I ran around the streets all the time just to get out of that house. My aunt's oldest girl loved babies, so I'd dump my brother on her and I'd . . . escape."

Theresa took another sip of tea and decided it wasn't

all that bad without cream and sugar. "Where would you go?"

"Edgewater Park, in the summer. I'd sneak into the Brookside zoo in the winter. Hardly anyone was around and the one old maintenance guy got so used to seeing me that he must have thought I belonged to one of the people who worked there and never asked me anything. I got in through the elephant cage. The elephants never cared. Ever been there in the winter? You should see the polar bears in the winter."

"I'll have to do that sometime."

"But I'd also go down and watch the trains a lot. I had a girlfriend, Doris, in the fifth grade and her father was a conductor on the Erie Railroad, so we'd walk down West Third Street to the yards and wait for him to come back in from Pittsburgh. He lost his job after the crash and they moved out to Illinois for some job, but I'd still go down there to watch the trains, and wonder where they were going, and wish I could go, too. I think that's what really started it."

"Started what?"

"Why I wound up in the Navy when they came for recruits. As young as I was, I figured nursing was a job I could take anywhere. I'd never get stuck in one place, like my mother."

"And that worked?"

"Almost too well—had some hairy times in the Philippines, let me tell you. But I'm getting ahead of my story. So there I was, fifteen years old, hanging around the rail yards, which I hope no self-respecting fifteen-year-old girl would do today, and I made some acquaintances, after a sort. There was a conductor who went back and forth to Chicago every day; he would always give me a peppermint candy. He had kids of his own and I guess he'd look out for me. Then there was the ticket taker for the passenger line; he'd talk to me about horse racing and how he'd lost everything he owned on Ticker Tape. Not the stock market, a horse named Ticker Tape. I still don't know if he got sort of obsessed with the fact or he just thought it was funny. A woman named Sophie hung out on the platform and she'd give me a cigarette. She would fix my hair once in a while, put it up in a twist that I've never been able to duplicate. She was a prostitute, I realize now, though I didn't then and would have had only a vague idea what that meant if someone told me. Kids were different in those days."

Theresa glanced past her to a photo on the bookshelf. It showed a young woman in a military uniform, leaning on a brick wall with a cigarette between two fingers. Irene couldn't have been more than twenty at the time, tall and strong with a tomboyish glint still in her eyes.

"My point is, I wasn't afraid of the people I encountered there. I'd never had any reason to be, and that, as it turned out, was a problem. More tea?"

"Sure." Obviously Irene Schaffer would tell this story in her own way and her own time, and Theresa stopped trying to rush her. She wondered what had happened to the three children but knew she didn't have time to hear each one's history. And Irene might say that they never called or visited, and Theresa did not want to hear that. So was this the way the world ended? You lived all your life and did all these things and wound up with nothing but half a room in a building full of strangers, tethered by your own failing body?

She told herself that Irene didn't seem miserable. "Why did you knock over a bank?"

The woman giggled like a teenager with a delightful secret. "If you want that story, young lady, you'll have to come back for another visit. You *will* come back and see me again, won't you?"

"Yes."

"All right, then. So one day," Irene said after the microwave *bing*-ed for the second time and two hard-of-hearing friends holding a conversation in the hallway had moved on, "I began to chat with this man sitting on the bench by the Pennsylvania tracks. It seemed as if he was waiting for the train, though it didn't occur to me to wonder why he'd be by the freight lines. Anyway, I kind of hoped he'd come across with a cigarette or, better yet, a piece of candy—people often gave children candy in those days; I suppose guys like this is why it became such a no-no—and I finally dropped a hint or two. Then he said I should avoid candy as it would put too much sugar into my bloodstream and from the yellowish tint to my skin he could see that I had a touch of jaundice. Well, I *had* had jaundice at birth, my mother had told me that often enough. Actually two of my three kids had it as well—now I know how common it is, but then I thought it might be some flaw in my physical makeup, a weakness that could kill me, or at least keep me from seeing the world before I died. He went on talking about my liver function and all these other words I didn't understand—hell, I was only fifteen and I had avoided school as much as possible. So he said he could tell me what I should and shouldn't eat and what vitamins to take to stay healthy. But I needed to come to his office. So I popped right up and we went off to his office." Irene shook her head as if in disbelief. The movement fluffed up the ends of the brown flip.

"And this was 1936?"

"April tenth, 1935. I'm ninety-one now."

Theresa felt as if she should say *congratulations* but refrained. "Do you remember the address of this office?"

"Forty-nine fifty Pullman." Irene squinted over the top of her cup. "Why do you *think* I called you?"

Theresa squirmed, feeling dumb. "And you walked there from West Third?"

"Sure. I had time and it was a sunny day. We walked everywhere then. Only rich people or businesses had cars. That's why the whole country wasn't obese, like nowadays."

"Good point."

"It never occurred to me to wonder why he had been at the train station if he didn't need to meet a train."

Recalling the information from the city directory, Theresa chose her questions carefully. "Do you remember this man's name?"

"I'll never forget it. Louis. Dr. Louis, he said."

"And his office occupied which unit of the building?"

"I don't know if it had a number. When you walked in the front door, from Pullman, you went down a hallway and turned right into the first office."

"Do you remember anyone else in the building?"

"I heard sounds. I think I saw another open door up the hall and I heard people moving upstairs, so I figured the other offices were occupied but I didn't actually see anyone."

"What did his office look like?"

Irene shrugged. "Kind of bare. He had a desk and a bunch of shelves, with books and jars."

"Jars of what?"

"Things floating in liquid. I didn't want to look at them. Medicine has changed a lot over the years, let me tell you. People didn't go to doctors for every little thing like they do now—you didn't want to. Hospitals were scarier than jails in some places."

"So you began to get nervous about this Dr. Louis?" Seventy-five years later, the bony fingers still entwined in her lap, pressing hard against each other.

"I asked if this would hurt, and he said no—you believe that? The bastard said no, that he only wanted to fill out a questionnaire about what I ate. He sat behind the desk and took out some papers and I sat in a chair. He asked if ate oatmeal, if I ate cherries, if I took aspirin, and he'd make little notes on these papers. It seemed to take forever. I remember I got bored until he gave me a bottle of soda pop out of a little icebox. Ginger ale. A whole bottle, just for me. That perked me up, for a while. Only a while, because that must have been what he put it in."

"Put what in?"

"Whatever it was he gave me to knock me out, because the next thing I remember, I woke up on a cot in another room and Dr. Louis was unbuttoning my blouse."

Theresa could barely breathe. "What other room? What did you do?"

"I couldn't move at first, my arms felt so heavy. He kept saying I shouldn't worry, that this wouldn't hurt, he was only examining my jaundice, but even at fifteen I wasn't that stupid and I would have clocked him one if I hadn't been so groggy. But when he got my brassiere off and put his lips—well, I clocked him one anyway, groggy or no."

"What did he do?"

"Fell back on the floor—he'd been perching on the edge of this cot, and I guess he was off balance. . . . I jumped right over him and out the door, which led into his office. We were in a little closet, or storage area, behind his desk. Lucky for me he hadn't locked his office door, and I went right out it and out of the building and didn't stop running until I got to my aunt's house."

"Did you scream?"

"The whole way home."

"Did anyone from the building come to help?"

"It was dark by then. I don't know how long that bastard had me in there, but it had to be at least six hours. He drugged me, then waited for everyone else to go home."

Or he had afternoon appointments he couldn't cancel, Theresa thought, *and wanted plenty of time alone with his prize.* Detectives had long theorized that the Torso killer had lured and drugged his victims, to explain why they had no defensive injuries and remnants of a last meal in their stomachs.

But on the other hand, the Butcher had preferred young adult males, sometimes older males, and rarely women. Never young girls. Though perhaps after meeting Irene Schaffer he had decided they were too much trouble.

"Did you tell your mother?"

"I told everybody. My uncle called the police, and they came to the house. The next day they took me back to the building to identify this Dr. Louis, which I did, plain and simple. Nearly peed my pants, but I stood between those two cops and pointed right at him."

"What did he say?"

"He nodded and smiled and told the police I would come around the offices sometimes, begging for a handout, and he'd felt sorry for me and gave me an apple once and a peppermint. He said the day before he'd had nothing for me, and that I got angry and said he'd be sorry."

"They believed him?" Theresa could picture the man in Edward Corliss's photo, tall and well dressed, describing his version of events with that clipped, professional tone that still swayed juries more than any female could.

"Things were different then," Irene Schaffer repeated. "Doctors were gods. I was a truant tomboy and there were no witnesses. Apparently he had no record and in those days they didn't have computers that gave you a map of where all the mashers live."

Theresa chewed at her thumbnail. "And you think this man could be the Torso killer?"

"They always said he was a doctor, and the office is right on the banks of Kingsbury Run. Dr. Louis hung out at the rail yards, down by West Third and the Abbey Street Bridge, where they found some of the bodies. Don't bite your nails, dear."

"The detectives checked every person in the city with a record of sexual offenses. Maybe they would have investigated him." Theresa didn't bother wishing to read all the original police reports. She knew from books on the subject that nearly all of the voluminous case material had been lost over the years.

"Not that chubby cop," Irene said, her mouth set in a hard line. "The skinny one, I think he believed me. But there was nothing he could do."

"Which cop?"

"The one whose body you found. James Miller."

CHAPTER 19

Theresa drove home in a daze. So much information, so many years. James Miller had been killed in 1936 in the same building in which Irene Schaffer had been nearly molested—by a doctor with, one would assume, the anatomical knowledge to cut up a body. Did James go there to confront the doctor about Irene, over a year later? Why? Had James found some evidence in the meantime? Did he then stumble on the Torso killer?

Or did the doctor kill James to prevent his own arrest for the molestation, and both incidents had nothing to do with the Torso killer? After all, the serial killer liked to dump his victims, not preserve them for posterity.

And he had dumped two nearly on the doorstep of 4950 Pullman. Seventy-five years later, someone repeated the process. Why? How?

It had begun to rain again, and Theresa slowed to negotiate the sharp curve from 480 onto southbound I-71. The car behind her insisted on riding four inches from her bumper. Missing a headlight, it winked at her in her rearview mirror and the rain pelted her windshield even harder as she sped up.

From his notes, however, James had been investigating the Torso killings. He might have completely forgotten about Irene and wound up entombed in 4950 Pullman as a coincidence.

But James had believed the young girl, in a world where no one else would.

Speaking of young girls, now they had Kim Hammond. Unlike Dr. Louis and the Torso killer, the sick bastard who had decapitated Kim still walked the streets, and like the Torso killer he did not intend to stop. Who were these two male victims? Did the killer know them, these mannequins in his diorama? Did he realize that, while he imitated a 1935 murder, Theresa would not be imitating 1935 investigative technology? Science had come a long way since then and she meant to utilize all of it.

What helped the Torso killer remain anonymous then had a great deal to do with the inability to identify his victims. They must have been transients, members of the uncounted, unseen forces riding the rails and looking for work. Very few people lived that way anymore; even today's version of that group, the homeless, was somewhat monitored and not so mobile.

Once home, she pulled her car into its spot but left the garage door open. She would go out again to walk next door and say good night to her mother.

Rachael had called. The blinking light on the answering machine let her know this as soon as she entered the house. It had to be Rachael—no one else ever called her besides Frank, who would use the Nextel. Theresa dropped her purse and empty lunch bag on the table and pushed the black button on the console.

It won't be her, she warned herself as she waited for

the tape to rewind. *It will be a dial tone left over from a computerized sales pitch, or the library calling with a book on hold. Or even Chris Cavanaugh.*

"Hi, Mom, it's me. Just wanted to tell you everything's fine. Talk to you later, bye."

Rachael. Why hadn't she called on the cell? She should know Theresa wouldn't be home, that she'd be at work or en route, so call on the cell. Instead Rachael rang when she knew Theresa would not be there, to avoid wasting twenty minutes on a conversation with her mother. That was okay, though. Her daughter sounded healthy and had been alive as late as this afternoon, and that was the important thing.

Theresa checked the caller ID: 6:00 P.M. She *should* have been home by then but had dallied with the cellar at 4950 Pullman, a couple of dead bodies, and Irene Schaffer.

Okay. Rachael had attempted to voluntarily call her mother. *Life is good. Life is just as it should be.*

And it gave her a reason to call her back and apologize for missing the call.

No answer. She left a message.

Theresa washed her face, changed her clothes, thought—not seriously—about cooking something to eat, and wandered into Rachael's room, as she did at least once a day, just to make sure the cat wasn't sleeping on the bed and the dog hadn't made off with one of the stuffed animals. Which of course they hadn't, because Theresa kept the door shut. But she checked anyway. The room remained in perfect order, which told her, more than the silence or the untouched food in the refrigerator or always finding the TV remote right where she left it, that her daughter was gone.

Rachael's window faced the street. A single car passed slowly by, with one dark headlight.

Theresa made sure to close Rachael's bedroom door behind her. Then she walked through the strengthening rain to the next home, where she asked her mother if her great-grandfather had ever mentioned the Torso Murders.

Agnes sat at her kitchen table, sorting recipes, gray hair bouncing in classic curls. "I don't think so. Do you think apple turnovers are better with cheese or with a honey glaze?"

"I think they're better with vanilla ice cream. What about Grandpa Joe?"

"He liked the honey glaze."

"The Torso Murders, Mom."

"Oh, that. I don't remember. It was before his time."

"But Great-grandpa would have been working at Boys' Town right after Eliot Ness founded it."

Her mother looked up from the stained pieces of paper. "Oh, yes. Joe used to mention that now and then. Usually when you two would be watching repeats of that *Untouchables* show—the one with Robert Stack. He shouldn't have let you watch that stuff."

"Or I wouldn't be a practicing ghoul today, I know." Theresa didn't try to explain that "all that stuff" was the only stuff she'd ever cared about. If other people found that odd, she couldn't have cared less, so long as it seemed normal and fine in the eyes of the man she admired above all others.

"Honey, I don't think you're a ghoul. I just hate to see you dealing with all those terrible people."

Murderers, she meant. "They're long gone by the time I get there." Tonight had been an exception.

Her mother merely raised an eyebrow. Several incidents in Theresa's past had disproven that statement.

Theresa ignored those memories and said nothing about Kim Hammond or the two men on the hillside.

Luckily, her mother never watched the news and, if the angels of peace were on Theresa's side, might be too busy at the restaurant to pick up a paper.

The horror of the Torso Murders, however, had faded with time and could be safely brought up. "What did Grandpa say?"

Agnes gave the question some thought. "He said your great-grandfather Gabriel always thought Ness looked in the wrong places. He said that gangsters were easy because you always knew where to find them. Ness couldn't figure out a guy who was insane, but then, neither could anyone else."

Theresa let her mother sort recipes for a while as she pondered this point. In the 1930s, no one would have ever heard of a serial killer. They would have approached the investigation like any other—rounding up the usual suspects, criminals, what they used to call sexual deviants. Of course that encompassed a lot more than now, since it used to be a crime to be homosexual or have an interracial relationship. "In that day they'd be looking for a man who stood out. Knowing what we know about most serial killers, nowadays we'd look for a man with a steady job, who doesn't bother his neighbors and has no or a very minor criminal record. Someone who *doesn't* stand out."

"Then how do you catch him?" her mother asked.

This stumped Theresa. "Evidence, I suppose. That's where I come in."

"Your great-grandfather Gabriel told your grandpa one other thing, too. He said it had to have something to do with the railroads."

"Because the victims were found around the train tracks?"

"I have no idea *why* he said it, he just did. You should go to bed, honey. You look tired."

"Were you going to make turnovers?"

Her mother smiled. "Not tonight. This weekend, at the restaurant. Come for dinner and for two forty-nine you can buy one."

"Highway robbery." Theresa stood up and said good night.

"And don't forget about Friday."

"Aw, *Mom*!"

"We always have birthday parties with the family. Especially a big one like this."

A small house crowded with aunts upon aunts and cousins upon cousins. Theresa loved them all, but not when they were trying to convince her that the irretrievable loss of her youth was something to be happy about. "Why should I *celebrate* turning forty?"

"Every birthday is one to celebrate," her mother said in a way that made Theresa feel ungrateful, which, of course, had been the idea. Mothers were good at that.

Theresa said good night and trooped through the rain, now faded to a heavy mist, to her home. The trees whispered above her and tossed a few cold drops down her neck while she ordered herself to get into the habit of leaving lights on, now that Rachael would not be there before her with every bulb blazing, the TV going, and the stereo bulging the walls. But Harry, her dead fiancé's dog, stood guard with tail wagging to let her know the perimeter had been secured, so lights did not seem that important.

A truck drove by, the name of a roofing company emblazoned on the side. No other cars, with or without missing headlights.

She tucked herself into bed with James Miller's notes and a business card. She dialed the phone before glancing at the clock and then debated whether she should hang up. She was still debating when he answered. "Mr.

Corliss? It's Theresa MacLean. I'm sorry to call so late."

"Not at all, young lady. I'm something of a night owl. What can I do for you?"

Helpful hint for women of a certain age, Theresa thought: Hang out with people at least twenty years your senior and they will make you feel youthful. "I need to learn about trains."

"Then you've come to the right place," he said, chuckling. "So to speak."

CHAPTER 20

TUESDAY, SEPTEMBER 24
1935

James Miller dallied with his partner only long enough to drink a cup of coffee before he left Walter to the tender ministrations of a middle-aged waitress and moved out into the bustle of the Terminal Tower. His stomach growled, but he told himself he was too interested in the investigation to eat. It didn't work.

He carried the coat, in its paper bag, after Walter refused responsibility for that particular piece of evidence. "I'm not eating my lunch with something that pervert touched on my lap. Now either sit down with me or scram."

James scrammed. There were no less than three drugstores scattered throughout the two floors of shops. All three were popular, but at two P.M. he did not have to deal with the lunchtime or after-work throngs. He headed for one on the lower level, marveling at whoever had come up with the idea of planting retail shops squarely in the path of travelers. People waiting for trains with time to kill and commuters who rushed from tracks to office and needed convenience were provided with the perfect outlet for their hard-earned funds. From inside this bubble of commerce, one could barely tell the Depression existed. Strolling along the gleaming marble walkways, a man felt prosperous even on an empty stomach.

The drugstore counters thronged with kids on their way home from school. James wondered where these children got the dimes for an ice cream soda when there were grown men outside on the streets begging for those same dimes. He didn't begrudge them; indeed, it seemed a hopeful sign that at least some of the nation's offspring were having a happy childhood.

He had to wait to speak to the druggist while a portly lady with a small dog described her nightly tossing and turning. James thought of telling her to spend some time in a trench in Europe and she'd learn to sleep through mortar attacks, but thought better of it. It wasn't her fault that he'd probably never sleep through the night again.

The man in the white coat listened with great sympathy, gave her a packet of powder, and sent her on her way before turning to James. "If I had a nickel for every whiny dame who comes in here I would own the place. What can I do for you? Anemia?"

"Uh, no."

"You sure? You look a little pasty. Just a cold, then?"

James identified himself and pulled out the blue coat, which the druggist, unsurprisingly, did not recognize. The pills from the pocket were another story. He picked up a magnifying glass and examined each pill, holding them one at a time in the palm of his hand. "Nothing bad. No kind of mass-produced barbiturate or narcotic—that's why you're asking, right? You think this is something that can dope somebody up?"

"I need to know what it is, even if it's harmless."

"Well, that would be my guess. Harmless. This one is probably a vitamin—vitamin A, see the *A* stamped on it? People are nuts about vitamins these days, think that all the alphabet minerals can cure everything that ails. Not that there's anything wrong with vitamins, of course, they're important, but they're not the bee's knees. But the customers don't listen. I guess any sense of security is better than none."

"Is the other one a vitamin, too?"

"I don't know. It might be a custom job, one that some guy like me brewed up special. I can't tell without sending it for chemical testing. You want me to do that?"

"No." James took the pill back before the man could think about it. "No, I need to hang on to that."

"Besides, don't you guys have your own lab that can do all that fancy stuff? I read about it in the paper. You've got Ness in charge now, after all. The reporters seem to think he's going to turn the police force into a bunch of angels."

James ignored this last sentence, thanked the man, and walked out past the kids. He found another drugstore and received the same information, this time from a dour old man who left out the speculation regarding the future of the Cleveland police force. Then James put the pills in his pocket and trotted down the steps to the train platforms.

Forty-five minutes later he found Walter window-shopping outside a tobacconist's shop. The older cop now carried a parcel wrapped in brown paper and an unlit cigar—both, no doubt, "gifts" from a grateful citizen. "I found a baseball suit for Walter Junior's birthday," he told James, eyeing his partner with a piercing glance. "Where have you been?"

"Haunting the platforms. Why, did you think I was

informing on you to the Untouchables?" James joked, nodding at the parcel.

He realized his mistake a split second later when Walter's face darkened and he stepped closer to hiss, "Don't razz me about that, Jimmy! It ain't funny!"

James flushed, more from the stares of the shoppers within earshot than from having the same argument one more time. "Nothing's funny about being a cop these days. Look around. The people we're supposed to work for expect nothing but a shakedown. They don't look to us for help. Nobody thinks we're heroes."

"Is that what you need, Jimmy? To be a hero? Then go find a war somewhere and leave us mere mortals to the business of making a living."

This was pointless. "Look, Walter—I checked out the pills and asked around to see if anyone recognized the blue coat. That's all."

Walter's shoulders relaxed a bit. He tucked the parcel under his arm and the unlit cigar between his lips, though his face retained its tense lines. "And did they?"

"Maybe. I got a bunch of maybes. The strongest one is positive they saw a man wearing a similar coat loitering by the loading platform about two and a half weeks ago. They couldn't pin it down to a day."

Walter nodded. They fell into step, doing a slow circuit of the shop windows as they headed toward Public Square.

James outlined what he had learned from the druggists. "They both said at least one is a vitamin. I know everyone's vitamin crazy these days—"

"Quackery is all that is. My granddad lived to ninety-five and never took a pill in his life."

"—but it started me thinking. Remember the tomboy?"

Walter pushed open the thin glass door to the bustle

of Euclid Avenue, his face smoothing into a thoughtful plane. "Yeah."

"Remember where she took us?"

Walter tucked the cigar into his breast pocket. "Yeah."

"I think we should pay the good doctor another visit," James proposed. "Now that you've had lunch and all."

CHAPTER 21

THURSDAY, SEPTEMBER 9
PRESENT DAY

The autopsy room in the sixty-year-old Medical Examiner's Office had been built for easy cleaning. With stainless steel sinks and counters, a drain in the floor, and ceramic tile over the floor and halfway up the walls, it could be scrubbed down night after night, year after year, without evidence of any real wear and tear. Each evening it appeared to be the cleanest room in the building, though the result was tidy rather than sterile. The victims could no longer be infected and the staff did not worry much about germs. For years they had worked with formalin and X-rays, been exposed to the insides of victims with tuberculosis, HIV, hepatitis (A, B, and C), and occasionally meningitis, and remained healthy. Surrounded by death they, like the rest of humanity, smoked, rode motorcycles, ate fatty foods, and drove too fast. Familiarity breeds contempt.

The two headless males were not, by a long shot, the most disturbing or most bizarre deaths the doctors and dieners had ever seen, and so had to compete with the baseball scores for attention. The Indians were third in the division, with wins and losses about even. One pathologist and two dieners thought that the team had made some good trades in the past year and were sure of a place in the series, maybe couldn't win it, but could at least participate. Another pathologist, another two dieners, and a deskman put these odds at slim to none. They had been through this heartbreak too many times. One pathologist, Christine Johnson, abstained, sharpshooting being the only sport to which she paid any attention.

Before her lay the body of the older victim, the head by itself at the top of the table. She had noted all the external information she could—injuries (a scrape to the right wrist, a healed cut on the left index, and of course the wounds to the neck and groin), old scars (appendix), moles (two large ones, as well as a host of smaller ones she didn't bother to note) and tattoos (none). She saw no puncture marks or abscesses on the arms that would indicate drug use, no swelling of the chest or stomach that would indicate trauma, tumors, or hernia. The body did not yet show too many signs of decomposition. She guessed the time of death to be twenty-four hours previously but collected a syringe of fluid from one eyeball to help her narrow that down. The potassium level of vitreous fluid increases after death.

Christine's assistant for this autopsy happened to be a young man by the name of Damon, and as she made the last notation necessary before beginning the internal autopsy, he took a scalpel and made the Y incision from the man's shoulders to his belly button, without waiting for her instruction to do so. At the medical examiner's, as just about anywhere else in society, doctors occupied the top rungs of status, influence, and power. Damon felt it his duty to bring these demigods down to earth and had a myriad of small ways in which to do so. Christine let it go. She understood the desire to keep humans on an equal footing. Besides, civil service made people nearly impossible to fire and she had to work with Damon almost daily, and besides *that*, he did excellent work.

The victim's skin parted like the Red Sea, and yellow globules of subcutaneous fat welled up from inside. Not much, relatively speaking, as the victim had not been significantly overweight. With quick slices of the scalpel, Damon stripped the flesh back from the ribs and got out the long-handled pruning shears. The bones made soft cracking sounds as he snapped through them.

Theresa MacLean entered the autopsy room. She did not express an opinion on the Indians' chances other than to wish them well, any more than she would have gotten involved in a discussion of politics. In Cleveland, the former could be a more volatile subject than the latter. She did ask Christine how it was going, a less nagging way of asking for information.

"Nothing interesting so far. What did you find?"

Theresa said, "A few fibers and adhesive residue on the wrists and ankles, of both men. But I don't see any bruising like they struggled against it, do you?"

"Nothing visible. I'll check under the skin."

"I scraped their nails but haven't had a chance to look at the material yet. No defensive wounds. Makes me think the tape merely made their bodies easy to transport, but then something must have knocked them out. I hope you can tell me what."

"We'll see." Christine never made promises.

Damon made the small incision into the pericardium, the membrane surrounding the heart, again without waiting for her instruction. A normal amount of fluid oozed out. An excess amount would have put the heart under too much pressure to function. Christine made a note and Damon removed the rest of the pericardium.

"You really think this is a copy of some 1930s murders?" Damon asked.

"Yes. These two were left in the same place and the same circumstances as victims one and two in 1935, circumstances too bizarre to have occurred by accident."

"Well, why not?" the young diener said in agreement. "People do those Civil War reenactments, with uniforms and horses and muskets and all that shit." He reached for the heart with an evilly sharp scalpel.

"Damon," Christine said, a note of warning in her voice. She hadn't finished her notes on the pericardium.

The young man shrugged and waited. He had made his point for the day, and the rest of the autopsy would proceed smoothly. Tomorrow he would start all over again. The battle to establish equality among all never ended. "What about that chick they found at the air show? Where does she fit in?"

"I think she's supposed to be victim zero," Theresa said. "It's too much of a coincidence that she turned up in the same week. But I can't be sure. There's nothing unique about men dismembering their girlfriends."

"I'll take the heart now," Christine said.

"And I didn't find any adhesive on her wrists—but then I assumed she had already been cut in pieces when transported. Not as difficult to move around as the nearly complete body of a full-grown male, and he moved them. Just like in the original cases, both men were clean and drained of blood with no signs of insect activity. We found no blood or a way to wash the bodies at the scene, so it had to be done somewhere else."

"What does that mean?" Damon asked, slicing through the top of the aorta. "Or do I want to know?"

"He has a workshop," Theresa said.

"I didn't want to know."

"Do you have everything you need this time?" Theresa asked them. "No missing sections of neck or anything like that?"

"Nothing missing," Christine assured her. "Even their genitalia is accounted for. Your guy removed stuff but didn't keep it. Any idea who these two unfortunate gentlemen are?"

"Yes, actually." Theresa followed the doctor over to the cutting board next to the sink to watch her dissect the heart. She didn't expect any clues to result from this, but she found cardiology interesting. "They've both been identified. Your guy is Levon Forrest, fifty-two, married with two grown children. Lives on East 119th, takes the Red Line from the Euclid station to the Brookpark station, and walks to his job at the Ford plant. Despite a nasty cold he left his house at six. But he missed his seven o'clock start time this morning, which was so unlike him that his supervisor called his wife, who called the cops, who, unsurprisingly, were not too interested in the case of a grown man missing only four hours. That ID isn't written in stone yet, but he matches the description exactly and the wife identified a photo of the head. His head."

The pathologist opened up Levon Forrest's heart with quick, sure strokes, then measured the thickness of the chamber walls. They were normal, with the left ventricle, of course, being much thicker than the other three as it had to push the blood throughout the length of the body. The valves had no abnormalities. The tiny coronary arteries covering the outside surface of the fist-sized organ showed some stiffening and blockage from atherosclerosis, but no more than average for a man his age. "I hope they didn't get the neck in the photo."

"No, of course not. Frank planned to ease into the

decapitation part of the story, figuring she didn't really need to know the gory details in the same breath with 'You're now a widow.' Poor woman. At least the time of his abduction is narrowed down to an hour. The officers are questioning everyone they can find along the route."

Christine kept some sections of the heart, dipping the scalpel into a small jar of formalin and swishing it until the tissue washed off, then returned to the body. "Has he got any history?"

"None. Some minor scrapes as a juvenile, but nothing as an adult. Apparently a law-abiding, loving husband and father and you-can-set-your-watch-by-him employee."

The doctor moved on to the lungs. "What about the other one?"

Theresa paused to stretch a crick out of her back, completely unaware that this action garnered a surreptitious glance from every male in the room. Had she been aware, she'd have lived with the crick. "We have an ID on him as well, for utterly different reasons. No one reported him missing, but he had a record as long as one's proverbial arm."

Christine Johnson ran her hands over the lungs of the dead man, feeling for any spots where they might have fused to the inside of the chest cavity. Prior surgery or tumors could cause this, but Levon Forrest's lungs were smooth and free, so she cut through the primary bronchial attachments and weighed them. The lobes weren't exactly the healthy pink of youth, but they weren't bad. She sliced off three thin sections of tissue and added them to the formalin soup in the plastic quart container. "So who is he?"

Theresa stood between the two autopsy tables, her back to the sink, so that she could talk to Christine and also the doctor preparing to autopsy the man of whom she spoke, the other victim of their modern-day Torso killer. "His name is Richard Dunlop, and he couldn't be more Levon Forrest's opposite. Different color, much younger—twenty-three—and if he ever held a job it must have been under another name. He lived on the west side, more or less. His last known address was a friend's house on Wade Avenue off Twenty-fifth. No one knows who he's been flopping with recently, or they're not saying, according to Frank and Angela."

"So little Richard has no visible means of support." The doctor opened Forrest's half-full stomach, pouring the contents into a fresh quart container. They would have to be tested for drugs as a matter of routine, and Theresa might want to examine the solid matter to corroborate details of his last meal.

Theresa's nose wrinkled at the thought. She hated gastric exams. "Visible, yes. Legal, no. He's been arrested every year or so since his teens for loitering, prostitution, possession, solicitation, more loitering."

Christine Johnson finished dissecting Levon Forrest's unremarkable organs as Damon sliced his scalp open with a scalpel. Then the doctor took over with the small instrument, like a flat chisel, used to separate the flesh from the white bone of the skull. With no other apparent cause of death, she wanted to examine every inch of it for trauma. "So he's a hustler," she said of the other victim.

Theresa nodded. "Looks that way. Not a difficult person for our killer to find and abduct."

"Yeah." Damon waited, bone saw in hand. "Just open the door and wave a twenty."

"Also without a firm timeline, like Mr. Forrest here. The last time anyone will admit to seeing Dunlop was three days ago."

"Maybe it was a doctor," Damon said.

"Why?" Theresa asked.

"The chick was an addict, the first guy had a cold, and the second guy is another malnourished lowlife."

"You have a point," Theresa said.

"Who else would know how to do this?" Damon gestured toward the severed neck. "And don't say me."

Christine said, "Here we go. I thought that felt a little too cushy."

A flat, wide blood clot had formed under Levon Forrest's skin, directly above the top of the neck, where the head had suffered a trauma and broken blood vessels leaked between the flesh and the skull. The doctor sent Damon to get Zoe, the photographer. This injury would have to be documented.

Theresa inspected the glossy red mass. "Someone socked him in the back of the head. Would that be enough to make him unconscious?"

"Why do you always ask me that?"

"Why will you never tell me?"

"Because it varies from person to person. This was hard enough to crack the skull but not hard enough to break the skin. Very blunt impact. It might have knocked him out, it might not have. That's all I can say."

"No other blows?"

Christine finished flaying the flesh from the bone of the skull. "I don't see any."

"Okay. How about a time of death, then?"

"Five hours and twelve minutes," the doctor said immediately. Christine rarely joked, but this was one of her favorites. No one else found it as amusing. Zoe even rolled her eyes.

"Seriously," Theresa demanded.

"I'm happy with twenty-four to thirty-six hours. Rigor has come and gone and he's been refrigerated since you found him last night, which should have slowed the process. He was cold when you found him, right?"

"Not Popsicle cold, but definitely cool."

"Right. So all the signs could easily fit into that window between when he left for work and when his shift began without him."

Theresa said, "In only one hour he ran into Richard Dunlop, or our killer, or both at the same time. But he spent most of that hour riding the Red Line."

Christine gestured to Damon, who started in with the bone saw to take the top off the cranium. As always, Theresa retreated to the man's feet and leaned up against the stainless steel sinks, away from the bone dust wafting into the air. She raised her voice over the whining saw to say to the doctor: "How does someone strike and drag off a fully grown man from a moving car packed with dozens of commuters?"

"He doesn't. He must have attacked him before he got on the rapid or after he got off."

"Frank found a few people who say he was on yesterday morning's 6:08, but he's taking that with a grain of salt. You know commuting—you get your regulars and they get into their habits. The whole process becomes a blur, so these witnesses aren't completely sure if it was yesterday or the day before, or the day before that. They've all seen the news last night or the paper this morning and now they're so freaked they can swear they saw Elvis."

"But if they're right, then the killer grabbed Mr. Forrest here after he disembarked."

"That gives us a window of fourteen minutes between the time he'd get off the rapid and the start of his shift, during which he should have been walking to the Ford plant. The cops are hitting the Brookpark parking lot hard."

Damon finished with the bone saw and pried the section from the top of the head. This took some muscle, and he quickly found it a different sort of proposition when the body didn't weigh down the neck—without it, he had no anchor to pull against. Christine put her hands around the torn neck and the hair at its nape and hung on as best she could, and they wrestled the bone apart. Zoe waited, camera in hand. As they did this, the doctor suggested to Theresa, "Maybe the killer attacked Dunlop and this guy"—meaning her victim—"tried to help and wound up in the cross fire."

"I thought of that—Forrest sounds like the kind of person who would come to someone's rescue. But the killer meant to kill two. He needed them to re-create the 1935 murders. Two fully grown, unhelpless men. This guy knows how to approach people."

Levon Forrest's brain came into view, pink and convoluted and looking so exactly like what one expected a brain to look like that it seemed unreal. But its neatness had been marred by the small clot on the occipital lobe. Christine ran her fingers over it and muttered to herself, "Coincides with the skull fracture."

Theresa leaned in, peering as well. "Would that have made him unconscious?"

"Why do you—I don't know. Possibly. I doubt it killed him—my guess is it's not big enough to really interfere with the brain's functioning."

"What did kill him, then?"

"Cutting his head off," Christine said. "Yeah, I think that did it."

She cut the brain free, the spinal cord sliding out easily since it had already been severed from the backbone, and dropped it onto the scale. Damon began to dry out the inside of the skull with a rag to get ready for more photographs while Zoe, as always, waited with what patience she could muster. The other pathologist in the room did not have Christine's brisk style and had not yet finished the external examination of Richard Dunlop, dutifully noting each blemish on Dunlop's young skin, bruises, abrasions, needle tracks. Theresa decided not to wait and left the autopsy room, to the disappointment of the male pathologist and his diener, whose conversation wandered back to the Indians and the deservedness, or lack of same, of their division ranking.

CHAPTER 22

James Miller entered the building at 4950 Pullman. It had not changed much in the half a year or so since Irene Schaffer ran from it, screaming and half undressed.

As before, he and Walter found Dr. Louis Odessa in his office, ushering a well-coiffed lady in a smart wool jacket out the door. She thanked him profusely for whatever services he had offered and departed, trailing promises to take note of every single thing she put in her mouth, every single thing. James shot his partner a warning look, knowing too well the sort of comment Walter would make after an opening like that.

Odessa invited them in, apparently not concerned about their unexpected appearance. His office still lacked décor but had gained more bottles and books on its shelves. "Good afternoon, gentlemen. What can I do for you?"

Walter sprawled in one of the cushioned chairs meant for guests—or patients, as no doubt Odessa would have insisted. "We were in the neighborhood, thought we'd stop by and see if you have any young girls tied up in your closet."

The man chuckled. It made James's blood begin to rush at the memory of the day he found the narrow cot exactly as Irene Schaffer had described it. He clenched and unclenched his hands, closed and open.

"I remember now," Odessa said. "That excitable girl. At least she embarrassed herself too badly with that wild story to come around here anymore."

"So you don't make a habit of bringing underage girls by to . . . *analyze* them?" Walter injected the verb with an insulting amount of skepticism for someone who hadn't believed Irene Schaffer. He thought her a fast girl who had picked the wrong guy to hustle.

James, on the other hand, figured if Irene did anything in the street it was probably to play baseball.

The doctor only made it worse by chuckling again. Most men would not be so cool when accused of mashing, especially of a girl Irene's age. "A typical example of my clientele left just before you, officers. Do I appear to be a man who needs to waste time with unwashed urchins?"

James turned away from the smarmy idiot to look over the contents of the shelving, pace a bit, fiddle with the faucet on a small sink at the inner wall, and bounce on his toes, anything to relieve the tension. "Mind if we check?"

"Go right ahead. There's nothing in there but paper and empty bottles." The doctor didn't even watch as James strode behind him and opened the door to the little room. Smart guys often cooperated with police, thinking it would allay suspicion . . . which it didn't.

No girl stretched on the little cot, of course, and the rest of the area appeared as Odessa described it. James closed the door again and moved back to the shelves.

"Why do you keep a bed in there, anyway?" Walter asked as if from the idlest curiosity.

"I catch a nap after lunchtime. It helps with the digestion."

"And that's what you're all about, isn't it? Digestion?"

Odessa spoke to Walter. "Digestion is only half of the puzzle. Coaxing the body into absorbing the right things entails giving it the right things to absorb. Our bodies are incredible machines, but without proper maintenance they do not work at peak efficiency, or they wear out prematurely."

"And you're here to save people from themselves."

"Someone must."

James stole a glance at the man while pretending to read a bottle label. For the first time, the doctor looked like a doctor, somber and serious as he lectured: "The Great War shook this country from its sleep. We had to go to war and found out that one-third of our eligible soldiers had to be turned down for poor health. One-*third*, gentlemen. And it's not only our bodies, but our minds, too—we couldn't find enough men in the general populace suitable to become officers. That's why education is now mandatory in all forty-eight states."

"But we wind up paying for people who don't need it." Taxes were a pet annoyance to Walter. "Like Negroes, and girls."

"All are part of the whole," Odessa argued. "Ignorant people only create more work for those who are not. Raising up individuals raises up the entire society."

"What sort of doctor are you?" James asked, both to throw Odessa off stride and because he had no interest in debating education with Walter once again. Baby John would go to school, period, for as long and as well as James could afford.

"I have a degree in nutrition science," Odessa said.

"Is that like an M.D.?" James knew it wasn't, since he now stared at the framed certificate on the wall and it said nothing about being a bachelor's or doctorate. He didn't know much about college but felt fairly certain that real degrees used one of those two words.

"No. I treat the whole body, the intake and outflow and the interaction of the same with our living cells. I don't saw off limbs or look at your teeth or deliver babies." He added this as if such trivialities were beneath him.

"Vitamins?"

"I beg your pardon?"

"Do you give people vitamins?"

"Yes. Vitamins—and minerals, too—are the single most important line of defense between ourselves and our graves."

Walter took over. "Do you have any vitamin A?"

"Yes. Why, Detective, do you suffer from night blindness?"

"Huh?"

"A deficiency of vitamin A causes night blindness, a difficulty seeing in dim light. But just as importantly, it can interact with—"

James placed photographs of the two Jackass Hill victims on the man's desk, hoping especially to shock this smarmy bastard with the half-decomposed face of the second victim. "Do you recognize these men?"

"No."

He had decided that quickly. "Are you sure?"

"Yes." Odessa waited for another question, switching eye contact from James to Walter. He did not look at the photographs again.

A hustler and a transient, James thought, *killed by a guy swell enough to own a car with which to transport the bodies. How would a guy like that get acquainted with a punk like Andrassy? He must be a chameleon, or he's got the kind of job that gets him accepted every-where. Like a doctor.*

James pulled out the unidentified pill and set it on the desk. "Do you know what this is?"

Louis Odessa picked up the tiny lump of whiteness and took a magnifying glass from his desk drawer. After a long examination, he set it back down on the edge of his desk and said, "I would guess it's either niacin or fo-lic acid. I have some here. . . ." After retrieving two bottles from his collection, he pronounced it most similar to the thiamine tablets he bought from a large pharmaceutical company in New York. "Not exactly the same," he added, though the pill certainly looked identical to those in the bottle as far as James could tell, "but I'll bet it's some brand of thiamine. There's really no way to tell without chemical testing."

"Why would a doctor prescribe it?" James tried a little grease. Walter rolled his eyes at the idea of prescribing pills to otherwise healthy people.

"It works against beriberi—a common disease to Orientals, the poor ones who live on rice—and diabetes. Alcoholics, also, can have a deficiency of thiamine and need supplements."

"And you're sure you've never seen these men? Separately or together?" James asked again.

"No, I haven't. Would you two care to go over your diets? I have a few minutes before my next patient. No? Are you sure? Because you need either fresh fruit or vitamin C tablets or you'll wind up with scurvy, and you"— he switched his gaze to Walter—"need to eat less-caloric foods."

James's portly partner did not care for the direction in which the conversation had turned and stood up. "No, thanks. We gotta go. But we'll be around in case you bring home any more little girlfriends."

Odessa continued to smile, but the edges appeared brittle.

James followed his partner into the hallway. Sunlight streamed in from both the front door to the north and the back door to the south. Lettering on the frosted glass across from Odessa's office read MADAME MORELLI, ME-DIUM. KNOCK TO ENTER. James heard low voices inside, one punctuated with a gasp. Laughter spilled from an open office door while two men stood outside on the south lawn. James tapped Walter's elbow and went toward them.

Both doors farther along the hallway had opened. James glanced into the one on his left without making his interest too obvious. Three young men in shirtsleeves drew at sketching tables, two of them throwing mild and apparently amusing insults to each other. They were reproached by a pretty young woman at a typewriter.

The office on his right held an empty desk, two chairs, a small sink, shelves filled with books and rolled-up drawings and disheveled stacks of newspapers, and a sleeping dog. James walked on and out the south door. Walter did not follow and instead dipped into the architects' office, no doubt to make the acquaintance of the pretty secretary.

Of the two men outside, the shorter man had turned away, heading toward Kingsbury Run in a stained cardigan and trousers so frayed that the pattern of his underwear showed through. He had a peculiar step, picking up his right foot higher than his left, and James watched for a moment before he figured it out—the sole of the man's right shoe had come loose in front so that the wearer had to take care or he'd fold it in half with each step.

"Good afternoon," said the other man. His trousers were not threadbare and his white shirt was clean and crisp. He had a full head of brown hair and light blue eyes with even lighter spots. They reminded James of ginger ale, not the color but the fizz. He appeared to be about thirty-five. "How are you this beautiful afternoon?"

"Fine, and yourself?"

"Quite well."

James nodded in the direction of the shuffling man. "Where's your friend going?"

The man gave a gentle smile and sat on a low bench, on which sat a plate with two sandwiches and three black soda bottles. "Probably to hop a boxcar back to Pittsburgh to look for work there. I don't know him, we just got to talking and shared some dinner. I have some corned beef hash here from Mike's on Thirtieth and some cookies my housekeeper made. Would you like some?"

"No, thanks."

"Or some soda pop? It's Mission Orange. I can't get enough of the stuff."

The man's gaze came to rest on James's shoes at the same time that his resolutely friendly tone penetrated James's mind. This guy had taken him for a hobo. A bum, looking for a handout.

His stomach chose that moment to growl, a sound loud enough to be heard on the next street. He should have had lunch at the Terminal building with Walter. "I'm a cop."

"Oh. I'm . . . sorry. I should have asked after your occupation. It's just that so many men who wander through this city don't really want to talk about who they are."

Or remember who they were, James thought. "They know you're a soft touch?"

"No, but since we're next to the tracks we get a lot of men passing through here." James could see what he meant. The wide valley made a perfect spot to hop on and off the trains for illegal rides across America. "They're all half starved," the man went on. "I've been lucky in my life, and I feel compelled to share that with my fellow man."

"What makes you so lucky?"

"My name is Arthur Corliss. I own the LEP—the Lake Erie–Pennsylvania Railroad." He stood again and shook James's hand with a kindly but crushing grip. As tall as Odessa but with Walter's weight, in muscle instead of paunch.

James asked, "You give handouts to the same bums who are going to ride your rails?"

"It's not their fault that this country's situation collapsed into rubble. Besides"—Corliss gave him a sheepish grin—"I convince them to use the B&O lines."

James laughed and let go of having been mistaken for a hobo. He knew if he bothered to look in the mirror it wouldn't be such a stretch. His shirts had been washed and worn for so many years that the weave had loosened. His cheeks had begun to sink into his mouth.

"Are you familiar with your neighbor Louis Odessa?"

"Dr. Louis? Yes. Why?"

James gave him a story, making it sound as if they had consulted Odessa for help identifying the vitamin pill. "He seems to have some highfalutin clients. Does he mind you feeding bums on his stoop?"

"No, no. Louis is generous in spirit, if not in cash. I merely give them something to eat, but Louis helps them decide what to eat for the rest of their lives."

"You're interested in vitamins and minerals and all that health stuff?"

"Absolutely. If you don't guard your health when you're young, it will be too late when you're old. At least that's what Louis says. He tells the architect boys that, too, but they won't listen."

James pulled the photos from his pocket. "Have you seen either of these men?"

Corliss took the picture, studied it. "No. Good Lord, this one barely looks human. Why do you ask?" A cloud passed over the sun. The darkening sky reflected in his light-colored eyes.

"We're doing a routine inquiry."

The man stared at James for a moment longer, blankly, no doubt wondering where he had seen the photos before. *Every citizen of Cleveland should see them in their sleep,* James thought, *with the attention the papers are lavishing on the case.* The people were both fascinated and repulsed, but most of all they were frightened.

But Corliss only nodded and solemnly asked, "It's about the man's wife, isn't it?"

James's blood picked up speed. "What about his wife?"

"Or his daughter, or whatever. Louis likes women," Corliss explained as if it were a condition Odessa couldn't help and should be pitied for. "Perhaps too much."

James merely smiled, nodded, gave up trying to link Louis Odessa to the two dead men on the hill, and went to retrieve Walter from the architects' office before leaving the building at 4950 Pullman.

CHAPTER 23

THURSDAY, SEPTEMBER 9
PRESENT DAY.

Theresa returned to the trace evidence lab. Their secretary huddled over her computer monitor, sneaking in a game of Solitaire while Leo's voice came as a steady hum from his office. Their boss could rival any teenage girl for hours spent on the phone. Theresa could also hear Don in the DNA rooms to the rear of the lab, singing quietly as he filled microtubes with extracted samples.

Theresa settled into her nook behind the FTIR and put on a mask before opening the samples she had collected from the two dead men, not to keep her breath from contaminating the fibers but so that an unexpected sneeze or sigh did not scatter them across the lab. Then she placed the glassine paper under the stereomicroscope to unfold it.

A single fiber, about an inch long, had been stuck to the inside of Richard Dunlop's wrist. Theresa used a fresh disposable scalpel to cut a piece off, then placed that section between a glass slide and a glass cover slip.

A drop of mounting media would hold it together—permanently—and make its form clearly visible under a transmitted light microscope. A red fiber, with a trilobal shape, exactly what she had found stuck to Kim Hammond's hair. A micrometer scale confirmed the diameter. Because it took only a minute, Theresa switched the slide to the stage of her ancient polarizing microscope, under whose light the fiber appeared in colors of preppy green and pink. Polyester again—like what had been found on Kim Hammond. To confirm this finding Theresa cut another piece of the fiber from Richard Dunlop. It took several minutes and a few muttered curses to get the substance, once flattened, to stick to the window and not to the pick and the roller, but eventually it became situated in the path of the light beam. Polyester. It had to be carpeting; fibers of that thickness and with a trilobal shape would not be used in clothing or upholstery.

Theresa sighed. On TV a scientist would have a handy database of every carpet ever manufactured in the world and some way to find the customers who bought each one. In her real and much more inconvenient life, this data did not exist. The closest she could come was to e-mail the fiber's description and spectrum to the FBI so that they could compare it to their automotive carpet database. It had its limits and involved only carpeting made for automobiles. This fiber seemed too thick and too bright to come from a car, but even a remote possibility was well worth a try. And she liked to stay in touch with the FBI lab. They were friendly and helpful people.

After that, she would have to take her fiber and its specs and hit every carpeting supplier in the area, a monumental task for which she would never have the time. Surely red could not be a common color—though current interior decorating did seem to favor the jewel tones, especially in restaurants—but most carpets were a combination of colors. The overall color of a particular rug could be anything—say, beige—but with tiny colored flecks here and there. This would not be listed in anyone's inventory as *red*.

She repeated the process with the other fiber found on Dunlop, a round, black thread that turned out to be nylon. It could have come from nearly anything—a coat, a bag, sports equipment, a tarp. The other victim, Forrest, had the red fiber on his ankle and no black fibers.

Swabs of the adhesive residue from both men told her that it probably belonged to duct tape, an item most criminalists saw far too much of. Every rapist and serial killer kept a roll in their "kit." She could identify the adhesive as consistent with the killer's roll of tape, if she had the killer's roll of tape. Had he bound Forrest's wrists while he cut off his head? No, bruises would have formed as the victim struggled for life—unless he were still unconscious from the blow to the head. But the killer might also have taped his arms and ankles to make the body easier to work with as he moved it to the hillside. Either way, simply knowing that he had used duct tape would not help them. The stuff was simply too ubiquitous.

The killer had murdered them somewhere else, cleaned and prepped the bodies, then taken them to the hillside for display. Like the original Torso killer, he had carried the bodies of these two grown men down the hill—their skin had not been dragged through the undergrowth. *Carried,* and Forrest had to weigh close to two hundred pounds.

A shudder of relief ran through her that the man had run from her foolish pursuit last night. He could have taken her apart with his bare hands.

Theresa forced her mind from these gory images back

to the forensic evidence. It didn't seem like much, so she decided to follow James Miller's example and make a list. *Kim: missing part of neck—strangled?; red fiber; brown paint. Richard Dunlop: decapitated; red fiber; black fiber; drug history; adhesive. Levon Forrest: bludgeoned, decapitated; red fiber, adhesive.*

"What have you got?" Leo appeared without warning, as he was wont to do, shoving her papers aside to perch on the edge of her desk across the aisle. This disruption to her desktop made her want to slap him upside the head with the polarizing microscope. Unlike him, she refrained. "Not much."

"Not much is not what I want to hear."

"Well, we have one thing in our favor. If this guy truly wants to re-create the Torso killer's murders, then we know where—"

"The next victim will turn up," Leo interjected.

"And who it will be, at least the gender. The third victim, actually the fourth if you count the Lady of the Lake, was a woman named Flo Polillo. She was found on a freezing January morning behind a manufacturing plant around East Twenty-second. Half of her, I mean. They found the other half about two blocks away."

"Yeah, he, um—" Leo stopped there and waited for Theresa to fill in the details he clearly couldn't remember or had never known.

"He cut her body into pieces and left the pieces wrapped in newspaper and burlap bags, placed in bushel baskets. A dog found them. Can you still get bushel baskets?"

"Can you still get burlap bags?"

"Our killer has a problem, though, according to Google Earth."

Leo raised one eyebrow and sipped his coffee. He would not ask, of course.

"The back of the Hart Manufacturing Plant is now an I-90 interchange. Today's killer might have to break with tradition."

"Shouldn't play in traffic," Leo agreed, then made a show of checking his watch as Theresa gathered her jacket and purse, in order to clearly illustrate how fifteen minutes remained until quitting time. "Leaving early?"

"Not exactly."

CHAPTER 24

THURSDAY, SEPTEMBER 9
PRESENT DAY

The pleasant hum that trains made when a comfortable distance from one's ears changed to a heart-rattling, eardrum-shattering, colossal banging when up close. And if they blew their horn, forget it. Five years of your life would be shaved off, at a minimum. Of course she had already learned that the night before; oddly enough the sound was no less shocking in the light of day.

But she loved them anyway.

"I can't help it," she told Edward Corliss. "I can't help but admire something whose design has not essentially changed in, what, two hundred years?"

They sat on a polyurethane bench designed to look like an ancient wooden one, next to the tracks near West Third Street, only a mile from Jackass Hill but on the other side of the river. The day had taken a turn toward winter and the breeze across the river chilled her skin more quickly than the sun could warm it. Theresa snuggled farther into her woolen blazer and added, "But I suppose that's silly. I don't really know a thing about trains."

"No, no, I agree completely," Edward assured her. "The propulsion systems changed over time, from wood to coal to diesel, and some to electric. But the structure of the cars and the tracks is the same as it was when people tied up their horses in front of the dry goods store."

The train in front of them, which had been moving slowly, finally came to a halt and then reversed, causing a new series of the deafening clangs to echo up the row as the coupling of each car collided with the next in line. Theresa put her hands over her ears. She swore the vibration plucked at every vein in her body as if they were overtightened guitar strings.

Then she felt Edward's hand on her raised elbow. "Do you want to walk along the tracks a bit?" he shouted.

She nodded, not at all sure that she meant it.

The tracks near the station had been kept in good order, with fresh gravel filling the gaps between one set and another. The stones crunched underneath her feet as they walked. The rails could have been there for a hundred years, the tops rounded and smooth from the weight of the trains. The air smelled of diesel fuel and fish.

Six sets of tracks passed rather close to each other, with only ten feet of clearance between them. A short train rumbled along the outermost rails, still close enough to rattle the ground. She looked about her constantly, afraid that with all the noise caused by one train, another could sneak up without warning. Hadn't Irene Schaffer said something about sneaking into the zoo through the elephant cage? It must have felt like this, passing through a pen of tame but still dangerous animals.

Corliss pointed to a section where two sets of rails

converged into one, where a train coming into the station would either continue on the original track or veer off on another one. The rails at the point of convergence formed a sloping X shape. "Those point blades—see the rail that yellow warbler is sitting on?—can slide from side to side, so that the train will go to the left- or the right-side track. The flange of the wheel catches the inside of the rail. That's what keeps a train on its track."

She expected to see some heavy piece of machinery present to move the rails, but only a squat motor no bigger than a garbage disposal sat on the ground to the side of the rails. An unlabeled red sign in the shape of a hexagon protruded from the top to mark its location. "I'm guessing you no longer have a person stand out here to throw the switch."

"No, it's all done by remote now. The switch engine is operated from inside the station. Even when they were hand-operated it was still done from inside the station—they just ran an underground cable from the switch to the operator."

Another train approached, one track over. Its trail of cars stretched into the distance, and perhaps the engineer saw Edward and Theresa, because he blew the whistle, or horn, or whatever one would call it. All Theresa knew was that she had never heard a louder sound in her life and her skin tingled where she must have jumped out of it temporarily. Her muscles ached as they froze solid in instinctive terror. She would never have believed one simple, loud noise could have such an effect on her. The cars chugged by, both pushing and sucking the air around her so that her body swayed.

Edward Corliss took her upper arm, gently but firmly.

When the noise subsided as the train continued to slow, she asked him, "And people used to hop on and off these things?"

"Like a moving walkway at the airport," he said. "If you wanted to go to the next town and couldn't hitch a ride or find the money for bus fare, trains became your only option. And as the Depression wore on, the bums who moved around the country had no money and no friends. My father said one day he had to rout out eleven guys from one set of cars."

"It's hard to picture how devastating the Depression was to this country."

"It is. Although," he added, as if it might cheer her up, "hopping trains was around long before the Depression. Soldiers did it to get back home after the Civil War ended."

"The army didn't give them a ride home?"

"Nope. Once the war ended they were on their own, and trains were the fastest form of travel."

She thought about this, watching her step over the gravel. "It must have been cold in the winter."

"They looked for cars that had something in them to use as shelter—bales of hay or livestock, mailbags. They'd use anything they could find, sometimes make small fires if they got desperate enough. That's why the railroads worked so hard to rout them out, to keep them from damaging the cargo."

The cars beside them now moved at a slow crawl.

"That's what they'd call an easy rider," Corliss went on. "A slow-moving train, easy to hop. They wouldn't get on and off here in the rail yards, of course, not within sight of the station. They'd wait a couple thousand feet up the line or even outside of town, at any curve or junction where the train would have to slow down."

She stared at the cars, painted in different, muted colors, coated with the grime of the valley, scratches and scars and rust evident on every surface. When she glanced at Corliss he smiled at her, a hint of mischief around his lips. "Want to try it?"

"No," she said. Then, "Yes."

"What kind of shoes are you wearing?"

She lifted a battered Reebok.

"Those should give you decent footing. Just hang on to the rungs for a few yards and then jump off, okay? You have to land solid and away from the car. Getting off is a lot more dangerous than getting on—you have to fall away from the wheels, not toward them."

Maybe this wasn't such a good idea. "Okay."

The train blocked the river breeze, and she began to sweat. She was in the train yard, the Torso killer's old haunt, and the next victim would be a woman.

"This one." Corliss pointed to a freight car rolling toward them, a green color with lettering too small to read at that distance. She shook off her mood and watched the train. Ten feet . . . five feet . . . she grabbed an upper rung with both hands and half pulled, half jumped up until her feet found a bottom rail, much higher off the ground than she would have expected. The wind tossed her curls into her face and her heart beat wildly, at least until she realized that the train was moving slowly enough for the older Edward Corliss to walk along beside it.

The distance between her and the gravel made her more nervous than the speed. Also, the rungs she used seemed an impossible distance from the sliding door. To swing from the rungs into an open boxcar, you'd have to be both agile and strong. And fearless.

"What do you think?" Corliss called to her.

The vibrations of the heavy cars no longer seemed to be such an assault on her senses, now that she had become part of the train. The air patted her face with fumes of oil and steel. "This is kind of fun."

"Ready to get off?"

She looked down. The ground seemed to be moving

faster now that she had to land on it, and it sloped toward the median's center. She needed a more level spot.

"The people driving these things still don't like it when we do this, you know," he said, prodding further.

She let go and jumped, focusing all of her mind on her two feet and the gravel beneath them, planting them hard and pulling in the arms that one naturally puts out to the side for balance except in cases where to the side rode a large steel machine with huge turning wheels that one should fall away from, not toward—

Corliss grabbed her, two firm hands on her waist, and she grasped his sleeves and tottered in a completely ungraceful motion. "That was cool."

"There, now." He kept his hands on her sides until she had steadied, then let go and guided her another few steps back from the train. "You've ridden the rails."

They walked, following the train's path toward the station. "I imagine actually climbing in and out of cars would be a lot more difficult, especially at higher speeds."

"Oh, yes. It could be quite dangerous—that was the fun of it, for kids. For the down-and-out it was merely an acceptable risk."

"Thanks for the opportunity."

"Any time you want to hop a boxcar, Ms. MacLean, just say the word."

He led her to a small, recently painted building. "This is the old West Third switch-house—now the headquarters of the American Railroad History Preservation Society."

The inside had been recently painted as well, with the large, airy space set up like a museum. Photographs and lithographs filled the wall space between each set of windows; the pictures showed Cleveland-area railcars from the late 1800s to the present day, as specified by

engraved plaques. Large metal pieces of the engines—
a cylinder, a pressure gauge—had been restored and
placed on pedestals dotting the floor. Theresa paused
before a pen-and-ink drawing of a locomotive, marveling at the intricate detail.

Corliss stood beside her. "That's my favorite. It's a
Hudson J Class, one of the finest engines ever built. They
were developed in the twenties and most were built here
in Lima, Ohio. The model city you saw at my house? I
have all Hudsons in that array."

A man emerged from the hallway to their left and
Corliss added with a slightly raised voice, "And here's
the man who drew this picture, our resident artist, William Van Horn."

Theresa offered her hand to the gaunt man with the
shaggy mustache. He shook it, the muscles of the hand
firm beneath thin skin. "It's beautiful."

"Thank you. I feel it *is* one of my better works. Are
you interested in becoming a member of our society?"

"Um, no, actually."

"I'm sorry?" he asked.

"Ms. MacLean needs a crash course in all things
trains," Corliss explained, again raising his voice.

Van Horn beamed a thin smile in her direction.
"Then I would love to help. I have been the president of
the Cleveland chapter for eleven years and will continue
to be until my retirement, except in the very unlikely
event of an upset in the coming election by the VP here."
He waved a dismissive hand in Edward Corliss's direction. "You will not find anyone in the United States who
knows more about railroad history than I do. How can
I help you?"

Theresa smiled, the slow, sweet curve that her mother
said made her look like the saint she'd been named for.
Then she slipped her hand through her guide's tense arm

and enunciated clearly: "Thank you, but Edward is taking quite good care of me."

The man switched his attention to Corliss, as if wondering how that could be, and Theresa left him to it as she and Corliss wandered toward the back rooms. Her companion seemed to step a little higher and ushered her into a book-filled room with a flourish.

The wooden floors did not give out a single creak. The lead-paned window let in the afternoon sunlight, its beams falling on a small table and three chairs. "This is our reference collection," Corliss explained. "We should be able to find the answer to any question you have in here. What *are* your questions, by the way?"

"I'm still working on that. This case has—had—so many details that it's impossible to make them all fit one scenario. The killer did many things that made no sense."

"Like what?"

"Like why did he dismember some corpses and only behead others? Why did he throw some in the river and leave others where they were sure to be found? Why kill both men and women?"

"That's unique?"

"Relatively unusual, yes. Though the Night Stalker in California was all over the board like that, too, with different genders, ages, socioeconomic statuses." She paused in front of a large, framed map, with lines to illustrate the track system for the northeastern United States. "This is my biggest question, though. New Castle, Pennsylvania."

Corliss joined her at the map. "What about it?"

"Before, during, and after the Torso killings in Cleveland, bodies showed up in a swamp in New Castle, Pennsylvania. At least eleven were killed between 1923 and 1941."

Her companion said nothing, and Theresa glanced at him. At times she forgot that not everyone could discuss violent death as casually as she had become accustomed to doing. But he seemed perplexed, not horrified, and asked: "Are you allowed to tell me these things?"

She burst out laughing. "It's a seventy-six-year-old case, one that's been extensively studied. I'm not saying anything—hell, I don't *know* anything—that you couldn't find in a library book. It can't even really be considered an open investigation . . . more of an intellectual exercise." He nodded, a bit reluctantly, and she went on. "I surfed the Internet a bit this week and found that New Castle is a major railroad hub—then *and* now. Most of the Cleveland victims were assumed to be transients, hobos. Many were found near the tracks. Three of the New Castle dead were actually found *in* an unused boxcar. Another one had been left by the rails."

"And you think the Torso killer picked his victims from trains?"

"I think the killer *came* from the trains."

CHAPTER 25

Thursday, September 9
Present Day

Corliss turned to her as if she had uttered a mild blasphemy. "A railroad employee?"

"Specifically, an employee who worked in both Cleveland and New Castle, Pennsylvania. Would there be any way to get a list of such employees?"

His expression changed from consternation to shock. "At this point in time? I doubt any company would still have records. On top of that, there are so many jobs surrounding a railroad. Especially at that time—unskilled labor might be hired for only a day or two, for peak season or a special cleanup job. Sweeping the station or loading, tasks like that would be given out on a piecemeal basis. Then you might have skilled labor called in for some particular electrical or welding job so that you'd have men working here who weren't officially employed by the railroad."

"Like a contract employee."

"Exactly. Though that wouldn't be often. You might

also have men who would be laid off from one railway and picked up by another, so they might have had steady work in the area, but with a variety of companies. On top of *that*, so many of those railway companies don't exist today . . . in fact practically none of them do. Somewhere in here we have a list of defunct U.S. railroad companies, and there's at least two thousand. Around the turn of the century they all began to merge and combine until now there's CSX and Norfolk Southern and a few others."

She sighed. "Impossible, in other words."

"Pretty much, yes." He seemed disappointed to have disappointed her.

"Let's go at it this way. What sort of job would a man have with the railroad that would entail traveling back and forth between New Castle, Pennsylvania, and Cleveland?"

He sat down at the table, resting his chin in one hand. "Brakeman, fireman, the engineer. Railroad police—the bums called them bulls."

"Bulls." James had included that word in his list, right under another notation about the railroad.

"Conductor—they had conductors on freight trains, too, not just the passenger rails. If you're talking a passenger train with dining and sleeping cars, then you have porters, maids, cooks, waiters, and bartenders."

She sank into a chair across from him. "On every train?"

"Every train." He gave her a rueful smile. "Your next question will be which trains ran between New Castle and Cleveland, right?"

"Right."

"Hundreds. Freight, passengers . . . even by 1935 there would have been cars belonging to fifty different companies. That's why the Terminal Tower was origi-

nally called Union Terminal—a union station mean that
the trains were not all from the same railroad. Anyway,
yes, New Castle was a hub. Railways from all the eastern states went through there."

"How many originated in New Castle? I mean, were
there any railroads that ran only from New Castle to
Cleveland and back again?"

"I'll see if I can find some references, but it's not likely
that records would exist on a company that small. Most
railways went at least to Pittsburgh, beyond New Castle,
like the Alliance and Northern and the Pittsburgh and
Lake Erie. But there's something else."

She looked into his blue eyes and waited.

"Railway workers weren't like stewardesses or business travelers; more like commuters. A conductor or
brakeman might have made the run to New Castle on a
daily basis, but they didn't stay there overnight or over
the weekend or anything like that. The train would be
there long enough to unload and load back up and then
they'd be heading back to Cleveland. For example, one
of the many jobs my father had was brakeman on the
Trenton branch of the Pennsylvania Railroad. He went
across Pennsylvania every day, from Glenloch to Mor-
risville and back again, and would still be home in time
for dinner."

Her shoulders sank as she saw what he meant. No
time for a Cleveland worker to be hanging out in New
Castle killing people. "They didn't have layovers?"

"Only as long as it took to unload and load, which
could be hours, sure. But the workers had to work, not
sit around idle."

She tried another theory. "What about railroad employees who didn't work on the moving trains?"

"Sure . . . the yardmaster, who controlled which cars
were coupled to which trains . . . baggage handlers, sta-

tion agents, an operator to work the telegraph. Section hands—those were the men who maintained the tracks. A dispatcher, mechanics, and welders."

"Could a worker hitch a ride on the company's train, like sort of a professional courtesy? Like I'm guessing pilots could let flight attendants hop a ride from one city to another if the plane had an empty seat . . . at least before 9/11."

"I don't really know, but I'm sure they did. Depending on whom you were buddies with, you could probably ride in the coal car or even the engine or just an empty seat. That would be easier on a train than any other form of transport because there are so many areas available. The engineer and fireman are all the way at the front of the train and the brakeman and conductor are in the very last car, the caboose. A person hitching a ride probably wouldn't even have to work for that particular railway company . . . as you said, a professional courtesy. Especially for the higher-up positions in the company. But it would have to be someone who fit that criterion, not just some pal who didn't want to pay for a ticket. It would have been too easy to lose a job over something like that, and especially in the 1930s . . ."

"People couldn't afford to lose their jobs."

"Exactly."

They were silent for a moment, contemplating the various possibilities, as her optimism dispersed like dust motes in the sunlight. Narrowing the cast of suspects to one industry had not helped, not in an industry as extensive and varied as railroads.

Corliss put both his hands on the table, fingers loosely interlaced. "Then there could be employees who didn't even work for the railroad. Mail cars had postal employees aboard each one, because they would spend the trip sorting the mail."

She found that interesting. "Multitasking."

"Exactly. So perhaps your killer did not work for the railroad but rode it?"

"And stayed overnight?"

"The mail carriers would not have, true, but traveling salesmen were common at the time. I'm sure business travel did not occur as often then as now, particularly during the Depression, but surely larger companies with offices in different cities sent employees back and forth."

"So I need to find an organization that had branches in both Cleveland and New Castle."

"One that still has employee records from seventy-five years ago."

Now she rested her chin on one hand, shifting her bottom on the hard wooden chair. Every cop in the city had worked on the Torso killings when they occurred. Surely many of them had to have had the same ideas she did, back when all the corroborating information could be easily obtained. Yet they had not found the killer, so how on earth could she? Especially from three-quarters of a century away?

Not that she would rest until she'd exhausted every possibility, of course. When you started something, you finished it. Her grandfather had been very clear on that.

"You think it's my father, don't you?"

She blinked in surprise, having hoped this conclusion would escape his notice. Then she would not have to feel guilty about picking his brain while placing his ancestor near the top of her short list of suspects. But Arthur Corliss had spent his life in the rail yards and a dead cop had been found in his building, and his son was not a stupid man.

"Not necessarily. He owned 4950 Pullman, and he owned the railroad. But as you've just pointed out, so many people and professions interacted daily with the train system without being part of it. Then there were the other tenants in your father's building, who could fit our criteria. Maybe that firm of architects had a branch in New Castle—after all, who better than architects to build a secret room into their office—or perhaps it's as simple as the fact that one of them grew up in Pennsylvania and went back now and then to visit."

This did not cheer Corliss much. "I hope you can find out, after all this time. I hate seeing my family name in the papers."

"That won't happen through me," she said in the same sober manner, reflecting that he and Frank saw eye to eye on that subject.

"I wasn't worried about you. That Mr. Jablonski has been hovering around me like some kind of vampire bat ever since you found those two bodies on the hillside. He calls, shows up on my doorstep, and leaves messages to ask about my father and the building on Pullman. No matter how much I try to explain, he doesn't understand my father—and neither do you. He *liked* human beings, and they liked him. He had a great compassion for people from all walks of life—more, frankly, than I do. He felt lucky to have wealth at a time when some had lost everything they owned, to be well fed while others literally starved to death, to be clean when they lived in cardboard shacks." He covered her hand with his fingers and looked into her eyes. "He never renounced a person until they failed to live up to their humanity. I *know* this. So you see, Ms. MacLean, it's not merely an intellectual exercise to *me*."

Theresa tried to extricate her fingers, found them too well pinned, and thought: *This is why I could never be a cop.* How did they look into the eyes of a mother who thought her son to be pure and sweet and tell her that he had raped a schoolmate? Or prove to a husband that his wife had emptied their bank accounts of her own free will, to run away with her lover? Tell a small child that their parent valued their drugs more than their offspring?

That perhaps Edward Corliss had seen only the side of his father that he wanted to see, or had been permitted to see. Ted Bundy had been quite the charmer as well. "I wouldn't—"

A third voice interrupted her. "Finding everything you need?"

She jumped. William Van Horn stood in the doorway, staring at their commingled hands. The sneer on his thin face seemed as irrational as it did obnoxious, and yet it made her heart thud as if she'd been caught chewing gum in study hall.

"Yes, thank you," she said.

Edward Corliss removed his hand.

When Van Horn dematerialized from the doorway, she leaned across the table and whispered, "What is up with that guy, anyway? Will this become an election scandal, you caught canoodling with a nonmember?"

He laughed, the air exploding out of his nose before he could stop it. "And in the library, no less. No, no particular reason for William to look so superior. He just always does. It doesn't win him any friends, but he enjoys his own company so much he doesn't mind."

Now she snickered. "Then why is he president?"

"Because his great-uncle was the last CEO of the Pennsylvania Railroad and left all the artifacts of its one-hundred-and-twenty-four-year reign to William. He parcels these out to the society a few at a time, and only as a loan. The pressure gauge in the lobby and the photograph of the Congressional Express are examples."

"Oh."

She must have worn a blank expression, because he

went on. "The Pennsylvania Railroad was a behemoth. It absorbed eight hundred smaller companies during its reign."

"It's not operating now?"

"The lines were eventually divided between Conrail and Amtrak. Twenty years later, Conrail's lines were divided between CSX and Norfolk Southern. It's a heartbreaking business, now that you mention it."

"You said your father worked for the Pennsylvania Railroad?"

"Yes, but as a lowly brakeman, not CEO. I have no claim to William's collection, so he will continue to ransom them for social acceptance. Ah well, one does what one must, I suppose."

Theresa shook her head, couldn't think of anything else to ask, and thanked him for a most interesting afternoon. "Thank you for teaching me how to hop trains. Not that I intend to make a habit of it."

"You're very welcome. And I will continue to poke around my house to see if anything has survived from my father's business concerns. I doubt I'll find any items of interest, but I'll let you know if I do." He patted her arm as they left the building, but she had the distinct impression that he would carefully weigh the significance of any such item beforehand. If it could possibly implicate his father she might never hear of it.

But she couldn't do anything about that, and couldn't blame him. Who would want the world to know they were the progeny of a serial killer?

She thanked him for his time and got into her car. As she pulled out of the parking lot she caught his image in the rearview mirror, watching her leave, suddenly looking his age as his shoulders drooped and he frowned. The vitality he'd shown earlier seemed to fade as if his mind now followed tracks it did not care to travel.

CHAPTER 26

SUNDAY, JANUARY 26
1936

James had not forgotten the two headless men on Jack-ass Hill, but he no longer carried the blue coat or its pills around with him. After he and Walter exhausted all possibilities for identification, they had turned it over to the identification unit for scientific analysis. Then they personally drove fifteen possible relatives of the uniden-tified man to the morgue to view the decapitated victim. The staff there would drape a sheet over the ragged bot-tom of the neck to spare the men, but to James the sharp falling-off of the cloth where a body should have been seemed worse, the situation made even more bizarre by trying to make the gore presentable. And they brought only men there, even if there were mothers or wives who might more easily have recognized the missing person. The morgue was no place for a lady.

Some of those men had fainted straightaway, and all insisted that the dead . . . *thing* did not resemble their missing relative or friend or neighbor. It did not help that the body's lack of not only clothing but genitalia convinced every adult in the city that the murderer had to be extremely perverted, and what would their friend or relative or neighbor have been doing in the company of any such man? James worried that someone might recognize the man and simply refuse to admit it.

Officers probed the background of the first victim—identified as petty criminal Edward Andrassy—and his family, friends, and habits, but every lead petered out without revealing the killer.

James kept up with the investigation, pestering the main detectives with questions and carefully absorbing any drop of office scuttlebutt, but he knew that the odds of finding a solution grew smaller with every passing day. He and Walter had plenty of burglaries, assaults, and domestic complaints to keep them occupied; at home Helen did not abandon her quest for new dishes and baby John caught a cold. James consoled himself that the killer had been a hobo who had sensibly hopped a boxcar and left town even as the bodies cooled on the hillside. That way it did not keep him up at night, despite the savagery of the murders. Every cop knew there were ones you weren't going to solve, and you either made your peace with that or you got into another line of work. James wasn't even the lead investigator, anyway, just a rookie gold shield who didn't take bribes and therefore wasn't trusted.

So he left the two victims to the angels and continued to plod through his daily life. He never expected there would be more.

James had that Sunday off, which had dawned crisp and very cold. Frost covered the windows and Helen didn't even consider going to church services and exposing baby John to the winter air. James had been awake most of the night, lying on his side, facing the bassinet, listening to each breath moving in and out of his son's tiny chest. The cold—little more than a case of the sniffles—did not truly threaten the baby but still he worried, and besides, concentrating on John gave both James and Helen a break from thinking about each other.

Twelve noon found him at the kitchen table eating a portion of soup, thin but hot, when someone pounded on the door. James opened it to a gust of unheated air and his partner, who began speaking immediately. "We got another one, Jimmy me boy, and I'm told it makes those two bums on the hill look like a school picnic. It's the most disgusting—good afternoon, Helen. How is little John coming along?"

James felt the soup turn to ice in his stomach. "You mean—another body like—"

"But it's Sunday, and you're not even scheduled," Helen protested. "You can't have to work on a Sunday."

Walter grimaced along with her. "I guess we never sleep, just like those Pinkertons. But we ain't got a choice—every cop in the city will be working this one."

James got his coat and muffler as his wife repeated, "But it's Sunday. I thought we could go out this evening, leave John with Mrs. Tsolt downstairs and see a show—"

The winter months were hard on her, confined to these four walls with only a coughing baby for company. "I'm sorry, honey. But there's nothing I can do."

Her scowl indicated that she found him less than credible.

"You'll have to come over for dinner real soon, Helen," Walter put in. "The missus has been asking about you."

Walter was a nice guy in a lot of ways, or maybe he found Helen his biggest ally in the attempt to get James around to the right way of thinking. In either case, her scowl lessened, and after one more check on the sleeping baby, James went with his partner into the icy streets.

The temperature had been arrested well below freezing; he could tell from the way his nostrils stuck together when he inhaled. Between that and its being Sunday, the roadways were largely empty. Their department-assigned car spluttered a bit before it would start.

"Only one this time?" James asked.

"Yep. And in more pieces than the first two. He didn't only remove the head, he separated the body at the waist and cut off the arms and legs."

Bile rose at the back of James's throat and he swallowed hard, then told himself it was only the exhaust fumes seeping into the closed vehicle. "Where?"

"In an alley at East Twentieth and Central."

"Who found him?"

"Her," Walter said, correcting him. "This one's a woman."

This surprised James more than the body being found on a city street instead of an isolated hillside. He had been assuming the killer was some kind of sodomite, but perhaps his tastes were more omnivorous. Or he had tried to be clever and mutilated the first two bodies to make it look like a sexual thing so that the cops would waste their time chasing perverts.

Or whoever murdered this woman was a different person entirely and they had two killers running around out there, outdoing each other in savagery.

James didn't know which option would be better.

They passed East Thirtieth, tires sliding over the occasional patches of ice. Walter filled him in. "Officially, the reporting party is a dog. Barked for hours until some Negro woman got tired of it and goes to shoo him, and finds two half-bushel baskets with burlap sacks on top of them. She peeks under the burlap and sees what looks like meat wrapped in newspapers. Now this woman figures it belongs to a meat market around the corner so she goes over there and tells the owner there's some hams sitting out in the alley. He thinks he's been robbed, goes rushing out to investigate, and gets the surprise of his life."

"It's not hams," James muttered.

"It's not hams," Walter confirmed. "At least the guy's market didn't get robbed. You gotta look on the bright side."

They left the car on Twenty-second since cop cars already lined both sides of the streets ahead. Well-bundled officers milled about, coming and going or just talking.

There should be a better way to do this, James thought. *What about a house-to-house search? Are there footprints? He had to leave a footprint in all this snow—but twenty cops would have trampled it by now.*

The alley in question ran alongside the Hart manufacturing plant, which didn't operate on Sunday, and was choked with police officers. Their hurried conversations rose into the air in puffs of white condensation. The words came faster the closer James and Walter got to the haphazard pile half buried in snow against the brick wall of the factory.

They stared. Even knowing what it was, James couldn't sort out the image in his head. He saw a basket, the rectangular kind with a handle used to carry fruit, with a piece of newspaper and a flesh-colored cylindrical object inside. Nearby lay two more bundles of . . . something. James couldn't blame the Negro woman for not recognizing it as a human body. He knew and still couldn't make it familiar.

Then he noticed the white ball protruding from the red mass in the basket—the rounded part at the top of a femur where it fits into the hip socket. He'd seen one before, sticking out of a broken soldier.

He moved closer, noting a right arm with the hand still attached. The nails were short and gnawed. She couldn't even have scratched her attacker with those.

Something nudged his knee. James looked down at a large brown dog.

As at Jackass Hill, a uniformed cop stood watch by the body; unlike at Jackass Hill, the cop's feet were cold and proximity to the limelight did not make up for it. The young man's teeth chattered as he told James, "That's your witness. Her name's Lady. Belongs to some kid around the corner."

James patted the dog's head. Her eyes pleaded with him, to either solve the murder or perhaps get her out of the cold. He patted the animal again to apologize for doing neither.

He and Walter turned away and found their captain, giving orders to his officers with the halfhearted air of a man who knows he's been overwhelmed. To James and Walter, he said, "You two help check the whorehouses, see if they're missing anyone. I've got guys on Twentieth going west, so you start at Sixteenth and come east. Don't rile the girls. This city's already hysterical and this will make it worse." He nodded toward a group of people at the end of the alley. "Reporters and neighbors and nosey parkers. They're risking frostbite to stand there, but they won't budge."

"Any footprints, Captain?" James asked.

The sardonic tone of their chief's response let James know he had sounded like a kid at Christmas and also confirmed his fears. "Look around you, Miller. This place has been wall-to-wall people for the last hour and a half. Any footprints this schlepper left have been trampled by the dog, the Negress, the butcher, forty cops, and half the neighborhood."

"What happened to her?" Walter asked.

"The . . . *madman* sawed the body in half, chopped the legs at the hips and the knees, sliced the right arm at the shoulder."

"Did he cut her head off?" James asked.

"Cut it and kept it."

"What?"

"It's not here." The captain lit a cigarette, striking the match nearly hard enough to ignite the whole book. "Neither are the feet."

"Did he"—James tried to find the words—"cut her in a perverted way? Like the men on the hill? Her—you know—"

The captain smiled, without any sort of humor in the expression. "I think you're blushing. Look, McKenna, your partner's blushing."

"He's a genteel sort, Cap." Walter didn't even try to smile.

"The answer is no, so far as anyone can see here. Maybe cutting her legs off sufficed for him. We're guessing she's a hooker because no one has come into the station yet to say their wife or mother or sister is missing. She's someone no one would bother to report, like a whore."

"Or someone from Hooverville," James said, referring to the shanties along the lakefront where the hobos lived, though the male residents vastly outnumbered females.

Suddenly Walter sucked in air, excited by a theory. "Maybe the husband killed her, and that's why he hasn't reported her missing. He read about the bums on Jackass Hill and figured we'd figure it's the same guy."

"Then what, he kept her head for a souvenir? Get out of here and check those whorehouses. And don't tell me you don't know where they are, McKenna. I know you better than that."

CHAPTER 27

THURSDAY, SEPTEMBER 9
PRESENT DAY

Teddy Morgan had been a cop for six years and had spent every day of them wondering if he might be better off in some other line of work. Every time a punk kid put on their sassy hat, or a drunk puked in the back of his cruiser, Teddy wondered if being an accountant would be as boring as it sounded. Since his utter lack of knowledge of resolution and f-stops kept him from applying as a photographer of Victoria's Secret models, maybe counting up numbers wouldn't be so bad. The hours would be regular.

He felt this way only when some part of cop work proved tedious, as it did tonight. Teddy Morgan was driving in circles. Down East Twenty-second to Orange, toward downtown to get on 90, immediately getting off 90 again at Central, then making a smaller circle around to Eighteenth past the Tri-C College district offices, on to Carnegie, then back down East Twenty-second to start the circuit all over again. Keeping his eye out for, get this, an unknown guy dumping pieces of an unknown woman wrapped in some unknown fashion. *Pieces*.

Teddy had received these instructions from the shift sergeant at roll call that evening. Six years and he was still on nights, he would grumble to anyone who would listen, but the truth was he liked being on nights. The less he and his wife saw of each other, the better they got along. "Who got murdered?" Teddy asked.

"Don't know."

"She hasn't been identified?"

"She hasn't been found or even reported missing. For all we know she hasn't been murdered yet." The same nut who beheaded those two guys by the Fifty-fifth rapid station and was almost caught by that girl from the M.E.'s office (and what the hell was up with *that* story? Teddy wondered) was apparently reproducing murders that happened in the 1930s. The next murder back then had been a woman cut into pieces and wrapped in burlap and newspaper and left at the two locations assigned to Teddy. Problem was, neither I-90 nor 77 had existed at the time. The geography of the situation had changed and there was no way to know how that would affect the killer's plans.

"And he's going to dump this woman, who we don't even know is dead, tonight?" Teddy asked.

"Maybe tonight," the sergeant said. "Maybe tomorrow night, or next week or next month. The real murder, I mean the original murder, occurred four months later in January, so who knows. That's why we can't spare the manpower for a full-scale stakeout. We're short already, what with the buyouts and the hiring freeze."

Teddy didn't care about the financial state of the city. He cared about a twelve-hour shift of nothing but tedium. "But if this guy wants to dump a body, won't a marked car make him think, *Wow, maybe this ain't such a great idea?"*

"Good. Then he can go dump it in one of the 'burbs. We can't spare an unmarked right now. One's in the shop and the others are working that drug cartel out on 110th. And the chief won't approve overtime for a detective to do it."

Teddy shot his last arrow. "Why me?"

" 'Cause you got those eagle eyes," another cop said with a smirk.

"You might as well," said another. "Then you'll have an excuse for not making any arrests."

"Why *not* you?" the sergeant asked.

No answer to that, so Teddy had listened through the rest of roll call, tested the charge level of his Taser like everyone else until the room filled with a buzzing, snapping sound, and headed out to his vehicle. Cut into pieces and wrapped in newspaper and burlap bags. What the hell *was* burlap, anyway?

At least the areas he needed to patrol were open, slivers of grassy lawn boxed in by a maze of major roadways. Any idiot carting around body parts would stand out like a missile silo in a cornfield.

So he drove, and drove, and drove, past the post office, the hospital, and the Tri-C building, getting practically freakin' *dizzy* going in circles like that, and wondered how long it would take to get a degree in accounting.

Night fell as the last of the commuters hummed down I-90 and the office buildings downtown stretched their glittering diamond windows into the black sky. He slowed down to take a hard look at someone waiting at the bus stop across from the post office facility, but as he watched a 76X picked the guy up and no bloody parcels remained at the stop.

This made him think: Being a cop really sucked at times, but at least he could afford a car.

Back on 90, it occurred to him that the number of sport utility vehicles had surpassed that of regular cars. Except for his police cruiser and a Ford sedan, every other vehicle in sight was a friggin' SUV. Officer Morgan sighed and continued to drive the half mile between the two points of interest. Around and around.

He stopped for a drunk who staggered along East Twenty-second and shouted dire predictions at the post office facility, and waited until the responding backup transported the guy to St. Vincent Charity's ER. He got out again at the edge of Broadway after noticing movement on the slope to the tracks down in Kingsbury Run. A brick wall separated the road from the valley, but it petered out near East Ninth. The activity turned out to be three kids and, without getting too close—since he really was supposed to be patrolling for this one guy instead of getting distracted with minor trespassing, even though the stupid kids would probably get hit by a train, and then who would be in trouble—he told them to get out of the rail yard. They shouted at him with language he wouldn't even have used himself but were still little enough that they actually listened and ran off toward East Ninth.

He climbed the few feet back to the crest of the hill. A Ford sedan had paused along this deserted stretch of Broadway but pulled slowly away as he got back in his car. Without thinking he noted the make and license number. Maybe the driver was lost and stopped to ask him for directions, then figured it out or was too embarrassed to ask. Or maybe the driver wanted him to leave or get tied up so he could dump a body in peace. Teddy Morgan pursued the Ford from a discreet distance.

It merged onto I-90 and got off at the next exit, making the same circuit Teddy had been instructed to drive. He continued to follow but didn't call it in, not yet. There were two disturbances downtown, a fatal traffic crash on the inner belt and a smash-and-grab on Prospect, and the dispatchers were going nuts. Some could handle stress better than others, and some scheduler with a vicious sense of humor had put all the high-strung ones on the same shift—his, of course. So he'd wait to ask them to run a plate.

The Ford turned off Carnegie, heading down Twenty-second. Passed Cedar. Passed Central. *Keep looking around,* Teddy reminded himself. *Don't want to miss the bad guy because you were stalking some kid from the suburbs who expected drugs to be available on every street corner in the big bad city.*

The Ford turned into the parking lot of the St. Vincent Charity medical building, across the street from the main hospital. The driver stopped to take a ticket from the machine at the entrance.

Okay, Teddy thought. A nurse or doctor who drove around wasting gas instead of going in to work a minute early. Someone who hated their job more than Teddy sometimes disliked his.

The Ford drove to the north edge of the parking lot and stopped. The driver got out but did not walk toward the hospital. He simply stood at the front of his car, facing the grassy area between the lot and Central Avenue.

Morgan took his little ticket from the machine and drove in, moving among the sparsely parked cars. He pulled the cruiser into a space between, what else, an SUV and another friggin' SUV, as quietly and calmly as if he were there to visit poor Uncle Moe in the cardiac ICU. The cars would hide at least part of the lettering on his vehicle, but nothing could be done about the rack of lights on the roof. Idiot detectives. He might as well have a neon billboard on top with the words *I'm watching you, so if you were going to do anything incriminating you might want to wait until after my shift.*

But the figure by the other car got the hint anyway, because he had disappeared.

Damn.

Teddy Morgan turned down the volume on the portable radio clipped to his shoulder and exited the cruiser. The night had gotten chilly, the temperature dropping at least ten degrees since roll call. One hand on his gun—if this guy did those two bodies on the hill, then he had to be a complete psycho—and the other on his radio, he moved closer to the Ford. He made his feet light over the asphalt grit crunching beneath his boots and knew the noise from I-90 would drown that out. He did not see the driver inside the vehicle.

He reached the Ford. Vacant, as far as he could see, and he didn't want to use his flashlight. Between the lot and the freeway lamps he had a fair amount of ambient light. No figure.

Morgan whirled suddenly, worried that the killer might materialize behind him like in some B movie, but the pavement remained empty. He turned back. Grass and trees extended to the 90 off-ramp. Nothing moved.

A flash of darkness near the trees and Teddy saw the figure separate from one tree and move toward another. It didn't seem to be carting any bodies, only looking for something. With a flashlight.

Teddy considered his options, since no crime appeared to be in progress. The man could be a really eccentric doctor or a drug dealer picking up a stash. Maybe Teddy should run the plate first—

The figure let out a small sound, like a muffled shout.

The hell with this. He charged across the grass, unsnapping but not drawing his gun. "Police! Stop right there!"

It turned. Dark coat, dark pants, face covered, or maybe the head was turned down.

Teddy pulled the gun out of its holster at the same time it occurred to him that the guy might not be able to hear him over the noise of a tractor-trailer now roaring by on 90. So he flicked on his flashlight with the other hand and aimed the beam square in the guy's face. "Police. What is your business here?"

The head snapped up and a woman stared at him in amazement and not a little fear, her mouth gaping in a red oval.

"Cleveland Police," Teddy said during a lull in the freeway noise. "Who are you and what are you doing here?"

"We're too late," she said.

She turned one wrist until the beam of her flashlight caught an object placed on the grass between two maple trees, and what Teddy Morgan saw in that light would give him nightmares for the rest of his life.

He really needed to get into another line of work.

CHAPTER 28

THURSDAY, SEPTEMBER 9
PRESENT DAY

Officer Morgan seemed distinctly unimpressed with Theresa's medical examiner's credentials, her relation to a Homicide detective, and her explanation for stalking the Torso killer's old haunts. Perhaps he thought she might be one of those unbalanced investigators who committed the crimes themselves, like the arson investigator who set fires so that he could swoop in and be the hero. She couldn't blame him. Stumbling upon three bodies in two days did seem a bit much.

He alerted the Homicide unit as Theresa explained, trying to sound scientific and sane and still speak as quickly as she could because they needed to *go! Now!* "As near as I can tell from texts on the subject, Flo Polillo's remains were found between Twenty-first and Twenty-second and Central, behind a manufacturing plant that isn't here anymore. I suspect I-90 would run smack through the middle of that plant if it were. So if the killer wanted to repeat the original murders as closely as possible, he needed to come here."

"Who is Flopalillo?" the young officer asked. He kept looking at the milk crate and its contents with quick glances, as if the image might be less horrible if taken in measured doses. Theresa doubted this would help him. The lower half of a female torso, both thighs, and the right arm and hand had been stacked on their ends in the crate, the raw, gory edges peeking from the top of the newspaper they had been wrapped in, the fingers protruding as if they might wiggle in a friendly wave at any moment. Nothing could make it less horrible.

She explained about the Torso killer's fourth victim.

"So you came here tonight because you thought this guy *might* kill again and he *might* do it tonight and he *might* dump the body here," he asked with some skepticism. Never mind that he was there for the same reason—he had been *assigned*. It was different.

"It seemed a distinct possibility." The double murder on Jackass Hill had come immediately after the Lady of the Lake, *if* Kim Hammond was supposed to be the Lady of the Lake, so why not telescope the rest of the series as well? "And that means that *at this moment* he's dropping off the rest of this woman's body somewhere around 1419 Orange Avenue. We have to go there. *Now*."

"There's no *we* here, um, ma'am," the cop said, trying for a combination of stern and courteous and missing both. "A car has been sent and they don't need help. This is our job, not yours."

He was correct, of course, in that she was not armed, not trained, did not get increased pay for hazardous conditions, and had no authority to apprehend or arrest anyone. But he made it sound like none of that mattered. All that mattered was that she was not a cop—not one of them.

"I understand. Besides, you can't leave this crime scene unsecured," she told him. "However, I can."

She walked to her car before he could argue, feeling fairly sure he wouldn't shoot her. *Fairly* sure. She hastily threw too much money to the young woman in the toll-booth for the half hour of parking and turned right on Orange, Fourteenth, then East Twenty-second. Down to Broadway, turn right. Once upon a time this area had been referred to as the Roaring Third, a rough conglomeration of bars and tenements. Her great-grandfather would have known that.

In the sparse grass north of Broadway as it intersected with Orange, she found it.

"We could have caught the killer," Theresa complained to her cousin an hour later, "if that kid had come here when I told him to."

"Wasn't an option. He couldn't leave a dead body unattended. Besides, the killer could have dropped this off and been back in his car in ten seconds. He was probably halfway home by the time you found the first body—the first pieces of the body." Frank straightened up, towering over her and her find, his back to the phalanx of mobile news vans corralled behind the yellow tape. Their lights nearly blinded her, but she could see Brandon Jablonski front and center, his gaze fixed on her.

"We could have caught him," she said again. A gust of cool wind hit her face with no effect upon her internal temperature. They'd been so *close.*

Frank showed her no sympathy. "He could have caught *you,* wandering around like that. Or any of the other assorted killers, rapists, and general miscreants that roam this city after dark. What were you thinking?"

Angela Sanchez had gone to the post office building to

see if they had outdoor cameras that might have caught the killer's brief stop by the side of the road. Two officers, armed with small but brilliant lights, combed the grass, but Theresa doubted they would find anything. The killer most likely placed one milk crate, made the twenty-foot walk back to his car, and did the same to the second. No dirt to retain tire tracks or shoeprints, no reason to hang around dropping a cigarette or a bloody glove.

Theresa said, "I was thinking this guy has to go to certain places to live out his little fantasy of re-creating the Torso Murders. All we have to do is be there. He should be the easiest killer to catch in the history of forensics and instead he drove right past us!"

"Don't shout," Frank warned her, jerking his chin at the reporters. "Those guys have parabolic mikes. But at least now we know he apparently plans to complete all twelve murders in twelve days. I won't have any trouble getting the manpower we need to get him tomorrow night. It's not too late."

"It's too late for *her*," Theresa said, nodding at the victim's calf. It protruded from the milk crate like a prop from the kind of late-night movie only bored teenagers watch.

"I can see that," Frank snapped. "What is here? I mean—"

"The upper half of a female torso, the lower halves of both legs, and the left arm. Exactly what we should have. He's read all the books."

"No head?"

"The cops in '36 never found Flo Polillo's head."

"Is that newspaper?"

After photographing the milk crate and its contents from every possible angle, Theresa had removed the arm and laid it in the clean body bag Don Delgado brought from the office. "Yesterday's *Plain Dealer*. It should be both the *Plain Dealer* and last year's issue of the *Cleveland News,* but of course the *News* has been defunct since 1960."

"Any ID so far?"

"There won't be. No wallet, no jewelry, not a scrap of clothing. They identified Flo Polillo—one of only three of his victims positively identified—by her fingerprints."

"Maybe we'll do the same. It worked on Kim Hammond."

"I don't know." A cool dampness worked its way through her pants as she knelt over the palm, examining the skin with a halogen flashlight. "Nails are neat and conservative, no polish. No track marks. She's healthy but older."

"You can tell that from her fingernails?"

She cracked a smile for the first time that evening. "No, the arm itself. We show our age in the elbows and knees. You can exercise, eat right, get plastic surgery, but the elbows and knees will always betray you."

She unwrapped the next piece. The killer had cut through the leg at the hip and the knee, leaving the two ends of the femur only slightly damaged. Theresa closed her eyes, opened them. In this job she did not have the luxury of turning away.

"He did that neatly," Frank said, his voice sounding oddly strangled.

"He did it carefully," she said, correcting him, forcing herself to examine the flesh. "Not neatly. He made numerous cuts into the skin, leaving the edges ragged. Then he got through the tendons and cartilage with some kind of saw, I think."

"Handsaw or electric?" Frank still sounded oh-so-deliberately casual. Behind him she could hear the murmur of the paparazzi shouting questions to anyone who came near them.

"I can't tell. We need Christine for that. But he took chips out of the bone to get it done. It looks neat because he washed it all up so well. There's no blood. He let the body drain, then cleaned the pieces. He probably even dried them because the paper didn't stick too much."

Frank coughed.

She frowned at him. "You're not going to throw up in my crime scene, are you?"

"Wouldn't dream of it. Notice the paper?"

"Yeah, it's—" She looked down. In the too-bright light she recognized the photograph that had been rolled around the victim's thigh. Herself, standing on the hillside below 4950 Pullman, her head bent toward a flash of white skin on the ground. It had been taken the evening before by some reporter with a quality telephoto lens.

"This guy could be sending you a message, Tess."

"I doubt it." At her cousin's snort she added hastily, "He's throwing this series of murders together day by day and we have only one newspaper in town. It's not like he had a choice."

"Could have used the *Beacon Journal*," Frank grumbled.

She took the illogic of this as a measure of his agitation. "The Torso killer used Cleveland papers. Akron wouldn't count. Relax, cuz. He doesn't kill another woman for four or five more murders yet."

"Oh, comforting. So tomorrow's victim will be a man?"

"Yeah. His head will be rolled up in his pants and his body found about a thousand feet away."

"The Tattooed Man. Yeah, I remember. Where did he turn up again?"

"Back near Jackass Hill, in the valley under the East Fifty-fifth Street bridge. Within sight of 4950 Pullman."

Frank lit a cigarette, striking the match too hard and breaking it. He put the ends in his pocket and used a second one. "Then we'll get him there. I'll have every cop in Cleveland in that valley, from side to side. He won't get away this time."

She didn't want to pile on, knowing how awful he felt, but the dead pieces of flesh before her forced her to point it out: "There's a man out there right now to whom that will come as no comfort."

CHAPTER 29

SUNDAY, JANUARY 26
1936

Sunday mornings were quiet in the cathouse business. No customers, and the staff catching up on their rest after the busy Saturday-night trade. Consequently doors were opened to James and Walter only after a long wait and then by lined faces with tousled hair, faces none too happy to find cops on the doorstep but especially unhappy to be awakened earlier than usual on such a frigid day.

The first such madam they encountered told them so in no uncertain terms. Police were usually made welcome in exchange for their lack of enforcement of standing vice laws and a phoned tip whenever they were forced to make a raid in order to let the public think that cops occasionally did their jobs. Apparently the madam felt different rules applied in the harsh light of day, or she was just too tired to care. "What do you want? Get the hell off my doorstep. Oh, come in, or I'll freeze to death right in this doorway, with all the neighbors staring."

"As if you care what your neighbors think, Rosie," Walter said, stamping the snow from his shoes onto the welcome mat in a show of politeness.

Rosie had deep lines in her face, a mouth set like granite, and a man's figure. A strong man. "I do. Some of them are my best customers. What do you want, this early on a Sunday? I know it ain't a visit with one of my girls, or you wouldn't have brought *him* along."

She meant James, with an inflection that made it sound as if he came from outer space. Did everyone in town know him as the police department oddity, the bum who can't figure out what's good for him?

Walter said, "Rosie, I got one question and one question only. Answer it and we'll be on our way and you can get back to your beauty sleep. Are you missing a girl?"

The woman blinked at him, then the sleepiness cleared. "Why, you found one? You got a girl in jail? You got her, you keep her, she's got nothing to do with me."

"Rosie, just tell me if you're short a girl, that's all. No trouble for you, I promise."

"Hah," she said before turning away. "*That* makes me feel a lot better, the word of a chizz."

When she had climbed the creaking stairs with the threadbare rose-patterned runner, James turned to his partner. "I see you two have met."

"So have you. Remember, we arrested two of her girls last year for rolling that drunk at the Soldiers' and Sailors' Monument. At least it's warm in here."

"I suppose it has to be, since most of the people in it are undressed at any given time."

"Can't have the clients catching cold," Walter said in agreement.

"A cold would be the least of my worries," James said. Upstairs, he could hear the groans and protests as Rosie went from room to room, rousing the prostitutes.

It did not take long. The madam thumped back down the steps and said to Walter, "They're all here."

"Every girl is accounted for? It's really important—"

"I got fifteen girls in this house, and all fifteen are upstairs in their beds. Now go away and let me get back to mine." She opened the door, hiding behind it to avoid the arctic blast from the street. "And don't come back unless it's paying business. You used up a free time with this little stunt."

Walter grinned his chubby little-boy grin. "I'd be upset if I thought you meant that."

"*Out.*"

Out they went, and climbed into the freezing car. Walter gave a shiver as he started it up. "Isn't she a dilly? Her place sure looks a lot different during the day."

"Let that be a lesson to you."

Walter laughed. "Yeah, yeah. You should come by here sometime, when Helen gets on your nerves. Rosie's girls will do you right. They even play that Negro music you like."

"Ragtime."

"Yeah."

They repeated the process at three more cathouses before two detectives from the Third Precinct caught up with them. They could stop waking prostitutes; even without a head, the dead woman had been identified by her fingerprints. James found that impressive. Those Bertillon unit guys did some interesting stuff.

"She's a drunk named Flo Polillo," they were told by one of the detectives. "The Bertillon unit had her prints from a prostitution arrest. Didn't work at it steady, though, either waitressed in gin mills or mooched off any man she could get, not that she could have gotten a lot. I saw her mug shot. Forty-one and she looked sixty. Your captain's at her place," the detective added, and gave them the address. "We're heading to the Feather Company over on Central. That's where the burlap bags came from."

"And I'll bet you're just tickled," Walter said.

"Ain't you a gas."

James and Walter climbed back into the car. Any heat the engine built up inside instantly dissipated in the cold and they had to wait for it to warm again before driving to Flo Polillo's apartment at 3205 Carnegie Avenue. A fretting landlady let them in.

The shabby little room bulged with cops, but at least their gathered bulks warmed the air. Whatever her lifestyle, Flo Polillo had kept her place neat, with a dozen dolls arranged on the bed and bureau. Their tiny black eyes seemed to follow the activities of the men. James got the idea that even if the toys could talk, they would choose not to. Dolls could not be killed, could not suffer.

He and Walter found the captain at a small desk, poring over a notebook full of scrawls while an officer from the Bertillon unit crouched next to the radiator and poked with one hand at a tray of debris he held in the other. James detoured over to the metal pipes, which kept the room at a comfortable temperature. Picturing the city as a map, James figured that the body had been found about a mile away. Flo would not have willingly left her warm apartment to walk to her death on such a cold night. Her killer must have had a car.

He asked the cop, "What have you got?"

The Bertillon unit guy looked up through glasses perched on a red and running nose. "Bunch of nothing I swept up from the floor. Dirt. A button. Piece of wood." He rubbed the half-inch sliver between his fingers and sniffed at the residue. "Smells like creosote. Coal tar."

"That's used in railroad ties, isn't it?"

"And electrical poles, and roads with wood bricks,

and floors in most factories, and docks. Any place they want to preserve the wood."

"You think it's from the killer?"

The guy sniffled and dropped the sliver of wood back into the tray next to the white flower-shaped button. "Sure. Or the victim. Or her landlady. Or off the shoes of one of the twenty cops who walked around in here before I swept. I don't believe the killer ever came here. There's no blood in the place, not on the carpet, not in the bathtub or sink. I'd like to see him cut up a body like that without blood."

"What if he washed it up?"

"It's not like a shaving nick. The benzidine would still find traces, with that much being splashed around." He gestured to a wooden case that lay open on the floor. "It's a chemical, turns blue when it comes in contact with blood. Then we could do another test to find out what type the blood is—A or B or—"

"I know," James said. "We had a tour through your lab once."

"Hey," Walter called.

James thanked the cop, left him to his tray of dirt, and returned to his partner's side.

Their superior did not look pleased to see them, but he hadn't looked pleased before he saw them, either. James could swear that the man's bald spot expanded and contracted in response to stress. Right now it seemed to be pushing the fringe of brown hair out until it crowded his ears and forehead like a flapper's bandeau. "What are you doing here?" the captain asked as he flipped through the small journal.

"Came to help," Walter said.

"Well, ain't you the Boy Scouts."

"What did they find on the body?" James asked.

"That her diary?" Walter asked.

"No, it's her money—she made three payments to a doctor named Manzella—and wages, at least the legal ones. This hag worked as a barmaid and waitress in about six different restaurants and juice joints. I'm going to need you to hit every one and question the owner, the busboy, delivery clerks, each and every customer. Got it?"

"Right, Cap."

"What was found on the body?" James asked again.

The captain gave him a considering look, the kind that usually preceded the comment that perhaps James would be happier in another precinct, but he said only, "Newspapers—yesterday's *News* and the *Plain Dealer* from a day last August. Dog hairs. Fur, I mean, but then that's who made the initial report, so to speak. Found by a dog. Hell of an epitaph. Besides that there was coal dust and cinders, like maybe she'd been laying on lump coal at some point and it left dents in the skin."

"A coal car," James said promptly. "He killed her down by the tracks, like the other two, and carted her back up here in pieces. He hid the pieces in a coal car until he could go back for them. The coal would absorb the blood and the stains wouldn't show against the black lumps."

"Great, Miller. By the way, what's your house heated with?"

James's flow of words hit a bottleneck. "Coal."

"And it's kept where?"

"In the coal cellar."

"Great place to hide a body, wouldn't it be?"

"Yeah. But, Cap—"

"And the other guys weren't killed by the tracks, were they? Just dumped."

"We think that because there weren't any pools of blood by the rails. But that could explain what happened to it—he killed them in the coal car, which then rode out of town."

"Except he didn't only get rid of their blood, he washed it off the bodies as well. And we didn't find any coal or cinders on those two dead guys. Aside from the heads coming off, I see more things different than the same here. The first time, the guy obviously had a sex problem with men, he only took the head off and didn't cover or wrap the bodies in anything. No newspaper, no coal. This time the doc says the cuts were neat—like a doctor or a butcher—but he wrenched the bones apart like he was in some kind of fit."

Walter made a face and clutched his stomach.

"Don't think about upchucking here, McKenna," the captain warned him. "It's got to be some kind of crazy doctor. Who else would know how to do something like that *neatly*?"

"Someone who's practiced it," James said, thinking aloud. "Helen's squeamish about most everything, but she can debone a chicken in minutes with a few quick slices."

"You think your wife's killing people, Miller?" the captain asked without a smile.

"She grew up on a farm and got good at certain things. Maybe this guy did, too."

"Nah," Walter said. "A chicken's a lot different than a person, and a doctor would have the equipment, the workroom, a car to dump the bodies—"

"Maybe," the captain said, rubbing the bridge of his nose. "But this lady wasn't no society Jane, if you catch my drift. She couldn't have afforded no doctor with a car. No, I'm guessing this bitch got on the wrong side of a boyfriend who'll have a line of arrests going back to when he wore short pants. How he learned to cut up bodies, we can ask him when we arrest him. So get out there and find out who she's been making whoopee with. You two ever find the source of that blue coat from the two guys on the hill?"

"Yeah—" James began.

"Bailey's department store had three of them," Walter cut in, his technique smooth from practice. "Sold one, and the guy still has it. The other two didn't sell and some do-gooder in the bargain basement donated them to St. Peter's soup kitchen."

"Not bad. After you report everything there is to learn about Flo Polillo's waitressing career, get to that church and find out where those two other coats went. And, Miller—"

James had half turned and now stepped back. "Yeah?"

"When you're done with that, you can check out the rail yards. But do the restaurants first."

Walter brightened more than he had when told to visit the whorehouses. "Restaurants?"

James sighed.

CHAPTER 30

FRIDAY, SEPTEMBER 10
PRESENT DAY

The temperature had begun to dip in the mornings, creating a fog that hung over the old steel mill and the river and Kingsbury Run like an unreliable shield, shifting and dissipating and then, unexpectedly, revealing. Now it lay wet and chilled against the back of Theresa's neck as she gazed out over the weeds poking up between the railroad ties. On her last visit, there had been two dead bodies on this hillside with her. If there were more today, the fog hid them.

Behind her sat the hollowed-out building at 4950 Pullman. On her left, the ravine stretched another mile and a half to the west to end at the Cuyahoga River. To her right, the East Fifty-fifth bridge spanned the gorge, concrete legs picking their way among the train and RTA tracks. Almost nothing had changed in this valley for seventy-five years, except the graffiti.

This place had never given up a clue to the Mad Butcher's identity and wouldn't now.

Theresa turned away from the slope and crossed the grass to the abandoned building. Another fifteen minutes and she would miss the M.E.'s morning viewing conference, ensuring Leo's ire, but her crime scene would be demolished by sunset. Councilman Greer's construction would remain on schedule.

The teardown crew had already returned to work and now only four central pillars and the wall studs remained. The floor had been cleared and the ceiling removed until she could see straight up to the inside of the roof. The place seemed bigger without the walls, and brighter now that they no longer blocked the light from the broken-out windows. The fog-coated sunlight softened the stones and turned the shadows to gray.

Armed with only a Maglite, Theresa scanned the area for signs of life. The smell of urine told her that the city's homeless had been making use of the place, but no one seemed to be around now.

From Edward Corliss's description and the photograph he gave them, she could assume the original layout. Half of the ground floor, the half on her left, had belonged to the architects and the medium. The area on the right had made up Louis Odessa's and Arthur Corliss's offices. She wandered to the space where they had found the table, where the two offices would have backed up against each other.

Outside, a stray cat or dog moved through the uncut brush around the building. The faint rustling began, then faded near the northwest corner.

The construction crew had done too good a job. Nothing remained on the studs to indicate where a wall had gone straight or turned, what might have been a doorway opening to the front office or the rear. She crouched, brushing the remaining plaster dust and a few stray leaves off the floorboards. If one of these areas had been James Miller's murder chamber or Louis Odessa's closet—or if the two cubicles were one and the same—there should be a wear pattern in the floor leading into and out of it.

A train clattered in the distance. Twenty feet above, the roof creaked as if the fog pressed on it.

The floor had been polished at some point and no doubt carpeted at another. The solid tongue-in-groove planks showed scratches and nicks and nail holes from tenants past. She followed the line of studs along the floor, trying to keep her pants off the dust but eventually giving up. Normally she waited until she got to work to get dirty, but not today. "Sometimes," her grandfather had often told her, "you have to get down on your hands and knees." She always thought it had been his way of warning her against pride, but perhaps he'd meant it literally.

Wait, she had gone at this wrong. The building had been nearly new when James Miller became entombed there—the closet entrance became a solid wall for all subsequent tenants. She should look at the gaps between the studs that did *not* show evidence of traffic in and out.

More time spent on the knees, without any real findings. Not even seventy-five years of feet had worn down the hefty planks in any discernible pattern. Arthur Corliss or Louis Odessa? Which one had walled up James Miller's body? Or did she have the floor plan backward, somehow, and the architects had occupied this space, surely more skilled at creating new walls than a medium would be?

The tiniest sound, almost a vibration more than an audible noise, reached her. It could have been the cat outside leaping to a windowsill, or the tiniest shift of a ceiling beam in the fall breeze. But she didn't think so.

She stood, flicked off her flashlight, and moved across the building to the cellar staircase. Her footsteps made only a whisper over the wooden planks, a series of small creaks.

At the top, she stopped and listened. It would be stupid to go down there, of course. If the sound came from anything other than a stray cat or a raccoon, it would probably be one of the vagrants who had used the upper floor as a toilet recently and retreated to the basement when she approached. Perhaps a camp had been set up— the earthen cellar would have been warmer during the night than anyplace on the surface. Homeless men—or women—were most likely timid and nonviolent . . . but she shouldn't take the chance.

She lowered her foot to the first step, heavy and solid.

But what if she were to find some descendant of the Mad Butcher, an apprentice who carried on his work? Someone who had not been surprised by the discovery of James Miller's body. Someone who knew how and why he had been laid to rest on a crude table in a secret chamber.

Someone who *knew*.

She took two more downward steps, waited. No sound, save for her own breathing.

This was stupid.

But wasn't it just as stupid to be afraid of the dark? It was only a cellar, after all. So what if a murder had happened here years and years ago?

Another step. She didn't believe in ghosts, anyway. If they existed, they didn't hang around crime scenes or even their old bodies. She'd spent enough hours with both to know.

Pity, really. She would have enjoyed meeting James Miller's ghost.

Her toes found the next board.

Though it wasn't ghosts one needed to fear here, not in an abandoned building in a large city with no one close enough to hear you scream.

Almost there.

He waited until she had one step to go to blind her.

The ray of light that struck her eyes seemed too bright for a handheld lamp, but rather like the startling beam of an approaching train. The toe of her Reebok slid off the edge of the last step and she fell even as her fingers clutched the Maglite. Her legs buckled and she would have wound up in a heap on the hard-packed earth if the man hadn't been in the way.

His flashlight fell away; it pointed toward the steps and provided a backlight with which to silhouette the man. He rose to his feet, unfolding a dense form that kept rising and rising, and the only thought in her mind became *They were right. He really is a monster.*

And now he stood between her and the only means of escape.

She had managed to hold on to her Maglite, but he was on her before she could either swing it or turn it on, yanking her up by her shoulders hard enough to leave bruises on both arms. She opened her mouth to scream.

"What the hell are you trying to do, kill me?" said this demon of the depths with a puff of onion-bagel-scented breath.

"Jablonski!"

"What are you doing here? Are you finding evidence? Are you *planting* evidence?" He gave her a little shake, *little* meaning it didn't completely loosen her fillings. "You have to tell me!"

Initial relief—at least she knew her attacker—turned to renewed fear. "Let go of me!"

He didn't. "Who is he? Who is this new killer? You know, don't you?"

Enough of this. At the risk of kicking a sleeping psychotic, she used the flashlight as a battering ram into his solar plexus. "Let go of me!"

"Ow," he said with a surprised and offended tone. "What did you do that for?"

Don't back down. Show strength. "Why did you blind me, trip me, and then try to rattle my brains?"

"I didn't mean to put the beam in your face like that," the researcher told her, using wiry arms to set her back on her feet. "You scared me."

"*I* scared *you!*"

He retrieved his flashlight but kept it pointed at the floor so that she could see him, the lean face, brown hair gone awry, a fresh set of fashionably casual clothes. Two camera bags and a large, square Kodak dangled from one shoulder. "I didn't know you were here. This building is so solid. . . . I don't know why Greer keeps saying it's unsafe."

"What were you doing down here?" Her voice still rang an octave higher than normal and her breath came in short gasps.

"Taking pictures." He hefted the Kodak an inch for illustration. "Damn, I'm going to have to solder this strap mount again."

She sucked in some air, held it, and let it out slowly. *Calm down. You have nothing to fear from this guy.* "Is that a digital?"

"Yeah, an ancient model that I got for ten cents on the dollar. Unfortunately, given how fast the technology advanced, I still overpaid. But I got to thinking about this cellar and figured he had to bury more bodies here. No one knows how many people he killed, you know. With all the transients moving through this town at that time, it could have gotten up in the triple digits. We still can't be sure how many Bundy killed, right?"

"No." She shifted a few inches to her left, the first step in a cautious circle back to the stairway, not wanting him to see how much he had spooked her.

"*Yes.* He probably only walled up that guy because he ran out of room down here. I figured I'd better get in here before Greer sends the wreckers. I have a shovel in the car."

"I mean no, there aren't any bodies buried here. A geology team from CSU came out here yesterday with ground-penetrating radar. There's nothing beneath us but dirt."

He seemed disappointed. "Yesterday's killer still won't leave us any clues, and today's killer drives right by us all and gets away."

Theresa moved to the stairs. " 'Us all'?"

"I patrolled that area, too. I saw you, and that cop. You couldn't miss the cop, they sent a friggin' marked unit. All three of us driving that circuit, and we still missed him."

She started up the steps, nearly tripping in her haste to see daylight again. "You were there last night? I mean—"

He stayed right behind her, confessing his proximity to the crime scene in a completely natural tone of voice. "Of course. It was obvious where the next body would be left—somewhat obvious, anyway—and what a story it would be if I had found the killer."

She emerged onto the ground floor, Jablonski close behind, and took a deep breath, hoping for the crisp fall air. Instead she sucked in dust and memories. "Speaking of stories, what I told you about my grandfather and great-grandfather, Mr. Jablonski, was in a casual, personal conversation. I didn't expect to see my family relationships become the focal point of your article."

He blinked in the sudden light, motes dancing in

the space between them. If he'd been much younger, he would have looked hurt. "But you seemed so proud of them. I thought you'd like to tell the city about them."

She couldn't lie, not here in the light. "I did. I do—I mean, I love talking about them. But my cousin wasn't so happy. I can afford a certain amount of sangfroid, but he has to work in an intensely competitive environment. You never let people know what's important to you in that setting."

"Sure, they'll tease him. But I've been in this business for a while, and believe me, as long as you're not being indicted, there's no such thing as bad publicity. In the long run it will help his career. Trust me."

Almost certainly true, but she didn't care for such a cavalier attitude toward other people's lives. She would have to chalk it up to a lesson she should have already learned—reporters are never off the record. She moved to the door, which was now nothing more than a stone arch.

"Besides, it gives the story a human face, a way to bring the past alive. The city has forgotten one of its most fascinating chapters, and it's up to us to remind them."

"Us?"

"You and me. We seem to be the only two people around who know their history."

"I very much doubt that."

Jablonski advanced, invading her personal comfort zone—but then, her personal comfort zone had a larger diameter than most people's. "That's why I need you to go to Pennsylvania with me."

"What?"

"You know about the New Castle connection, right?"

"The string of similar murders? Yes."

"Not just similar. Some bodies were found actually in

unused train cars. One had newspapers from the same day in July, *three years* previously, from both Cleveland and Pittsburgh."

He exited the building, then turned to take her arm for the few stone steps leading to the ground. She watched a train chug through the valley and said, "I think those murders were committed by the same person, yes, but it's not a new theory. They knew about the similar murders in the thirties, too, and got nowhere with it."

"But now we know the killer not only had some connection with that city, this city, the railroads, but also this building. That narrows the suspect pool. It gives us an advantage the cops in 1936 didn't have. We need to go there."

"I need to go to work, Mr. Jablonski."

"*Work?*" He laughed. "He killed men and women, one by one, and put them in that swamp until they turned to skeletons. You tell me—how long does it take to strip all the flesh from a person's bones?"

"It depends on a lot of things, temperature, the conditions of the water, marine life," she explained on the way to her car. "Possibly as little as a month, but probably longer. A swamp is actually better than a river for that sort of thing because the water doesn't move; the body just stays in one place and decomposes."

"That's what this guy did. He not only killed these people, he erased every bit of their identities, took away everything that made them individuals. He wiped them from the face of the earth." He leaned against her car as she unlocked the door. "Come on, Theresa. Play hooky with me."

He could be as charming as Chris Cavanaugh, in an even sneakier way, but that wasn't what tempted her to take him up on his offer. The Torso killer had so little respect—or so much hatred—for his victims that he had taken his victim's identities along with their lives. He had done the same to James Miller, hiding him away from the rest of the world, letting his family think he had abandoned them, a man who had only tried to make the world a safer place.

But James Miller had been dead for seventy-six years, and she needed to concentrate on the man who would die today, who might be saved if she could find something useful in what the killer had left behind last night. "I'm sorry, Mr. Jablonski. I have more immediate obligations."

"Suit yourself." He stepped back, giving her room to open the car door. "I guess I'll see you here tonight then."

She frowned at him from the driver's seat. "Tonight?"

"The fourth victim. The Tattooed Man." He swung the door shut on her. "I wouldn't miss it for the world."

CHAPTER 31

SUNDAY, JANUARY 26
1936

St. Peter's Church at Superior and Seventeenth sprang upward from the concrete sidewalk as a soaring edifice of stone and stained glass. The last Mass had just ended, and parishioners spilled out of the massive wood doors to find their Sunday garb inadequate against the biting air. The church stood less than a mile from the lake, without enough barriers in between to stop the wind. The two cops clutched their coats.

"I wonder what he looks like," James said aloud, his breath appearing as a misty puff.

"So does everyone else in the city," his partner grumbled.

"I mean when he's killing them, the expression on his face. Calm? Crazed? Terrified? I saw a lot of different looks on the battlefield. I wonder where this guy falls."

"That's a swell thought, Jimmy. Thanks for the heebie-jeebies."

It had taken the rest of the morning, but James and Walter had visited Flo Polillo's prior places of (legal) employment. They had to eat in each place, of course, and by the third one James's stomach had grown so full that he had the staff box up his tiny portions to take home to Helen. It would help make up for having to spend her Sunday trapped in a chilly set of rooms.

Walter insisted it would relax the staff and clientele to see them as customers instead of policemen, and it worked. The staff talked. The customers talked. While the two detectives sipped coffee and ate a sandwich, the horrible news filtered through the city and agitated its inhabitants until they could not *stop* talking.

Not that James and Walter learned much. At first they would be told that Flo Polillo had been a fine waitress or barmaid, a cheery, roly-poly, hardworking woman. After the speaker relaxed into their role, the description would inevitably be refined to include the fact that she drank quite a bit, which would make her pecky and argumentative. She would be seen with one man for a while, then another, then another. Though not a bad worker when she worked, Flo eventually proved so unreliable that management had to let her go.

"A typical drunk, Flo," the owner of Mike's tavern near Central told them. "One day she'd be down in the dumps, sayin' nobody in the world cared about her, so what did it matter if she drank herself to death. Then she'd go to St. Peter's and get all inspired with the do-gooders there, decide to reform. Sure I can't interest you in another sandwich? Best corned beef in the city." He gave what seemed like a relieved sigh when Walter turned down the offer.

At least all the free food put Walter in a good enough mood to trot up the steps of the church without hesitation. As a good Irishman he went to Mass as often as his wife could drag him, and the fortresslike exterior did not daunt him.

James followed with less enthusiasm. He had not set foot in a church since returning from Europe. He had not made a conscious decision about it; without his mother to coerce him, he had simply stopped going. Helen rarely went herself, and then only as a social event.

Once inside, he discovered that he still *liked* churches, the soaring arches overhead, the glass pictures that glowed even in the cold winter light, the quiet. Especially the quiet.

They found the priest in the vestry. Father Donatello had wasted no time in removing the vestments and adding a heavy sweater and then a coat. When he spoke, his breath misted. "What can I do for you gentlemen?"

They explained the need to retrace Flo Polillo's steps.

"You can ask the ladies in the kitchen," the gray-haired man said as he led them to a large building behind the church. "But we have so many people come to us for help. Sometimes we give food to eight hundred men a *day*."

A heavy door revealed a large room with opaque windows and chipped linoleum. It smelled of stewed cabbage and body odor. Tables and a motley assortment of chairs had been set up, and most were filled with men, though plenty of women and children sat among them. James's gaze fell on one, a too-thin toddler on her mother's lap. Her long lashes and porcelain skin contrasted with the patched, stained little coat. She reached for a roll, but her mother kept it out of reach and broke the stiff bread into smaller pieces, giving her one at a time, either to keep her from choking or to stretch the meal out. The child stuffed each piece into her mouth and set to chewing with a determined motion of her tiny jaw. The girl's father, hollow-eyed and with an expression one muscle short of a snarl, noticed James's scrutiny and glared until the cop looked away.

You'd let your son starve for your pride. . . .

Would he?

The priest was leading them toward the kitchen. "We never know from one day to the next what we're going to be given to work with. Many grocers will be generous with old bread and meats, but it's awfully hard to get decent vegetables, especially in winter. Everything is harder in the winter. We keep the heating at a minimum to divert funds here, but on top of all that, we have more people to serve."

"Why?" Walter asked. "Because they can't survive in the shanties in this cold?"

"No, there's just more *of* them. Once the lake freezes, the port closes for the winter and that ends a lot of jobs. On top of that, some of the mills and auto plants in Detroit closed down and those men came here. Is this about that poor woman they found in the alley?"

"What do you think about a bas—a man like this, Father?" Walter surprised James by asking. "Is he controlled by the devil, or just a rotten man?"

"I get asked variations of that question all the time, my son, and I've not yet found a perfect answer. I believe it's a combination of both."

He introduced them to three ladies dressed in practical and similar garb, with no other characteristics in common: a teenage girl, dull and pockmarked; a woman of about thirty with a peaches-and-cream complexion; and a hatchet-faced matron. Not one recalled Flo Polillo.

"Well, thanks anyway, ladies—" Walter began.

James interrupted. "Father, what's that?" He gestured to three large crates that someone had labeled with white paint: MEN'S, WOMEN'S, and CHILDREN'S.

"This is where we put the available clothing. The ladies here dole it out as best they can based on size and need. It doesn't last long."

Resting on top of the women's pile sat a bright blue summer frock, too cool for this time of year and too frilly for everyday use. A rich girl must have cleaned out her closet.

James pulled out a photo of the blue coat from the first victim. He explained—very briefly—why they were looking for the owner of the coat. The occupants of nearby tables paid no attention to them but continued to eat with solemn focus and little conversation.

The priest said, "Even if it came here, these are only the odds and ends. Most of the clothing is given as direct relief, with shelter and food—over thirty-two thousand families last year. So I really can't guess where your coats would have ended up."

"I understand, Father," James said. But then the matronly one took the photo and said, with faint German overtones that raised the hair on the back of James's neck, "Yah, I remember. We got two of them."

"Yeah?" James couldn't believe their luck.

"Goot inseams. Extra stitching at the cuff. Donated by Bailey's."

"The department store," James said. They had been able to find the origin from the tag. "You know your coats."

"I supervised the line at the shirtwaist factory until the crash." She surveyed his frayed cuffs and worn buttons.

"Did you see who took it?"

The girl and the peaches-and-cream woman shook their heads, but the older one said, "I helped a gentleman into one of them. I don't know what happened to the other."

"What man? What did he look like?"

"Short for a man, and stocky. Dark hair. The color suited him. He seemed pleased when I told him so."

At least ten questions threatened to burst from James at once, so he made himself take a breath and pull out his notebook. Walter let him handle it, more interested in the visual examination of Miss Peaches and Cream.

"What was his name?"

She shrugged.

"When was this?"

"Early summer, I zuppose. Still cool at the night. I remember thinking he could use a light coat."

"Did he stay here at the church?"

The priest answered that. "No, we don't have anything like that. We help find houses for families, sometimes, but we don't have the resources to provide both food *and* shelter."

"Ma'am, did this man tell you where he spent his nights? Or even his days?"

"I don't remember. I juzt happen to recall the coat, that's all."

"Then did he say anything about the coat?" James asked in desperation.

Her face cleared. "Yes, I remember now. He seemed quite pleased with it, like I said, and said perhaps it would help him get a job like he'd had before."

James refrained from grasping her arm. "What job?"

"Oh, *ich weiss nicht*—I don't know. Looking for work is all these men do, all day, every day. Poor souls."

A man at the closest table glanced up at them. His eyes blazed at the description before reality snuffed out the flame and he turned his face downward once again.

"But what kind—"

"Mechanic." Apparently another wisp of memory had surfaced, and she massaged her chin with strong fingers as she thought. "That was it. Mechanical zuper-visor—heavy machinery, steam engines, that's what he zaid. He called them turbines."

James digested this. Walter tore his gaze from the younger woman long enough to question the woman further, but she could not add anything more.

James and Walter thanked the quartet and went out into the freezing day once more.

After the car warmed up and thawed out their jaws, Walter said, "This doesn't quite fit. Unless this guy gave the hawk-nosed lady in there a line, he's a reasonably pleasant, formerly hardworking joe. Why would he hang around with a punk like Edward Andrassy?"

"Maybe he didn't. We found them together, but they weren't *killed* together. The coroner said the guy with the coat was dead a week or two before Andrassy."

"And he went looking for a job. Great. That narrows it down to half the guys in this city. Probably more."

"But he'd have been looking for a mechanic job. Who'd be hiring for that?"

Walter waited for a bundled-up family of four to cross the street in front of them, which allowed him to look like a nice guy while using the time to light a cigarette. He offered James one of the Luckies and for once James didn't have the inclination, or willpower, to refuse. They puffed companionably before Walter said, "Garages. Factories, the few that still operate."

"Trains."

"You and your trains again! Ain't it that guy you're always quoting who says never theorize ahead of the facts?"

"Sherlock Holmes."

"Yeah, the limey. You're stuck on this railroad thing and now you see trains every way we turn. I thought you liked that masher doctor for it."

"Odessa. Who picks up his marks at the train station," James said.

"The dead whore don't have nothing to do with trains," Walter argued. "She had a place to stay and wasn't leaving town."

"Same with Andrassy. And the woman had coal on her."

"The city runs on coal!"

"I know, I know. But what else do we have to go on? Two guys found by the train tracks and four months later we still don't even know who one of them is."

"And probably never will, by now. That's why we should concentrate on Andrassy and this woman. It's easier to trace their movements since people knew them."

"The whole city's been working on Andrassy for four months, and every cop will be working on Flo Polillo now. Why duplicate efforts? I say we stick with the man in the blue coat."

"The captain said to track down the doctor the Polillo hag made payments to. Remember?"

James finished the cigarette and cracked the window only enough to toss the butt out. Then he put his hands in his armpits to keep them warm. "Okay, you're right. Let's compromise."

"I hate it when you say that."

"We'll go see Odessa. The mook claims to be a doctor, maybe he knows this Manzella. And we can also ask if he saw our guy in the blue coat while trolling the train station last summer."

"He won't say even if he did," Walter predicted. "That chizz has every angle figured."

CHAPTER **32**

Friday, September 10
Present Day

The body pieces found in the crates apparently belonged
to a thirty-eight-year-old mother of two who worked the
early-morning hours at the West Side Market, unloading, cleaning, and stacking fruit for display. Two other
merchants remembered her being there about 5:00 A.M.,
but when her boss arrived at six he found the job only
half done and no sign of Peggy Hall. The scattered personnel at the market probably would have seen her ab-
ductor if he had entered the pavilions, police concluded,
but Peggy made several trips to the Dumpster to throw
out empty boxes. She always flattened them properly
and took them to the one marked for recyclables. Peggy
Hall believed in being green. She must have encountered
the killer in this dark corner of the lot, as the Cuyahoga
quietly streamed by.

"Interesting, that Dumpster," Theresa said to Don as
the DNA analyst prepared microtubes in order to confirm Peggy's identity. "The milk crates he used didn't

come from it. I found—aside from another strand of that black nylon that keeps turning up—dried spaghetti with sauce, a healthy little clump of it."

"You can't get spaghetti at the West Side Market?" Don asked. "Isn't that against the order of nature or something? I thought you could get everything there."

"Oh, you can. But we didn't see any in that Dumpster, or in any of the Dumpsters. I think he picked up the milk crates somewhere else. That makes more sense—he would have had all his props in place before choosing a victim. He would already have the crates."

"And this spaghetti?"

"If he's smart—and he is—he picked them out of the garbage somewhere, so they couldn't be traced to him or his place of business."

"Aha. So you think he stole them from a Dumpster behind a restaurant that serves spaghetti?"

"Yep."

"Wow. That narrows it down. In a city the size of Cleveland. Tess, everyone from Bob Evans to Hornblower's serves spaghetti."

"I know."

"Of course you can take a sample and run it through our spaghetti sauce database."

"Not funny." She rubbed her eyebrows. The few hours of sleep she had managed to catch at home had not helped.

"If this were a TV show, we'd have one."

"If this were a TV show, I'd be twenty pounds lighter and twenty years younger. And Leo would be chosen *People*'s Sexiest Man Alive."

They spent the next thirty seconds giggling. Theresa's laugh held a tinge of hysteria.

"Seriously," she said, wiping her eyes. "We ID'd Peggy Hall off a missing person report filed by her sister, who was sleeping over to watch the kids while Peggy worked. The husband has been in the hospital for two months after an accident at work—something to do with a forklift—and he called the sister to see why Peggy hadn't come by for her daily visit on her way home from the market. She has no record. She was a perfectly nice woman, working her butt off to keep her family going."

"Wow," Don said. "Sister's going to be watching those kids for a very long time."

"We've got to catch this guy, and we've got to do it tonight." Since the killer seemed to be an early riser, to-night's victim had most likely already been abducted. Every police department in Cuyahoga County had been alerted to contact the Homicide unit with any missing person report filed today, particularly those of grown men, as well as reports filed in the prior forty-eight hours. The media had been pressed into service and fed warnings about possible abductions. County residents were warned to take extra precautions for their safety and to watch for any suspicious behavior occurring around them, especially during the hours from dusk to dawn. This could make their killer change his habits or go to ground, and catching him would be that much more difficult. But they couldn't neglect the chance that for his next target, forewarned might prove to be fore-armed. "Frank will put cops at each of the four corners of a square mile at Fifty-fifth and Kingsbury, plus one at the rapid station. And he should have a more diffi-cult task tonight. The fifth victim of the real Torso killer was a young man—never identified, despite a boatload of tattoos—and they found a large pool of blood next to his body."

She got lost for a moment, picturing this, until Don prompted her. "Uh-huh?"

"So he was one of the few victims actually killed at

the scene. Most were killed somewhere else, cleaned, and then deposited. Our killer can't just dump the victim. He has to bring him, murder him, decapitate him, wrap the head up in the pants, and carry it a thousand feet away. That's going to be tough to do in an open valley surrounded by cops." Impossible, she hoped, for the city's sake as well as any future victims'. Councilman Greer, with his construction project cleared, had now guided the city's fear into a hot wave of righteous indignation at police incompetence, mentioning her and Frank by name. Bad enough that he let his bruised ego come after her, but to criticize Frank because he couldn't wave a magic mirror and spot the killer aroused Theresa's own virulent indignation. Only catching the killer would stop Greer's assault.

Don said, "I see. This guy will show up with tonight's sacrifice, and your cousin and half the Cleveland police force will be waiting for him."

"So will I."

Irene Schaffer sat in a wheelchair and stared out at the setting sun with a face so vacant that Theresa worried—perhaps Irene had good days and bad days, and this could be one of the latter. But when the old woman turned and saw her, the wrinkles in her face curved into smiles along with her lips. "You came back."

"Yes. I have some more questions, I hope that's okay."

"Let me check my busy social schedule. Sure, it's okay."

Theresa waited patiently for the tea routine, trying not to tap her foot. Her mother would kill her if she was late to her own birthday party, and she'd even hear it from Frank, since *his* mother was to host the shindig. They would both have to make a showing before cutting out to wait at the valley. But she couldn't rush Irene. Theresa might find herself in a place like this someday, with a visit from a stranger the only entertaining thing to happen that year.

She began, "We talked about your encounter with Dr. Louis."

"I've been trying to remember more about him." The old lady stirred her tea as delicately as any queen. "I came up with a white shirt with gold buttons. The buttons had an anchor on them."

"Really," Theresa said, just to say something.

"I got rather a close look at them. Does that help?"

"They thought one of the victims might be a sailor, the one they called the Tattooed Man. But I'm here to focus on the room, the little storeroom he put you in. The building is going to be destroyed tomorrow, and it's driving me crazy that we still can't figure out which office the room with the body belonged to."

Irene tapped her spoon on the cup. "Dr. Louis had a door behind his desk, and that opened into the closet."

"I understand that, but the other offices probably had such built-in closets as well. The door behind his desk—was it next to the outer wall, or the inner wall, by the hallway?"

For the first time Irene seemed unsure. "Neither . . . somewhere in the middle."

"Tell me again about the arrangement of the room. When you first walked in from the hallway—"

"His desk was on the left," Irene said immediately, "but not touching the wall. He had a chair behind it for him and two in front of it—"

"Closer to the hallway door."

"Yeah. On the right were two windows and shelves going almost to the ceiling, with books and bottles and things. He had a coat rack in the far corner, way behind his desk. That was about it. Kind of sparse, really. That also struck me as odd—most doctors' offices that I've ever seen, even today, are crammed to the gills with stuff."

"So the desk sat about midcenter along the south wall?"

Her face scrunched up in concentration. "Yeah, I think that's about right."

"And the door to the storage room, in the south wall behind it—would you say that was closer to the outer wall, or the hallway wall?"

Irene thought so long that Theresa had to gasp out a breath she hadn't realized she'd been holding.

"The outer one, I guess. Otherwise his desk would have been in the way of the door."

"Okay. When you entered the room, the little storage room, did the space open up to the right or the left?"

"I see what you mean. God, I tried not to think about this for so many years—"

"I'm sorry."

"Don't be. Okay. I woke up on the cot. . . . I pushed him and ran past the shelves. . . . I think the storage area would have stretched between the middle of the room and the outer wall. When you looked into it, it opened to the right. The cot lay in the back corner. I had to get past him, out the door, around the desk, and out the door to the hallway."

Theresa pondered this with a mix of exhilaration and disappointment. The area in which they found James Miller lay farther into the building. If that section of floor had not belonged to Dr. Louis's office, it moved Arthur Corliss up to number one suspect. Corliss, the adored father of her new friend Edward. Maybe—Odessa could have installed the table after Irene's attack and before James's murder. "And this was a cot, not a table?"

"A cot, canvas thing about two feet off the floor. Standard military issue, I learned a few years later."

"Did you see any plumbing in there? A sink, a toilet?"

"I didn't really stick around to inventory the place, dear. I only remember shelves, bare wooden things made out of two-by-fours. I grabbed on to one to haul myself up. It gave me a splinter."

"What did he have on the shelves?"

"Not much, as I recall. Bottles and jars, like his outer office. A stack of paper and a typewriter, I remember that."

"Any medical instruments? Like a stethoscope, or . . . knives?"

Irene grinned to show that the delicacy had been wasted on her. "To chop up his victims with? I don't remember any, but again, I didn't take the time to look around."

"And then you ran out."

"As fast as my chubby little legs could carry me."

"And you saw no one else? All the other tenants had gone home?"

"Yes. Yes. . . ." Irene sipped tea.

"You seem unsure about that," Theresa said, pressing her.

"I didn't *see* anyone. But—oh, that was it. The dog."

"Dog?"

"The man in the next office must have had a dog. I heard him whining and scratching at the wall next to me, as if he heard us in there and knew I was in trouble. Animals can always tell, you know. They sense it. Or maybe he just wanted us to come and let him out." She shook her head, the badly dyed locks going every which way. "Funny, I forgot all about that until now. Probably because when you asked I thought you meant *humans*."

James Miller had made a notation about dog hair in

his notes. "And you're sure this dog was in the other office? Not in the hallway or outside the building?"

"No, the scratches were close, and on wood. Real clear."

"Did he bark?"

"Yeah, once or twice. Obviously no one was there to hear him, except good old Dr. Louis—the bastard."

"Why would someone leave a dog in an office overnight?"

"Honey." Irene Schaffer's eye twinkled over the rim of her teacup. "People didn't have electric alarms that called the police when a burglar opened the door or smashed the window. And thieves were thick on the ground then. People were desperate."

"I see. Irene, I'm going to try to get a blueprint of the building and bring it here to show you. Then we can make some notations about the layout."

"Sure, bring it by. I'll try to make time for you."

"Thanks." Theresa set her cup gently on the doily-clad end table. "I have to go now, or I'm going to be late to my own birthday party."

"How old are you?"

Theresa made a face. "Forty."

She expected the ninety-one-year-old Irene to point out that forty made her a mere child, but the woman said, "That sucks."

"Yes, it does." At the door, strangely reluctant to leave, Theresa turned back. "Say, you never told me about robbing the bank."

Irene's eyebrows pushed the wrinkles on her forehead up to her hairline. "I wouldn't rob a bank, dear. I've never taken a thing that didn't belong to me, no matter how tight things got."

"But you said—"

"I said I knocked one over. That's different."

Theresa waited, returning the older woman's grin.

"It was the Union National Bank Building on Euclid. They demolished it in the fifties to build a Woolworth's. My boyfriend at the time—Harold something-or-other—worked for the demolition company and I got to sit with him in the cab as he swung the wrecking ball."

"I see. You knocked it over."

"That we did. Every time that wrecking ball smashed into the walls, the ground shook all the way up through the machine until my teeth rattled. My heart bounced around in my rib cage. It was something to feel, all right."

"Cool."

"Actually, after a while it got a little tedious. They didn't go just *bam, bam, bam*. They had to stop after every swing and take a look at what they'd done and decide where the next blow needed to be. It all had to do with the weight of the upper floors and the placement of the supports. Harold knew all about that stuff and I wanted to know everything about Harold. Always date interesting men, dear. Life is too short to waste on boring people."

"I'll keep that in mind," Theresa promised as she left.

CHAPTER 33

One glance told Theresa that her aunts had won control of the cake. Had it been up to her cousins, they would have had it decorated with black icing and perhaps a vulture or two. But her cousins were no doubt busy with their own children and jobs and households and left it to the aunts, and the aunts had picked out a round white concoction with pink roses and yellow bumblebees. The fact that it would have been more appropriate for a preschooler made her feel not the slightest bit younger and certainly no less self-conscious about the entire celebration.

That would not, of course, stop her from eating as much of the frosting as she could get.

"Don't stick your finger in that," Frank warned.

"Too late."

"It will make you fat."

"Too late for that, too."

"Are you guys going to kick out a death certificate on Kim Hammond soon?" he asked. "Her mother calls us every day about it. I keep referring her to you, but she calls us."

Theresa let her aunt's German shepherd lick the frosting residue from her finger. "Christine said she was having some kind of problem with it—not the cause of death, she's going to keep that a generic 'bodily trauma' and then list 'decapitation' and 'exsanguination' as factors. But paperwork is holding it up. She's still trying to get the medical records and birth certificate."

"Another reason why the mother needs to call you and not me."

"Go ahead and tell her to." Theresa paused to hug one of the many children of her many cousins, then turned back to Frank. "You getting anywhere on Kim?"

"No."

"Not at all?"

He sipped red punch from a plastic cup, making a face she knew meant it would taste better with some rum in it. "Snaps to the girl for staying off the drugs and all, but it seems that all she did with her new free time was sit around her mother's apartment and watch TV. As far as we can tell, she didn't contact her old gang, didn't return to her old haunts. She went downtown now and then, but what she did there is anyone's guess. Probably just shopped. Her mother did say she'd go to the West Side Market once in a while."

"Where Peggy Hall worked?"

"Yeah. But no one ever saw them together."

Another cousin stopped by to hug Theresa. "Happy birthday."

"Thanks."

"So, you're over the hill now, huh?"

"And speeding down the other side." Theresa would have laughed at the comment from anyone other than Heather, the youngest and perkiest cousin, the daughter of the youngest and perkiest aunt. Heather's butt probably wouldn't fall until she drew social security no matter how many beautiful and perky children she pushed out.

"Well, you look great."

"Thanks," Theresa said. "But from now on I'll only look great *for my age.*"

Frank frowned in confusion, because he was, of course, a man, and didn't understand.

"It's one of those lines you cross," Theresa explained to him. "It starts when people start calling you *ma'am* instead of *miss,* as if a memo had been sent out to everyone in the world except you. Then in a few years you find your normal poundage has been shifted upward, and even if you lived on plain lettuce, your high school weight has become an impossibility. Then you find that you can walk past a group of young men without hearing any suggestive comments."

"Depressing," Heather said.

"Actually, that's the only good part of aging I've found so far," Theresa told her. "Sometimes I like being invisible."

"That's what Kim seemed to have been," Frank said, giving the punch another try. "Invisible. If she went anywhere or did anything in the weeks before she died, we have yet to find out about it."

"Then look at home. What about that creepy guy on her floor you told me about?"

Dead girls didn't interest Heather, who interrupted with: "Is that hostage-negotiator guy still chasing you?"

Theresa leaned against the table to give the muscles in her butt some relief from the onslaught of gravity and considered this. Chris Cavanaugh called her rarely and inconsistently, which hardly constituted *chasing.* And yet nothing gave her the impression he had *stopped* calling. "I suppose."

"Are you going to let him catch you?"

"Actually"—Theresa sipped and inwardly agreed that the punch did need some rum—"I've been seeing another man. Older. Distinguished."

Behind Heather, Frank rolled his eyes.

"Likes trains," Theresa went on.

Perky didn't equal dumb. Heather apparently suspected a put-on and left to steer her toddler away from the punch bowl as he poised himself to fish for the floating lumps of sherbet. Theresa and Frank escaped for some fresh air.

The backyard of Frank's mother's house ended in trees, and Theresa watched the setting sun turn them into an inferno of reds and golds. Forty years old, and still the only person she wanted to talk to was her cousin. Maybe Leo and Irene Schaffer and everyone else were right. She had a gap in her life and needed someone to fill it.

She asked Frank, "Did you find out any more about James Miller's work history?"

"Not much. Hired in 1929, made detective in '32. His partner's name was Walter McKenna. Human Resources did find a few reports relating to Miller's disappearance; they were in with the paperwork to dismiss him from the rolls for apparent dereliction of duty. The partner had no idea what had happened to him. They had been working on the investigation of the third victim, the one killed in June 1936."

"The Tattooed Man. The one who should die tonight. I mean, the murder our current killer should be planning to re-create tonight."

"I know what you meant. Anyway, at the end of the day McKenna went home to dinner and they parted ways. He never saw Miller again. Miller's wife said he never came home. End of report."

"So he ran into the killer by coincidence, or he followed a lead he didn't tell his wife or his partner about."

"Or the partner's lying," Frank supposed.

"Why would he?"

"Cleveland was pretty wild then. Organized crime ran the city and most of the cops were helping them do it. That's why they hired Ness, to clean up both the city and the department."

Clouds were creeping up to block out parts of the sunset and she hoped it wouldn't rain on tonight's stakeout. "You think Miller worked for the mob and they killed him?"

"Or he didn't, and dirty cops killed him."

It surprised her that he would suggest such a thing, but then, it had happened a long time ago and it would hardly reflect on today's police force. "You think so?"

"No, not really. I can't see a cop cutting someone's head off. The mob would at least have had a little more practice at it. Maybe they intended to plant the body in a way that would make everyone think the Torso killer did it, and lost their nerve or changed their minds. Or it really *was* the Torso killer. Who knows? If they couldn't solve it in 1936 I doubt we can now."

"Maybe we can. At least we've narrowed the suspects down to the tenants of that building," she said, aware that she was echoing Brandon Jablonski's earlier words.

They stood in silence for a few minutes, thinking. A V of geese flew above them, heading for the dusky southeast sky with a round of startlingly loud honks.

"Weird, isn't it?"

Frank lit a cigarette. "What?"

"This case has fascinated Cleveland for three-quarters of a century. I just keep wondering what Grandpa would say if he knew we were working on it."

Frank said nothing and puffed, staring at the trees.

"We used to watch *The Untouchables* all the time,"

she said. "When I got older and started reading true crime I'd tell him about every case I read. Most of them he already knew."

"And I'm the one who became a cop," Frank said.

His words settled through the air like a layer of dust, and suddenly she *heard* what he had been trying to say, possibly for years. He had been one of the boys in a sea of girls. He had listened to Grandpa's tales and had gone into the same line of work. If anyone became their grandfather's favorite, it should have been Frank. Not her.

Frank had spent as much time with him as Theresa had, at least before her father died. After that no one had been around Grandpa as much as she had, or rather, no one had been around Theresa as much as Grandpa.

It would never have occurred to her that Frank resented that relationship, never in a million years, but now it seemed so obvious that she felt stupid.

"But you had a father," was all she could think of to say.

He ground the cigarette into the grass, twisting hard as if to make sure the embers were out. "Not much of one."

That was true.

"Frank—"

He didn't look at her. "Come on, let's go in. You have presents to open so we can get out of here and back to the stakeout. I got you Scott Joplin CDs; sorry to ruin the surprise."

"But, Frank—"

"It's a boxed set. Better rip into them now." The sun, beginning its nightly dip, turned his face to scarlet. "We're going to have to go."

CHAPTER  34

MONDAY, JANUARY 27
1936

James and Walter had to wait until the following day to find the doctor in. To James's frustration, they had neglected to get a home address for him during the Irene Schaffer investigation and he had no listing in the city directory. But Monday, despite the cold, found the building at 4950 Pullman full and bustling.

Odessa, of course, not only denied being Flo Polillo's Dr. Manzella but denied knowing a Dr. Manzella. He showed no concern over the name, merely added a new bottle to the sparse collection on his shelves, moving the items already present so that there would be equal spacing among them all. "I don't wish to be crude, gentlemen, but I don't include common whores among my patients."

"As opposed to uncommon ones?" Walter asked.

"She wasn't a whore," James said, though he knew this to be largely untrue. "She held a job, most of the time."

Odessa said, "I'm not trying to be elitist, but you've seen the type of lady who leaves my office. If any of them needed to work they wouldn't be able to afford my services. It's a pity, really, for the lowest classes are the ones who need nutrition counseling most of all. If we had a government that cared for all its citizens equally—"

"So you don't know a Dr. Manzella?" James cut in.

"No." The bottles arranged to his satisfaction, Odessa turned. "Never heard of him."

"And you don't have any drugged young girls in your closet?"

The man actually laughed at that. "No, Officer, I do not."

"Mind if I check?"

"Jimmy . . . ," Walter said with a note of warning.

"Not at all." Odessa gestured toward the closet door with a gracious sweep of his hand. "Though if you continue to make a habit of this, I will make a report of harassment to your superiors."

Now Walter bristled. "Go right ahead, mister. Our superior has a daughter about Irene Smith's age."

James didn't bother to correct the girl's last name in light of Walter's sudden support. He pulled the door open and entered the storage room, flicking a switch to illuminate the bare bulb that hung from the ceiling. He didn't really expect to find a girl. What he wanted to look for was blood.

The room appeared much as he had last seen it, bottles of pills and herbs with handwritten labels, a short stack of towels, and a supply of writing paper. No dark spots stained the rough wooden walls or floor. Two spots appeared on the edge of the cot frame, and James could only pray they did not belong to some poor girl with less luck than Irene. But he saw no signs of Flo Polillo's body having been brutally dismembered in that small space.

And yet he swore he could smell it, that damp and

rotting odor of blood. Murder, war, it all smelled the same.

"Satisfied, Officer?" Odessa asked when he emerged.

"Detective."

The man came close to rolling his eyes. "Detective. Then I will bid you good day. I have a client due to arrive in a few minutes. Take a look at her, and you will see why I would not waste time with the Flo Polillos of the city."

"You know our victim's name," James pointed out.

"The papers have written of nothing else. Everyone in Cleveland knows her name."

They emerged into the hallway as he said this, and a woman unlocking the door across the hallway said, "Whose name? Mine?"

"Sorry, Auralina. The detectives were speaking of that woman found so brutally murdered."

The glass in the door read AURALINA DE MORELLI— MEDIUM and the woman dressed the part in an outlandish getup of flowing purple and crimson that did not even resemble a dress, per se, and yet still managed to hint at a perfectly feminine figure. Her face, while coated in too many colored powders, had a similarly pleasant shape. "I read all about it. You need my help, gentlemen. I can contact the dead woman and ask her who tore her limb from limb."

"Really," Walter said with a less-than-convinced air. James didn't bother to respond but surveyed the rest of the hallway. A burst of laughter sounded from the architect's firm. The door to the railroad man's office remained closed, with no light behind the glass.

But de Morelli knew her business and qualified her statement. "That is, if she wants to tell us, if she even knows. But you can't be sure until you ask. It could solve the whole case for you."

Walter's gaze did not budge from her bosom. "Just like that."

She braced her back against her open doorjamb, the better to display herself. Auralina de Morelli had become schooled in the finer arts of salesmanship, James could see. "As I said, you can't know until you try. The spirit of this troubled woman will be straining to find expression in this world."

"Thank you anyway, ma'am," James said. "Let's go, Detective McKenna."

"Sure." Walter did not move, however, still captivated by the straining breasts of the de Morelli woman, and meanwhile the front door opened to allow in a burst of arctic air.

The medium smiled at Odessa in a way that made James think the man did not have to drug *all* his partners. "A client comes for you, Louis, or perhaps for me."

But only Arthur Corliss entered. He carried a paper parcel that smelled good. "Hullo. Are we having a meeting in the hallway?"

Odessa introduced the two cops, as if they were his guests at a party. Corliss's gaze rested with more recognition on James, but he said only, "I've been out getting provisions. Would you gentlemen be needing some lunch? It's the best corned beef in the city."

"From where?" Walter asked, of course. Only food could get his attention from a female body.

"Mike's."

"Oh, yeah. Good stuff."

"No, th—" James began to say. Then he stopped himself. "Actually, that would be great."

Walter stared. "You don't even like—"

"Always thinking of you, partner. Let me help you with that, Mr.—Corliss, isn't it?"

"Yes."

James left the other three people in the hallway and followed Arthur Corliss back to his office. In the time since James had seen it last, the man had accumulated more items: more papers, more books, more newspapers in separate stacks (apparently he read all three: the *News,* the *Press,* and the *Plain Dealer*), a good supply of Mission Orange soda pop in their signature black bottles, a large table now crowding the desk and scattered with reports and diagrams. Unlike his fellow tenant, Arthur Corliss did more with his office than rape young girls and sell pills to society ladies.

The dog remained. He opened one eye at James's entrance but chose not to leave his spot in front of the radiator.

"Well, Detective, what brings you by?" Corliss asked as he unwrapped his parcel.

"Just keeping an eye on your neighbor, that's all, making sure the good doctor's lady friends are all of legal age."

"The ones I see are well above that, I can assure you. Louis never lacks for lady friends."

James did not press this. "I had a question for you as well. If a man wanted to work for the railroad, would he come here to talk to you or go to the station?"

Corliss straightened from his task as if both astounded and delighted by the prospect. "Are you considering the railroad police? Excellent! We can always use experienced men. I used to be one, you know, a detective like you are."

"With the railroad?"

"In my younger years. I wasn't much good at it. I felt too sorry for the unfortunates in this country who couldn't afford a ticket—and there's so many more now." Corliss found a knife in a drawer and sliced one of the sandwiches with an agitated *whack!* "Of course too many of them *can* afford it; they simply don't want to part with the cash, and the railroads have to protect themselves. Once I grew into a man I learned that it takes a great deal of money to establish a railroad and even more to run it, and I can't let that all fly away because criminals think a depression is an excuse to appropriate my property for their own uses. It's a battle out there every day, you know. Practically a war. Sandwich?"

"No, thank you, but I'll take a slice for my partner." The man's face fell, so James explained, "I've never cared for cured beef. My father cured everything when I was a boy. He considered it the only trustworthy way to preserve food."

"Your partner doesn't understand, does he?"

"Curing?"

"War." His gaze lingered on the worn hem of James's coat, on the practically threadbare thighs of his trousers. "And fighting it on one's own terms."

In that instant James wanted nothing more than to pull up a chair and talk, to this man or even to his dog, about the difficulty of coming up with excuses to get out of working protection for a gambling joint or collecting the department's take from a cathouse, about Helen and baby John, about the cold seeping up through the tape around his shoe.

He didn't, of course. He could not bare his soul to another; men didn't do that. And he had some concerns about the tenants of 4950 Pullman. The first two bodies had been found on the slope outside, only a few hundred feet to the west of this building. The man in the blue coat might have come to Corliss looking for work. And Flo Polillo had tended bar at Mike's. "About a job with the railroad, I didn't ask for myself. I am trying to retrace the steps of a man who might have come here looking for work as a mechanic."

A young man with tousled dark locks and a pencil behind one ear bounced in through the door behind James. "Got the grub?"

Corliss held out a sandwich. "Here you go, Mr. Metetsky. Though you know it's a crime to eat corned beef on anything but rye."

"So you say. Did your housekeeper send any biscuits today? No? What a pity." The architect plucked the wrapped food from the man's hand. Then he bounced back out, but not before taking in James's form from the softened hat to the shoelaces mended in three spots. He said nothing, though, and merely added over his shoulder to Corliss, "I'll settle up later, okay?"

"I doubt I'll ever see it," Corliss said to James. "He's a bit of a chizz, that one. Hasn't learned that those who fail to contribute their share fail in their very humanity."

"Young men are often careless." James pulled out his notebook. "The man I'm tr—"

"But there's no excuse, in his case. He earns a good amount of money at his trade. What I paid them in design fees for this building alone could buy a year of sandwiches." Corliss continued to stare at the door as if waiting for the young man to return, and with sufficient coinage this time.

The dog decided to scratch, sending a shower of its yellow hairs onto the floor beneath the radiator. The sound distracted his master.

"Well, young men, as you say." Corliss sliced part of the meal off for himself. "They thrill at nothing so much as getting away with something. Who did you say you were looking for?"

James explained about the man in the blue coat. "He may have come here inquiring about work as a mechanic. It would have been late spring, early summer. June, probably, perhaps July."

"Six months ago? Detective, I get ten men a week begging for work, any work. And those are the skilled ones—the rest apply at the station and never get to me. I'm sorry, but I can't possibly remember—"

"He did have skill—he might have been a mechanical supervisor. And this is the coat." James pulled out the color photograph he had hounded the Bertillon unit into making for him, insisting that the style of the coat would not stick in people's minds, that it became memorable only with the color.

Corliss took the photo with one hand, holding his sandwich in the other. He peered at the blue coat. He set down the sandwich. The hand holding the photo began to quake, very slightly, yet his expression did not change, the helpful curve of his lips still in place.

Louis Odessa appeared in the doorway. "I forgot to get my lunch. You still here, Detective?"

James made no reply, and Odessa didn't seem to care. He picked up his parcel and, unlike the young architect, left his share of the bill on Corliss's desk blotter. Corliss watched him approach, take, and leave, without saying a word.

Then he held the photo out to James. "I've never seen this. Nor do I recall the man you describe. I'm sorry I can't help you, Detective."

"Are you sure?"

"Quite sure, I'm afraid. I have a fairly good memory for people—not perfect, of course, but good." He held out the wrapped corned beef. "Here, give this to your partner. You'll need it to lure him from Auralina's charms."

Still stuffed from their restaurant rounds, Walter showed a rare indifference to the food but willingly departed from the medium. Apparently she had a habit of talking money more than sweet flirtations, and Walter didn't care for conquests with an entrepreneurial bent. "Did you show him your little picture?"

"Yep."

"What'd he say?"

"Didn't ring a bell."

"Big surprise there. Nobody would remember some bum's coat from six months ago. Well, *you* would, but nobody else." They got in the car and began its sliding ascent toward East Fifty-fifth.

"He's lying."

"Huh?"

"He recognized that coat. It startled him. But after his buddy Dr. Louis walks in and out, then he's never seen the coat before. We always wondered how one guy carried two full-grown men down a steep hill. Do you think there could be two of them, working together?"

"I think your imagination is working overtime, that's what I think."

James wrote *Corliss lying* in his notebook and circled the second word in heavy pencil.

CHAPTER

35

FRIDAY, SEPTEMBER 10
PRESENT DAY

They drove separately. Frank might have to leave the crime scene at some point to chase down a witness or a lead and Theresa hoped to need the supply of equipment she kept in her trunk. But it also forestalled any conversation.

Perhaps this was just as well. There was nothing she could think of to say that would not sound condescending. She could not tell Frank that their grandfather had loved him as well, because he knew that. She could not tell him that their grandfather had beamed for days after Frank's graduation from the academy, because he knew that. She could not tell him that Theresa had not been the favorite grandchild, because that was not true.

So she would say nothing at all.

Now she drove through the dying light, leaving the Cuyahoga River behind, following the access road to the RTA station and administrative offices. The task force would meet up there, the only place in the valley where cars coming and going would not seem like unusual activity, and it had parking to boot. Frank had suggested they use the building at 4950 Pullman, but Theresa had vetoed him in the hope that their copycat might consider it some sort of shrine and stop in to pay his respects. Cops were secreted in the woods and at the electrical station to keep an eye on it.

She drove past the slope where she had found the two dead men, starting for a moment when her headlights caught a pair of glowing eyes. Raccoon. She patted her chest, drove under the East Fifty-fifth bridge, and found the employee parking lot.

RTA had loaned them a conference room and set up a number of monitors with feeds from their station platform cameras. All three transit lines—Red, Blue, and Green—passed through the East Fifty-fifth station. This might make a getaway easier, or it might not, as the Red Line boarded from the west end of the building and the other two lines at the opposite. At this time of day a train left at least every fifteen minutes. To use them as transportation with cops in pursuit, the killer would have to employ split-second timing and the driver could easily be radioed to stop the train at any point. Theresa figured their killer was smarter than that.

Frank went over the facts of the original case. Angela Sanchez had Theresa use a map to point out the locations of the original body.

"This is guesswork to a large degree," she warned the men. "But I believe they found the head—wrapped in pants, so it might not be immediately obvious—south of the tracks roughly between Fifty-fifth and Kinsman. Directly across from this building, in fact. They found the head just east of the Fifty-fifth bridge, but between the sets of tracks. Those are my calculations, made with case studies and Google Earth. The killer might come to different conclusions, so we need sharp eyes at least a half mile west of Fifty-fifth as well, level with the building on Pullman."

The fifteen or so uniformed and plainclothes cops in the room stared at her without expression. This did not mean they were not listening—she had spent enough time around cops to know that—only that they could not appear impressed by anything except themselves. But she felt good about them. Even the ones who didn't look old enough to drive seemed bright, fit, and a hell of a lot more awake than she was. This killer would be caught tonight, webbed in by his own obsessions.

Angela said: "And don't forget about the trains, even the rapid transit. He might use them to arrive or escape. It's unlikely since he needs to bring an abducted male with him. Whether the victim's conscious or unconscious, it would be difficult."

Frank added, "We expect a lot of rubberneckers and reporters. Anyone who's been reading the papers could reach the same conclusions Theresa has and come out to watch the action, so there may be people in the valley tonight who wear dark clothing and don't stop when you shout at them. Go for your Taser first. Picture the headline 'Cop Shoots Innocent Teen in Botched Police Operation' splashed across tomorrow's *Plain Dealer*."

Angela muttered, "I bet Brandon Jablonski shows up, rain or shine."

"Who?" one cop asked.

Frank explained about the Web-news reporter and his interest in the case.

"So if he does come around, just escort him out of the area?"

"No," Frank said. "Let's consider him a suspect for now."

Theresa bit her lip before remembering that Jablonski

made an ideal suspect. If anyone knew where to leave all the bodies, he did.

The officers all filtered out to their assigned places to make themselves inconspicuous.

She pointed out a spot on the map to Frank. "We should wait here, between what used to be the Nickel Plate Railroad and is now Norfolk Southern, and the RTA rapid tracks, which used to be the New York Central Railroad."

"If he's reading the same books as you, and if he doesn't decide to call it off because he's smart enough to know we're going to be here, or because it's raining out and he likes the idea of us running around like wet idiots. And when did you become such a railroad historian?"

"Since I met Edward Corliss. Come on, we'd better get out there before it gets completely dark."

"What do you mean *we*? You're going to stay right here."

"*Why?*"

"Because you have neither a gun nor an *S* on your chest and I'm not going to have you running around a dark valley with a bunch of trigger-happy cops, not that I don't feel a little itchy-fingered myself."

"But—"

"Besides," he continued, "if you find one more body I'm going to have to bring you in for questioning."

"But—"

"There are no coincidences, isn't that what you're always telling me? Cheer up, cuz. At least you'll stay dry and close to the coffeemaker."

And then she was left alone on the white linoleum of the RTA conference room. Theresa exhaled sharply enough to fluff up her bangs, got a fresh cup of coffee, and turned out all the lights in the room so that she could watch the activity outside.

The room at the east end of the building gave her a wide view of the tracks on both sides and the station platform. The south side of the tracks turned into a steep hill of dense brush, unlit and apparently empty. To the north of her position, at least ten people milled about on the station platform, waiting for either the 8:41 or the 8:42, depending on whether they wanted to head downtown or toward the eastern suburbs. Overhead lights clearly outlined their body language. A girl stood between two pillars, facing Theresa with either a bag or a pile of books clutched tightly in both arms. She did not turn to look at the three young men twenty feet away no matter how much fun they seemed to be having, no matter how boisterous their horseplay seemed to get. A weary soul leaned forward on the bench, feet splayed. Two other men of similar height and weight shifted around, hands in their pockets. They did not speak to anyone and moved slowly but constantly. Everyone else on the platform shrank from them, ever so slightly, whenever they approached. They would be the cops.

The 8:41 arrived. The three young men boarded. The girl remained, but her shoulders relaxed.

Theresa could not see the area to the west of the building, the patch of grass between the two sets of tracks and just east of the Fifty-fifth Street bridge. This irritated her.

Her shoes squeaked across the floor as she paced from window to window, and she wondered who else remained in the building. The rapids ran more or less all night, pausing only for a short period in the wee hours of the morning. Surely there would be some manager on hand to deal with emergencies, mechanical breakdowns, or a bunch of armed police officers running around his territory.

Theresa had assumed that the killer would hop a

train with his victim, kill him, and then throw the body and head out as the train rumbled through the area. But now other scenarios began to present themselves. What if he dropped the two body parts from the Fifty-fifth bridge? Inelegant, yes, and the head might unroll from the pants during the fall, but perhaps he did not value ritual as much as she assumed. Did Frank have men on the bridge?

So much depended upon the killer's concern for historical accuracy.

Two older ladies and two teenagers joined the people on the platform. None of the four seemed to be traveling together.

The 8:42 arrived. The girl did not board, but the weary person from the bench got up and shuffled into the car.

Otherwise the killer had to carry a body to the patch of grass between two wide sets of train tracks. He could drive to the spot, but only through the RTA building lots and past a handful of waiting police officers. It would take nerves of steel. The head, on the other hand, should be left on the outside of the tracks, at the base of the south slope at the far east end of Kingsbury Run. He could wind through that small forest from Bower and Butler avenues and have at least, she estimated from her window, thirteen hundred feet of lush foliage for cover. Frank and the cops had one or two officers watching that stretch of ground. If the killer was so inclined, he could rewrite history a bit and drop the head from the bridge like a macabre depth charge, wait until the cops found it and clustered around, then putter quietly to the end of Berwick and dump the body in the dark and tree-covered spot, instead of putting the body by the bridge and the head on the slope. Then the killer would drive away and leave the cops to explain this failure to the citizenry, already tempted to riot from fear.

The 8:57 arrived, and when it left it took the girl and three others. The girl had simply not wanted to get on the same train as the three young men, though traveling in the same direction. Theresa could remember being that young and that attractive.

And what about the pool of blood? The Tattooed Man had been one of the few victims killed at the scene. How could he possibly take the time to murder his victim on-site without attracting the attention of one of the officers?

Unless the victim *was* one of the cops.

The victim only had to be a man. There was nothing to say that that man couldn't be in uniform.

What a challenge it would present. Depositing Peggy Hall's body had been only a little risky. He had some leeway there when it came to location, since the original manufacturing plant had ceased to exist, and the cops were not yet convinced that he would stick to his one-a-day schedule. But now he had to know the cops would surround the tracks. How much more delicious it would be to come up behind one of the men who were trying to catch him, slip a loop of razor-sharp wire over his head, and pull on both handles with all his might—

Theresa burst from the conference room and through the lobby, out the lobby door, and into the night.

And ran straight into Councilman Greer.

CHAPTER 36

FRIDAY, SEPTEMBER 10
PRESENT DAY

Kingsbury Run had never been a populous place, in any era. So aside from the RTA riders and employees clustered at the station, the surrounding cops didn't have much activity to keep an eye on.

The officer stationed at the northeast corner of the area had parked his car in the lot behind some kind of old trucking terminal, long fingers of falling-down red brick that could warehouse a host of dead bodies, had he any desire to look through them. He didn't, content to pace along the patch of grass between Kinsman Road and the railroad tracks and experiment with a pair of night-vision binoculars he'd bought off eBay with his own money. Designed for use in the middle of the woods, they weren't much use in a city where the dark got interrupted at too many points by a bright streetlight or security light, nearly blinding him and overpowering the dimly lit areas he wanted to see. He crossed the weeds to stow them in his car. If any piece of equipment was going to get broken while he tackled a suspect tonight it wasn't going to be something for which he'd shelled out his own funds.

An older cop waited by the railing on the north end of the East Fifty-fifth bridge, high above Kingsbury Run, tucked into a small L where the sidewalk widened. Farther up Fifty-fifth a diner that had been closed for hours still managed to waft enough food smells to make him, in turns, both hungry and nauseated. On a typical night he'd have been breaking for "lunch" right about now, parking his unit on the East Ninth pier or maybe near the stadium and discovering whatever healthy thing his wife had decided he should eat that day. She would not let him pack his own meal, since he tended to wrap up stuff like leftover chicken wings, Funyuns, and Pop-Tarts.

At least it's not raining, he thought, approximately five seconds before the first drop of water struck the back of his neck.

The female officer had stashed her unit off the dead end of Berwick Road and waited in the copse of trees, south of the tracks, at the east end of the run. She stood mostly hidden under the low-hanging branches of an oak tree, secure in the knowledge that its wide berth had her back. She hoped the killer would not show before midnight, when her shift ended, so that she could remain on duty and get the overtime, important since her husband had lost his job at a GM dealership. She didn't mind the loss of income—they'd always been pretty sensible with money and should be able to weather this economic storm—so much as the loss of her "me" time. Working a rotating shift gave her days at home, him at work, the kids in school. She could watch TV, exercise, or take herself to lunch or a movie. Now he was home all day, every day. Not ideal.

A fourth officer, assigned to 4950 Pullman, had been

with the force for fifteen years. Way too long, he told himself, to let one empty building freak him out. Even a hollowed-out shell with heavy stone walls, isolated on one side by trees and on the other side by a steep hill leading down to the tracks. Even a building where a body—a *cop,* no less—had been walled up with his head between his feet for seventy-odd years. A building with nothing left in it that still managed to make a lot of noise. Rustles. A weird, muffled crackle every so often. When the wind picked up, entering through the southwest holes where windows used to be and blowing out the northeast spaces right at him, it gave a sort of keening wail, so faint he might have imagined it. But he had been a cop for fifteen years, so he was not freaked out. Not at all.

Detective Frank Patrick formed the center pin of the square, leaning up against one of the massive columns of the East Fifty-fifth Street bridge. Only fifty feet separated him from the RTA parking lot, and yet a woman had walked to her car without apparently noticing him in the deep shadows underneath the bridge. But she hadn't really looked around, either secure with or uninterested in the heavy presence of police on the RTA site. The killer would be more observant. So Frank Patrick stayed still, more or less, and sacrificed the idea of smoking a cigarette. He had sacrificed a lot for this job over the years.

He really, really hoped the killer would show up. Not just so that they could catch the sick son of a bitch, but so that Theresa wouldn't look like a crackpot for insisting he'd be there and that he, Frank, wouldn't look like the world's biggest idiot for believing her. It would take a long time to live down using department resources and making a bunch of cops stand for hours in the rain merely because he loved his pretty, slightly strange cousin who worked in the morgue. His fellow officers had cousins, too, but it didn't mean they chose to be around them all the time, and given their relative positions in the criminal justice system, if he and Theresa ever wanted to frame someone they could do one hell of a job. But worse, he might be sharing cop confidences with a noncop, and that made other cops nervous. Theresa was one of them and yet not one of them, probably smarter than most of them, and had gotten too old to be fun to flirt with. They thought Frank called her in more often than he needed to and wished he wouldn't.

At the same time Frank knew that all or most of this could be attributed to the typical human paranoia over the thoughts of others and shouldn't trouble him. The killer *had* to show up tonight—so far his re-creation of the original Torso Murders could not have been more accurate. He'd done everything but draw them a map. He would come.

Angela Sanchez stood about seventy feet to the north, along an even smaller spit of grass between train tracks. She did not know it but had proved much better at standing still than her partner, watching the terrain with slow, sweeping arcs of her head. The bridge stood too high to serve as an umbrella, even in a vertical rain, and her right sleeve grew damp. At the moment she felt no worry about the killer and his plans for the evening but instead fretted about her daughter's math scores. Math and science would be the way to make a decent living in the future and she didn't want the girl to get insecure about her abilities so early. Problem was, she'd always sucked at math herself and her daughter's homework might as well have been written in Greek. Too bad the girl hadn't inherited her father's talent for it. He'd been able to convert ounces to kilos before the dealer could finish counting the bills. Thinking of her ex-husband made her insist to herself, for the four billionth time, that he had no excuse. They had grown up in a perfectly nice neighborhood on the near west side, not some kind of ghetto. His parents were good folks who worked hard. No excuse. At least he'd had the courtesy to be caught and jailed in another county, which slowed the rumor mill just a bit.

So as she watched the valley around her she tried to recall which side of the graph was x and which was y, and what went over what to get the slope. She did not lean against the concrete column, having more concern for her clothing than Frank had for his.

The female officer in the trees heard voices to her right. Two or maybe three men were having a discussion in the middle of Berwick Road. So far it sounded friendly.

The male officer waiting on the Fifty-fifth Street bridge returned to his car for his raincoat. It said PO-LICE on the back, but he wasn't getting soaked to the skin for nobody. It took only wetness to change the cool of the fall evening from brisk to miserable, and cop work didn't pay enough to cover miserable.

The officer hunched by the building at 4950 Pullman, protected from the rain but still feeling its chill and, he hoped, invisible in the shadow of the stone wall. The wind's faint moan raised the hairs on the back of his neck. *Give me a matter-of-fact drug bust any day,* he prayed, Heat *instead of* Friday the 13th, *Ed McBain instead of Anne Rice.* He tried to rewrite the evening in his head, turning it into a funny story to tell his wife over breakfast, but nothing amusing came to mind.

Frank saw a woman emerge from the station and make a beeline for the north edge of the parking lot. He hoped it would not be Theresa but felt sure it would be.

She did not run or shout or use the radio. He pushed himself off the column and moved to the next one, took a careful look around it, and continued on to meet her at the edge of the lot. If the killer noticed her at all, perhaps he would see only an RTA employee going to her car.

He met her between a battered pickup truck and a shiny new Cobalt. "What are you doing?"

"Sorry. I got scared." She explained her fear that the next victim could be a cop. "It would be enormously appealing to him, to thumb his nose at us at the same time he continues his pattern. Not to mention the fact that if he knocks a hole in our perimeter, how much more does that increase his chances of getting away?"

"I see that, but my cops have enough on the ball to keep anyone from coming up behind them. Go back inside."

"I'd rather stay with you."

"Don't be dumb. This is a stakeout. I didn't bring you along just to have someone to chat with."

The rain picked up a bit and reached her scalp. "What about Angela? She's all bundled up with the Kevlar vest and sweatshirts—what if he doesn't get a good look at her, doesn't realize she's a woman?"

"What if he sees you running up to people all night and decides to dump tonight's body someplace else? Do you have any idea how stupid you and I are going to look?"

"He won't. He can't. Besides, is that the most important thing? How you *look*?"

"Yes. Yes, it is, because the next time I try to tell them a killer is on his way, no one is going to listen. Understand?"

"Yeah, yeah. Oh, and Greer is here."

"What? Why?"

"To make sure we do our jobs and protect the citizens of Cleveland, etc., ad nauseam. Meaning he sensed a photo op but the idea of meeting a killer turned him pale and sweaty. He's inside with the RTA staff and the coffee machine."

"Good. All the more reason not to blow this. Go back inside. If you have to contact me again use the cell. I have it on vibrate."

She thought, chewed the inside of her lip, and finally nodded her assent. But she didn't move, painfully reluctant to let her cousin out of her sight.

The train coming from the east continued to rumble and the track next to them began to vibrate. The 9:17 rapid appeared from the west. Frank crossed the closest set of tracks, staying within a line of deep shadow provided by a bridge column. Rain accumulated in Theresa MacLean's hair until it overflowed to the back of her neck, and she said "Frank!" in a fierce stage whisper.

He turned, only eight or ten feet away. "What?"

"About our grandfather—"

"Not *now*, Tess!" he hissed, and walked away, no doubt trying to stalk as unobtrusively as possible.

His cousin watched him. Theresa knew what they had at stake this evening, but all the killers in the world weren't more important than her family.

"He loved you," she said. He couldn't possibly hear her, not with the rapid transit roaring into the station behind her and the other train bearing down on him, the driver blowing his horn, no doubt wondering why RTA couldn't keep its passengers from wandering all over the valley.

Frank turned anyway, clearly visible in the bright headlamp of the train, and looked back at her just before the train passed between them, cutting him off from her sight. Theresa put one hand on the battered pickup to steady herself in the roiled air as the train rocketed through the night.

"*I* love you," she said.

Thirteen or so cars passed, revealing an empty valley. Theresa told herself that Frank had gone back to his place of concealment under the bridge, and not to be an idiot, of course the train didn't hit him and the killer didn't kill him. Now, how to get back inside the station without being too obvious about it, and before she got soaked to the skin?

The 9:17 departed while yet another train approached from the east, a short thing of only four cars. She let the rain pelt her head for another moment while she watched it flow up the tracks. Its driver, too, let out a short toot on the horn, a habit or perhaps a requirement with the busy rapid station nearby.

He had liked this area, the Torso killer, needing the trains to travel back and forth between Cleveland and New Castle and to troll Kingsbury Run for victims, but not *only* for those reasons. He came there because he felt comfortable there. It was home to him.

She crouched between the cars and opened her cell phone, practically burying her head in her lap in order to muffle her voice and protect her phone from the rain.

A man's voice answered. "Hello?"

"Mr. Corliss?"

"Ms. MacLean! It's nice to hear from you again."

"I'm sorry to bother you."

"Not at all. I'm just putting the boat away. It's a bit too windy for an evening sail."

She could hear the erratic humming of the breeze behind his voice. "I have a quick question that I should have asked you earlier. The two railroads operating in Kingsbury Run—the Nickel Plate and the New York Central—did they go to New Castle?"

"Sure," he said promptly. "Both of them. As I said, it was a hub. They'd stop for the Northern Ohio food terminal on Orange Avenue. It's the post office building now."

She stared at the track in front of her, wondering how that bit of information helped her.

A faint light shone on the tracks in front of her, growing in strength, and she felt the now-familiar rumbling. "I have to go, but thank you."

The clacking of the wheels grew in volume. "Theresa," Edward Corliss said, "are you near a *train?*"

"Yes. I'll tell you about it later."

"Just be careful," he said emphatically, and hung up. She had to grin. No doubt he thought letting non–train people in a train yard sharply akin to allowing children to play in traffic. But she had no intention of wandering onto the tracks.

Cleveland to New Castle. Trains. She straightened, cautiously, and watched this new row of cars appear from the west. She knew she should get back inside before her hovering spooked the killer, but she found herself lost in the physics of the sight. Trains were large and heavy, unable to operate without their tracks. Very heavy. The phrase "stopping in its tracks" was not accurate; a train couldn't just stop. They accumulated too much force behind them.

Momentum. Mass times velocity. Trains had a great deal of mass, and the velocity could get impressive.

A rapid transit car, basically a hollow aluminum tube, had much more stopping power because it had less weight. A shorter train could stop faster than a longer one. That train that had just passed, the one with four cars, would be able to throw on its brakes much more effectively than this longer one now approaching.

So if you wanted to get away, pick a long train. Even if the cops flagged down the engineer or got the dispatch center to call him, even if he threw on every stopping mechanism he had, the train would still be a mile away before it came to a halt, before the police could swarm it.

By which time you would have jumped off at any point in the stopping process, preferably by a main road where you could catch a cab or a bus, or, if you appreciate irony, the rapid transit. Though a rapid transit station could have cameras. For real irony, how about another train?

But how to murder the victim there at the scene? Forgo that detail? Or jump off the train from the front, decapitate the (presumably incapacitated) victim, then hop back on one of the rear cars? Difficult, but possible. Assuming the train moves slowly enough. And is really long. Like this one.

Obeying an instinct she did not truly understand, she burst into a run and sprinted across two sets of tracks with at least four seconds to spare. It only *felt* like less. The driver let out an annoyed blast from the horn, not caring to cut it close any more than she did. The earsplitting sound proved so startling that it shoved into her with physical force until she stumbled over the third set of tracks and wound up stretched across them like the hapless heroine of a silent movie.

Scrambling to her feet, she moved to a tiny strip of grass and scanned the other tracks for oncoming cars. Nothing. The rain pelted, let up, and pelted again, its dynamics affected by the push and suctioning of the passing cars and the gaps in between each one as they rushed by her. The large boxes alternately blocked and allowed the bright lighting of the RTA station to pass through, and some cars had lights. This inconsistency ruined any night vision, effectively blinding her. She turned away, looking up and down the ten-foot-wide sliver of dirt and sparse weeds that ran along the tracks under the bridge.

She thought the killer should leave the corpse near the bridge, but that seemed too risky. If the cops were present—and, unless completely insane, he would assume they were present—that's where they would hide.

He would pick a new spot, farther east or west of the bridge, where he could do his grisly work and be gone before they discovered it.

Theresa moved under the bridge, better hidden by its deep shadow. Frank would be poised on the other side of the next pylon. She knew she shouldn't move around, yet they had too much ground to cover and too much of it became hidden as trains passed by.

Under the bridge, to the west, stood a low structure, probably an abandoned platform. She crept closer to it. The train continued to rumble by.

The original killer had not only murdered this victim at the scene, but he had left the head and the body in two different places—only a thousand feet apart, but far enough that the body had not been discovered until the following day. What would today's killer do about that? Ignore it? Jump off, decapitate, leave the body, and jump back on the train with the head, then toss that out farther up the line?

That would work, actually. The body had been found near the bridge, with the head found between the bridge and Kinsman Road to the east. Her thighs ached but she moved a few more feet along the platform in a low crouch, keeping her head below its surface. The rain had penetrated her cloth jacket and reached her skin, and this, she told herself, caused her trembling.

Movement.

At the west end of the abandoned platform, a flicker of darker against dark. An animal? A bush blasted with violent air from the passing train? A cop, wondering who the hell she was? Maybe lining up his sights right now?

Another step. Definitely movement.

She crept forward, feeling, curiously, no fear. The killer would not harm her; she was not male and killing her would ruin the authenticity of the scene.

But then, Peggy Hall should have been a heavyset sometime prostitute over forty. Perhaps authenticity was not his top priority.

She moved faster. She thought she could hear the rustling of his movements now, but that could not be possible, not over the roar of the train. It was probably Frank, and they'd scare the bejeebers out of each other like they did as kids playing Spotlight in Uncle Glenn's basement.

He appeared. A tall bundle of raincoat and hat and nothing where a face should be. He was not Frank, nor any other cop. Some sort of black mesh hid his features and he held a bundle in his arms. She knew exactly what that had to be.

He stood completely still for a moment, watching the train pass. She did not move—she couldn't—and yet his head snapped to her direction as if she'd jumped up and down.

Now she felt fear. Paralyzing, gut-twisting fear that squeezed every molecule of air out of her lungs.

He leapt toward the tracks and neatly caught the rungs protruding from one side of a boxcar, pulling his body up with much more feline grace than either she or Edward Corliss would be able to command. He melded with the train car as if he were part of it, mercury joining back into mercury with one hand, the other still clutching the bundle.

Her legs carried her forward before she knew it, as he passed on her left, until she reached the end of the platform. A body lay splayed across the dirt and weeds, with no clothing, and no head.

She turned and launched herself toward the train. He had done it.

She could, too.

Another car rushed by her in a dizzying blur. This next one—see the rungs? The weak streetlights shone down from the bridge and glinted off each metal protrusion. *Grab, pull. Just make sure your feet come up and don't swing into the wheels, to be chopped off at the ankles and pulverized.*

She reached out a hand.

It collided with a rung hard enough to break bone, and she stumbled, landing on the gravel shoulder only inches from the clacking metal wheels.

She looked ahead. The killer watched her from only three cars up, hanging easily off the side and facing back toward her, so the train could not be moving that fast. It was just the momentum. Mass times volume.

"Frank!" she shrieked, in a presumably hopeless attempt to alert the officers, and bounded up and along the side of the cars. That's how they did it in the movies, lessen the difference between the train's speed and yours.

It still outpaced her. She would have to grab the rungs of the next car.

It did occur to her to wonder what she would do if she caught it. She had no way of moving forward on the train toward the killer—unlike a passenger train, this one would have no pass-throughs between cars—but at least she could see where he jumped off. She could jump as well, pursue him, though once out of the crime scene he need have no qualms about ruining the effect by tacking on an extra murder.

But she had to catch the damn thing first.

She vaguely registered a sound that might have been Frank calling her name and hoped it was. The end of this car, the coupling between them, reach out and—

The killer pitched his bundle, tossing it underhand as one might abandon a basketball once the game ended. It landed in the narrowing strip of grass, directly in her path. If she didn't stop running she might step on it.

Her right hand connected with the rung. It hurt slightly less than the other one had. Then her right foot slid in the loose gravel and she went down, instinctively curling into a ball to keep all fingers and toes and arms and extremities off the tracks and out of the blender of moving parts underneath the train cars.

Her body came to a stop with her face in the gravel and her knees only an inch or so from the rails, but without losing any bits of itself.

She opened her eyes to find someone else returning her look, but with the unwavering, unseeing gaze of the dead. The killer had thrown the head, wrapped loosely in a pair of pants, just as she had expected him to do, just as the original Torso killer had prescribed.

He still watched her from up the tracks, receding farther into the east with every split second, the train picking up speed as it moved out of the more populated downtown area. Could he see her reaction from there, or did he simply enjoy letting his gaze linger on the tableau he'd created?

Frank caught up with her. "Tess. I saw you fall, are you hurt? What the hell were you doing?"

"He did it. Surrounded by cops, he still did it."

Frank clicked on his flashlight to see the head, though it was clearly visible in the parking lot lights strobing through the passing cars. He opened his mouth but apparently couldn't think of a profanity bad enough to express his thoughts and pulled out the radio instead. He'd arranged for a link to the downtown train yard dispatch center and now asked them to tell the driver to stop the train, though they both knew that when he did, the killer would be long gone.

"He did it," Theresa repeated.

"Damn," Frank said.

CHAPTER 37

At least it had stopped raining.

The body at the far end of the abandoned platform could tell her only this: that it belonged to an older man and that it had suffered no violence other than the loss of its head. The hands appeared clean and neatly manicured. Scraggly gray hair covered the chest, the shape of which would have benefited from a few more pounds. A deep red pool had spread from the shoulders.

It took a while to recall the train to the area, backing the cars slowly over the tracks—after, of course, examining the tracks closely for any evidence. The Conrail locomotive pulled a chain of fifty-seven cars bound for New Castle—a detail that caused her an extra frisson of dread—with a variety of cargo. Each car had been searched by teams of cops and Don Delgado, who found nothing. No pieces of ripped clothing, no murder weapon, and not a drop of blood.

Theresa also failed to find a trail of blood from the

tracks to the body, so it seemed unlikely that the killer had decapitated the victim on the train. If he had, he could have simply tossed the body from the train without jumping off himself. No, he had wished to re-create the original murder as closely as possible. He had leapt from the train with the apparently unconscious man, cut off the head, then reboarded the train. He would have to be very strong, but then she already knew that. Like the original killer, he had carried two full-grown men down at least part of Jackass Hill—not a task for the feeble.

Had he at least undressed the victim while on the train, or had he not only decapitated but undressed the victim there at the end of the platform, as she crept ever closer to him? She couldn't believe that. Every moment of this evening seemed to have happened in slow motion, but surely he had not had time for all that activity. He knew officers would be watching, and he had a train to catch.

She combed the ten or so feet between the tracks and the body three times before giving up. The killer had not dropped any handy clues to his identity, which she found quite unsporting. Bad enough he made them all look like fools—he could at least throw her a bone for her efforts. Surely the man wanted to be caught, or he wouldn't stick to a blueprint that told them the whens and wheres of his next murder.

Which murder came next? Another man, the only one found well out of the downtown area. On the west side, in the Metroparks.

The killer might be picking him out right now, coming up behind him, putting a tire iron to the skull or some chloroform to the face or simply asking for help getting his car started. She had no idea how he gained control over his victims. She had no idea how he chose them. She had no idea how to save this unlucky male who would die before the first golden glints of tomorrow's sun warmed the sky.

She needed to catch this killer. Then she wanted to squeeze the life out of him with her bare hands. This no longer had to do with a fascination for history or making the ghost of her grandfather proud. She *wanted* this guy stopped, brought down, trussed up like a calf, and forced to look her in the eye.

The night-shift body snatchers, too brightly alert for her, lifted the limp form into a white plastic body bag, and she hiked up the track to the group of cops around the head. Frank had frozen all the heavy train traffic through the area so that they could work without fear of disruption. Theresa shuddered at the thought of encountering another train any time soon. Every time she thought of falling along the tracks, so close to those whirling, slicing wheels, her mind turned away and closed off the picture until it could fade to black.

Portable halogen lights again turned the area into a live display of harsh beams and deep shadows, where the cops' faces were made even more pale and the browns and greens of the woods washed into a million shades of gray. At the center of it all lay a splash of bright color that only seemed more surreal given the neutral palette around it.

A light blue shirt, almost turquoise, glowed under the lights to near fluorescence. It had been ripped at one shoulder and the blood splashed across the front seemed oddly bright even though it had dried. A pair of khaki pants, similarly torn and bloody, wound its legs around and under the shirt and along the leaf-strewn earth. A belt and a pair of worn leather loafers stuffed with what should have been the man's white socks had landed next to the pants. Among all these items lay the head. The third disunited head she'd encountered in less than a week.

That wouldn't have been so bad, in and of itself. The only shocking part was how familiar the head looked.

The gray hair, the thin cheeks, and shaggy mustache . . . "I know him."

"What?" Frank said at her elbow. How long had he been there?

"I know him. I mean, I met him. His name is William Van Horn. He's the president of the American Railroad History Preservation Society. Was. He *was* the president. For the past eleven years, possibly only because of the Pennsylvania Railroad."

"Are you okay?"

"I'm fine." It was only the humming of the electricity along the rapid transit tracks and the brightness of the lights that made her dizzy. "I'm just very confused."

Frank shifted his weight, snapping a twig under one shoe. "Join the club."

"Aren't you going to ask how I know he was president of the preservation society?"

"Because you met him the other day, you told me that. And because that's what his wallet says."

"He had ID?"

"Driver's license, a membership card from the train society, credit cards, and fifty-two dollars in cash."

Theresa shook her head as she attached the heavy flash to the top of the Nikon, and Frank asked what was wrong. "He's got everything right in this series except the victimology and the ID. None of the Torso victims had any identifying item found with them and he didn't kill young girls like Kim."

"She was a prostitute, now and then, like Flo Polillo," Frank pointed out.

"Yes, but with very different looks. And this victim is a wealthy local man. Hardly a bum who wouldn't be missed."

"The killer might not have known that," Frank said. "He sees some guy wandering around the train tracks and either doesn't notice the designer clothing or doesn't care. Please don't tell me you're annoyed with the killer over his lack of historical accuracy."

"If he's going to do this"—she crouched next to the head—"he should do it right."

Van Horn wore, improbably, the same sneery look she had seen on him earlier, albeit with a slight cast of surprise. His right cheek had a light scratch with a trace of blood in it; otherwise the head seemed unmolested except for having been cut from the body. The slices there were not as tidy as on Kim, and the neck was the appropriate length.

From what she could see with a Maglite, the mouth had nothing in it but blood. Small flecks spotted the gray hair and appeared to be tiny leaves blown there from the surrounding weeds. Blood had been patted onto his right temple, probably from coming into contact with the wet pants. But the head seemed otherwise clean. The clothing, too, was only stained in spots and not soaked, the shoulders only spotted with blood. Definitely removed before decapitation.

Theresa let the heavy camera dangle from her shoulder while she sketched, still muttering to herself over the consistencies, and inconsistencies, of the murders. The ID bothered her. The original Torso killer had taken pains to keep his victims from being identified, with great success. Names had been found for only three of the twelve, and only two of those with complete certainty. Kim might still have been Jane Doe if it hadn't been for her criminal history.

But a lot had changed since 1935. They had identified all his victims so far, without too much trouble, so perhaps he decided not to worry about it.

"Has this guy's family been notified?" she asked Frank as she worked.

"Sanchez is at his address now, but apparently he lives alone. She woke up his landlady, who reports that Mr. Van Horn had no kin and not many friends. His life revolved around his job and the railroad preservation society."

"What job?"

"Draftsman at an architectural firm on Fifty-fifth."

"That makes sense. He was quite an artist."

"But he never got ahead."

She peered at him.

"At the firm. Never got a-*head*?"

"Haven't you heard a pun is the lowest form of humor?" she asked, thrilled to have Frank joking with her again. He didn't hold their grandfather against her, not really.

"I've heard it. I just don't believe it."

"When was the last time seen?"

"His landlady talked to him yesterday evening. When the firm opens up tomorrow morning we'll find out if he went to work. What's the matter?"

"I don't know. I just didn't want to be the last person to see him alive." She couldn't have said why, only that she did not want to get in the habit of meeting victims *before* they died. She preferred to have a completely impersonal relationship with the people on the gurneys. "I'm deeply unhappy about something."

"Turning forty? Get over it, cuz. You could still pass for thirty."

"I meant having met a murder victim before he became a murder victim."

"It's creepy," he said in agreement.

"It's giving me bad feelings about my new friend Edward Corliss. He introduces me to Van Horn yesterday, who today becomes the victim of our neo-Torso killer."

"Does Corliss have a motive to kill this guy?"

"Aside from the power and prestige of the presidency of the American Railroad History Preservation Society?"

"Don't laugh. Men have killed for a lot less."

A shudder ran through her. "I'm not laughing."

Frank shook his head, the bright halogen beams glinting off his sandy blond hair. "I'll admit that if that's a coincidence, it's an uncomfortable one. But here's what I'm thinking: This guy's unmarried, no family, not many friends, and Kim did occasional hooking. What if Van Horn was one of her occasional clients?"

This seemed quite probable to Theresa. Her impression of Van Horn had been that he was a smug and stuffy man, probably quite lonely with no idea what to do about it. He might want a young girl to play the role of adoring student, or simply to be someone he could feel superior to, in order to be comfortable during their encounters. And he would have felt vastly superior to Kim Hammond. Theresa asked Frank, "So whoever killed Kim decided to kill her john as well? Is that the pool from which he's been culling his victims?"

"Happily for us, she did not seem to have a very prolific career."

"Would her mother know Kim's clients or friends? The junkie lived in the neighborhood. Peggy Hall worked up the street."

"I got the idea her mother preferred not to know much about Kim at all."

Theresa looked around again, the wind lifting the hair from her face. Van Horn must have spent a lot of time in this area, drawing trains, hanging out at the preservation society headquarters only a short walk up the river. And Kim lived by the West Side Market, not even three miles away. Their paths could have crossed. She didn't believe in coincidence, but . . . "There's something else, too." She explained how she had spoken with Edward Corliss not ninety seconds before seeing the killer by the platform. "He said he was on his boat."

"How did he sound?"

"Not like he was perched on a train platform juggling the phone, a naked dead man, and a bundle of clothing, that's for sure."

"I can't see a guy that old jumping from a train any-way, much less clutching a body."

"Watch who you're calling old. We're going to have to hold this scene, you know." She could never see a valid reason to search a crime scene in the dark. Even the brightest halogens could not substitute for daylight, and the deep shadows they created could do more harm than good.

"Of course. But for now, go home, get some sleep. We'll start again in the morning."

"Yeah."

"Oh, and"—he tossed one arm around her shoulders and brushed her temple with his lips—"happy birthday."

CHAPTER 38

FRIDAY, SEPTEMBER 10
PRESENT DAY

Theresa drove home, intending only to shower, change into dry clothes, arm herself with every caffeinated drink in her fridge, and go back to the lab. When she pulled into her own driveway with almost no gas in the tank and rumblings in her stomach, it occurred to her that she should have at least brought a piece of her birthday cake home. It would have hit the spot right then and perhaps she would have had some energy to deal with whoever had invaded her home in her absence.

Her garage door stood open and light glowed from behind the ill-fitting door into the house. She really would have to get that fixed. Perhaps even start locking it.

Not that she expected a burglar or assassin. Such stealthy types would hardly drive a flashy sports car, or park it in front of the home they were attacking. Perhaps—her heart leapt at the idea—Rachael had gotten a ride home from college. Though who did she know who could afford such a car, and surely she would not go on a trip through several counties with a boy she had just met? Unless it was a girl, a fellow student who had borrowed her parents' car—

Theresa turned the knob and entered her kitchen.

Chris Cavanaugh, the police department's star hostage negotiator, sat at her table with a bottle of something in an ice-filled steel chiller and several open manila files that did not belong to her. He glanced up from his writing as she walked in. Apparently he'd been catching up on his paperwork as he waited.

Her watchdog, Harry, lay on the floor at his feet and opened one eye at her arrival. The young and normally unsociable cat perched on top of the bookcase behind Chris, as if she'd been reading over his shoulder.

"Happy birthday," he said.

"Chris." She shut the door behind her and strung her purse over the back of a chair. "What are you doing here?"

"I brought you a bottle of bubbly to celebrate." But he said this more with grim determination than cheer.

"Big help you are," she told her dog, who got up and pushed his snout into her thigh by way of apology.

"You shouldn't expect a lot out of a golden retriever. They're too friendly," Chris told her.

Exhaustion overtook her knees and she slid into the chair. "Chris. I haven't seen you in a month."

"You keep track? I'm flattered."

"I mean, I just don't get you. We've never slept together and probably never will. I'm not one hundred percent sure I even *like* you, and I can't imagine why you show any interest in me other than a desire to bed every last woman in Cleveland regardless of age, marital status—"

While she talked, he stood up and retrieved her only two matching wineglasses from the top shelf over the stove—choosing the correct cabinet immediately, which made her pause long enough for him to say: "That's just the birthday baggage seeping out. I keep talking to you because I like you, and you keep talking to me because I'm cute. You and me just get along." He set a glass in front of her, bent over, and kissed her lips, which, as always, made her blood churn and pitch in her veins.

He *was* cute.

He had good skin, she reflected as he unwound the wire frame that held the cork in place and peeled off the foil covering with a thumbnail. And the dimples, which made up for the receding hairline and the touch of smarminess. But could she *talk* to him? *There is no you and me,* she thought. "Christopher."

"I'm cuter than your friend, anyway," he added with that oddly flat affect.

"What friend? And if you ever break into my house again I'll have you arrested."

Pop!

"Theresa, while I admit to feeling a steady and magnetic attraction for you, I would never stoop to a felony to get your attention. Your friend let me in."

Her heart began to pound again.

He poured the clear and bubbly liquid into her glass. "Nice boy. Young for you, I would think, and without much fashion sense. He's upstairs working on your computer. Apparently you need virus protection."

She stood. "I need protection, all right. *Jablonski!*"

Her voice should have split the floor above her to let him fall through it, but the house remained silent for a shocked second or two before a slight creak sounded from the office room above.

"*Jablonski!*"

Steps pounded across the upstairs hallway and down

the stairs. The reporter trotted into the kitchen and tried for a sheepish grin.

"Why did you break into my house?"

"I'm sorry to borrow your computer, but I had to get tonight's murder in a half hour ago for tomorrow's edition—"

"What are you doing in my house? On my *computer*?" She turned to Chris. "I can't believe you let him browse through my computer."

"He was here when I arrived." The negotiator defended himself while filling his own glass. "And I'm hardly in a position to refuse other men access to you."

"You know why? Because we hardly know each other, that's why!"

"A situation"—he sipped—"I came here to remedy."

She whirled on the young man again. "Jablonski!"

"I didn't break in."

"I'm sure I didn't leave my home unlocked."

"Um, no. Not exactly." She glowered with what felt like nuclear strength until he added, "I guessed the code for your garage door opener. It's your birthday, which is not the best code for you to use, you know, for that reason alone."

"How did you know my birthday?" She turned to Chris as if this might have been some sort of conspiracy, but he threw up his hands to proclaim his innocence.

"I'm a reporter. I have my ways." Jablonski attempted the rakish grin, but the look on her face must have convinced him that it wouldn't work this time. "I went to the scene but your cops wouldn't let me in. Your cousin threatened to arrest me if I tried. He has a real attitude, by the way."

"You have not yet *seen* an attitude." Then she added, "You were at the train yard? I didn't see you."

"I knew he'd come there to re-create the Tattooed Man. I'd have been there much earlier but a tractor-trailer overturned and the turnpike became a parking lot west of Streetsboro . . . anyway, I saw *you,* with the gloves and the camera and the evidence. You're a formidable woman in your element, you know that?"

He looked at her with soft brown eyes full of admiration that normally would have melted her on the spot, but today the idea that she had been flanked by two men who felt free to invade her space at will simply because they were handsome irritated her to no end. "Both of you need to leave now."

"But—" Chris protested.

"But," Jablonski said, "I went to New Castle!"

She should not have been swayed. Finding unexpected people in her home had startled her, particularly unexpected men with whom she did not have a blood tie. But . . . "And?"

"I think I know who the killer is."

"The Torso murderer, or the current one?"

"Both."

Her eyes narrowed. Jablonski obviously found the mores of polite society quite negotiable. But on the other hand, he might have something interesting to say.

"All right," she said at last. "Look in the cabinet over the stove and find a glass that isn't chipped."

"So," Jablonski said, once he sat at the table and plucked the champagne from Chris's ice bucket, "I drove to New Castle, Pennsylvania. It took me—could your boss maybe toss me some reimbursements to cover, like, my gas? Maybe?"

"No." Theresa sipped the bubbly liquid, which was not her favorite. Champagne in general had too many calories and not enough alcohol to suit her.

"The print media deserves the support of its community," he repeated like a mantra.

"I agree, but it's a police department investigation."

"I'll ask your cousin then."

She snorted. The boy did not understand government budgets.

Chris said nothing, with an expression that came dangerously close to pouting. Theresa began to feel glad Jablonski had come, if only to throw a wrench in Chris's suave plans.

"So, New Castle is kind of interesting. It started because some guy went out there to double-check surveys of land that the government donated to Revolutionary War veterans. He found that, oops, they screwed up and left out fifty acres. So this surveyor figures, *No one's going to come looking for these fifty acres, I might as well help myself,* and laid out his own little city."

"When was that?" Theresa asked.

"Seventeen ninety-eight."

"Very interesting. What did you find out about the 1920s and '30s?"

"It's also the hot dog capital of the world."

"Uh-huh."

"Really?" Chris asked. "Why?"

Trust a man to perk up at the mention of food.

Harry caught the discussion of dogs and laid his head on the young man's thigh, glancing upward with imploring eyes until he got petted. "Something about Greek immigrants making chili dogs. I never really thought of chili dogs as Greek food, myself."

Theresa stopped sipping. "Did you find out anything relevant to the building at 4950 Pullman?"

"I think so. This swamp where all the dead bodies turned up is almost directly south of the city of New

Castle, toward Pittsburgh, by a junction where all the railroads come together at a large station. And this swamp, well . . . it's a swamp, not much there. So then I went to the historical society and found the city directories for 1925 through 1935, and looked for the names of the 4950 Pullman tenants."

"I thought your victim died in 1936," Chris said to Theresa.

"He did, but the murders in New Castle began in 1923 and continued off and on until 1941."

"Why'd he stop?" Chris wondered. "World War II? Was the guy drafted?"

"Or the government protected the railroads so well that security got too tight for him to operate."

Jablonski sipped the champagne and gave Chris Cavanaugh an up-from-under glance. Chris's shoulder shifted like lava welling up from a dormant volcano. "I didn't find any mention of Corliss—well, actually I found two Corlisses, but they were residential addresses for a John and a Henry, I think, and no business listings."

"And the nutritionist?"

"I'm *getting* to that." Clearly Jablonski wanted to tell his story his way, so she listened. "I found a Dr. Odessa listed under physicians, without a first name noted. Then I tried business listings. No individual practice, but in a section for hospital staff I found a Dr. Odessa at the Shenango Valley Hospital from 1926 through 1930. Still no first name and he disappears after 1930."

"Specialty?"

"Anesthesia."

Theresa pondered this, twirling the stem of the glass between her fingers. "That's interesting."

"Why?" Chris asked.

"It could be a different Dr. Odessa, of course. But our Dr. Louis knew how to slip young Irene a mickey, and if he had made a habit of using his wares on female patients he might have been run out of town on a—well, on a rail."

"A mickey?" Chris asked.

But Jablonski ran with it.

"So he moves to a new city and a new job."

"He stays off hospital staff and doesn't have a partner, so there's no one to monitor his activities."

"And you two think this guy is the Torso killer?" Chris asked, resting his elbow on the pile of paperwork he'd brought with him.

"Yes," Jablonski said. "Maybe."

"Not necessarily," Theresa said. "The Torso killer killed many more young men than women, and none of them teenagers. On the other hand Odessa may have had access to the room in 4950 Pullman where we found James Miller's body, so we can't eliminate him."

"This killer is amazing, really," Jablonski said with that now-familiar glow of enthusiasm for the subject. "Going back and forth between the two cities, lopping off heads, never getting caught by either police department."

"He's not that amazing," Theresa said with annoyance. "Communication then was not what it is now, and forensics was severely limited."

"But they connected the New Castle cases after the sixth or seventh murder, right? So he killed one after another in two different locations, and they still never caught him."

"The New Castle murders weren't that steady. There were gaps—I have a chart of it around here. Hang on a second."

Theresa went up her steps two at a time and retrieved a legal pad from the desk in her small home office. She bumped the computer mouse as she did so, and her annoyance increased as she saw that Brandon had left a Web page open. A picture of one of the Torso's victims appeared, the one known only as the Tattooed Man. Jablonski had been doing research as he waited for her. She moved the cursor to the X in the upper right-hand corner and then hesitated. They might want to use the PC to look up some piece of information, so she figured she might as well leave it on.

Her gaze fell to the text on the page. She had assumed it to be a factual history of the murders, but it seemed to be one person's fantasy about the case from the killer's point of view. Certain words jumped out at her, with a heavy emphasis on the sexual aspects of the killing.

She minimized the page, deciding to come back and check the history of Jablonski's time on her computer after the two men left.

She returned to the table. "The New Castle murders began in 1923, with three bodies found that year and two in the following year, mostly skeletons. Then nothing until 1936. That's a thirteen-year gap."

Jablonski said, "Maybe he went to other cities. Like here."

"One skeleton turned up in Youngstown in 1939, which is also on the rail route from New Castle to Cleveland. But nothing else."

"That we know of," Chris said. "As you pointed out, communication was not what it is now."

"But the Cleveland cops would have been watching for similar cases, especially after connecting with the New Castle bodies. I'm sure they would have found any similar murders that were out there to find."

"How did he go back and forth without anyone figuring out that there's something strange about the dude?" Jablonski wondered aloud.

"Because a whole lot more people rode passenger

trains then than now, and, if my theory is correct and he worked on the railroad, then he wouldn't have been noticed under any circumstances. Besides, there's really only one New Castle murder that occurred while the Cleveland murders were going on, and that was in 1936."

"You think he moved to Cleveland from New Castle and then moved back again?" Chris asked. "Or he did the 1936 case during, what, a visit to the dear old homestead?"

"Could be. Or he traveled between the cities every week for twenty years, and simply went in streaks as to where he preferred to pick his victims. Who knows?"

The cat came down from the bookshelf and jumped up on Jablonski's lap, swatting the dog's nose until he conceded petting privileges and moved on to the next man. Jablonski sniffed at his glass again. "Hardly Dom Pérignon, is it?"

For a rare moment, the silver-tongued hostage negotiator remained speechless, though his eyes spoke volumes.

"Anyway, then I looked for the other names I had. I got nothing on the medium, Morelli. But get this . . ." He paused, watching as both of them waited for him. Theresa allowed him his moment of drama. "I did find one of the architects' names. Richard O'Reilly."

"Huh," she said.

"He had an office in the center of town, but his residence listing was way down on Route 18, almost to Mahoningtown."

She stared at him with what had to be a blank expression.

"Just north of the murder swamp, in other words."

"Now that *is* interesting."

Chris said, "In cop circles, that's what we call suspicious."

"Richard O'Reilly is not listed after 1933. Actually there were two other Richard O'Reillys there during that time, but their addresses don't change and they were still listed in the city directory in 1935, when the architect guy we're interested in was living in Cleveland and working at 4950 Pullman."

Theresa nodded. "I don't know what, if anything, it proves, but it certainly is interesting."

The young man beamed, but not with pride—something more reminiscent of a cat who had recently made the acquaintance of a canary. "I'm not done."

He waited so long this time that her patience eroded. "*What?*"

"The Lawrence County Historical Society—that's where New Castle is, Lawrence County—is housed in a mansion built in 1904 for a tin plate magnate. I'm not sure what tin plates are, actually, but I know what *magnate* means. That means he had a lot of money."

"Uh-huh," she said, prompting him.

"This magnate's name was George Greer."

"Uh-huh."

Jablonski peered at her. "Greer."

"Uh—*oh.*"

"What?" Chris asked. "Greer who?"

Theresa said, "As in Councilman Greer. The councilman who's so hot on having 4950 Pullman razed to the ground."

"Maybe to cover up an old family secret." Jablonski nodded his head and topped it off by swigging champagne with a theatrical flourish, though he ruined the effect by coughing afterward.

"And maybe," Theresa said, "Greer is simply a common name. We haven't come across anyone named Greer in connection to the building."

"Other than the councilman."

"He just wants to collect his fee for building the recycling plant." His fear at the crime scene had been real, and he couldn't possibly have gotten from the RTA station onto that train with the victim in time to encounter her by the tracks. Not possibly . . . "Did you see him there?"

Jablonski drained his glass. "Who?"

She explained her encounter with the councilman.

"He wasn't in the crowd outside the tape when I arrived," Jablonski said insistently. "I milled through everyone present, trying to get tidbits and reactions. If he'd been there I would have interviewed him."

No, she thought, *impossible.* "Feel free to work on that angle, Jablonski, because my boss is already unhappy with me for getting on Greer's sh—um, list."

"But it would make sense, wouldn't it? Everyone always said the killer came from a wealthy family that covered up any clues to his guilt, and those politico types have usually been in that line of work for generations—"

"*Everyone* also said he had to have had medical training in order to dismember his victims, and I'm not one hundred percent down with that theory, either. People said a lot of things. They always do in unsolved cases."

"But—"

The door to the garage opened suddenly, letting in the crisp fall air and Rachael, who carried a stack of books, a purse in the shape of Hello Kitty, a backpack, a bottle of water, and a duffel bag approximately as large as her torso slung across her back. "Hi, Mom. I wondered whose car that was—"

"*Honey!*"

Harry barked in excitement. Even the cat leapt from Jablonski's lap in welcome.

And then her daughter, who had apparently not been murdered, been raped, flunked out, or been found dead in a ditch somewhere after a bad car accident, was in Theresa's arms. "Did Tonya give you a ride? Are you hungry? Did you eat dinner? How are your classes? Do you like your teachers? What about your roommate?"

"I see you have company," Rachael said as she allowed her mother to divest her of the heavy accoutrements. "Are you celebrating your birthday?"

"Hi, Rachael," Chris Cavanaugh said, shooting a triumphant look at Jablonski.

"Hi, Chris."

The duffel bag thudded to the floor. "No, we were talking about a case. You know Chris, and this is Brandon Jablonski, he's a newspaper researcher. Thank you for the information, Mr. Jablonski, but you both have to leave now."

The young man didn't notice Chris's smugness or Theresa's hint, too busy taking in every inch of Theresa's daughter until his mouth gaped open a bit. "Wow."

"Especially you," Theresa added.

SATURDAY, SEPTEMBER 11
PRESENT DAY

Theresa bustled off to work bright and early on Saturday morning, intending to finish her examination of William Van Horn and his bloody clothing and get home before Rachael rolled out of bed. A month at college and still in teenager mode—without any classes to attend, her daughter would not rise before lunchtime.

A stern look combined with a mental pat on the head for his good work in New Castle had gotten Jablonski to shuffle out of her home without much difficulty, though she locked every door and window behind him. Chris Cavanaugh left only after a firm and excellent kiss in her cold garage, so that she went to bed flush with happiness, flattered at his continued (though sporadic) interest—*always date interesting men*—but mostly glad that her daughter had returned home safely and voluntarily.

Even the half-rotten-groceries smell that had long since permeated every ceramic tile in the old building seemed to greet her like a close friend as she waved to the deskman and plucked Van Horn's ripped pants and shirt from the drying rack. She poked her head into the autopsy room, where Christine Johnson met her with a baleful expression and asked, "Do I have you to thank for this?"

"Yeah, I thought it might save you some time if I started cutting at the scene."

The pretty doctor laughed, then contradicted that by saying: "You are so not funny, missy. I heard you met him the day before he turned up like this. Is that true?"

Theresa said yes. It still felt odd to her. She felt as if she should call Edward Corliss to express her condolences but didn't know quite what to say. *I'm sorry the friend you introduced me to was murdered by a modern-day Torso killer. Which wouldn't be you, would it, by the way?*

She gathered what information she could from Christine and then went into the amphitheater to spread out the khaki pants. The pair of Burberrys was torn at the back; the pants found with one of the original victims, known only as the Tattooed Man, had also been described as ripped in the back. As in 1936, a white men's handkerchief nestled in the rear pocket. She put that aside without unfolding it.

After noting the size, condition, staining, and label of the pants, she got out the 3M packaging tape and eight-and-a-half-by-eleven sheets of clear acetate paper and "taped" the front and back, inside and out, for hairs and fibers. As always, even a clean-looking piece of clothing gave up a myriad of loose trace evidence. A few black fibers, pieces of dead grass, and a dog hair.

She folded the pants—stiffened with blood—loosely and stuffed them into a paper bag. On a fresh, smaller piece of paper, she unfolded the clean handkerchief that had been found in the back pocket. A single bloodstain marred its snow-white material. She opened it carefully, with a magnifying lamp hovering above. She taped both sides and smoothed the tape onto the acetate, then moved the handkerchief to its own brown bag.

The tapings showed only minute particles of lint, except for one dark fiber and three white specks. They seemed to be round and flat. She would have to run them through the FTIR to be sure, but they seemed very similar to the ones found on Kim Hammond.

Theresa covered the table with a fresh piece of brown paper from the large roll mounted at the end and repeated the process with the shirt. The shirt did not offer any new insights, only a few splotches of blood, most likely transfer from the severed head. No particular staining on the shoulders, which supported her theory that the clothing had been removed prior to the decapitation.

When she had finished taping the shirt, she covered the table with yet another fresh piece of paper and placed the shirt on the upper half and the pants on the lower half, both facing upward. Then she pulled out the loafers and held them in her hands. Dirt, dead grass, and a few pieces of fine gravel had been wedged into the treads.

Frank appeared in the doorway. "Mornin', cuz. I finished your birthday cake for breakfast. Hope you don't mind."

"Not at all—what, you stayed at your mother's last night?"

"I don't know about *stayed*. Stopped in for a shower and a change of clothes."

Theresa felt guilty. She should have spent a sleepless night working on the case, too, but motherhood had interfered. "But why—"

"A certain young lady didn't take our breakup well

and tends to call and pound on my door at odd hours. It's not worth changing my number—she'll get over it before long."

"*Frank*." Sometimes she wondered where his restlessness came from. No one else in the family was like that. He hadn't learned it from his father—whatever bad habits his father may have had, philandering wasn't one of them. Theresa sighed and didn't bother to tell him that it was high time he grew up and started dating nice, sensible women like Angela Sanchez. The tone of her one word said it all.

He ignored both her tone and her meaning. "What do we have so far?"

"Christine said his coronary arteries would have taken him out in a few more years if someone hadn't cut his head off."

"Is he missing any sections of neck, by the way?"

"Nope. Both halves fit perfectly. Christine also thinks there's a blunt force injury on the back of the head, and no defensive wounds. Not even a bruise."

"So the killer got up close without much difficulty. Like it was someone he knew."

"He seemed a bit hard of hearing when I met him. It might not have been difficult to sneak up on him. So then the killer takes him to the train, undresses him en route, and jumps off for the decapitation."

"Why undress him on the train? How do you know that?"

"Because there's no staining on the shirt that would indicate he had it on at the time of the decapitation, no staining on the shoulders. It seemed to me there should have been more blood at the scene, so maybe he killed Van Horn by slitting his throat somewhere else, but there's no spray or flow down the front of his shirt. No, he undressed him first to save time, then killed him at the scene because that's how the Torso killer did it. He brought a live victim to that valley, just to slaughter him right at our feet."

"Don't take this personally, Tess."

She looked at him as if he'd begun speaking Swahili. "How am I *not* supposed to take this personally? Aren't you?"

He didn't confess what she knew he believed—*It's different for me, I'm a cop*—and instead asked, "Did you get any sleep last night?"

"Did you?" she shot back. "What about his house?"

"Shipshape and buttoned up. The man was a neat freak of the highest caliber, and you were right, he had pretty much no life at all outside the preservation society. His datebook had their official doings written in for the next six months and nothing else. No lunch dates, no business meetings. Not even a doctor's appointment."

"Unless he kept two. One for society business, and another for personal appointments."

"Good thought, cuz. But we didn't find a second one and no sign of someone else rifling through his possessions. Besides, the landlady confirmed his loner status. Their lobby is locked and only residents can enter. Of course someone could have buzzed in a delivery boy or the killer could have ducked in behind a tenant. Sanchez has a couple of uniformed guys and they're canvassing the neighbors now. And the scene is still secure—we had to let the rapids start up again, but aside from that—so you can see it in the daylight. Though the two on duty there were going to do a second search as soon as the sun came up."

"Then I don't really need to go, do I?"

He raised one eyebrow. "Do you?"

"I can't see why," she thought out loud, trying to convince herself more than him, or perhaps the ghost of their dead grandfather. Family vs. job she could decide easily. But family vs. family? "I won't see anything the cops won't. I don't have X-ray vision."

"No. But you met the victim."

With a sinking feeling she knew that to be true. She might see the significance in an item the cop with no knowledge of William Van Horn's personality or habits might dismiss. What little she knew about the man was still more than nothing. "All right. I'll go there on my way home."

"Besides, what else do you have to do?"

As she taped the unremarkable turquoise shirt she told him Rachael had come home for the weekend in honor of her birthday. Frank sympathized but did not discourage her from revisiting the crime scene. The department did not waste two cops guarding a hunk of land lightly. "How does it feel to be over the hill?"

"Terrific. Just great. Two new wrinkles just this morning." Theresa sealed all the bags of clothing with red tape, scribbled her initials, and locked them all in the storage room in record time. Then she collected her sheets of acetate and written report and nudged her cousin, who dozed in one of the many seats in the old amphitheater. "Why don't you go home and get some sleep?" she told him. "I'll call you if I find anything significant."

"I was hoping you'd have some coffee. Then I have to start interviewing Van Horn's acquaintances, if Sanchez finds any worth talking to."

"Come along, then, and we'll forge an assault on the Braun." They trudged up the three flights of stairs to the trace evidence lab.

Peace and quiet reigned there. Usually Theresa enjoyed her assigned Saturday mornings at the lab—giving up part of the weekend was worth it for the uninterrupted time. But this Saturday she would have preferred to be at home, planning breakfast.

The fibers trapped in the tape's adhesive appeared to be the usual conglomeration of debris every person carried around with them: lint, khaki-colored and turquoise-colored fibers almost certainly from the clothing items themselves (though she would confirm that), and pieces of vegetation. But she also found a black fiber on the trousers and made a mental bet that it would match the fibers found on Richard Dunlop, one of the two men from the side of the hill, and the fiber from the bottom of the crate that held the body parts of Peggy Hall. She cleaned this new fiber with xylene to remove all traces of the tape's adhesive and folded it into a piece of glassine paper to wait for the FTIR. She cleaned the yellow dog hair and mounted that on a glass slide. Organic materials—like hairs and natural fibers—were not uniform enough to yield a reliable spectrum on the FTIR. She would have to do a microscopic examination on the hair, and should they find a dog to compare, the root could be tested for the animal's DNA.

The front of the shirt had not yielded much. But the back of it gave her another dog hair and other animal hairs, too fine and black to belong to the yellow dog, and also a number of white cotton fibers. Terrific. The killer had worn the one fiber so ubiquitous in the world it was considered to have no forensic value whatsoever. White cotton also had other advantages. Any bloodstains would be easy to bleach from white cotton, at least to the point where DNA would be unusable. As a natural fiber it would burn clean, if he chose to go that route, and not leave the gloppy mess that synthetic fibers could. He could bury it and the fibers would disintegrate completely within a few years, provided the killer felt comfortable waiting that long.

The soles of the shoes had two blue, trilobal fibers, and as her cousin returned with a steaming cup she asked him how Van Horn's apartment had been decorated.

"Heavy, ugly curtains; a decent leather sofa; and blue carpeting that should have been replaced twenty years ago."

"I'll need a sample of that."

"Gotcha." He yawned and propped his feet up on the edge of her worktable. If she didn't know better, she might have thought her cousin was now waiting around to talk about their respective relationships with their grandfather and any inequities in same. But she knew better. Frank never talked about his feelings. Frank didn't admit he even *had* feelings.

She didn't do much of that herself.

No, he hung around for the coffee and a few moments of peace, period.

"Did he have any pets?" she asked.

"Van Horn? Not so much as a goldfish. No animal lover he—except for birds, he had pictures of birds, but nothing live. I expect he didn't want the place messed up."

One of the white specks from the handkerchief flattened easily and stuck to the salt window after only a few seconds of fiddling. Once the stage had been moved so that the light beam could pass through the material, the spectrum popped up on the computer screen. Polyethylene and some titanium dioxide to make it extra white. But why the shape?

Frank sniffed the air. "I smell something musty. Is the stuff from the dead cop up here?"

Theresa allowed that James Miller's notebook lay humidifying in the fume hood. Frank's curiosity must have overcome his weariness because he wandered over to the hood and switched on the light.

Theresa called up the spectrum for the white flecks she had found on Kim. No surprise there. "Hey," she said.

"Hey!" Frank said.

"The white flecks I found on Kim Hammond are identical to the white flecks I found in Van Horn's handkerchief."

"This notebook has the same handwriting as the one in Kim Hammond's apartment."

They stared at each other over the top of her microscope.

"What?"

"*What?*"

Frank said, "When we searched her belongings, she had a little notebook like this one with the same handwriting. Her mother said it belonged to Kim's father."

"James Miller couldn't have been Kim's *father*." Theresa felt silly even thinking such a thing. "But—"

"He could have been her grandfather, or great-grandfather, or whatever. I've got to go talk to her mother again. What did you say about white somethings?"

Theresa explained about the specks found stuck to the paint in Kim's hair. "They're identical to the ones I just found in Van Horn's handkerchief. Granted, there's not a lot to their composition—polyethylene and titanium dioxide and a few trace elements—but they're identical."

"So she *was* the Lady of the Lake."

"This guy began his copycat spree with James Miller's granddaughter? *How?*"

"That's what I'm going to find out." Her cousin no longer seemed a bit tired. Coffee forgotten, he pulled on a glove, snatched up the notebook, and absently planted a kiss on her cheek before barreling out the door.

"You can't take that without—" She heard the stairwell door open. He hadn't wanted to wait for the creak-

ing elevator or to sign the property form to check out
the notebook. She laughed in his wake but felt fairly
reenergized herself. At least Kim Hammond had been
linked—and how—which meant they had only one
crazed decapitating murderer preying on the citizens of
Cleveland instead of two.

This man had killed five people in as many days and
had probably already abducted the next young man in
the series. Yet like the original Torso killer, he remained
a ghost.

But at the same time, all she wanted to do was go
home. At only ten o'clock she had more or less completed all reasonable work on William Van Horn. She
had only to stop by the crime scene on her way home and
then call her cousin to release the patrol officers. Every
cop in the city would be working on this case. Surely
they could spare her long enough for her to make her
only child some breakfast.

With a pang she reminded herself that both James
Miller and his only descendant had been wiped from
the earth.

She analyzed the fibers found on Van Horn. The blue
carpet fibers were made of polyester, and the black nylon fiber matched the ones found on Kim and Richard
Dunlop. The khaki and turquoise cotton fibers could not
be assayed on the FTIR, of course, but a microscopic
comparison with sample fibers from Van Horn's shirt
and pants indicated a common origin.

This left only the animal hairs, and she plunked the
dog hair down on the microscope stage. She could be
out of there in twenty minutes. Fifteen minutes to drive
to the crime scene, maybe ten given the light weekend
traffic . . . though she still wanted to pay Edward Corliss
a visit to express her condolences, since he had intro-

duced her to the victim and all, but that could wait until Monday. A phone call would do.

She had not found any animal hairs on Kim, but then they had never found Kim's clothing. The hairs would stick to cloth much more easily than to skin; she knew that from constantly picking the fine wisps off her own clothes. Animal fur was insidious, and Theresa often swore that after the current set she would never get another cat or dog, no matter how adorable, soft, or funny they were.

She kept a reference library of animal hairs mounted on glass slides in an undersize metal filing cabinet designed for exactly that purpose, and she began to put one slide after another on the stage opposite the hairs found on Van Horn. With the comparison microscope she could view both slides at once.

The yellow dog hair reminded her of a retriever like her own, and using the reference slide for comparison she decided that the killer had one as well.

Exactly like hers. She had used Harry's fur for her reference library, and the dog hair on Van Horn appeared to be identical. Of course, it didn't mean much—all golden retrievers looked pretty much the same, didn't they?

But Harry was not purebred. In fact, Harry had belonged to Theresa's deceased fiancé and she had no idea of his actual ancestry, except that he had come from a pound and his fur had always seemed darker than the classic gold of that type of dog.

She wrote *One dog hair, app. gold retriever* into her notebook and went on to the finer, dark hairs. They were nothing like Harry's, of that she felt certain.

The thicker guard hairs of cats and dogs were quite easy to tell apart by the distinct roots. The roots of dog hairs ended in a smooth spade shape, while the cat's ended in an uncharacteristically awkward mess of tendrils. But the thinner undercoat or fur hairs, which kept the animals insulated, were not so easily separated. Often the roots appeared to be a cross between the two.

The medulla is a channel running through the center of the hair. It could be clear, if filled with cells, or black if hollow. The medulla in these three hairs appeared as a series of black bubbles, known as a string-of-pearls medulla, usually found in cats. The overlapping scales making up the outer cuticle were long and thin, or spinous, which indicated a cat. She got out her cat fur slides.

The hairs were solid black, with no coloration or banding to give any indication of breed. So she really could not consider it significant that the hairs were alike in every way to those of her own cat.

Anubis, named for the stern-faced Egyptian god, had been given to her by a neighbor of her cousin's. He had been an only child, the offspring of a gray Persian mother and a father who snuck into the yard one night under cover of darkness and never returned. This made him fairly unique, and not only in his own mind.

The hairs matched perfectly, something she would never say in court. No, in court she would say that "the microscopic characteristics of both sets of hairs are such that they could have had a common origin." Right after she explained how she contaminated a victim's clothing.

Theresa had no illusions about her ability to do just that. Animal fur got everywhere, and she felt sure it could be found on every item of clothing she owned if she only looked hard enough. But she had worn a disposable lab coat when examining the clothing downstairs, and at the crime scene . . . though the cuffs of her long-sleeved T-shirt peeked out from the rolled-up ends of the Tyvek sleeves. Could she have brushed those cuffs to the shirt and pants as she moved them around?

Had she brushed against Van Horn at the preservation society headquarters? No, she'd only touched his hand. Besides, he had been wearing dark pants and a white shirt at the time, so he must have changed clothes later in the day. Of course the hairs could have transferred from the first set of clothes when he picked up the second. They could have clung to the chair she sat in when speaking with Edward Corliss, and then Van Horn sat there later and picked them up. The chairs were hard wood, no upholstery, which made it unlikely but not impossible. But four hairs?

Her heart began to beat faster and she told it not to. She had no reason to be upset. Golden retriever mixes and black cats were hardly uncommon in the Cleveland area. She had no reason to believe that these particular hairs came from her two particular animals. Perhaps Van Horn's landlady also happened to have a golden retriever mix and a black, half-Persian cat. Last night the woman had spoken to the victim. Perhaps she and Van Horn were more than friends.

And perhaps Theresa needed to be a whole lot more careful about how she handled evidence. Any defense attorney in the city would jump at the chance to point *that* out in court. *Isn't it true, Ms. MacLean, that you have a letter of reprimand in your personnel file for contaminating evidence?. . .*

What to do now? She could note the hairs and their description and leave it at that. She could note the hairs and add "possible examiner contamination" and hope that no one would ever delve deeply enough into the case to notice. Or she could tell somebody. This would invite at best a tongue-lashing from Leo, or at worst some sort of disciplinary procedure that he would probably make up as he went along and might involve everything from remedial training to suspension. And with Rachael in college, Theresa couldn't afford to lose even a few pennies from her paycheck.

Didn't matter. She'd have to inform her supervisor, and the sooner the better. In any sort of law enforcement position, the cover-up always screwed you worse than the actual crime.

Theresa got her purse from her desk, locked up the lab, and headed for the crime scene.

CHAPTER 40

SATURDAY, SEPTEMBER 11
PRESENT DAY

"I don't get it," Angela Sanchez said to her partner as they climbed the steps at Riverview Towers once more. As if she had read his mind at some point during their earlier trip, she had made him go first so he could not observe the tilt of her hips as they ascended. It made the journey less interesting to Frank. On the other hand, the hope remained that she might be observing *his* rear in motion, and the thought buoyed him through the last two turns. He needed a boost after being up all night.

She went on. "You really think Kim Hammond had James Miller's notebooks?"

"Yep." Short sentences allowed him to hide the pants of breath. Theresa was right, he should stop smoking.

"How?"

He came to their destination and knocked. "That's what we're here to find out. Mrs. Hammond?"

He had called ahead to be sure she would be at home, and she answered the door promptly. Nothing had changed since their last visit, except the woman's clothing. The dingy windows, the smell of yesterday's coffee, all Kim's worldly possessions kept in a few shoeboxes under the futon. Frank sighed in relief at the sight of them, having worried that Mrs. Hammond might throw them out. She didn't seem too sentimental to him. Grieving, but not sentimental.

"We need to go through Kim's things again," he told her mother, and went to his knees on the floor, risking the fleas and who knew what else living in the carpet fibers.

"Do you know who killed her?"

"Not yet."

Mrs. Hammond sat on the plaid sofa. "But you're still working on it."

"That's why we're here."

"Good," Kim's mother said.

Frank found the notebook exactly as he'd left it, next to the eagle medal on the faded ribbon. A momentary curiosity won out and he held up the medal. "What is this?"

"That belonged to Kim's father."

"And he left when she was in junior high?"

"No, that was her stepfather."

Aha, Frank thought. That was why Dr. Christine had trouble finding the birth certificate—because Kim hadn't been born with the name Hammond. "Mr. Hammond was her stepfather?"

The woman nodded without any great interest. "Eladio married me and adopted her when she was ten. I had high hopes. I think we both did, Kim and I. But he ran out on us a few years later, just like my first husband. I really know how to pick 'em."

"And your first husband's name?"

"John Miller."

Even though he'd been expecting it, the news shot through Frank like an electrical charge. This, he knew, was where the case would all come together. "And John Miller's father's name?"

She rubbed her eyes. "Um—another *J.* Jake . . . no, James. Jim."

"James Miller."

"Yeah. I guess he'd be Kim's grandfather. That medal belonged to him. He was in World War I."

"In the Marines? It's a Distinguished Service Cross."

"I guess." Now she peered at him. "Why?"

"Did this notebook come from James Miller, too?"

"Yeah. Lord knows why Johnny kept it. Or why I gave it to Kim, or why *she* kept it. Probably because when you've got nothing else . . ." She stood up and went to the kitchenette, pouring a cup of too-strong-smelling coffee into a cup without milk or sugar.

"Did you ever meet your father-in-law?" Sanchez asked.

The woman snorted. "Of course not. He ran out on Johnny and his mother before Johnny could even walk. He left that woman in the middle of the Depression. Men couldn't even *buy* a job then, much less a woman. She—I don't know how she survived. Johnny wouldn't go into details."

"What else did he tell you about his father?"

She leaned against the wall as she spoke, as if she no longer had the strength to remain upright. "Nothing, other than he hated the guy with a passion."

"But he kept his notebooks?"

"Like I said, when you've got nothing else . . . Johnny figured he would have had an okay life if his father had stuck around, if he had had enough to eat and a decent place to live. He could have at least finished high school. Instead he had to scrape by, stealing what he couldn't con people out of. I felt sorry for him, so, like an idiot, I married him." She finished her cup with one desperate gulp. "Again, I had high hopes. He was a lot older than me. I thought that would make him more stable. Hah! All that happened was he ran out on me and Kim before *she* could walk. Don't they say history repeats itself?"

History repeats itself.

Frank asked, "Where is Johnny now?"

"Dead. They found him in an alley off of East Seventy-first."

"When was that?"

"Hell, I don't remember. I think Kim had just turned five."

Eighteen years before. Frank turned this fact over in his mind as he got off his creaking knees and pulled up a wooden chair. "What did he die of?"

"Natural causes. My guess is he had a heart attack banging some hooker, but I hate to think that because it would mean he died happy. I never told Kim. . . . I mean, I told her he died of a heart attack, but not the circumstances. She had already started to ask if he would ever come back for us, and I didn't want her to spend her life waiting."

History repeats itself.

"Why?" Mrs. Hammond demanded again, sinking into the plaid sofa once again. "What does her grandfather's old things have to do with her getting killed?"

Frank and Angela Sanchez exchanged a glance, and she asked the question: "Did Kim mention a news story in which a body had been found in an old building off of Fifty-fifth, by any chance?"

The furrow between her eyes deepened with each question. "What?"

"The newspapers and TV news all reported—"

"Newspapers are one of those little luxuries I don't

have, and I never watch the news. Kim did, sometimes, but she never said nothing to me about some body. *Why?*"

"We found James Miller's body in a building at 4950 Pullman."

They let this sink in. It took some time. Frank had an image of her mind approaching the concept like a timid animal to a strange object, coming closer, then backing away to get another perspective, unsure whether this was something valuable, or dangerous, or simply irrelevant.

"Johnny's father? Damn . . . but what does that have to do with Kim?"

Frank said, "That's what we're trying to find out. She never mentioned it? Had she brought up her father in the last few days? Ask questions about him or her grandfather?"

"No. I'd remember. I don't think we've talked about Johnny in years. I tried not to bring him up. There were too many—what do you call it, parallels? All these things that seemed the same between their two lives, Kim and her father. I didn't want her to end up like him. Kim thought the same way Johnny did—that life had not been fair to her, so she deserved a break. I think it's the only thing she inherited, besides that medal and those notebooks."

"Notebooks, plural? How many were there?"

"Two."

"There's only one here now."

The crease between her eyes threatened to become permanent. "There were two."

Frank thumbed through the pages. The first date noted read May 5, 1935, and the last August 8 of the same year. The one in Theresa's lab began in April 1936. That left eight months. James Miller had made some notations during those eight months that made Kim Hammond think that she knew who killed him, and she had not shared this theory with her mother or her friend— meaning there was money involved, money that Kim didn't want to share.

"The last few days before she died, who did she talk to, visit, go hang out with?" He had asked that question before, but perhaps a memory had come back in the meantime.

"I don't know. I was at work."

"She didn't mention looking up any old friends—"

"I told her to stay away from her old friends. She was, too. Like I told you before, the only suggestion I have is that bastard down the hall."

"Okay." They would have to interview the drug dealer again for any hint of where Kim had been headed, what plans had revolved through her little mind. She had learned that her grandfather had died in the building at 4950 Pullman. She should have been happy that he had not run out on her father as all had supposed . . . but perhaps not. Perhaps that made the ruination of Johnny's life all the more poignant.

But it had not depressed Kim. It energized her. Why?

The building—

"Mrs. Hammond." His voice burst out so suddenly it startled him as well as the grieving woman. "You said Kim worked one summer at city hall?"

"Yes."

"Doing what?"

"Clerk-type stuff, I guess, for the zoning and planning office. Filing plans, typing up allotment forms."

"Did she stay in touch with any of her coworkers there?"

"Kim wasn't the staying-in-touch type," her mother said as if that were an endearing trait.

He tried to hone in by different means. "She was in

high school then? Did she get along with everyone in that office?"

Her brow smoothed out as she remembered a more hopeful time. "She was only seventeen, and they made quite a pet of her at first. Then she said the older ladies got snooty, which probably meant she had gotten on their nerves. But there was one girl she liked—just out of college and young, so they had more in common. But I don't know her name, if that's going to be your next question."

Frank smiled. "It was, yes. Please try to remember."

The woman tried, pressing her back into the sofa with her arms crossed. Sanchez raised an eyebrow at Frank but would wait until they left to ask why he asked.

"Sorry, I'm a total blank."

"That's all right. It was just a hunch."

"I remember she got pregnant just before the summer ended. I had hoped they might hire Kim to fill in during her maternity leave, but they didn't."

"That's helpful. Thank you." He stood up and gave her his card for the second time, asking her to call if she thought of anything else and telling her that they would be in the building for a while longer, reinterviewing her neighbors.

She pressed it into her palm and then crossed her arms again, balled fists underneath her armpits. "You really think Johnny's father's body turning up is the reason Kim got killed?"

"Mrs. Hammond," he confessed, "I don't know what else *to* think."

Theresa prodded a flattened McDonald's cup with her toe and decided it had been on the scene for years and was unlikely to have been on his body when it had been dumped. Besides, she couldn't see Van Horn eating in a McDonald's. John Q's, maybe.

Occasional bursts of sun made the buildings in the distance glitter as if studded by diamonds. The cries of birds and insects, one class of animal thinking about migration and the other about death, filled the air. A perfect day for a stroll by the railroad tracks, except she wouldn't have considered strolling here without some sort of escort—in this case one of the patrol officers guarding the scene—and she'd rather have been strolling through her kitchen, deciding what to cook to entice her teenager out of bed. Eleven o'clock. Rachael would still be asleep, unless Harry decided to wake her.

The patrol officers had already walked a grid through the area, so she really didn't need to do this. Surely they would have found anything of significance. She knew she should just tell them to release the scene and go home. Frank would let her know if any significant facts developed from the interviews, and she could use the time to figure out a way to tell Leo about contaminating the victim's clothing with her pets' hairs.

Yet she continued to walk from the pool of dried blood to the train track and back, widening the swath with each step. Perhaps the killer had dropped something. How she would know that something when she saw it became the question, so any item that had not yet become encrusted by rain-soaked dirt bore closer scrutiny. So far she had not found an object to match that description.

The patrol officer watched her from the concrete platform, bored in his little cage of yellow tape. She'd have to release the scene after she finished—she couldn't justify tying up a road officer because she wanted to go home to her daughter. And the railroad wanted their train back.

A dirty matchbook, a bundle of filthy yarn. She

walked on. The sun flowed through her hair to her scalp and she took off her sweater, tying it around her waist. The valley smelled of diesel fuel and dead leaves.

A broken plastic fork. A penny. A rumble sounded, and she looked up. The Red Line 11:08 chugged off to the west.

A used condom. A piece of surprisingly clean white paper.

She stepped carefully over a stand of dead goldenrod to pluck up a piece of torn paper. The piece had been torn from the upper left corner of an unlined spiral notebook but the black pencil used on the paper formed not words but a series of lines and dots, some very straight, some wavy, some forming another corner, the deep slashes against the white somehow reminiscent of—

She turned her face up to the train in front of her. The rear edge of the boxcar, with its small rung at the bottom and the coupling sticking out, matched the piece of drawing. Someone had been sketching a train.

She couldn't prove it without finding his sketch pad but would bet that Van Horn had been drawing one of his favorite items—a train—at some time in the previous day. Standing near the tracks, where a train rattling by would deaden the sound of someone approaching from behind, ready to bludgeon, catch, bundle into a waiting car. Perhaps the victim's hand clenched on his drawing, ripping the paper. Perhaps the notebook had been left behind at the site . . . by a train track. There were too many miles for herself or the officers to scour. She should start with the preservation headquarters, the most logical place for Van Horn to do his sketching.

SATURDAY, SEPTEMBER 11
PRESENT DAY

Frank knocked on the door. The Brookpark bungalow was neatly kept, with the grass trimmed and the leaves raked and only a few scattered toys to make it look homey. At least on the outside.

With Sanchez at his side, he knocked again, hoping the husband would not be at home. When he interviewed married women, in Frank's experience, husbands always took up too much time. They wanted to *know* everything. He would be the first to admit that men were, in general, paranoid. Maybe they'd learned to be while evading saber-toothed tigers or something.

The inner door swung inward, pulled by a short, slender woman with light brown hair and a chubby baby perched on one hip. She left the screen door in place. Behind her, a little boy as round with baby fat as his sibling peered at them with dark eyes, his hands reflexively clenching a Tonka truck. He must have been the pregnancy that engorged the woman while she worked with Kim Hammond at the zoning and planning office.

"Sonia Kettle?" Frank asked.

"Yes?"

They showed her their badges, told her their names, and said they were there to ask about Kim. That this did not seem to surprise her at all convinced Frank they were on the right track. She pushed the screen door open with her free hand and told them to come in.

There were more than a few scattered toys on the inside of the house. In fact, the living room seemed more like a well-scrubbed toy box than a place for adults. No husband emerged, though a motorcycle magazine and a pair of men's sunglasses implied that he did exist. Good thing, Frank thought, since Sonia Kettle appeared to have her hands full. As soon as they sat at the kitchen table, the baby started to squirm and the little boy plunked the Tonka on Frank's knee.

"I have a truck," he declared, as if daring Frank to deny it.

"That's great." *Now go away.*

"I read about it in the paper," Sonia said. "First about the body in the lake, and then the next day I caught a little paragraph somewhere about it being Kim. I couldn't believe it."

"You worked with her in the zoning and planning office?" Sanchez began.

"Yes. That was . . . geez, four, five years ago, I think, right before I had Brent. Kim was just a kid. So was I."

"The back goes up," Brent continued, demonstrating how the dumping part of his dump truck worked by unloading a Super Ball onto the oak table.

"I see," Frank said.

"I can put a motorcycle in it." The kid zipped off, and Frank wasted a moment hoping that the quest for a motorcycle suitable for demonstration would keep the tot busy for a while, but he returned before Sanchez could finish asking, "Had you seen her lately?"

"Yes. Isn't that why you're here?"

The baby screeched until Sonia relented and set her— her? the diaper had pink flowers on it, so probably—on the living room floor. The baby immediately made a bee-line back to the linoleum and her mother.

"Yes," the woman began. "She came to see me at work, last week. I'd wonder from time to time what happened to her, because she seemed a little wild to me back then."

"It's a spider motorcycle," Brent said.

Frank didn't recognize the term, until he glanced at the toy to see the Spider-Man logo on it. "That's nice."

The kid squinted at him. *That's nice* was not something men said, not even to a five-year-old. "Do you have any motorcycles?"

"Brent," his mother said, "Mommy is talking. Don't interrupt."

The boy shared a murderous look with his truck, then flounced off, nearly stepping on his baby sister on the way out. The sister reached Sonia, who plucked her up for deposit in a playpen in the living room. Brent beat her back to the table, however, with a plastic Sponge-Bob doll.

"He talks," the boy announced.

Great, Frank thought. *Another country heard from.* "Wild how, Sonia?"

"The drugs. The things she did with boys. The things she did with boys to pay for the drugs. I chalked some of it up to bravado, but most of it—most of it she didn't seem to be proud of. She wasn't bragging, just shooting the breeze, which struck me as sadder than any sob story she could have given me."

Brent pushed a button, and the toy uttered a comment Frank couldn't quite catch, not that he tried very hard. "Why did Kim come to see you last week?"

The baby began to protest.

"Just a visit, she said at first. She had been kicking around downtown, thought she'd come in and say hi."

The cops waited. SpongeBob made another pronouncement as Brent walked his bendy little feet across the table, nudging Frank's elbow.

"She seemed good. Relatively healthy; her eyes were clear. But she had that old look."

"Look?" Sanchez said, pressing.

"You can talk to him," Brent reminded Frank.

The baby wailed.

"Brent. Show SpongeBob to Bethie. Try to make her laugh. *Now*," she added in one of those iron tones that all mothers eventually learn. It worked on Brent. It would have worked on Frank if he'd thought she meant him.

With toys and babies momentarily quieted, Sonia Kettle made the most of her break. "Like she was up to something. When we worked together, I could always tell when she'd be about to hit me up for cigarettes or money or to help her cover up a long lunch hour. She'd get this glinting look in her eyes, suddenly be real interested in everything about you. And when she showed up last week, I wanted to think she'd grown up, got her life together, and that maybe I'd helped with that process in some small way. But she hadn't."

"What makes you say that?"

"Same thing, different day. She chatted, made a fuss over pictures of the kids, then asked for a favor. She wanted to see blueprints from a building. That's not a big deal, really—I mean they're not exactly state secrets and she did used to work there. . . ."

Frank nodded encouragingly. He didn't know if Sonia had violated some code, but knew he didn't care if she did.

"The problem was, they were from 1935."

"Forty-nine fifty Pullman?"

For the first time Sonia Kettle looked surprised. "Yeah. How'd you know?"

"Long story. Did she say why?"

"She said her grandfather used to own it, and they were going to tear it down, and she wanted to see what it had looked like. It didn't make a lot of sense to me, but Kim would go off on tangents like that. She'd get obsessed about a movie or a car or a breed of dog and talk about nothing else for a few days, then lose interest."

"So you didn't get them out for her?"

"No, I did. I figured she'd nag me until she got what she wanted—same old Kim. She'd gotten off the drugs, but nothing else had changed." She gave an abrupt shrug. "Maybe I'm being mean. Anyway, we went down to basement storage and dug through the drawers until I found what she wanted. Got dust all over a new blouse, too."

"The blueprints?" Frank asked as the baby started up in the other room. "We requested those and were told it would take a week because they had to come from remote storage, or something along those lines."

The young woman nodded. "Requests are processed in the order they're received. Unless you get, like, the mayor to call us and say it's an emergency. Otherwise it goes into the queue with the others."

Frank wished he'd known that. But the fresh bodies turning up had taken priority over James Miller's murder for everyone except Theresa. "So you—"

"I did her a favor, yeah. Isn't every job like that?" she asked with a hint of defensiveness. "Don't you fix people's parking tickets?"

"I try," Frank said to soothe her. "Sometimes. Did

anything in particular interest Kim about the blueprints? Did she just want the general layout?"

"I don't know. She seemed real interested in them, that's for sure, but I couldn't tell you why."

"Did you make her a copy of it?"

"No! You need the oversize copy machine to do that, and that sort of thing the boss *will* get mad about. Kim didn't even ask. She just wrote down some of the information, like the date and the name of the architect." The baby wailed again, not loudly.

"Anything else?"

"Yeah, but I didn't pay attention. By that point I wanted to get her out of there and back to work before the boss came looking for me."

"Mommy! Bethie threw up!"

"Excuse me." Sonia left the table and went into the living room.

Sanchez leaned over the oak surface. "What do you think? Kim knows it's her grandfather's body in that building—"

"And she's got his notebook."

"—and she sees something on the blueprints that leads her to the killer? What?"

"Maybe it's Corliss. She confronted him and he killed her."

"Corliss is the only tenant we know about, but that doesn't mean he was Miller's suspect. Who knows what Miller wrote in that notebook?"

Sonia came back into the kitchen area and took the baby to the kitchen sink to rinse off the spit-up. Brent made a triumphant return to the table, legitimately freed from his exile, both the motorcycle and SpongeBob in hand.

"Mrs. Kettle?" Frank asked. "Can you show us those blueprints?"

"Sure. It will only take a minute now that I know where they are. Come by Monday morning and—"

"I meant now."

She looked up from drying her daughter's face with a paper towel. "Now? No, I can't—I mean, I don't have a key to our offices, they don't give keys to peons—and I think the building itself is locked—"

"If we get your supervisor to unlock the offices?"

She perched the baby on her hip with an expression of profound unhappiness. Brent, sensing a significant decision, swung his body from person to person as the exchange went on.

Sanchez asked, "Are you worried that your boss will be mad you showed Kim the blueprints?"

"No, he won't really care about that. It's just that my husband is at work and I don't have a babysitter I can call at short notice. We'd have to take the kids with us." She finished on a determined note. "And you'd have to give us a ride there and back."

Frank bit the figurative bullet. "Brent, how would you like to ride in a real police car?"

CHAPTER 42

SATURDAY, JUNE 6
1936

The dead man's head had turned up the day before, wrapped in (presumably) his own clothing and left under a willow tree just southwest of the East Fifty-fifth Street bridge, where any passerby would spot it. The passersby happened to be two Negro boys playing hooky that pleasant Friday.

The killer had not had to wait long for the rest of his handiwork to be discovered. A railroad detective regularly checked the area, looking for items stolen from the cars, and knew the macabre bundle had not been there the day before. "Right across from the railroad police station," Walter pointed out from their vantage point atop the edge of the Kingsbury Run valley. This detail seemed to disturb him more than any other. "Why do that? He gets off on the risk? Or he wants to rub our noses in it?"

James recalled Corliss's words. "Maybe he likes nothing so much as getting away with something."

"I'd like nothing so much as rubbing his nose in this dead guy's ass, that's for sure. 'Course he's probably already done that. Pervert." Walter spat out the last word but lacked the wind for any more as they picked their way down the slope, only half a mile to the east of where they'd found the first two bodies.

Then Walter puffed, "They are not going to be happy with us."

"It's not our fault."

"Has that ever helped, with a wife?"

"It used to." James couldn't blame his wife for being disappointed. She had been looking forward to spending this Saturday on a drive in the country with Walter and his wife after being cooped up all winter long. Summer had arrived, with at least as much certainty as one could get in Cleveland, where warm weather could never be counted on no matter the month. The women wanted to see the rolling green hills of Cuyahoga Falls. But once the body turned up, the detectives no longer had the day off. No cop in the city had the day off.

Helen's mood had already been foul enough after Friday, her personal wash day, despite the fact that she could now hang the clothes outside and away from the soot of the woodstove. Washing took the entire day and left her back aching and her hands blistered from the boiling water. James's interest in finding the building at 4950 Pullman mentioned in the newspaper—now reopened after renovations made necessary when a tenant cooked food on a hobo stove and set his office alight—had been met with a tight-lipped scowl from his wearied wife. James hadn't dared speak to her until well after lunchtime. Even his having splurged on the newspaper did not thaw her; only the proposed outing had brightened the horizon. When Walter arrived to collect him, they had thrown the news at Helen like a curveball and ran out before she could catch it and bean them.

"Who found it?" James asked his partner as they picked their way through the spring weeds, careful not to slip down the sharp incline.

"Two crane operators for the railroad. Every cop in the city looking for this bum's body, and a couple of joes stumble on it."

They reached the valley floor. Everything reminded James of the first two victims, the knots of cops standing around watching other cops beat the weeds for clues, a police captain smoking a cigar as if he wanted to punish it. The cluster around the dead, naked flesh on the ground. The rumble of a train along the tracks, warning them to stay out of its way. Everything except the air, which had the turgid feel of summer rather than the crisp breeze of early fall.

They approached the body and its attendants.

The dead young man, minus his head, lay on his side, tucked under the branches of a sumac bush as if this would provide enough cover to make it blend in with the surroundings. But if the killer had wanted to conceal the body, why not tuck it farther into the growth on the hill or dump it in the river? Why leave it practically on the doorstep of the railroad police for the Nickel Plate line? But then, if he wanted to mock the police, why not make it even more showy?

For the first time—and it startled him to recognize it for the first time—James wondered if the killer was insane. Naturally anyone who would do such a thing must be, his mind instinctively responded, but James had met a few men during the war who had illustrated the different shades of insanity. They had not given any sign of imbalance or shell shock and could converse and function and obey orders like any other soldier. Only their eyes gave them away, the slight smile that lingered around their lips when they drove a bayonet in more times than necessary. They *enjoyed* killing.

Walter and most men would chalk that up to evil, but James did not believe in evil. It smacked of the supernatural and seemed too easy an excuse for grown men who should take responsibility for their actions.

But if they weren't evil and they weren't insane, what were they?

Dangerous, he thought. *That's all I need to know.*

He and Walter weaseled past the gawking cops to see. Walter said, as if he hadn't quite caught his breath, "At least he left this one his balls."

"Look at those tattoos." The victim had colored patterns on both his arms and his legs—a heart, anchors, flags, the names Helen and Paul on one forearm, and a butterfly on the left shoulder.

"Sailor," Walter announced. "Who else would have all of those? He's got two anchors—but what the hell kind of man gets a butterfly? Pervert."

"Never know," said a plainclothes officer crouched by the feet, picking debris off the skin with a pair of tweezers. James recognized him as one of the Bertillon unit guys, the one who had made the photo of the coat for him. "It could have been his nickname for his girl or something."

"Only a whore would have a nickname like that."

"He's a sailor. What other kind of dame would he know? She's probably some island floozy, dances in a grass skirt." The cop paused in his work for a moment, apparently to enjoy the vision of a tropical paradise, with a sandy beach and coconuts and no dead bodies. "This is my day off. I had tickets to see the Indians play in that new stadium. They say it's really nice."

Walter snorted his lack of sympathy. "And I still say this guy's a pervert. Otherwise, how did he fall in with our Butcher?"

A uniformed guy James didn't recognize called to his partner, and Walter toddled off. As this happened a couple times per day, James didn't pay any attention to it. Instead, he asked the Bertillon unit cop, "Find anything?"

"Grass, weeds. A few dog hairs. Two black hairs that could be our killer's or could be his. We'll have to take a closer look."

"No other injuries? Besides . . . the—"

"Besides his head being cut off, you mean? No. He is otherwise unmolested. It only took a few slices, too, from the looks of it. This madman knows what he's doing."

"No ID yet?"

"No. Kind of odd. Nice-looking young guy, you'd figure somebody would miss him—at least that's what we thought yesterday when we only had the head. But with all these tattoos . . . if he's a sailor, he could have blown into town from anywhere. I have high hopes for the fingerprints, too." James noticed that the tips of the fingers had been blackened with ink. "But it's been an hour, so if he turned up in our files nobody's told me yet."

"Was this body here when they found the head?" James asked.

The Bertillon guy winced. "You can bet that's the question of the hour. Anyone in this gully yesterday is going to be called on the carpet and probably flogged for not searching past the bridge. We're only about a thousand feet away."

"Maybe it wasn't here. He hung on to the guy found with Andrassy for a few days before dumping them both. He could have kept the body a day longer than the head."

The cop picked another twig from the calf and dropped it into a jar before jerking his head to the east. "Even if he did, they should have found *that*."

James went to investigate. *That* turned out to be an irregular oval of dried, dark red liquid in the dirt and leaves, approximately two feet by three. The density appeared to vary, heavier where the dirt had more clay than loam, lighter over loose soil. The edges broke up here and there, as if some object had been dragged from the perimeter. Of the weeds that remained firm and upright with their cells brought back to life by spring, most had been painted with the stuff.

Walter joined him. "Not tough to guess what that is."

"But why is it here?"

"Gee, you think the headless corpse over there might have something to do with it?"

"But it's not like him, not tidy. He didn't keep that young man's blood in a bucket and pour it here. He *killed* him here, spraying all the weeds, see? The other bodies—"

"The other ones were killed somewhere else and then dumped." Walter turned as he surveyed the run. Trees on both sides hid the gully from the view of any nearby houses. "At night there would be no one here to see him."

"Except the trains."

"Yeah, your damn trains. All he'd have to do is drop down when one came by. It would be pitch dark out here."

"Exactly, so why?"

"There you go with the why again. Because he's a crazy pervert, that's why."

"I mean, why outdoors? Why not in his lair or workshop or wherever he holed up to kill the first three?"

They took a few steps back to the corpse. Walter said, "This stiff is a young guy, got a decent enough shape. Maybe he had second thoughts about his new friend."

"He tried to get away, and the guy had to work fast. That's possible," James admitted, "supposing the killer had the weapon along with him, and probably did. But I'm wondering if he did it outdoors because he had no choice."

Walter squinted at him in the sunlight. Behind him, the men from the morgue spread out a clean sheet next to the body. The Bertillon unit guy got ready to topple the body over onto it.

"Maybe he had to work outdoors because he lost his workspace. He's been kicked out of his house or his wife or some out-of-town guests arrived unexpectedly. Or his office had been closed for repairs because they had a fire." He told Walter about the notice in the paper.

"So who's your suspect? Corliss or Odessa?"

"Either. Both. The victims have been healthy men and one large woman. They'd be a lot easier to handle with a partner."

Walter shook his head. "Just because we've run across them, Jimmy, don't mean either one is the guy. Every cop in this city has a suspect in mind and good reasons to pick them up."

James looked down at the cop by the corpse, now plucking evidence off the side the body had been lying on. "What color are those dog hairs?"

"Yellow. Why?"

James raised his eyebrows at Walter. "Corliss's dog is yellow."

"So's mine, Jimmy. And Odessa only likes good-looking girls and Corliss is as milquetoast as any guy I've ever met. Face it—you ain't going to necessarily be the hero here."

James's face burned from more than the sunlight. "That's not the point."

"Yeah, it kinda is. Look, we'll let the captain know

about your little theory, and we'll go around and talk to that doctor *again*. But right now we've got a job to do." He nodded his head to the side and walked out of earshot of the men around the body. James followed with a sinking heart. They'd played this little drama before. The sooner they got it over with, the sooner he could get back to work.

Over Walter's shoulder, James watched the Bertillon unit guy put the dog hairs in an envelope. He wondered if they needed another man in that unit. Did they feel pressure due to their access to the evidence? How many hairs and coat buttons and shoeprints got "lost" on the way to the lab? Or did their scientific world stay removed from that of the beat cops?

"Ness is going to raid Harwood's place tonight," Walter said without preamble.

"Harwood."

"Commander of the Fourteenth."

"I know who he is." Captain Harwood perched nearly at the pinnacle of corruption in the city; no vice could exist in his region without his stamp of approval, or his hand in the till.

"Some city councilman out there has a beef with Harwood and he put a bee in Ness's bonnet about the Blackhawk Inn. We've got to help move the tables out of the back room before Ness and his handpicked band of saints get there."

"We?"

"Yes, Jimmy, *we*." It would have been funny under other circumstances, the jolly Walter wearing an expression of such grim determination. "You gotta make up your mind. Either be a cop like the rest of us, or—"

"Or *what*?"

"Or I swear to God I'll walk into the captain's office

first thing Monday morning and request a new partner. And you'll need to find some other line of work."

Because everyone else in the department would refuse to work with him. On the other hand . . . "Ness has the mayor behind him, and, as you said, it's an election year. Why not keep ourselves out of it and let Harwood clean up his own mess?"

Walter went straight for his trump card. "There's a double sawbuck in it for you."

Twenty dollars would pay his rent for the month, and Walter knew it.

"You could buy Helen those dishes she's been pining for. Harwood's boys are desperate for help. Every cop in the city is busy with *this* thing." He waved his hand toward the decapitated corpse as the morgue boys wrapped it loosely in its new shroud.

"We're busy with it, too."

"We're rubberneckers. The captain isn't here and we have no assignment. You're out of excuses, Jimmy. Face it."

"You face this, Walt. Harwood will go down. They'll all go down. Times have changed."

"Some things don't never change, Jimmy."

"Corliss is our killer, I'm sure of it." He wasn't, really, but he'd sooner encounter the Mad Butcher than help out the mob just so the other cops would play with him at recess.

"Are you *afraid* of Ness? Is that all this is?" Walter stared at his partner with both disappointment and a cold intelligence of which James would not have thought him capable. "All this time I thought it was integrity."

I did, too, James thought as he watched his partner walk away.

At least he was free to track down Arthur Corliss and his yellow dog.

The body had been hefted into a waiting hearse, but the Bertillon unit guy still crouched among the weeds where it had lain. He seemed to be puzzling over something in the palm of his hand.

"What's that?" he asked.

"Piece of glass." The guy held it up to the light. "I found it under the body, sticking to his calf. It could have been here already, of course, there's plenty of trash around. Odd color, though."

Something prickled at the back of James's neck. "Color?"

"I thought it was brown, like a beer bottle—that's mostly what you see down here—but it's actually black. Maybe a decorative thing . . ."

His voice faded into the distance as James sprinted up the hill.

CHAPTER 43

SATURDAY, SEPTEMBER 11
PRESENT DAY

Edward Corliss seemed surprised to find Theresa on his doorstep. "Well, hello. Do come in."

She apologized for dropping by unannounced and gave him her condolences upon the death of his friend as she followed him into the house. He thanked her but shrugged off the sympathies. "I can't say William and I were great friends. I'm sorry for him, of course, but selfishly sorrier for myself. It's strange to have violence strike so close to one. And at my age you begin to take the death of peers personally, as if time itself is reminding you that yours is limited."

And yet for all his calm tone, he did not head for the elegant living room, instead returning to the comfort of his model room. The trains were running, chugging through the fake buildings and hills, their tiny wheels making tiny clicks against tiny tracks.

Theresa circled the plastic city, taking in details she

hadn't noticed on her first trip. He had specks underneath the solid water in the lake that looked like fish. The top of the Terminal Tower lit up. The Waterfront Line rapid transit had a graphic on its side to advertise the Rock and Roll Hall of Fame. She browsed and waited for Edward Corliss to ask questions. People always had questions about a murder.

Except him, apparently. He crouched over the rust-brown Center Street swing bridge, soldering the seam on a piece of track. Where had she heard about solder lately? Jablonski, and his oversize camera after she fell on him in the basement of the Pullman building.

Jablonski, who had had no trouble getting into her house and making friends with her dog, or sitting on the chair in front of the computer, where the cat liked to sleep. Jablonski, in his comfy cotton clothes that everything stuck to. Had last night really been his first visit?

"Would you care for a cup of tea?" he asked.

"No, thank you. I've come to ask for your help," she said, and asked if William Van Horn often sketched near the preservation headquarters.

"Yes. Is that what he was doing when they mugged him?"

She didn't comment on what was almost certainly not a "they" and not a mugging. "I think so. I found a piece of a picture. I had hoped you could help me scout the area, figure out where he might have been sketching."

"Oh. That would be William. The only human part of him was the artist part." He straightened and unplugged the soldering iron, which left a gritty, metallic smell in the air. "I don't mean that as harsh as it sounded. He made an excellent president for the society and I'm going to have a hard time filling his shoes. But he was, well . . ."

"A hard man to get to know."

"Exactly." He tested the track with one finger and, apparently satisfied, stood up.

"I think you'll be an excellent president."

"Thank you."

"So the society gets the Pennsylvania Railroad files after all."

He raised one eyebrow slightly, as if he found that in poor taste but didn't want to embarrass her by pointing it out. "Yes. Let me set this down." He puttered at a small table in the corner for a moment and then came back with an open plastic container for her. "Would you do the honors, Ms. MacLean, before we strike out. to search the rail yard? I'd like to get this city winterized before winter actually arrives."

She took the container of paint-on snow. The faster she checked the preservation headquarters for Van Horn's abduction site the faster she could go home and see her daughter, but the man before her had nothing but trains and the memory of his father. She felt compelled to warn him of what might lie ahead if they identified that father as Cleveland's worst serial killer. Trains were all he had to keep from feeling as lonely as Irene Schaffer. She mixed the glop with one finger.

But could this be a case of like father, like son? Though she couldn't quite picture this older man jumping on and off trains carting the dead weight of a full-grown man, he still made at least as good a suspect as Jablonski or Greer.

The fake snow felt wetter today, sticking to her fingers as much as the rough branches of the plastic trees as she watched the trains go round and round. From Cleveland to New Castle, Pennsylvania. James Miller wouldn't have known about that series of similar murders; he died before the connection between the two cities had been uncovered.

Jablonski had flown with the theory, however. She had checked out the *Plain Dealer* that morning at the lab, and while the young man had thankfully restrained himself from quoting her as a source, he had put nearly every detail of last night's conversation into his story. When he ran out of facts he moved on to speculations. The man was truly obsessed. Perhaps too obsessed.

Though at least Jablonski wanted to preserve James Miller's final resting place. Councilman Greer had been agitating to destroy it since they discovered the body. Why? To hide a past crime? To destroy his connection to the current set of murders?

She gazed at the miniature Terminal Tower. Everything remained circumstantial. Just like the original Torso Murders, all the evidence was like a fog in the valley, constantly shifting in appearance and weight. Everything she'd learned in the past week added up to nothing.

"So." Corliss adjusted two pine trees in the Metropark system as he talked, encouraging their trunks to stand ramrod straight. "Do you still think my father might be this Torso killer?"

"I don't know. I'm not sure we'll ever know for sure. Unfortunately, James Miller's body was found in a space that, most likely, only your father had access to."

"How do you know that?"

She explained about her conversation with Irene Schaffer.

"Dr. Louis? That nutritionist?"

"Yes."

"He sounds like a much more suspicious man than my father."

"I agree. But the Torso killer never showed any interest in young girls, and her description of the closet puts it closer to the outer wall than the space in which we found James Miller."

"But you can't be sure. Perhaps the closets weren't of equal size. Perhaps Dr. Louis used them both. And even if there had been a door from my father's office, that doesn't mean my father used it."

She said nothing, having no reason to think the closets weren't of symmetrical sizes, and though one could say all one liked about proof it was pretty hard to explain away a corpse turning up in your storeroom. "It would help if we had the original blueprints."

"If I find them, I'll let you know."

She brushed whiteness along the branches of a fir tree, dotted it on the browning leaves of an oak. "I thought you had looked through all your father's papers already."

"I did. But they probably had to have the building inspected when they sold it, and any paperwork would be in the Penn Railroad collection. If I find anything, I'll keep it out for you."

"Thank you." Most people would not have been so cooperative with someone trying to prove their parent's guilt. But perhaps Edward needed to know as much as she did.

The trees at last standing to his specifications, he added, "But you know, I might even be mixed up in my recollections and that wasn't my father's office at all. Plus the architects who designed the building worked in it. They could have put in all sorts of secret rooms without anyone else's knowledge."

True, though unlikely. The floor had been too solid to be breached from the cellar, and the construction crew had not found anything to indicate access to the space from the second floor. Too craven to press him, she only asked, "Is that enough?"

He inspected her work, saying, "A little more."

Something tugged at her brain cells, wanting their

attention. The mention of their neighbor state had echoed a previous conversation, from her first visit to Edward's home. "You said your father worked for and then bought a railroad in Pennsylvania?"

"That's where it was based. The track system went from Harrisburg to Chicago."

He added the loose fake snow on top of her wet coating, creating a snowfall realistic enough to warrant mention on the Weather Channel.

"Winter has come to your city," she told him.

He let more flakes drift to the top of the music auditorium. Apparently Cleveland had had a blizzard. "Snow covers up a multitude of sins. Little imperfections, roof sections that don't perfectly meld."

Theresa's legs began to feel heavy. The late night and early morning had caught up with her. "My dad used to say that about paint. Covering up a multitude of sins, I mean."

Snow. Paint.

"Where did your father live in Pennsylvania? When he worked for the railroad?" To get his attention away from the model, she added, "The one he later bought."

He recapped the container. "Oh, a little town, you've probably never heard of it. There's pretty much nothing there except train tracks."

"Where?" she asked again, pursuing some body of thought that would not quite gel.

"New Castle."

And, just like that, the final piece fell into place.

Arthur Corliss fulfilled every requirement of the Torso killer. He had intimate knowledge of and free access to the railroad system. He worked in the Kingsbury Run area. He had lived in New Castle and had a business there. He owned and occupied not only the building but—apparently—the storage space where James Miller had been slain.

She felt drunk—but not with success, as she could not summon the slightest happiness for solving the Torso killings. For one thing, the evidence seemed damning but still completely circumstantial. For another, she felt dismay on behalf of Edward Corliss. "And your father never—" What? Gave any sign of a depraved violence? Talked about his victims? Displayed his trophies, if he kept any? She knew she should shut up now, put down the white goop, and search the rail yard on her own, leaving him to sort out his family's ghosts in private. She needed to talk to Frank. Between the two of them they would figure out what to do.

"Never talked to me about being the Torso killer?" Edward gave her a weary smile and straightened. "This is a hell of a job you have, Theresa."

"I know."

"The answer is no, he didn't. I'm sure he would never have mentioned it to Mother, either."

She felt her forehead crease in a frown, trying to make sense of this last part.

He took the container out of her limp hand. "She didn't know, you see. She believed him to be a great businessman and philanthropist—which he was—and only that. I would have spent my life believing it, too, if I hadn't crept into the cellar one day to pinch a beer and found a leg in the stationary tub."

She waited, the way one does when another person is talking too fast, hoping that if one gives it a little time one's brain will sort the words into an order that makes sense. Her problem was, they made too much sense already.

Edward went on, his light blue eyes dancing with

light reflected from the white walls. "They never caught him, you see. He didn't go to jail, his family didn't whisk him off to some fancy asylum. He simply got over the need for attention and learned to hide his victims where no one would ever find them."

"Where?"

Edward smiled at this and shook his head. "Always the scientist. I don't know where. After I found half a man in our basement—this basement, I'll show you the room—I toasted him with the beer I'd taken and went back to my studies. When my father returned from whatever errand he'd been on—probably disposing of the first half of the body—he didn't know his sanctum had been breached, and I never said a word." He picked up a stained towel and began to wipe the white stuff from her fingers as he spoke, gently tugging on each one. "All through the years, I never said a word, though I think I should have. The way he looked at me sometimes . . . he wanted to share it with his only child. That's natural for a parent, don't you think? Don't you share your secrets with your daughter? My father never told me, but I found my own way of coming and going from the basement so that I could watch."

"Wahssh—"

"But I never killed." He moved closer to her, watching her face for its reactions. "Whatever demons drove my father didn't drive me. Not even when temptation would strike—when you work on roads, Theresa, the one thing you learn about human beings is that most are sheep. They simply do the same things over and over until someone tells them to do something else, and then they'll do that over and over until redirected again. Boring things, really. But I never harmed a one of them until that blond whore showed up on my doorstep. I have to admit I'm disappointed in you, Theresa. It's taken you a week to discover what that little bimbo figured out in two days."

Theresa grabbed for the edge of the table and caught up the bottle of fake snow instead. She opened her fingers to let it fall, then thought better of it. If she damaged the model there was no telling what Corliss could do, and besides, the label caught her attention. Polyethylene.

"Granted, it was only a guess on her part. She found my father's name in that notebook—"

"Wha no—"

"Some little book from her grandfather. He had written about Arthur in it and then she found his name on the blueprints. I happen to be listed in the phone book, so voilà, she showed up on my doorstep."

Plastic snow. Polyethylene made to look like tiny snowflakes . . . circles.

She couldn't believe how slowly her brain was working. Had worked.

As liberally as he applied the fake snow, it must have settled on all sorts of things, just as her pets' fur did.

"She wasn't *positive* my father was the killer, but figured the evidence came close enough. I don't think she even cared. She only had this wild idea about us taking to the talk-show circuit, making the most of her fifteen minutes, I guess. But *I* knew, and I had to get that notebook away from her."

They had struggled here—Kim brushed her arm against the hot soldering iron as Corliss strangled her, damaging the freshly painted swing bridge, infuriating him all the more. The struggle lodged paint and fake snow in her hair.

Physical evidence could chase all the fog away. And now she had it.

Afterward Corliss took Kim down to his father's

workroom and removed part of her neck to hide his finger marks, and so that the death would resemble the senior Corliss's work.

"Wheresh the notebook?" she managed to ask, more or less coherently.

"I burned it."

One of her knees buckled, and she dropped the bottle to lean heavily on the edge of the platform. So little remained of James Miller and his time on this planet and Corliss had destroyed one more piece.

"I thought it prudent," Corliss added, perhaps at the pained look on her face. "Too bad I couldn't burn *her*. So I tried to make the most of it. I cleaned her up, just as my father would have done. And he'd never heard the word *forensic*."

And yet Corliss Jr. left trace evidence behind, she thought. The snow and paint from his model were stuck in Kim's hair. Fibers from his car trunk and living room carpeting stayed with the two men on the hill. Polyethylene snowflakes had been on the handkerchief—probably Edward's handkerchief—placed in Van Horn's pocket to make the scene more similar to the Tattooed Man's.

Her pets' fur on the victim's clothing hadn't come from Jablonski or been the result of her own clumsy cross-contamination. The fur had gotten on Edward's white cotton dress shirt when he helped her down from a moving train car and had transferred onto Van Horn when Corliss wrestled his unconscious form into the trunk of his car.

She saw it all so clearly now and felt strangely unable to do a bloody thing about it. "Whuu'd you do to m—"

"I'm sorry, my dear. It's Midazolam. When you turned down the tea I had to add it to the snow gel—with some DMSO, of course, so it could be absorbed."

"Dental anesthetic," she tried to say. Extremely fast-acting, but temporary.

"Borrowed it from the neighbor. I *did* tell you I minored in chemistry," he said, chiding her.

"You killed them," she said dumbly, her words so slurred she couldn't understand them herself.

"I did. I killed that little bitch and discovered how fun it was. Then you and that reporter showed up here, salivating over my father's work, and that gave me the idea. If I intended to follow in his footsteps, why not do it right—"

He caught her as her knees buckled and she fell, not gently, so that he had to tighten both arms around her torso firmly enough to leave bruises. Her foot slid into the bottle, scattering polyethylene flakes across the hardwood floor.

"You have no idea how much I regret this, Theresa," he murmured in her ear.

She felt his lips on hers, and then nothing else.

CHAPTER 44

The zoning and planning department's hallways were silent, the workers all home enjoying their weekend, and Brent made the most of their lack of supervision by tearing up and down the linoleum and listening to his screeches echo off the walls. His mother did not seem inclined to restrain him. Frank suspected she felt she deserved the officers' indulgence since they had interrupted her Saturday, or she wanted the kid to burn off all the excess energy he could before they returned to their bungalow. Frank could only hope finding this blueprint would help point them to Kim's killer, that this entire exercise would not be for nothing.

At least, once her supervisor had arrived to unlock the offices, Sonia Kettle had quickly found what they had come for, since only a week had elapsed since she last retrieved it. She carried the old paper in one hand, as gently as she carried her baby in the other, to a worktable in the center of the storage room. "Here it is."

"What is that? Let me see!" her son demanded as she spread it on the wooden surface.

"No, Brent. It's very old. *Do not* touch it," she added in a tone so stern that the child listened and contented himself with running up and down the aisles of cabinets. While shouting, of course.

The fragile papers contained an illustration of the outside view of the building at 4950 Pullman, then the upper floor, then the lower floor. Frank immediately honed in on the two offices on the west side of the layout. There, in neat and flowery script, the southwest corner room had been designated *Mr. Corliss's suite.* No such notation had been made for Dr. Louis Odessa. A logo reading *Metetsky-O'Reilly, Architects* appeared at the bottom.

Corliss's storage room extended from a doorway in the back of the office; a mirror image had become Odessa's space. However, Corliss's closet had an additional feature noted. A small circle had been drawn into the floor, and an arrow pointed to it from the word *drain.*

James Miller had been found in Arthur Corliss's closet.

But that would not have meant anything to Kim Hammond, would it? Had the newspapers mentioned the hole in the floor? Had Jablonski's elaborate stories discussed it? He had definitely interviewed the construction crew.

Frank scoured the rest of the blueprint. What else would have put Kim in the path of her murderer? "What did she say to you, Sonia, when you showed her this?"

"Brent! Quiet down, buddy. I don't remember—like I said, by that time I just wanted her to get done and go. But she thought it was cool, et cetera, liked the fancy handwriting."

"The architects are on here, too," Sanchez pointed out. Their office also had their names written on it, claiming that space for the firm of Metetsky and O'Reilly.

"Did she make any specific comments?" Frank pressed Sonia Kettle.

"No. She, um, she had a little notebook that she kept looking at."

Frank and Angela Sanchez perked up. "Notebook?" they asked in unison.

"Yeah, a really old-looking little thing. The pages were brown and dusty and crumbling. She'd have to turn them really carefully, and then she'd look back at the blueprint, then turn a page. I didn't bother asking about it, I knew her well enough for that. Kim kept her little plans to herself more securely than a Hollywood producer with the script to a sequel."

Frank and Sanchez met each other's gazes over the table. James Miller had jotted a note three-quarters of a century before that put Kim in the path of a killer. What had he written? And what did it mean in light of the blueprints?

"Brent! Be quiet! I wouldn't put too much stock in it, frankly," Sonia Kettle added to the officers, sounding more and more put out by such a fuss over an ex-employee. "Kim wasn't a bad kid, but in terms of brains . . . she had never been one to think things through, and from what I could see of her, that hadn't changed."

Frank's phone rang, and he snatched it off his belt with an irritated swipe. Perhaps the woman had it right—Kim Hammond had picked up the wrong john, and the mystery went no deeper than that. "Hello?"

"Uncle Frank? Do you know where my mom is?" His niece sounded even more annoyed than he and Sonia Kettle put together. "I mean, I caught a ride home to spend her birthday weekend together because I know this whole empty-nest thing has been getting to her, and now she's not even answering her phone."

CHAPTER 45

SATURDAY, JUNE 6
1936

It occurred to James, while making his silent way into the building at 4950 Pullman, that he did not even know where Arthur Corliss lived. This did not concern him much. The man had mentioned a housekeeper, and a woman in the throes of the cleaning process would certainly stumble on some telltale artifact were her employer carving up young men there in the household. If James moved a saucer from one cabinet to another, Helen knew instantly. Women had nothing but their homes and their children to occupy them, all day, every day. Hence the near obsession a set of Fiestaware could cause.

He could buy it for her if he went with Walter.

The top step creaked. Not that it mattered, really. The sun had only begun to set and the front door stood slightly ajar. James entered the hallway. Three of the offices were dark and closed, but light poured from Arthur Corliss's space.

He did not plan to take the man by surprise. He did

not feel 100 percent sure yet. Nearly everything that applied to Arthur Corliss also applied to Louis Odessa, except their preference for company. Arthur Corliss sought out the down-and-out men, the ones looking for work, the ones without relatives to report them missing. He spoke kindly to them. He fed them.

They would trust him.

He needed to follow up on his clues, and then he would turn his information over to the captain and ask for an arrest warrant. James could do nothing by himself. He knew that.

At the office door he saw Corliss inside, doing nothing more sinister than laying in a fresh supply of Mission Orange soda, his favorite, in their signature black bottles. Had Corliss offered one to the latest young man before killing him? Or had they broken during the fire and a shard lodged in the sole of his shoe, only to come loose when he dumped the body?

The shelves were clean and freshly painted, books and bottles and drawings returned, all except for the newspapers. Those must have gone up in the blaze. Flo Polillo's body parts had been wrapped in two different newspapers, dated five months apart. Who else would have a five-month-old newspaper handy but a man who made a habit of collecting them?

The yellow dog lay under the window, no longer interested in the radiator on this warm evening. He opened one eye, saw James, closed it again.

He could swear he hadn't made a sound, but Corliss whirled around all the same. "Oh, Detective. Good afternoon. Evening, really."

"I thought you'd be here. Moving your things back in after the renovations?"

The man chuckled and set the last bottle on his shelf. "They never really left, merely got shuffled around while the painters worked. The fire only damaged my table and the things on it, but the smoke got everywhere. Nasty stuff, smoke. The smell went through the whole building. Auralina had to throw out two of her robes, and did she get after me about that! I'll have to pay her three times what they were worth."

"The fire started here?"

"Oh, yes, I'm entirely to blame." He opened a carton and began to pull books out, setting them on the shelf one by one, in no apparent order. "I made a hobo stove out of tin cans and lit a little coal fire in it. I propped it up on two bricks on the table but then went outside to drink a soda with the men and—"

"What men?"

Corliss paused, book in hand. From a step or two closer James could see that the books were in alphabetical order by the author's name. "A couple of joes came by looking for work. One of them hadn't eaten in two days and I merely wanted to warm some beans for him. I should have taken the blasted thing outside, of course, but I didn't think it would get that hot. You're not going to report me to the fire marshal, are you? Doesn't matter, he already made a report."

"You used coal instead of oil?"

"I know, another silly thing. But such a tiny stove hardly makes any fumes, and I have a handy supply of coal." He tossed the empty carton on the floor and opened another.

"From your train cars?" James asked, feeling, under his blazer, the gun at his side.

"Yes. Stealing from one's employer, that's called. But I *am* the employer and I can't technically steal from myself, can I?"

"How long did everyone have to clear out of the building for?"

"A couple of weeks, it's been." He peered at James. "Why all this interest in my fire?"

Because that's why you had to kill this last one out-side, isn't it? Your building had painters and workmen crawling all over it and you decided you couldn't wait. "Well, you know how fascinated I am by Dr. Louis's closet."

Corliss chuckled again. "I suspect many ladies have been, too."

"What do you keep in yours?" James eyed the door behind the man's desk.

Did he imagine it, the momentary halt in Corliss's act of placing one more volume next to the others? "No young girls, I can assure you of that."

"I believe it," James said with sincerity. "Did the painters redo that as well?"

Another book, carefully placed. "It didn't seem worth painting a storage space. And the smoke barely penetrated."

"Mind if I look at it?"

Corliss abandoned the books and stared at him. "You want to see my closet?"

"If you don't mind." James didn't bother coming up with an excuse for the request, unable to think of one that would make the slightest sense.

Finally the other man shrugged. "Help yourself. If you'd like to bring out another carton while you're at it, that would be swell."

James skirted the inner wall, rounded the desk, and turned the knob to the storage room, all without removing his gaze from Arthur Corliss, who had gone back to unpacking books.

James entered the storage space, still moving sideways. The storage space mirrored Odessa's, except shelves lined only the north wall. The rest of the area had been taken over by a table made out of unfinished wood planks and two-by-fours, with a lip running around the edge. Some of the smoke had left its odor lingering on the air. Otherwise the small room smelled like the disinfectant Helen used to use on their sinks, back when they could afford to join the national obsession about germs. James sniffed, tried to detect that tinny blood-and-offal smell he remembered from the war and occasional visits to the morgue. Nothing.

Nevertheless, he did not turn his back to the door.

He saw what Corliss meant about the cartons. At least five were stacked on the table and he plucked one from the top of the pile before reemerging into the office, feeling a bit ridiculous. He must have been wrong, he thought. Odessa moved back to the top of his short list of suspects.

"I hope you found that edifying, Detective."

"Oh, greatly. It's the same size as Odessa's, I see. Where do you want this?"

"On the desk, if you don't mind." He continued to unpack, and James returned to the closet for another box.

James heard Corliss uncap two bottles of Mission Orange. "Here. If you're going to help, I can at least provide refreshments."

James hadn't had a soda in over a week, and he'd had to walk the two miles from the murder scene since Walter had taken the car. He accepted the bottle, formed from the black glass he had thought so incriminating, and figured that every drugstore counter in the city served the fizzy flavored liquid. What a pill he was. He drained half the bottle in a few swallows.

"You fellows have had a busy weekend, I see from the papers." Corliss tapped a folded pile on one shelf, already reestablishing his newspaper collection. "A murdered young man. Are you and your partner assigned to that case?"

"Only peripherally."

"Amazing, that such things could happen in this day and age. But I suppose vengeance never goes out of style."

"We can't even identify two of the four. They may not have known anyone in this town." *Except,* James thought, *for whoever killed them.* He perched one hip on the edge of the desk; it had been a long day. "Andrassy was just a punk and the woman never bothered anybody. Who would feel vengeance toward people like that?"

"Any member of society, I suppose. Given what they were." Corliss placed another book, squaring it until it lined up in formation with the others. "Thieves. Parasites. An army of them, men who used to be men, who have been reduced to little more than animals by a travesty of economics."

"I thought you . . . you seemed sympathetic to the . . ."

"The dispossessed? Of course I am. It's not their fault—you think I don't know that? But that doesn't change the fact that they have become a scourge upon those of us who are left, who still have productive lives."

James drained the rest of his soda pop and set the bottle down. "So someone killed them for the betterment of society?"

"Isn't that what you do? What men have always done?" Corliss took the last book from the carton and piled it atop the first empty one on the floor. "Soldiers killed in the war, to keep the American system from foreign invaders. You officers lock the criminals away, sometimes execute them, not because of what they are but to keep them from doing more harm in the future.

I would think if anyone understood the protection of society, you would."

Years ago James thought that was what his job was about. Now, thinking of his department, his fellows in the blue line, Walter's offer . . . they had become parasites and thieves, as well. The Butcher ought to have been stalking them instead of the downtrodden, because the cops had had a choice in what they became.

"Are you all right, Detective? I hope I haven't upset you."

"No . . ."

"Would you mind grabbing one more carton for me? Then I think I'll cease for the night."

James did, because it gave him time to consider his next move. Maybe he could pet the dog, collect some hairs. Could the Bertillon unit tell one yellow dog from another? Or could Walter be right, and James chased shadows only to avoid being chased by Ness's gang? He picked up a box from the surface of the table, revealing an irregular pattern of staining on the unfinished wood. At the same time he noticed that what looked like an extra leg in one corner was actually a pipe, draining from the table through the floor. This should have meant something to him, he felt, but he couldn't quite grasp it. It had been much too long of a day, and the idea of not having a job come Monday morning taxed his brain.

Corliss accepted the carton, opened it, began stacking books. He seemed about as dangerous as his dog.

"What do you use that table for, the one in your closet?" James asked.

"You *are* fascinated by my storage room, aren't you? Just storage. It holds plans and blueprints, since they don't fit comfortably on a shelf and the edge keeps them from rolling off."

"What's the pipe for?"

"Pardon?"

"Pipe. Like a drain. Going into the floor." What was the matter with him? He sounded only barely intelligible.

"Washing parts. I do still tinker with bits and pieces of the locomotives. I was quite a mechanic in my day. I've held every job one can have on a railroad. That's how I learned to run one."

James gave one more valiant effort to mold his accumulated suspicions into something resembling proof. "Including shoveling coal."

"Indeed. Dirty job, but it kept my muscles up."

Spots of light began to appear before James's eyes. "And you were a bull."

"Railroad detective, yes. I kept the army of parasites from bringing a working system down. Like you."

"No," James said, straightening. "Not like me."

Arthur Corliss was the Torso killer. James had to get help to make the arrest. He didn't feel strong enough to even lift a pair of handcuffs, much less get them on somebody. He headed for the door, or at least tried to, steadying himself with one hand on the desk. There would be a call box at the next corner, he could alert the station—

"Where are you going, Detective?"

"Haffa . . . haffa . . ." He'd never make it to the door.

Corliss grasped one shoulder and spun him around as easily as a rag doll.

Anger and fear powered James's arms, which shoved Corliss back a foot and surprised them both. That was it, though. He had nothing left with which to resist when Corliss grasped James's collar with his left hand and pulled James's service revolver from the holster with his right.

This could not be a good development, James thought. Then Corliss pulled the trigger and set the inside of his body on fire.

James felt as if he had exploded from the inside out, in addition to being vaguely surprised not to see the floorboards covered in gore as he slipped down to them.

With his last gasp of consciousness, James insisted, "Not like me."

"If you say so," Arthur Corliss conceded. Then he took both of James's hands and dragged him into the small closet.

Helen, James thought. *Johnny.*

CHAPTER 46

SATURDAY, SEPTEMBER 11
PRESENT DAY

Theresa smelled the earth before she felt it. Cool and firm, pressing against her back and legs; she should have been fairly comfortable but somehow wasn't. Her head ached, her jaw felt stiff, and the chill of the outdoors had seeped in and through every bone in her body. She shivered, convulsing. Only then did she realize her legs were tied down.

Her eyes, blurred and in near dark, could not tell her much about her surroundings, but they didn't need to. She knew instantly where Corliss had taken her.

She was in the basement of the building at 4950 Pullman, approximately underneath the room where James Miller had lain for seventy-four years.

Why hadn't Edward killed her?

Then she heard movement. He simply hadn't killed her *yet*.

A vague amount of dusky light filtered down the stairwell and silhouetted Edward Corliss as he straightened from the support column to which he had tied her legs.

Why would he bring her here? Some sort of symmetry with his father's crimes? To live out this fantasy of re-creating his father's crimes, as he had with Van Horn's body? But which of the Torso killer's famous victims would she be?

Then the noises from outside finally penetrated, and she knew that historical accuracy had little to do with it. She heard men's voices, distant and indistinct, and the rumblings of large diesel engines heavy enough to vibrate the ground beneath her. They were coming to destroy the building, to collapse the stone walls into the hole beneath them and pour concrete over the whole mess. Her body would never be found.

No, wait. Surely they would do a walk-through, one last check to make sure a kid or a homeless man or a cat was not still inside. Right?

But they must have already done that. Corliss would have waited until they took one last look around and returned to their equipment on the north lawn, between the building and the road. Then he carried her in via the south lawn, out of their sight, and got down the steps without being seen through the window cutouts. That's the only reason he would have cut this so close.

Any minute now the ball would swing and the stones would bury her.

She should have been unconscious, but absorbing a drug through the skin must be an uncertain business. He would have had a hard time calculating the dose. A small slip, but obviously the only break she was going to get.

She blinked her eyes until they cleared and saw him give a tug to the knot he had tied around the post. She wanted to point out that the first swing of the wrecking ball would collapse the northeast corner right into their stairwell, blocking his only avenue of escape, but the tight gag in her mouth prevented speech. Besides, why should she tip him off? Instead, she lay limp and still, hands tied together over her stomach, as he picked up the bundle of thick rope and wrists he had created. He wanted to check that part of his tableau, too. A perfectionist to the last.

When he did, she grabbed his shirt with both hands and bucked with both feet, pulling him down to the ground. If she would die down here, so would he.

Once he was on the floor she let go just long enough to strike at his chest with her tied-together fists. It didn't feel to her like she did much damage, so she tried again, hitting at his face. He grabbed her hair. She tried to knee him in the groin but didn't have enough slack in the rope holding her ankles. She heard the slight clink of metal as his keys slid from his side pocket, falling onto the packed earthen floor.

She rolled upright, sitting on his right thigh. Her hands came down again, missing his chin in the dark and hitting him in the right eye. He immediately released her hair and pressed both hands to his face, groaning. She ran her hands along the floor to find the keys, sometimes useful as a weapon, and found something much better.

He had kept his trusty folding knife in the same pocket.

Now she had to get it open with bound hands and a writhing man underneath her. Using her toes to scoot herself backward, she raised herself up an inch or two and then fell, planting her knee in his groin.

He doubled automatically, body-slamming her over backward, knife still clutched in her fingers. She couldn't do much to stop herself, not with her wrists tied together.

His assault paused; apparently he needed a second to

get air back into his lungs. During that time her fingers grasped the largest ridge on the side of the knife and pulled.

The sounds from outside became more distinct. One of the diesel engines began to whine in a higher gear. Someone spoke over a megaphone, his words ominous: "Stand clear."

Corliss would not stop attacking long enough for her to learn the technique of sawing at the rope around her wrists while still bound by it, so she drew up her knees and applied the blade to the rope holding her ankles. It was thick, though. She'd never get through it in time to move away from him.

The vague duskiness creeping down the stairwell provided just enough light for his fists to find her; he struck her shoulder hard enough to rattle her teeth and then grabbed her shirt. She tried to duck while continuing to work at the rope. His hands slid to her throat and began to squeeze.

She abandoned her ankles and sliced at his arm with the knife. It felt as if she'd only grazed his jacket, but he gave a surprised grunt as if she'd cut the flesh. His fingers found new strength, tightening enough in one split second to bring stars to her eyes.

She twisted her body toward him and with both hands thrust the knife upward.

A deeper grunt now, and he let go. She saw him press both his hands to his stomach, or perhaps she only imagined it.

Then he reached out to take the knife away from her, but his fingers found only its blade and she sliced him again without even trying.

"All clear!" yelled a man outside. The diesel engine gave another bellow.

Corliss backed off. He couldn't get the knife away

from her without risking more injuries, and besides, he didn't have time. He had to get out now or be trapped with her.

He ran.

She screamed, producing only a pitiful mewl that would not be heard over the machinery outside. Trying to pull the gag down from her mouth only caused her to scrape her cheeks with her fingernails and wasted one valuable second. She applied the knife to the rope around her ankles.

Corliss ran up the old wooden steps, on all fours from the sound of it.

Nearly through the rope, but the remaining strand held her ankles fast.

Then her world exploded in a thunderous boom of vibration and noise. The northeast corner of the building caved in, and the rubble of the heavy stone walls immediately broke through the floor. The old timbers gave way with sharp cracks, like a volley of rifle fire. Shards of stone flew everywhere, forcing her into the fetal position to protect her face while she felt sickening pain in her arm, back, and thigh.

Next came the dust, so that when she finally could take a breath the air had been filled with bits of mortar, sawdust, dirt, and sand. She coughed it back out, then tried to breathe only through her mouth. At least the gag could provide some kind of filter.

Light struck her from above. A blinding array of floodlights was aimed at the building. Couldn't they see her? They would stay a safe distance back, away from the flying shards and dusty air, too far away to see into the pit of the basement.

Then she discovered that her scrabbling had snapped the last rope strand, and her ankles were free. She stood, choking, her eyes closed to slits against the onslaught of elements around her, and hesitated for one fateful second.

Retreat into the back of the basement, and hope they knocked off for coffee halfway through the demolition? Or try to climb up that slope of broken rock to get out before the rest of the building came down on top of her?

Irene Schaffer had said they paused between each swing, to study the last blow's effects before deciding where to place the next.

Go with Irene.

She charged the northeast corner.

Hands still tied, she tried to run up the pile of rubble and immediately fell, forcing sharp pieces of stone into her hands and knee. As she pushed upward her feet collapsed the gravel underneath her, and she tried to angle her hands to use the rope around her wrists as a cushion. She might as well have tried to climb a sand dune implanted with razor blades.

Looking up, she saw that the very top edge of the building had not yet fallen but hung as an angled arch over the hole in the lower corner. The next strike would drop the remaining stones straight down. They might even fall on their own, right onto her.

Yet even as she climbed, waiting for a weighted ball large enough to encompass her entire body to swing directly into her skull, she wondered if Corliss had made it out. Was she now scurrying over his body?

The whine of the diesel engine slipped into a higher gear. She couldn't get enough air through the thick gag and had no choice but to suck in dust through her nose. Screaming remained impossible; she produced no more than a low grunting *uhh-hh-hh* as she climbed.

Her right foot slipped again, forcing splinters into her right knee until a ripple of nausea ran through her stomach. Three feet to go. It couldn't be more than three feet.

The call came again.

"All clear!"

The other foot slipped. Her fingers grasped, painfully, for a hold.

She crawled, more than climbed, the last foot to poke her head above ground level. *"Uhh-hh-hh!"*

Theresa could see nothing but brilliant light, not the ground, not the men behind the machines, not the huge iron ball coming her way. She didn't try, simply kept her head down and her body in a crouch and moved northeast, stumbling over the rubble. She had pictured herself bursting out of the wall to safety, but the outside of the building now stood as littered with broken stone as the inside, a sharp and uneven terrain.

"Hey!"

Still as blind as if she had no eyes at all, she heard the wrecking ball whistling through the air just as her foot touched something familiar. Grass.

Perhaps it was the column of air displaced by the swinging iron, or some sixth sense that allowed her to feel its location, but her knees buckled and she threw herself to the lawn, rolling and rolling and rolling over slivers of rock that cut her with every touch, until the night burst once more with thunder and a shower of broken rock. She pressed her face into the earth to protect it, curling her arms and legs in as best she could.

This time was better. Fewer projectiles struck her and the air became only a bit dusty instead of unbreathable. Even after the trembles in the ground faded away, she did not move. No sense getting in the way of the return swing. In fact, now that she was out of the building, no real reason to move at all.

Except that suddenly there were hands on her, lots of feet around her, and strained, excited voices.

"Holy shit, lady, what are you doing?"

"Why the hell were you in there?"

"She's tied. Look, she's *tied*."

The faces above her were visible now that they were all on the same side of the lights, the men illuminated with brilliant glare so that they seemed to be boys telling scary tales with the aid of a flashlight. She grabbed the one who had bent the lowest and used him to haul herself to a sitting position.

"You okay? Are you okay, lady?"

"Uhh-hh-hh."

A familiar click, and another man dug his finger under her gag. Then he slipped in a blade and sliced it off. She took a second to rub her jaw, which felt frozen in place. The habit men had of carrying pocket knives . . . *That's a good habit,* she decided.

"Hands," she said, although it didn't come out quite that clearly, and thrust her wrists toward him. He obediently sawed at the ropes with the swiftness of an adrenaline rush.

"Don't cut her," another man told him.

"Hardly matters at this point," she said, though that didn't come out so clear either. She could see the blood coating her hands, could feel it oozing down her legs as she stood. "The man. Did you see the man come out?"

They continued to ask her questions, so that she raised her voice. "Did you see a man come out of the building?" But even as she asked, she realized that of course they hadn't. If they had, they would have postponed the demolition until they rechecked the premises.

"A man?"

"What were you doing in there?"

"What man?"

"You mean that guy?" one said, pointing.

Everyone turned. Overflow from the dazzling lights lit up the parking lot and street enough to illuminate the only figure moving *away* from them, a man who wove through the heavy machinery to pause on the edge of Kingsbury Run. Corliss.

"Call 911," she said, pushed past the men, and ran.

She crossed the lot and dodged through the wreckers. With luck Corliss's injury had slowed him—no, he had probably wanted to watch, to see that she did not escape, that there would be no chance of her body being found. He would want to see the end of what his father had begun. She reached the top of the ridge and plunged over.

The slope had not gotten any easier to traverse since her last trip down it, still an irregular surface dotted with brush and rocks. A train rumbled in the distance. *What the hell am I doing?* The blood loss would probably bring her to her knees before she caught up with him anyway, and she had dropped the knife in her scramble from the building. They knew him now, his name. She would tell Frank, the cops would go get him . . . what could she do, by herself?

She kept running.

She had made it only halfway down the hill when Corliss reached the bottom and turned to the west, away from the RTA station, disappearing into the dark and a light fog. It hung in vague wisps throughout the valley as the ground cooled in the absence of sun.

A sparse but tough bush caught her midshin. She somersaulted the last ten or fifteen feet to the bottom but had at least gotten down the hill. A shout from behind her and a weak beam of light told her that one or more of the construction workers had located a flashlight and were in pursuit. But they were too far behind Corliss. So was she.

Then she heard him, a stentorian wheeze. Perhaps she could catch him after all. He *did* have an extra twenty years and a stab wound. Just then she tripped over a train track, slamming one elbow into a tie and nearly braining herself on the second rail.

Through a break in the mist she saw him, speeding up and over the next set of rails as if he had their locations memorized.

She knew she really should stop. It was not her job to chase murderers. She ought to call Frank. Did she still have her cell phone on her?

She hoped Rachael had not gone back to college.

Where was Corliss going to *go*, anyway?

Theresa pushed herself to her feet with her bleeding hands and continued, taking care to watch for the shadows of the tracks on the ground. It might not have been her job to haul Edward Corliss to justice, but maybe she didn't care so much about justice right then. Maybe she just wanted to beat his brains in.

The train she had heard in the distance had not stayed there. Heading west toward them, its headlamp made the fog glow like a living entity. Corliss raced across the run, trying to beat the iron monster and let it cut her off from him. His father had moved through Cleveland like a phantom for over a decade. Edward had learned how to murder from him. He might also have learned how to disappear.

The wet fog slapped her face, but it didn't help to dredge up more energy for her tired legs. She tried like hell to push another ounce of adrenaline from her glands, give herself one little boost. . . . *Try all you like,* her over-forty body let her know. *It's not there anymore.*

But he could *not* get away!

She kept running.

Corliss had only ten feet to the track, but he still had to get over it before the speeding engine hit him . . . perhaps the image of the cattle-catcher slicing his feet off at the ankles made him hesitate. Perhaps he knew he couldn't make it. He slowed and blew his chance of beating the train. The engine roared up the track in front of him, cutting off his escape and certainly moving too fast to jump.

As he stopped, Theresa's tired form began to slow as well, so automatically that her brain did not notice it for a second or two.

The mist worked both for and against her, taking the light from the construction workers above and diffusing it throughout the valley, making parts of the run easier to see than they would normally have been. But the fog's undulations made it seem as if the world were moving and made distances difficult to estimate.

For instance, she could see the train passing behind Corliss. But it seemed as if the end were approaching very fast, too fast, so fast that it would free Corliss before she could reach him. The train consisted of only five or ten cars, not long enough to imprison him.

Perhaps it was only a trick of the light. She peered into the fog for a better look, stepped into a hollow, and turned her ankle. The bolt of pain brought her to her knees.

Corliss began to run toward the rear of the train, increasing the speed with which it was passing him.

She pushed up with her good foot and sped on. The last car, a blue boxcar with a bright light on its rear corner, came toward them.

"Corliss!" Why she thought shouting would help . . .

The blue boxcar drew parallel with him for one split second, then went on its western way and left the track free.

Corliss glanced back at her with, she could swear, a grin of pure triumph. He might not escape detection forever, but at least he could best her on his home field, here among the trains. Then he leapt up and over the tracks as lightly as a man one-third his age.

But a second train had come from the west, moving in the same direction, its noise and lights obscured by the first train. Corliss stood dead center in the second set of tracks when it struck him.

It happened so fast that Theresa could not comprehend how one moment Corliss stood on the tracks, and in the next an iron behemoth swept across the landscape, slicing the night in two. She didn't understand. But her body did, and stopped running.

Footsteps pounded up behind her. She didn't turn, expecting it to be one of the construction crew.

"Theresa!" Frank grasped her with both arms, holding her, shaking her, even going so far as to cup her face in his hands. "Are you all right? You're bleeding."

"Sorry," she told him. "Broke my promise. Where did he go?"

"I went to Corliss's house but couldn't find—are you all right? Are you in shock?"

"Dunno. Where did he *go*?"

With his hands on her shoulders he answered in a patently reasonable tone that only annoyed her. "The train hit him."

"I know *that*," she snapped. "But where did he go?"

"The train would have flung the body forward, so we'll find him somewhere up there. Which side of the tracks, that's anybody's guess. Are you sure you're not hurt?"

"Oh, I'm hurt." Every inch of her skin seemed to be stinging and bleeding. Her elbow throbbed and her right ankle had already begun to stiffen. "But I'll live. I think."

He put his arms around her and she held on to him, bleeding all over one of his good shirts, and knew it didn't matter a damn who had been their grandfather's favorite.

Members of the construction crew had caught up with them, flashlights waving. "Did you see what happened? Who was that dude? Look over there."

"It's a crime scene," Frank protested. "You can't—"

"We won't touch nothing. Hey, is that blood?"

"Frank?" Theresa asked, her voice muffled by his windbreaker, her aching arms still wrapped around his body.

"What?"

"Did Rachael go back to school?"

A pause, during which he let her go in order to look at her rather oddly. "No. She's still home. She's the one who told me you weren't answering your phone."

"Oh. Good." She withdrew her palms and blew on them, not knowing what else to do for the stinging pain. "Good."

"Found him!" shouted one of the men from farther up the track.

CHAPTER 47

THE FOLLOWING MAY

The Law Enforcement Officers Memorial in Washington, D.C., is a graceful oval of stone and marble, located a few blocks northwest of the Capitol. The annual service to remember officers who died in the line of duty takes place each spring, the season of renewal. Theresa breathed in the light scent of cherry blossoms and wondered if Edward Corliss had repeated the Torso Murders to distract police from seeing his connection to the first and fifth victims, or because he really enjoyed doing so.

"Thanks for coming with me," she said.

"And miss a photo op?" Chris Cavanaugh scoffed. "As if."

The plaza thronged with people, even though it would be hours before the candlelight ceremony took place. For the third time in as many minutes, Theresa traced the engraved marble with her finger. *James F. Miller.*

"Good job getting him added," Chris told her. "Everyone got so hysterical about solving the Torso Murders, it would have been another seventy-five years before anyone thought about Miller."

"I just wish—"

When she didn't go on, Chris prompted her: "What?"

"I wish we knew what *happened*."

"To Miller? Yeah, I know what you mean. Did he know Arthur Corliss was the Torso killer? Did he stumble on it? He was in plain clothes—maybe Arthur didn't know he was a cop until after he'd already killed him. Then he figured he'd better not take any chances with this one and sealed up his little room. But he didn't stop killing."

A breeze wandered through, chilling the skin on her bare arms. "No. He didn't stop." Corliss had to have been right on top of him, the gun right up against his gut, to leave heavy gunshot residue on his shirt. How had he gotten James's service weapon away from him? Did James worry, with his last breath, that his son would grow up thinking he had abandoned his family? What about his wife? Why had she doubted him? Didn't they get along? Was he lonely? Or did he shut everyone and everything out, except his work, because sometimes life was more comfortable that way?

If so, did he regret that at the end?

Yes, there were many things she would have liked to discuss with James Miller.

Aloud, she said: "I wonder why the other cops didn't follow up on Corliss. If James had a lead, you'd think they would have picked it up after he disappeared."

"Maybe he didn't tell anyone. Either wanted to keep the glory, or"—he glanced around and lowered his voice, as if it were sacrilege to suppose such a thing in such a place—"he wanted to shake the killer down, collect a little hush money."

"I don't believe that."

"Those were desperate times," Chris reminded her.

"I don't believe that," she repeated, though she couldn't have said why. Her finger traced the engraved letters one more time. "Maybe the other detectives investigated Corliss but didn't have enough for an arrest. We can't know, since most of the records are missing."

"That's true. I'm just a little concerned, that's all. I think you're in love with the guy."

She jerked her hand away from the marble.

"It's a little tough to compete with a ghost, especially a heroic one." With a light and respectful touch he guided her chin up so she had to meet his gaze. "But he's dead, Theresa. And I'm here."

Life is short. Always date interesting men.

She linked her arm through his. "So you are."

NOTES AND ACKNOWLEDGMENTS

The Torso killer did indeed exist, and his crimes proceeded more or less as I've written them here, except for the clues I invented, such as the pills and the glass. Aside from the great Eliot Ness (and the suspect Captain Harwood), all the police officers mentioned in this book are fictitious. The coat James traced did exist, though I have no reason to believe the clues were divvied up at the crime scene.

Other historical notes: Fiestaware was not on the market until early 1936.

Flo Polillo did work as a barmaid and waitress, but I do not know if there really was a Mike's on East Thirtieth, or if they had the best corned beef in the city. St. Peter's had a soup kitchen until its recent closure; I do not know for sure if they had one in the 1930s, or if the figures I quoted are from one particular location, or if the diocese had more than one kitchen operating in the city. Also, I have it on good authority that neither the Nickel Plate nor the New York Central railroads served New Castle, Pennsylvania, an unhappy piece of information that blew my whole theory. Congratulations to Kim Hammond, who won the character name auction at Boucheron 2009, and thus commissioned her own surrogate murder.

I'd like to thank all those who assisted me with this book: my mother, Florence, who braved a frozen street to visit the Cleveland Police Museum with me; my sisters, who never mind pulling over on the way to lunch at Lola's so that I can jump out and take pictures of odd places; my husband, Russ, who knows the nooks and crannies of Cleveland better than I do; my invaluable critique partners Sharon Wildwind and Sheri Chapin; Tom Carey; Don Moore; Bernie Juszak; and Sheldon Lustig of the New York Central System Historical Society.

And of course this all would not be possible without Elaine Koster and Stephanie Lehmann at the Elaine Koster Agency, and David Highfill at William Morrow.

MURDERS OF THE MAD BUTCHER OF KINGSBURY RUN

Date Found	Victim	Victim's Age	Location Found
CLEVELAND, OHIO			
September 5, 1934	W/F (Lady of the Lake)	30s	Euclid Beach
September 23, 1935	W/M	c. 45	East 49th & Kingsbury
	Edward Andrassy (W/M)	28	
January 26, 1936	Florence Polillo (W/F)	41	2300 block of East 20th
June 5, 1936	W/M (The Tattooed Man)	20s	Kingsbury near 55th
July 22, 1936	W/M	c. 40	Clinton Road
September 10, 1936	W/M	20s	East 37th & Kingsbury
February 23, 1937	W/F	20s	Euclid Beach
June 6, 1937	Rose Wallace (B/F)	35	Lorain-Carnegie Bridge
July 6, 1937	W/M	35–40	West 3rd & Cuyahoga River
May 2, 1938	W/F	25–30	West 3rd & Cuyahoga River
August 16, 1938	W/F	30s	East 9th & Shore Drive
	W/M	30s	
July 22, 1950	Robert Robertson (W/M)	44	East 22nd & Lake Erie
YOUNGSTOWN			
June 30, 1939	W/F		near tracks

Date Found	Victim	Victim's Age	Location Found

NEW CASTLE, PENNSYLVANIA

Date Found	Victim	Victim's Age	Location Found
Spring 1923	skeleton		swamp
	skeleton		swamp
	head	40–60	swamp
1924	decomposed body		swamp
	skeleton		swamp
July 1, 1936	W/M		swamp
October 13, 1939	W/M	20s	by the tracks
May 3, 1940	W/M	30–40	boxcar
	James D. Nicholson	30	boxcar
	W/F	30s	boxcar
1941	skeleton		swamp

BIBLIOGRAPHY

Badal, James Jessen. *In the Wake of the Butcher*. Kent, OH: Kent State University Press, 2001.

Baden, Dr. Michael, and Marion Roach. *Dead Reckoning: The New Science of Catching Killers*. New York: Simon & Schuster, 2001.

Fletcher, Connie. *Every Contact Leaves a Trace*. New York: St. Martin's Press, 2006.

Green, Harvey. *The Uncertainty of Everyday Life, 1915–1945*. New York: HarperCollins, 1995.

Koehler, Dr. Steven A., and Dr. Cyril H. Wecht. *Postmortem: Establishing the Cause of Death*. Buffalo, NY: Firefly Books, 2006.

Kyvig, David E. *Daily Life in the United States, 1920–1940*. Chicago: Ivan R. Dee, 2002.

Nickel, Steven. *Torso: The Story of Eliot Ness and the Search for a Psychopathic Killer*. Winston-Salem, NC: John F. Blair, 1989.

Ramsland, Dr. Katherine. *The Science of Cold Case Files*. New York: Berkley Boulevard Books, 2004.

CHAPTER 1

WEDNESDAY

The first volley came in the form of a text message.

Cm quck. Sum1 ded here.

Standing on the twenty-third floor of the Justice Center with her cousin, Theresa MacLean translated slowly and aloud. "Come quick. Someone dead here."

"That from the lab?" Frank asked. He had met up with her after her testimony in an officer-involved shooting case, ostensibly to take her to lunch but more likely to get an update on the trial's progress.

"No," she told him. "It's from my daughter."

Now she and Frank pushed past the worn glass-and-brass doors into the vast lobby of the Terminal Tower, passing a microcosm of society on the way: panhandlers in ragged clothes with plastic cups, repeating "Got any spare change?" until the sound of their voice blended into the backdrop of bus engines and cooing pigeons; teenagers freed from home and school, dressed like gangsters in training regardless of socioeconomic background; young sharp men with crisply knotted ties and ladies arriving for lunch, armed with credit cards and fashionable scarves. Their voices bounced off the marble walls and echoed down the hallway before plunging into the cacophony of the Tower City mall.

The Terminal Tower had been built in 1928 by the odd but quite brilliant Van Swerigan brothers. It remained the tallest building in the world for twenty-five years. Its 708 feet spread from the rapid transit station in the basement to a glitzy shopping mall, two hotels, and floors and floors of offices topped off by an indoor/outdoor observation deck. This deck had been closed since the September 11 attacks, a policy considered extremely silly by locals—as if terrorists would target Cleveland. Clevelanders love their city, but have no illusions as to its status among the rest of the planet.

Theresa entered the lobby of the Ritz-Carlton, the heavy glass door closing on its own. Any sound from the streets, the mall, the rest of the city was sliced off and left behind.

"How long has Rachael been working here?" Frank asked. He had called his partner in the homicide unit to find that, indeed, a person had been found murdered at the hotel. Two other detectives had been assigned, but that would not dissuade him. From the body he kept in shape to the neatly trimmed mustache Frank lived for his job; besides, with no children of his own, he took on the role of papa grizzly when it came to his "niece." Rachael's own father checked in only between girlfriends.

"About two weeks. Front desk. She likes it, likes being downtown, says her boss is decent." The lobby spread out around them in tasteful shades of cream and beige. A man with bulky leather bags waited without apparent patience to check in, and a lean young waiter served a Bloody Mary to a delicate woman in a pink twinset as she lounged in an overstuffed cream armchair. "I—"

"Mom!" Rachael appeared, long blond hair flying, torso encased in a tidy uniform that didn't quite disguise her curves. At eighteen she had her mother's height and lean build but her father's excitability. "Hi, Uncle Frank. What took you so long? You look nice," she added, taking in Theresa's black skirt and somewhat styled hair.

"Court," allowed her to explain both. "What's going on?"

Showing a new sense of discretion along with her uniform, her daughter looked around and lowered her voice before speaking. "A guy called from the Presidential Suite and said there's a woman murdered there and it's really gross and bizarre, she's all tied up and there's blood everywhere—"

"Did you see this body?" Theresa asked, dreading the answer. Dead bodies were her job, not her daughter's. Never her daughter's.

"No. I was going to go up, but Shawna was on break and I couldn't leave the desk—"

Theresa felt herself making one of those "mother" faces. "Rachael—"

"I just thought I'd check it out! You know how you always say Dispatch calls you and tells you there's blood all over the place and then you get there and there's, like, three drops? So I wanted to go make sure it was really worth getting Karla out of the Housekeeping meeting, but like I said I couldn't leave the desk alone, so I did get Karla—she's the GM, general manager—and she went up. Then I guess she called you guys because she didn't call us back." Rachael didn't seem upset or even shaken, only stirred by this great drama, her hands fluttering as she spoke. The guest had taken his bag and departed, while the other young woman at the front desk studied Theresa with great intensity, no doubt having heard about her line of work. Rachael went on. "Karla said there's a ton of blood and William says that they can't figure out how she got in there and get this—"

"Theresa!" A homicide detective she recognized crossed the heavy carpet toward them. John Powell had thinning black hair and a layer of doughy fat under the skin on his face, but his body looked tough enough. He carried a small camera and a notebook with no hands left over for shaking. He glanced at Frank without much welcome and at Rachael with more, taking her in from toe to chest so skillfully that Theresa might have missed the absently sweeping look. She didn't. "Thanks for coming," he said to her. "We have a woman in the luxury suite. She—" another glance at Rachael. "I'll fill you in on the way."

"This is my daughter," Theresa said.

He nodded without interest—apparently taking in the teenager was simple male reflex—and then spoke to Frank, "What are you doing here, Patrick? Doesn't she go anywhere without you?"

"Good morning to you too, Powell. I'm just tagging along," Frank said, controlling the bristle. He and Theresa had worked a lot of cases together and those cases always seemed to be the insane ones; it had become a stereotype. Each detective in the homicide unit had a theory about this: that they were unlucky, or lucky, cursed, or somehow cheating. "Anything to get out of court."

"Well, you need to stay outside the tape unless you're assigned. No sense cluttering up the contamination checklist with rubberneckers—and there's going to be a lot of them," he added with a sigh. The mild belligerence leaked went out of him, deflating his shoulders. "This is going to be a cluster."

"Stay here," Theresa told Rachael, eliciting a groan of protest, and followed Powell to the elevators. But two hotel guests got into the car with them, precluding conversation during the trip. Instead Theresa's introduction came about in the form of a bright halogen lights set up outside the double doors to the delicately labeled Presidential Suite and a small army of policemen, hotel managers and two EMS responders. They were not needed, but lingered anyway and no one wanted to create the bad blood necessary to kick them out. Frank remained with them, firmly on the civilian side of the crime scene tape, no doubt gnashing his teeth.

Theresa stepped into the Presidential Suite, behind Detective Powell.

The trail began inside the double doors, only a few scattered stains across the fawn carpet. They could have been mistaken for dirt if she hadn't been so familiar with the black-red color of dried blood. Powell stopped to talk to another man but she ignored them and continued past a small kitchen with granite countertops and a conversation area with heavy armchairs, watching for any tiny scattered evidence before she placed each foot. Thick drapes had been pulled back and privacy sheers let the room fill with softened light. All seemed tidy. But through another set of double doors she could see the blood trail pick up.

A bedroom, large enough for a king-sized four-poster, a desk and more armchairs. The requisite fluffy comforter had been pulled back, the exposed sheets smooth and snow white. Crisp and perfect but with enough touches of old money, enough sconces and details and deep wood to make it seem worth the price. Theresa wondered what the room had smelled like before it took on the scent of raw meat that had been left in the refrigerator a little too long.

Against the opposite wall sat an end table and two armchairs; one cushion had been shoved out of place and a glass and a magazine lay on the floor. Blood drops increased now, accompanied by splotches, smears and vague suggestions of footprints. A man with a detective's badge stood to her left, jotting notes to himself.

Theresa stared, as the activity and voices around her faded to a distant hum. She saw death every day, and murder many days, but this—this was the sort of thing one should see only on television, and really not even then.

Thank God it hadn't been Rachael who found this.

The victim stretched across the middle of the carpet, almost equidistance from the foot of the bed, the armchairs and end table, and the bathroom. She lay on her stomach, head turned, right cheek resting on the floor with her hands stretched back to her ankles and tied there. She wore no clothes, and the bare skin had been spattered with blood. Long black hair obscured part of her face and blood obscured the rest, soaking the hair and spilling onto the carpeting. Except for two red slashes across the right shoulder blade, all of the killer's fury had been visited on the victim's head, the scalp split by at least three heavy blows. Theresa crouched down—something that would have been a lot easier in her usual working uniform of khakis and Reeboks—to get a look at the face, with its pale skin and already clouding brown eyes. And then she looked again. "She . . . I. . . ."

"We think it's Marie Corrigan," the detective explained—his name could be Nelson, but Theresa could not be sure—stood next to the bed. Closer to her age than Powell's and taller than both of them, he had receding brown hair, lively brown eyes, and a smile that made you want to keep an eye on him. "No ID, but it looks an awful lot like her, and her office said she's supposed to be here."

"It's her. I testified in front of her a month ago."

Theresa shook her head, trying to reconcile the dead person with the live Cleveland defense attorney she had known. "Why would she be staying at the Ritz?"

"She wasn't staying here. She was attending the convention." At Theresa's raised eyebrows, he explained. "The hotel's full of lawyers. They're having a convention for criminal defense attorneys, can you believe that?"

"Everyone has conventions," Theresa said. "Who rented—"

"That's just it. No one was registered to be in this room. I guess they can't make enough off their dirtbag clients to afford the Presidential Suite. Almost makes me feel a little better."

"Almost," Powell added, coming in behind her.

Theresa said nothing about their evident bigotry. She respected attorneys but often didn't like them, and had no doubt they felt the same toward her. It was simply a condition of the adversarial system of law. Nothing personal. At least not usually.

"So she wasn't staying in this room." It made sense, since there seemed to be nothing there save for the victim, her scattered clothing, and the hotel-provided magazines. Theresa could see into the thoroughly mirrored bathroom; it contained enough towels to stock a locker room, but no toiletries broke up the white-on-white accoutrements of the sink area.

"No, it was vacant. Except somebody got a key," Nelson or maybe-Nelson said. "They decided to ditch the latest legal scoop for a little luxury suite whoopee with no room tax. He and Corrigan get their kink on but then lover-boy gets out of hand."

"Any suspects? A boyfriend?"

"Don't know yet, but suspects? A hotel full of them," Powell said. "And I can't wait to question them. How are they going to lawyer up?"

"They'll each represent themselves, and say nothing," his partner guessed. "This is going to be oh so much fun."

"Marie Corrigan," she said, still trying to take it in.

"Yeah. The bitch finally got what was coming to her."

"Finally," Theresa breathed.

Many aspects of forensic science, Theresa knew, were not designed for the faint of heart. Among them: Zipping on a Tyvek suit that made her sweat in the dead of winter in order to move around an efficiency apartment with a four-week old corpse oozing across the kitchen floor. Or asking a pedophile to open his mouth so she could rub two large Q-tips on the inside of his cheeks to collect his DNA. Or searching through a series of kitchen drawers looking for a murder weapon while cockroaches the size of ore carriers scuttle out from under every item touched.

But the worst, the absolute worst, was having to put on a conservative black skirt and a pair of sensible heels and take a seat in a hushed, paneled room. A hot seat.

The last time she had seen Marie Corrigan alive, the seat had grown warm enough to sear.

"Can you tell us what's in that envelope, Ms. MacLean?"

Three months previously: In the witness box Theresa opened a manila envelope, the red seal already torn from the attorneys' examinations, and shook out a smaller envelope. From there she pulled a piece of glassine paper folded to about one inch square. "These are the fibers I removed from the suspect's shirt."

"Which you say came from the victim's sweater? This sweater?" Marie Corrigan held up an opened paper bag, helpfully giving the jury another peek at the blood-stained scarlet cardigan.

"They have all characteristics in common with that sweater," Theresa corrected. "I can't say they positively came from that sweater. I have no idea how much of this thread has been produced or how many sweaters are in circulation."

"You said they are"—Marie made a show of picking up Theresa's report from the defense table and quoting it directly—"alike in all discernible factors?"

"Yes."

"Can you show the jury those fibers?"

"They're very small," Theresa warned. Even the closest jury members wouldn't be able to see them, and if passed around they would surely be lost. Static electricity, a sneeze or clumsy fingers would see to that.

Marie said to do it anyway. As usual the prosecutor did nothing, did not wish to be seen as coaching or protecting the state's witness. No sense handing the defense grounds for an appeal.

Theresa unfolded the paper, then held up three fibers of neon pink. The jury could see them all right. The last row of spectators could see them, and a child could see they bore no resemblance to the blood-like color of the victim's sweater.

"These aren't the right fibers," Theresa said.

"I beg your pardon?"

"These are not the fibers that were in this envelope," Theresa said, unable to prevent a quaver to her voice. She had never had her evidence stolen before, much less in front of a jury.

"My chambers!" the judge snapped. "You, too."

Theresa unhappily repeated her assertion in the cramped, white-walled office while the judge glared at her, the prosecutor and Marie Corrigan. The fibers had been switched. Both offices had had access to the envelope and both attorneys insisted they had no recollection of even looking at the fibers, only the signatures and dates on both envelopes.

The prosecutor reluctantly accused Marie. "She's the only other person who could have—"

"Along with a dozen interns, paralegals and baliffs," she countered. "And you."

"And why would I torpedo my own case? The fibers are all we have since your client strangled this poor girl with his bare hands. No blood, no murder weapon, her nails too short to get his DNA, the cellmate he confessed to is in the wind. No one can locate him."

"Exactly. Fibers aren't conclusive; you knew you'd never get a jury to convict on them only. This stunt buys you time to find your mystery witness."

The judge turned to Theresa. "Are you sure those fibers have been switched?"

"Positive."

"Do you have any photographs of the original fibers?"

"Um," Theresa had to say. "No." Due to budget constraints in the suffering county she still used an ancient Zeiss comparison scope. It had an inconvenient and balky camera attachment, which required more talent with 35 mm film than she possessed. She could have asked the photographers for help, but . . . "No. But it's obvious I wouldn't have said the colors were identical when these are so radically different, your honor."

The judge pondered, seeming to tune out the protestations of the attorneys. Theresa pondered as well, wondering how this could adversely affect her career, affect the trial, and what might resolve it. No solution presented itself.

Finally the judge declared a mistrial and Theresa paused in the hallway to give her heartbeat a chance to return to normal.

The Justice Center in Cleveland loomed twenty-six stories into the sky, and Theresa pretty much despised each one. Not the court system—she had great respect for that—but the design of the building itself. Built to be chock full of people who had committed crimes and yet shockingly unconcerned with security. Some stairwell doors locked and others didn't. Hallways turned and twisted, taking one quickly out of the sight of others. Worst of all, courtrooms were clustered four to a floor, with offices and judges chambers placed around the outside of the building. The hallway to the courtrooms ran from the elevator bank to the east wall, where wide windows opened onto a stunning view of the city and the lake—even more stunning on a summer's day when the window tint only deepened the blue in the sky. But mere mortals could not visit this calm oasis because the judges' chambers opened onto the space. People waiting to appear in any one of the four courtrooms, people under stress, worried, upset, traumatized, with small needing-to-be-entertained children, who could have benefitted from the panoramic scene outside the glass, had to stay corralled in the 1970s modular seating next to the elevator bank, under the weak fluorescent lights.

Theresa loathed the Justice Center.

Two weeks later, with no other evidence and the mystery witness still missing, the prosecutor dropped the charges. Marie Corrigan's client was free to kill again.

And he did.

Three weeks later another strangled girl turned up in

the same alley. When the police went to pick up the suspect, they found nothing but ants and candy wrappers in his rented room. He had not been seen in Cleveland since and nationwide BOLOs failed to locate him.

And now Theresa loathed nothing so much as Marie Corrigan.

CRITICALLY ACCLAIMED THRILLERS BY
LISA BLACK

TAKEOVER
978-0-06-154447-7

A grisly death in a quiet suburb pulls forensic investigator Theresa MacLean into the case, and a terrifying hostage situation at a downtown bank makes it personal. But the nightmare truly begins when she gets inside.

EVIDENCE OF MURDER
978-0-06-154450-7

Jillian Perry has been found dead in the woods, leaving behind a husband of three weeks and a young daughter. Her body shows no visible marks, and the autopsy reveals no sign of foul play. Apparently it was a suicide—Jillian purposely wandered into the forest and succumbed to the freezing weather. But something doesn't feel right to forensic investigator Theresa MacLean.

TRAIL OF BLOOD
978-0-06-198936-0

Seventy-five years ago the Torso Killer terrorized a city with a horrific spree of murder/dismemberments. Now a newly slain body bearing his unmistakable signature leads Theresa MacLean to think a copycat is following in a madman's bloody footsteps.